Courtesy of the author

NADINE GORDIMER, who was awarded the Nobel Prize for Literature in 1991, is the author of fifteen novels, more than ten volumes of stories, and three nonfiction collections. She lives in Johannesburg, South Africa.

NO TIME LIKE THE PRESENT

•

NADINE GORDIMER

PICADOR

FARRAR, STRAUS AND GIROUX

NEW YORK

NO TIME LIKE THE PRESENT.
Copyright © 2012 by Nadine Gordimer.
All rights reserved.
Printed in the United States of America.
For information, address Picador, 175 Fifth Avenue, New York, N.Y. 10010.

www.picadorusa.com
www.twitter.com/picadorusa • www.facebook.com/picadorusa
picadorbookroom.tumblr.com

Picador® is a U.S. registered trademark and is used by Farrar, Straus and Giroux
under license from Pan Books Limited.

For book club information, please visit www.facebook.com/picadorbookclub
or e-mail marketing@picadorusa.com.

The Library of Congress has cataloged the Farrar, Straus and Giroux edition as follows:

Gordimer, Nadine.
    No time like the present / Nadine Gordimer.—1st American ed.
        p. cm.
    ISBN 978-0-374-22264-2
    1. Interpersonal relations—Fiction. 2. Interracial marriage—Fiction.
3. South Africa—Social conditions—1994– —Fiction. I. Title.
PR9369.3.G6 N58 2012b
823'.914

                                                                    2012930442

Picador ISBN 978-1-250-02403-9

Originally published in Great Britain by Bloomsbury Publishing

First published in the United States by Farrar, Straus and Giroux

First Picador Edition: February 2013

10 9 8 7 6 5 4 3 2 1

Reinhold Cassirer

12 March 1908–18 October 2001
1 March 1953–18 October 2001

Nadime Gordimer thanks those whose own works mean much to her—

Karel Nel, whose painting is used on the cover of this book, is a South African artist of world renown. Examples of his work hang in the collections of the Smithsonian Institute in Washington and the Metropolitan Museum in New York. A collector of African, Asian and Oceanic art, he advises museums in London, Paris and New York. He visualises art in terms of the continuing expansion of consciousness, his own work now in the exploratory vision where art meets science. He participates as artist-in-residence in an international astronomy project which is mapping two degrees square of the universe.

and

The poet Oswald Mbuyiseni Mtshali, 'Sounds of a Cowhide Drum', 'Fireflames', for his isiZulu translations.

and

George Bizos, invaluable friend.

History has to do with manifestations of human freedom in connection with the external world, with time, and with dependence upon causes.

—Leo Tolstoy, *War and Peace*

Though the present remains
A dangerous place to live,
Cynicism would be a reckless luxury

—Keorapetse Kgositsile, 'Wounded Dreams'

Glengrove Place. It isn't a glen and there isn't a grove. It must have been named by a Scot or Englishman for features of a home left behind, when he made money in this city at more than five thousand feet and entered the property market enterprise.

But it has been a place. It was somewhere they could live—together, when there wasn't anywhere to do so lawfully. The rent for the apartment was high, for them then, but it included a certain complicity on the part of the owner of the building and the caretaker, nothing comes for nothing when law-abiding people are taking some risk of breaking the law. As a tenant, he had the kind of English- or European-sounding name no different from others usual on the tenants' mailboxes beside the elevator in the entrance; a potted cactus decorative there, if there was no grove. She was simply the added appendage 'Mrs'. They actually *were* married, although that was unlawful, too. In the neighbouring country where she had gone into exile just over the border to study, and he, a young white man whose political affiliations made it necessary for him to disappear from the university in the city for a time, they, imprudently ignoring the consequence inevitable back home, had fallen in love and got themselves married.

Back home in South Africa, she became a teacher at a private school run by the Fathers of a Catholic order tolerated outside state-segregated education, able there to use her natal surname on non-racial principles.

She was black, he was white. That was all that mattered. All that was identity then. Simple as the black letters on this white page. It was in those two identities that they transgressed.

And got away with it, more rather than less. They were not visible enough, politically well known enough to be worth prosecution under the Immorality Act, better to be watched, followed if they might, on the one hand, make footprints which could lead to more important activists, or on the chance they might be candidates for recruitment to report back from whatever level, dissident to revolutionary, they were privy to. In fact, he was one of those who, while a student, had been sidled up to with finely judged suggestions either of the cause of patriotic loyalty or, maybe, youth's equally assumed natural lack of funds, and had it made clear to him not to worry, he'd be ensured of his own safety and no longer be so hard up if he would remember what was said in the huddles where it was known he was present and had his part. Swallowing a gob of disgust and mimicking the tone of the approach, he refused— not that the man recognised rejection not only of the offer but also of the man who had agreed to be a political police pimp.

She was black, but there's a great deal more to that now than what was the beginning and end of existence as recorded in an outdated file of an outdated country, even though the name hasn't changed. She was born back in that time; her name is a signature to the past from which she comes, christened in the Methodist church where one of her grandfathers had been a pastor and her father, headmaster at a local school for black boys, was an Elder, her mother chairlady of the church ladies' society. The Bible was the source of baptismal first names along with the second, African ones, with which white people, whom the child would grow up to have to please, deal with in this world, had no association of identity. Rebecca Jabulile.

He was white. But that's also not as definitive as coded in old files. Born in the same past era, a few years before her, he's a white mix—that was of no significance so long as the elements were white. Actually, his mix is quite complicated in certain terms of identity not determined by colour. His father was a gentile, secular, nominally observant Christian, his mother Jewish. It is the mother's identity which is decisive in the identity of a Jew, the mother whom one can be sure of when it comes to parental conception. If the mother is Jewish that is the claim for her son within the faith, and of course this implies ritual circumcision. His father evidently raised no objection, perhaps like many agnostics even atheists he secretly envied those practising the illusion of a religious faith—or was it indulgence for the wife he loved. If that's what she wanted, important to her in a way he didn't understand. Let the foreskin be cut.

There was a Pleistocene Age, a Bronze Age, an Iron Age.

It seemed an Age was over. Surely nothing less than a New Age when the law is not promulgated on pigment, anyone may live and move and work anywhere in a country commonly theirs. Something with the conventional title 'Constitution' flung this open wide. Only a grandiose vocabulary can contain the meaning for the millions who had none recognised of the rights that go by the word freedom.

The consequences are many among the aspects of human relationships that used to be restricted by decree. On the tenants' mailboxes there are some African names: a doctor, a lecturer at a university and a woman making a career for herself in the opportunity of business. Jabulile and Steve could go to the cinema, eat in restaurants, stay in hotels together. When she gave birth to their daughter this was in a clinic where she would not have been admitted—before. It's a normal life, not a miracle. It was made by human struggle.

He had been interested in science from an early childhood and studied industrial chemistry at university. His parents saw this as at least some hope of antidote, insurance for his future in contrast to the leftist activities against the regime that led to his disappearing apparently over the border somewhere for periods; he would have a respectable profession. They were never to know how useful his knowledge of chemical elements was to the group who were learning how to make explosives for targets such as power installations. When he graduated, the junior post he found in a large paint factory was indeed a useful cover for a suspect way of life, political and sexual.

Ambition. Wasn't a time, then, to think about what you really might want to do with your life. The compass within swung the needle firmly back to the single pole—until the distortion of human life in common was ended, there was no space for meaning in personal achievement, climb Mount Everest or get rich, all cop-outs from reality, indecent sign of being on the side of no change.

Now there was no reason why he should continue to research advances in the durability of paint for new varieties of construction and decorative purposes, from rooftops to jukeboxes, bedrooms to sports convertibles. He supposed he could have returned to a university to further his knowledge of other branches of chemistry and physics, not confined to appearances. But there was a child for whom he and she had to provide a home. He did his work well anyway without much interest, there was no spice left as there had been in knowing that at the same time as (literally) keeping up appearances for white industry he was making explosives to blow up the regime. The firm had a number of countrywide branches, he was advanced in this one, the headquarters where he had begun. If he didn't make a decision, as he kept considering, to reconsider test-tube chemistry and move into the other kind, between humans, non-governmental, non-profit making, he worked part-time voluntarily on a commission for land claims of communities dispossessed under the past regime. She studied by correspondence, economics and law, and was volunteer secretary to a women's action group against woman and child abuse. Their small Sindiswa was in day care; what little time was left they spent with her.

They were sitting on their Glengrove Place balcony just after sunset among the racks of child's clothes draped to dry. A motorbike ripped the street like a sheet of paper roughly torn.

Both looked up from companionable silence, her mouth slewed, the curve of the brows pencilled on her smooth forehead flown up. It was time for the news; the radio lay on the floor with his beer. But instead he spoke.

—We should move. What d'you think. Have a house.—

—Wha'd' you mean—

He's smiling almost patronisingly. —What I say. House—

—We don't have money.—

—I'm not talking about buying. Renting a house somewhere.—

She half-circled her head, trying to follow his thought.

—One of the suburbs where whites have switched to town house enclosures. A few comrades have found places to rent.—

—Who?—

—Peter Mkize, I think. Isa and Jake.—

—Have you been there?—

—Of course not. But Jake was saying when we were at the Commission on Thursday, they're renting near a good school where their boys could go.—

—Sindiswa doesn't need a school.— She laughed and as if in a derisive agreement the child hiccupped over the biscuit she was eating.

—He says the streets are quiet.—

So it is the motorbike that has ripped open the thought.

—Old trees there.—

You never know when you've rid yourself of the trappings of outdated life, come back subconsciously: it's some privileges of the white suburb where he grew up that come to her man now. He doesn't know—she does—lying in his mind it's the Reed home whose segregation from reality he has left behind for ever. How could she not understand: right there in the midst of enacting her freedom independence, when one of her brothers, the elder of course, dismisses her opinion of some family conduct directed by custom, she finds what her studies by correspondence would call an atavistic voice of submission replacing the one in her throat.

He is saying as he lifts Sindiswa flying high on the way to bedtime (fathering is something the older generation, white and black, segregated themselves from)—She'll need a good school nearby soon enough.—

In the dark, withheld hours of quiet, two, three, in the morning, you don't know what is going on in the mind-rhythm of the one breathing beside you. Maybe there tore through the unconscious an echo of what prompted the idea that sunset a week—some days—ago.

Jake Anderson calls to ask whether he and Isa had been forgotten lately, would their comrades come by on Sunday— whether this was prompted by he who slept against her, she wasn't told. Anyway, it meant that they bundled Sindiswa and a couple of bottles of wine into the car and took the freeway to an exit unfamiliar. It debouched on streets brooded over by straggly pepper trees drooping their age and what must be jacarandas, but not in bloom, whose roots humped the pavements. The houses all revealed somewhere in their improvements their origin: front stoep, room ranged on either side under rigid tin roof, although some had additions, sliding glass-fronted, somehow achieved in the space of each narrow plot within walls or creeper-covered fences defining the limit between neighbours. Apparently following Jake's directions Steve slowed at what appeared to be a small red-brick church peaking among the houses, but as he drove past to take a left turn, revealed a swimming pool contrived where the church porch must have been, and three or four young men or perhaps determinedly youthful older ones, in G-string swimming briefs were dancing and tackling one another in the water to the sound of loud reggae. In the small gardens of other houses there were the expected bicycles, garden chairs and barbeque jumble. Jake's was one of them. The standard stoep had been extended by a pergola sheltered by a grape vine. There was a car and a motorbike in the street at the gate, a party evidently. Well, no, just a few comrades remembering to get together, out of the different paths their lives were taking.

They're all young but it's as if they are old men living in the past, there everything happened. Their experience of life defined: *now* is everything after. Detention cells, the anecdotes from camp in Angola, the misunderstanding with the Cubans who came—so determinately, idealistically brave— to support this Struggle at the risk of their own lives, the clash of personalities, personal habits in the isolation of cadres, all contained by comradeship of danger, the presence of death eavesdropping always close by in the desert, the bush. Peter Mkize is at this Sunday gathering, taking a hand at expertly turning chops and sausages on the charcoal grill under the grape vine, a beer in the other hand. His brother was one of those who were captured and killed, their dismembered bodies burned at a *braaivleis* by drunken white South African soldiers and thrown into the Komati River, a frontier between this country and Mozambique. That history, may it not come back to him as he flips over the spitting sausages for the comrades.

Now everything is after.

Steve feels a breath of rejection lifting his lungs. What they did then, some of those present much braver and enduring hell beyond anything he risked, anything Jabu, herself black, inevitable victim, took on—it can't be the sum of life experience? To close away from this he tosses a personal distraction. —Jake, where's the house you were telling me about. Like to have a look at it.—

8

—Sure, plenty time. Have another glass of this great wine you brought, while the sun goes down.—

Jabulile smiles, the patronage of intimacy. —He has a sudden urge to move.—

Move on. Yes, let's move on. —Is it in this street?—

—No, but we'll still be neighbours. It's a couple of houses down from where you turned to our street.—

—Before that weird-looking place that looks as if it was a church? There were some guys dancing in a mini pool there.—

—Was a church, this is an old *ware* Boer suburb, no Kaffirs allowed to come to Jesus at the altar of apartheid, *blankes alleen*.—

Everyone laughing release from the past. Spread hands thrown up and head dropped in mock responsibility for the guilt of the generation of his mother and father, Pierre du Preez is the one who arrived on the caparisoned motorcycle parked outside, as elaborately accoutred as some royal carriage, flashing flanks, sculptured saddle, festooned with flasks and gauges. He's an Afrikaner who no more takes offence at the gibes than Mkize does at the outlawed word, Kaffir.

—Who are the frolicking owners who've taken over?—

Pierre answers whomever's question. —It's one of our gay families.—

More laughter—this is the final blasphemy, housed.

Jake signals to Steve, leaving Isa to take care of the comrades. Jabu in turn signals she is enjoying herself and doesn't want to be interrupted but Steve's arm goes gently decisive around her and the three move unnoticed to follow past the church swimming pool to the next street to look at the house with FOR SALE TO LET board on the wall.

—Shit, it seems it's not a show day, usually at weekends . . . where's the agent got to? I hope it hasn't been snapped up since I told you.—

9

—Live behind a spiked wall.— Steve hasn't counted on that.

Through the pattern of the wrought-iron gate they saw something of what is behind it. There is a modest representation of the setting of the house he grew up in: a rockery with aloes in flower, a jacaranda tree, a neat mat of lawn either side of a path to steps and the front door. No clue to the previous inhabitants—oh, except a rusted *braaivleis* grill and a kennel with half the roof missing.

—There's a garage at the back, another gate and, believe it or not, an old chicken run.— Jake is standing in for an estate agent's hard sell, in his purpose of making some kind of community out of dispersed comrades, in this suburb claimed against the past.

Back at Glengrove Place Steve holds a towel ready while Jabu coaxes their small girl out of the bath. In the steam haze his voice is softened as reflection rather than question, he doesn't want to press her.

—What do you think of it?—

The gathering, the house, the church as gay commune something to laugh about together; and something not to be avoided, the practical future there was no time to think about from Glengrove asylum, before.

She's a clear-headed person always capable of occupying her hands in some task while active elsewhere in her mind. —It's a nice house, far as you can tell from the outside.—

—Of course I'll get the estate agent to take us, or give us the keys, that'd be better, next week. But the set-up, the place.—

—How can I say. I don't have any comparison, I mean I've never lived in such places, suburbs, whatever, have I.— Smiling, whether at the wriggling child she was patting dry, or for him.

—I rather like the idea.— He doesn't have to explain, taking over from the *Boere*, if even Pierre welcomed the displacement of his own clan, although everyone is supposed to live together, no ghettos, luxurious or new black-and-white middle class.

Alone, if you can be said to be while those whose being you share are somewhere close by in kitchen or bedroom; not lonely, he wonders whether he really wants to prolong in some way the intimacy between comrades that was survival in detention or the bush, there's a resistance to nostalgia. And at the same time self-reproach; what will there ever be like the bonds between cadres, the rest will always be strangers.

Jake gave him the name of the estate agent and offered to accompany them to enter the house, but they wanted to be without anyone else's observations and went, after work, with Sindiswa; after all, without offering any opinion, she would be subject to any decision made. He found the bedrooms poky, you could knock out the windows and put in something more generous with light. There was a red-brick fireplace thirties-style in the living room and space enough for a good-sized table and chairs along with sofa, television and so on. A rather shaky sliding door, obviously an improvement on the enclosing box that was the original room, opened onto another improvement, a small terrace. They were pleased to walk out and find shrubs beyond that half-hid the wall that was overhung with shade from a neighbour's tree —Acacia.— But she was not interested in the identification. As a kid given every advantage he was taken to plant nurseries with his father and learnt to match botanical names to certain trunks, leaves and bark. She had learnt on walks with her grandmother in the forests of Zululand what wild fruits were safe and good to eat.

The kitchen was a surprise. She tried the four plates on the big electric stove—no result. —Just that the current's cut off, of course.— He reassured, opening cupboards. They moved their feet approvingly on the tiled floor; Jabu peered into the shelves to confirm capacity. The bathroom had a shower stall as well as a large tub, not bad, ay? The paint through-out was in good condition although candy pink in what was supposed to the main bedroom made him groan. —We could put a lick of white over it, I suppose—I don't know if you're allowed to make any changes in a house you rent?— They toured the rooms again, hand in hand with Sindiswa. —She'd have her own room, toys and all her gear— Jabu touched her head against his shoulder a moment; at Glengrove Place they shared the single bedroom with the child, strange to make love with even a sentient in the room; who knew how much a young child is aware of, perhaps the cries of pleasure sound fearful to an emerging awareness. They checked the sliding door to the terrace and locked the front door behind them in unspoken accord.

But next morning, the reality of Monday, driving the child to the day-care centre—Jabu took a bus to her school from there while he went on to the city—putting a hand down on the keys in his pocket —I'll go to the agency and sign for us.—

She drew her lips hidden between her teeth, her familiar gesture of acceptance. When she got out of the car to deliver Sindi, suddenly kissed him. Coming back to the car, her eyes were held narrowed as if she were seeing some inner vision. He read it as, we'll be happy there.

Decisions always divide into practice. They had to give notice of vacating Glengrove, and it turned out several months' advice in advance was required. He negotiated this successfully and the stipulation was reduced to one month. As for the house, Jake knew the agent well and the rent was not unaffordably higher than the apartment's had been, on the guarantee to the owner that although the woman was black these were reliable tenants who wouldn't fill the house with immigrant refugees or whatever they were from Congo and

Zimbabwe, property values must not be allowed to go down as the result of rowdiness. Well, at least the condition wasn't gender prejudice, they didn't have to worry about moving into a mini-community where that prevailed. The gays could enjoy their holy pool. Some of the things that had been made do with in Glengrove, second- or third-hand necessities given by comrades when they first clandestinely moved in there, were not worth taking; new purchases, in keeping with a house, had to be made. A table and chairs for the living room—at Glengrove they ate in the kitchen or off the coffee table in the all-purpose room. Jabulile wanted a large refrigerator and freezer, to be paid off along with the furniture on the never-never instalment plan, it was the usual way in the communities she knew, but Steve was alert to how business economy worked to its own advantage, charging hidden interest on the amounts the poor paid every month. He would buy only what they had money to pay for on purchase—these are just trivial differences born of background which come up not only between a couple like theirs. The curtains: on the other hand, she knew a woman in Kliptown (old Location), mother of a colleague teacher, who would make them in her home at a cost below any decorator's shop. They were completed and could be hung—Jake and Isa helped, it was fun—before the actual move to the house would take place.

On the morning of the move Jabulile took charge. She bustled authoritatively between the men handling the cardboard cases he and she had filled the night before, herself correcting the carelessness with which they ignored the bold FRAGILE with which some had been carefully marked. Her reproaches were joking, she laughed with the men encouragingly. Displacement made everything unfamiliar to him, out of mind, as if they had never lived there—he was already, as if going home, in the house. He thought it unnecessary when

Jabu made tea for the movers, just a delay. But she took mugs out of one of the boxes, talking in the language she shared with the men and he couldn't follow. To speed things up he broke into her hospitality and quickly took back the emptied mugs with a gesture that they be left behind, not bothering to wash and pack them up again. He became authoritative now, giving a heaving arm to despatch of the boxes to the elevator, ready when it rose again to load it once more. She continued the laughing exchange in their common language with the men, darting back to the kitchen and bedroom to check what she must have already known, that nothing was missed, left behind. With the last batch he squeezed in to go down and help, hasten the loading of the van. The movers had been put in a good mood and took their time, arguing about the placing, how the bed, those chairs, could go here, that box balanced there. At last the double doors were barred across. He and Jabu could follow, with keys to the new kingdom. He had already taken the car out of Glengrove Place's underground garage; for the last time.

The elevator was in use, he bounded up three flights of stairs three steps at a time as if he were a schoolboy again and called out at the top, Let's go!

His stride almost stumbled: she pressed further against the door frame.

—What's been forgotten?—

She moved her head slightly in dismissal, and he was stayed.

It was nothing he could put a name, a cause to, ask what's the matter would be some sort of intrusion. Although it's impossible to accept that there are times when the trust of intimacy fails. She said very distinctly, I don't want to go. It resounded in his silence as if she had shouted. She was so known to him, the pillars of her thighs close together, the line of her neck he would follow with buried face to her breasts, yet this was someone he couldn't approach in whatever was happening. How say stupidly, what's wrong.

Of course she is thrilled delighted with the house, the terrace where she's looking forward to putting out their child to play in the sun . . . she had planned zestfully how the rooms would serve them, she agreed that he could sign for occupancy. I don't want to go. She knows it has no meaning; they are gone, it remains only to close the door and drop the keys with the caretaker.

Nothing could break the moment. Carrying the bride over the threshold was in his embrace. She didn't cry but took a few rough broken breaths. Her breasts pressed familiarly against him. He didn't ask, she didn't tell.

Leave behind, a drop into space. From the place that took them in when nowhere, no one allowed them to be together as a man and a woman. The clandestine life is the precious human secret, the law didn't allow, the church wouldn't marry you, neither his for whites nor hers for blacks. Glengrove Place. The place. Our place.

Isa, Jake and Peter Mkize surprised them that first night, arriving with Isa's chicken and mushroom stew to heat up for the first time use of the stove, wine for which glasses were dug out of packing boxes. Jabu was putting Sindiswa to sleep alone in her own room. —*Khale, Khale*, take it easy getting her accustomed to things. If I were you I'd keep her at her old day care for a bit before you move her to the one that's nearer.— Isa, the senior resident, wants to be useful. *Slowly, careful*. Comrades, even if white, find expressive the few words in the languages of black comrades they've picked up. The presence of the three neighbours in the impersonal chaos of displaced objects is order of a kind. They slept well, the new tenants.

On Sunday someone shook at the wrought-iron gate for attention and there was one of the dolphin-men from the church pool holding a potted hibiscus. —Hi, welcome to the residents' association, there isn't one but make yourselves at home anyway.— In shared laughter of the unexpected they gestured him in for coffee but he couldn't stay, was due to make a jambalaya lunch, his turn to cook. —Come and swim when you feel like it, it's a teacup, but it's a cooler . . . In the afternoon when they tired of unpacking Jabu decided they should take Sindiswa on a walk and they passed the fondly mock-wrestling water, as they had seen the day they came to find Jake's house. Jabu lifted Sindiswa's little arm to wave a hand at the revellers.

You shift furniture about: this way, that, not in the relation bed to door, sofa to window these had before, back there. And the new purchases must find the right relation.

Commonplace physical acts can lead to the jolt of other, acceptedly established arrangements. He had gone back to the chemistry of paint as decoration, protection against the weather, after concocting Molotov cocktails in local adaptation. With the need of the demand of using it illegally in the cause of revolution that had somehow justified his rather random choice of a career, was he to stay in the paint manufacturing industry as the meaning of his working life. It came to him—again. A shift implied. Wasn't there some other, a need of now, that would verify a working life in some way, as concocting a Macbeth witches' brew had been imperative in another time. *A luta continua*, the avowal goes. The battle has been won; it continues in the practicalities of the abstract, the big word, justice for all. Where does an industrial chemist fit in.

He replied on impulse to an advertisement for a position as lecturer in the chemistry department of the faculty of science at a university. Again, a move came from him, but this time not with a motorcycle ripping the street as a sheet of paper torn. He raised the subject, the shift, before making application. That also brought to light the difference between her working life and his, its meaning. Education a primary right of justice that was doled out, table scraps to blacks, before. She is teaching the freed generation, there's continuity between her part in the Struggle, her detention, her having taught at the Fathers' school even while clandestine in Glengrove Place.

She had perhaps been waiting for it to come to him that part-time do-good associations are not enough to justify the life of someone like him, like her. When he was called to an interview she crossed her arms and hugged herself for joy.

—I'll earn a lot less, way down from what I do now, Jabu.—

—So what. I'm probably going to be Deputy Head of Junior School next year, that's for sure, first woman among the Fathers, and with your degrees and your Struggle record—well yes, it must count—you'll end up a professor!—

The university was in transformation.

Not alone had the intake of black students been advanced by various scholarships; the attitude of some of the white lecturers towards blacks had come into question.

He's an academic of the new kind, particularly apposite since in the needs of the country and the policy of Black Empowerment, blacks must be encouraged to study science rather than favour, as they do—Business Management against Engineering—for the ambitions evidently dangling on the capitalist side of the country's Mixed Economy. Getting on in life? And as luck would have it, he's turned out to be a gifted lecturer to whom his students respond with alerted intelligence; another kind of comradeship—in the learning process. His facility of rousing response when speaking at political gatherings, toned down for a different situation, unexpectedly responsible.

A personal transformation.

Occupying a house in a suburb is a sign of the shedding of whatever remnants of the old clandestinity, the underground of struggle and defiance of racial taboos.

If either his parents or hers—so far apart in every South African way—had come to know about the clandestine couple, they had not been told by the son or the daughter. Once sexual segregation laws had gone with apartheid Jabulile arrived in KwaZulu one day to present rather than introduce him to her father and mother—for her very much in that order of whom she needed to inform of how she was conducting her life. No difficulty for him; he was accustomed from birth, one might say, to adapting naturally to the different tribal customs of his father's Christian family and his mother's Jewish family, as later with comrades he took part in the customs of blacks, Indians, any DNA mixture of these. That underlay what mattered: ethos of liberation. Jabu had been less at ease with the idea of being produced for his mother and father to meet his choice—for him very much in that order. (Jewish women and their sons.) But the self-confidence in having taken her own emancipation from any restrictions on her freedom from custom in the sexual relations of her own tribe, meant she entered his parents' home as if she were an unexceptional guest.

The presentation, in both places, passed without any more familial exchange than general light conversation, avoidance of politics as if these would draw attention to the consequence of politics; the daughter's choice of a man, the son's choice of a woman, to whom now the law, at least, gave its blessing.

When the baby was born, there was a different result of political overturn. Of course, both sets of parents had grandchildren from their other offspring but this grandchild Sindiswa was the first infant progeny of a new age, for them. There's a whole population who share the subtle skin colour toned by her mixed blood, and nature's arbitrary intriguing decisions to pick this bone structure or that, which nose which flesh-line of lips to perpetuate from this or that different progenitor. Once she was there, alive, with Jabu and Steve in what was no longer a clandestine Glengrove Place but nevertheless was the origin, the place of her conception, the grandchild already had brought about a different relationship between her parents and grandparents. Occasional Sundays Steve and Jabu took her to visit the Reed parents—he had to be reminded by Jabu that this was necessary. Whether this means Jabu was closer to her family—cliché sentimental concession of whites to compensate for depredation of blacks' other characteristics—was not remarked by him, or claimed by her as a reproach to him; reminder of a son's duty was enough. When the baby was a few months old there was the visit to KwaZulu where the women carried her away, daughter Jabulile's first-born, once the infant had been presented to the grandfather. No one, particularly Jabulile's Baba, showed any expected reaction to the light-skinned face and clutch of miniature hands. A baby born to one of their own, the extended family, is in itself a rejoicing of them all, their being.

Moving to a house is more than arranging furniture. There's the child, however small and young, now in possession of a room of her own. There's the planting of the gift hibiscus in a private garden; the acknowledgement that there is a neighbour, neighbours, not only comrades Isa and Jake, the Mkizes. The gay commune, all moving to a middle class of a kind. It involves something Steve is not sure about—subscription to a communal security patrol. —They're almost certainly former *impimpis*, bastards who betrayed and murdered comrades. Who needs to be protected by traitors?—

Jabu teases. —I'll pay the fee.—

A house. It implies home, not a shelter wherever you can find one. Home is an institution of family, his come to visit now—lost touch with when it was better for them not to be known as relatives of political activists, exposed to police questioning. But their Reed children are Sindiswa's cousins. She squeals with excitement when they play with her. Son Steve brother Steve, his wife and child, are expected more often than they would like, to arrive at the obligatory Sunday meal at one or other family home. It would have been nicer to drive out somewhere into the veld and picnic alone, Sindi playing with her toys on a rug and the Sunday papers handed between them. Jabu seemed to mind the obligations less than he did. He doesn't know or doesn't want to know that the family, his family, intend to show they accept (for some must swallow hard the prescription, non-racial democracy) that Steve's wife is black. One sister-in-law, wife of Steve's brother Jonathan, rather overdoes it; Brenda flings her arms round Jabu, kisses, rocks their bodies together, pulls back her face to look at Jabu as in delighted discovery. This with every arrival and departure from a gathering.

There is continued avoidance of any discussion of politics out of consideration of people's feelings on both sides. It is salutary for the comrade-husband, comrade-wife to see how social relations can imply this; despite all that has happened to everyone, if differently. Occasionally the invitation is for an evening with one or other of the couples who comprise his siblings. The gay one, Alan, takes them with his current lover to an African restaurant, new venture in the city, offering traditional mopani worm snacks, tripe and *usu* with beans. —Is this because of me?— Jabu opens the uninhibited mood of the evening. —No, we like this place, exotic for us whites, nê.— Alan's manner is flirtatious but brother Steve doesn't have to worry because (so far as he knows?) this sibling is not bisexual in his desires, which are obviously centred on the lover. Brother Alan, in family congenital variation of physique and face, looks a more manly man than Steve, which, without vanity, Alan amusingly concedes himself. —How'd a guy like you manage to kidnap this girl, what'd you cook up in your paint lab to spike her drinks.—

—He was cooking up fireworks to blow up pylons.— She can speak this out aloud now, in certain company, it's a qualification of honour.

—She loves me for myself.— Steve enjoys the banter.

But here with Alan politics are not to be considerately avoided. The lover, Tertius (what a name—only Afrikaners would lumber a kid with it) is a journalist regarded by many of his family as a traitor to the *volk*. Whatever his paper will publish of his gleeful post-mortem of his people's past as a hangover in the present—in the case of reconciliation the press must be prudent with the truth—brings punching denial from readers.

Alan himself took no part, neither in the Struggle nor safe liberal ones signing protests, those times. As he once told his brother in the handy dismissive style that invoked their secrets of shared childhood —It's a Struggle to deal with gay-bashing. Enough, enough shit already.— Yet Steve knows he shared revulsion against the regime that denied human reality in the time and place to which by birth both belonged. Steve could go, once when he had to disappear quickly, to Alan, confident there was somewhere to be concealed for a few days. Alan was not afraid. This was not brought up now to claim comradeship with Steve and his woman.

—What do you two in-the-know think of the heir apparent so far?—

Steve claims. —Mbeki's keeping up, so far. Except for what's unbelievable—that he takes it on himself *not* to believe AIDS is a virus. He appoints a Minister of Health who prescribes African potatoes and—what is it—garlic and olive oil as a cure. Mandela had to deal with the morning-after when we all woke up from the party, FREE-DOM FREE-DOM FREE-DOM. But the hype was there, the thrilling possibilities the—how d'you say—absolute reassurance of Mandela in person while he was leading, making the changes—the immediate ones that could be brought off. Now it's a different story . . . Government has to pick up the spade and tackle where we bulldozed apartheid. How long are whites going to dominate the economy? Who out of the handful of blacks who managed to gain the knowledge, know-how that qualifies, will really be able get into that powerful old boys' cartel? Who's going to change the hierarchy of the mine bosses—from the top. The goose that makes the country rich—blacks, they're the ones who continue to deliver the golden eggs, the whites, grace of Anglo-American and Co. make the profit on the stock exchange.—

—Blacks are becoming shift bosses and mine captains, used to be only whites.— Jabu in the habit of their arguing enlightenment together, rather than interrupting.

—Underground! Kilometres down! Mine managers? No Radibes or Sitholes sitting in the manager's chair, my girl.— She's a Gumede or was until she became partner in the postbox identification at Glengrove Place, Mr and Mrs S. Reed. Twitch of a smile, eyes of others not following, meant for her. —I'm not looking at promotion at shaft levels, there'll be no real change until there are black chairmen of the boards of directors. Black owners! Minister of Industries has to work on that. Trade unions have to work on *him*.—

—State ownership of mines, that'll be coming up. Ask the unions—

—Mine managers . . . co-option to the capitalist class!— Is Tertius trotting out a label or expressing his own politics? Alan has a private laugh with his man.

—But Stevie, what about Mbeki's high style, he quotes poetry in his speeches, English, Irish poets, what the hell does Yeats mean to your mine workers coming off shift—

—Sure. It's always a mistake to be an intellectual if you're a president. The Man of The People knows your rat-a-tat street march slogans, quotes from the fathers of the liberation. He's got to get used to being sharp-sharp, eh, you're saying. Cool. As if the way we gabble has anything to do with policy drive, getting change done.—

—It has, it has! The way people feel about power, it's parodied in the way we express ourselves.—

—Madiba could—he had to concentrate on the country within its borders. The chaos of the old regime left, the chopped-up map people were fenced in, ghettos, locations, Bantustans called Separate Development, Madiba dealt with the dismantling at home. Our identity wasn't a continental task then, OK. But we're the African continent. Just as Europe is not Germany, Italy, France and so on, individually. Mbeki has to integrate us as a *concept* if we are ever going to be reckoned with in the order of the world. Seeing us, the country individually, it's the other hangover, from when we belonged piecemeal as Europe's property. Backyard. Grant Mbeki sees that.—

—Democracy begins at home. That's what locals say.— Tertius flourishes the wine bottle. Jabu puts a hand over her glass. —No no? Congo's been the DRC since the sixties and they're still fighting each other regionally. Mugabe's good start in Zimbabwe has careered off into dictatorship. We can't pretend other neighbours aren't in trouble or heading for trouble and we won't be involved.—

Jabu's lifted hand tilts. —There are girls from the Congo out on the streets near where we used to live, the local ones complain they take away their customers—

—Darling, that's always been the first form of international trade.— But Steve is not sure either, whether his quip is stale repartee or solidarity against a liberation which has not

24

changed the last resort of women—to go into the business of trading entry to their bodies for survival.

—So you're back on the Sunday lunch circuit. Oh ho.— A swap to family politics. Alan to Steve, although he's turning a shoulder, mock coy attention to Jabu. —You and I, they have to give us a seat at the table. It's the new democracy, ay. Which doesn't extend further to our kind— He catches Tertius's earlobe between thumb and forefinger. —We still have the tattoo Queer setting us aside from the bear-hug. We've been beaten up by bully boys when we danced together in a night club, and Tertius's dominee brother thunders to his congregation God's love-wrath at ours—the love that dares not speak its name. There you are . . . quoting high-falutin' like Mbeki.—

'A seat at the table' will not be recognised by the lover or the brother's wife, and maybe Steve himself won't get the allusion, either, he's removed by revolutionary distance from the maternal Jewish connection that is the reason for all three of them, the brothers, being circumcised males.

The seat at table is laid at the Sabbath, Friday night family dinner, for the stranger whom the head of the household leaving the synagogue after Sabbath service shall invite to share a meal. Ancient, it is a meaningful origin of charity with dignity. Alan once studied religious faiths—including the secular one of his brother Steve. This on his way to trying out Buddhism. Maybe the 'research' had not to do with any gods but with his adolescent need for some explanation why he was not after girls, as all his friends were. He read poets alongside—what he retained was to have no discrimination against what was evidently the poetry of political ideology; it was poetry that was holy to him; why shouldn't Mbeki quote Yeats—lines, images recalled that distilled what he wanted to invoke better than in any way a politician could. If he, Alan, could have chosen to be anything he would have been a poet rather than a revolutionary; that's the revolution against all limits of the ordinary.

He's a copywriter in an advertising agency.

Jabu didn't always expect, or even want Steve to come with her on her return home—that other kind of home he didn't have, couldn't have as his ancestors were of another country or countries, for that matter; they had come to this one, at best, only some generations back. Her parents and extended family lived in what had been a 'location' for blacks outside a coal-mining town in what remained a rural area. There had been and still were large farms long owned by whites, where location men who didn't dig coal were labourers. But the 'location' was not the urban slum of city ghettos. Her father's house—her grandfather's house—was a red-brick villa in the adopted colonial 1920s-style of those provided by the mining companies for its white officials. It marked the standing in the 'location' community of the Pastor of the Methodist Church for blacks, which her grandfather had been, and that of her father, an Elder, Diakone, in the church and headmaster of the high school for black boys. There were round annexes in the yard, mud walls smoothed by the women builder-occupants under thatch of straw gathered by them. Collaterals lived in these.

The women were accustomed to leading a woman's life alongside a man in a bed but sharing, apart, their own preoccupation with care of children, cooking, maintenance of the family commune in their activities, from growing vegetables to building shelter. Jabu has always been her father's child. She wasn't kept at home while a brother, males always first in line for education, went to school. Her father found a place for her at a mission school, paid the fees and a younger brother waited his turn for entry.

Elias Siphiwe Gumede was not a tribal chief yet he was the man of authority in recognition that he had managed to get himself educated to a high standard with letters after his name, BEd., due to his own proud determination dismissive of the difficulties for a rural black boy; but sisters' and cousins' husbands did not take the example of favouring girls, although nobody would contradict him with disagreement over the way he ignored the correct procedure of the people. At first her mother endured, with silence like consent, the disapproval of the women to be read in their faces when they chanced to look up from private gossip; then the daughter brought home excellent reports, the mother proudly walked in on the enclaves to announce, 76 per cent in arithmetic, 98 in isiZulu, 80 per cent in English, each term further success. The girl child's learning achievement. Well, English, that was something, but isiZulu—that's our language of course she knows—from home, from the time she learnt to speak.

Her father was not aware either of the gossip or the counter boasts, or if he knew was not concerned; he expected to have her homework presented to him every night and equally could not be expected to fail to see where her attention had strayed or she had scamped what should have been pursued. She soon did not resent this strict condition because of the way in which he presented it, it was as if it was some special occupation, special game only she, among the children, shared with him. And as she grew up she realised how much she had gained in the process of real comprehension, from her father, beyond the instruction by rote, of school.

Was it his intention or her idea that she go away over the border to Swaziland to a teacher's training college?

The one over the border was not restricted by colour. This was not the advantage mentioned when the possibility of her entry was discussed, it was the quality of degree offered which, her father insisted to his wife, was decisive, the standard of the teachers—and he knew who they were, people who had studied in Africa and overseas, universities in Kenya and Nigeria as well as in England.

The mother did not want a child of hers to disappear, out of sight in another country, even if neighbouring. —So young, young still, this year seventeen, our child should stay with us a few years and then when she's more ready— She broke into English from their own language.

—Jabulile has done well. You want her to forget how to study? What will she do?—

—A teacher's training somewhere we can see her. Later on she can study away, plenty of time for that.—

His own studies never ended, not only did he read biblical commentaries borrowed from the White Fathers' mission, he had roused the shamed Christian conscience of the white librarian of the municipal library in the town at the fact that, high school headmaster, he could not be a member, and for years she had been secretly supplying him with the loan of books he requested, taking them to her house from where he could collect them. There came to his mind, stayed with him, maxims he had read and that remained meaningful to his own particular place and life—'No time like the present,'—breaking into English: one of them. He'd used it often as a reproach for tardiness among pupils and his children. It could now have been an admonition to his wife, but for his daughter it was a signal she was to be granted a venture over the border, independent, the way she and her father wanted for her.

Apparently he was not a member of any political formation, banned or still tolerated, although some churches were under surveillance as taking the revolutionary example of Jesus as contemporary; but he certainly knew Swaziland harboured activists on the run from apartheid police or sent out by the liberation movement to contrive smuggling of arms to the cadres at home in South Africa? He must have been aware that she, his daughter, would be living in a different atmosphere—of acceptance, support of the revolutionary struggle next door, even though Swaziland itself was ruled by a king—if still kind of ward of the dwindling British Empire. The influence she'd be open to. He did not speak of this to her, no fatherly warnings despite the confidence between them. She went in all innocence and ignorance to her teacher's college, happy to be boarding not in a hostel but with a distant relative, great-aunt on her father's side who had married out of the Zulu clan, to a Swazi. In 1976 headmaster Elias Siphiwe Gumede confused the African National Congress members, whose gatherings he had never attended, and that they disappointingly interpreted as fear of losing his position as headmaster in an apartheid state school, by intervening between the boys and the police who arrived with their armoury of dogs, batons, tear gas, to break up the boys' demonstration of solidarity with riots in Soweto against 'Bantu Education' and Afrikaans as the medium of instruction in their state schools. Natural authority somehow prevailed—some of the police might have been ex-pupils of the school?—he stood with his back against the chanting toyi-toying boys, arms outstretched as a shield before them: the sergeant strangely distracted by the old authority enacted the same stance, but to hold his men back. The boys continued their defiant dance and song as the sergeant and the headmaster stood face to face in discussion. Their headmaster then took his place quietly again before the triumphant uproar while the police left the school grounds with their dogs straining to bark. What had he said to the police? The amazed community never learnt; he ignored questions as if he had not heard them.

His daughter was recruited by Freedom Fighters from South Africa in Swaziland, he was informed by the great-aunt who came back home apparently on a usual family visit, bearing pineapples and litchis; she talked to Jabu's mother and the other women only of how happy the girl was at college, how many new kinds of friends she'd made, how pretty she was, how helpful in the house, everybody loves her.

He sent back money and two books he had bought for her by James Baldwin and Lewis Nkosi, not guns but arms of the mind.

When she was deployed on a mission back to the home country, arrested and detained for three months, he applied for parental right to visit her in the women's prison in Johannesburg and was refused.

He went to Johannesburg and persuaded the chief wardress, entitled 'matron', to accept clothing sent by the girl's mother and what he declared as study materials, from him, her father. In which textbooks he sent messages by turning down dog-ears on certain pages and marking words to be linked up from the text. He had introduced himself by caringly enquiring what church the matron belonged to (over her uniform collar there was a crucifix) and it was indeed Methodist, the denomination of worship where he informed her he was himself an Elder.

So long as he's happy.

Pauline pronounced on their son, to his father, Andrew.

A mother always goes to the essential, she's right, but the father came to have other more objective, if supportive reasons for approving Steve's choice of the woman. The physical attraction goes without saying—she's extremely pretty in her way as any man knows the distinctive attractions of a blonde as different from those of a brunette, although he himself has never (so far; all changes possible at all ages in the wonderful mystery of sexuality) been attracted to a black girl. He finds her intelligent, beyond question, quick on the uptake with opinions of her own and respectful of those of others, also you don't have to feel you must be careful of what you say because experience of the world they happen to live in has been different (like the looks you don't share). Her manner. She is neither unspokenly aggressive in some reprisal for whites' denigration of black; whether or not Andrew Reed ever held it? Her presence is not the hostile proud grudging one of some blacks now; making clear it's no privilege to be accepted in white circles. She's simply herself. And he, he's not simply a Father, he's a new individual in her life she's getting to know.

So long as he's happy.

Andrew Reed's parents: somewhere unexpressed to him might have had the same thought when Andrew married Pauline Ahrenson. They were not anti-Semitic—of course not! Discrimination is unchristian. But if as they were reluctant to think, he might have become not just neglectful of observance but an unbeliever, he was still Christian by his father's background, ethics and culture.

They got on well enough with his Jewish wife Pauline. Maybe she too was non-observant of her religion. She and Andrew brought Steven, Alan, Jonathan to sit cheerful and expectant round the Christmas tree with cousins, receiving their presents from the hands of grandfather Thomas Reed beard-disguised as Father Christmas. Pauline and Andrew exchanged gifts for each other secretly placed under the tree and opened between laughter and embraces. His parents had not remarked on not being invited to any baptisms of Andrew's children; he didn't see the need to tell them about the circumcisions.

Steve remembers from childhood those Christmas celebrations as the only family occasions. And his mother once saying guiltily with a mock thankful grimace something he didn't understand because he didn't know of the occasion she referred to, she never had to spend those Friday nights sitting around a Sabbath table listening to her brother's responses to the groaned blessing. Andrew went along with her to the weddings of her collaterals in synagogue just as they attended marriages of his in church. Their own community was that of his business associates and their wives with its own rituals of dinner parties in favoured restaurants, gala cocktail parties at the golf clubs where the men discussed the stock exchange and shots from the rough and the women traded experiences of their leisure-time diversions. Pauline belonged to a book club and took up silk-screen printing in private recognition that this was the limit of the talent as a painter she once believed she had. What an irony one of her sons should have ended up an expert in an industrial paint factory as his first career—her sense of this wasn't seen by her husband who had been impressed by her daubs when they met, part of his falling for her, as the expression went in those days; her wry, bright irony in respect of many circumstances perhaps comes from the Jewish side she brought to the marriage. Somehow paid her due to what she was, always would be, by the odd obeisance of her sons. Alan was the only one of their children who turned out to have any bent for the arts. In the circles in which she and Andrew move round accepted ideas, there was one that there was a predilection among men with ambition in the arts to become homosexuals, expressed in the usual epithets, Queens, Moffies. Did what had become Alan's sexual choice along with his passion for poetry come from her blood. He had suffered for it, his worldly mother was his confidante, she knew the doors that had slammed on him because he was gay—what an irony (again) that misnomer was, no gaiety in being sneered at and despised. But what a great result of whatever his brother Steven had done to bring about a revolution—it hadn't only freed the blacks, now it had given the same Constitutional rights in legal recognition that men like Alan, who love other men, are entitled to! She knew too well this was a—what's the word—reductionist view of what freedom means, but it's her minority experience of it, as a white privileged by oppression of the others in the too-close past. Andrew, his father, had accepted that this son among his sons made 'love' to men (yes, entering the place of shit) a version of sexual desire; he couldn't understand how this chosen deprivation of the love of women, the place for perfect consummation in their lovely bodies, could come about. He loved his son and continued to show it, and did not let appear what he felt on his son's behalf. Not disgust: regret. He could not go so far as behaving exceptionally welcoming to Alan's lovers, as Pauline did, as if they were the same as the other sons' wives, the producers of grandchildren. Hard for him to dictate to himself: so long as he's happy.

Steve brought students to the house. There would be peanuts and cartons of fruit juice dumped on the small terrace for hospitality, although they might have preferred beer and good pot. These were not seminars, their prof (as they called him although he was still only a senior lecturer) invited them as young friends. That most of them were in what used to be called the 'non' category, non-European: African Black, African Indian, African-God-knows-mixture-white, something new to the science faculty at the university, as company was nothing new to Jabu and him as it was for many who might receive them in their homes as people other than servants. Struggle had no non-categories among identities of comrades. There was no sense of inadequacy of a white comrade in that he didn't know the languages of the cadres where he was minority with communication only in his native English. The few friendly colloquialisms of African tongues he had picked up as every kind of collective with shared aims, activity, conditions, has its own jargon, made do; after all, there were the Cuban cadres most of whom didn't even know two words of lingua franca English, brothers though they proved themselves, coming from vast distance other than that between the black and white cadres when they were boys.

That was then. Now the allowance made—to himself, and by his black friends, Mkize and others, the students attracted to the subjects he had taught—it belonged to the dead and the buried. He was an African although he didn't understand, couldn't communicate in any African language—allowance made by his lover, mother of their child, Jabulile herself? Had never spoken to her those intimate words that must be

35

known to her more committing than darling my love etc., the second-hand.

And Jabu was a teacher.

She was surprised, curious when he announced: You're going to start teaching me Zulu. What other tongue should he learn; it was her own. She lightly used the everyday English endearment —Darling what's it with you?—

A new thought. —You talk to Sindiswa in Zulu. Already she's able to say quite a lot. Demanding what she wants . . . I don't understand her. She won't understand me.—

Jabu laughed. —I talk to her in English too, and you do.—

—She'll grow up talking to me in a language she and I share, and I won't be able to speak to her in a language that's also hers but we don't share.—

—Is that so bad. Many people have one parent who doesn't know the language of the other, that's passed on to the child.—

—I'm not a foreigner.—

To have the need to bring up again, now to her—he's a white who has earned his identity, not non-black: African.

—So when do we begin? It's going to be fun. I'm strict you know. What about tonight. No, we're due at the Mkizes', her sister's back with the Ghanaian she's married, big excitement. He's some kind of special surgeon, hoping he's going to get a post at the medical school, wants to talk to you about the university.—

—Oh there's no hurry, I've remained dumb so long, whenever you can take me on as another one of your Holy Father's school kids.—

So one of her father's maxims comes back from childhood. —No time like the present. Say with me *Ngingumfana ohlankiphile eckasini lika thishela uJabu?*—

—Which means . . .—

—How are you going to pay me for my after-school classes.—

—Only if you stop sniggering at my pronunciation.—
Hugging her, which led him to her mouth and the deep kiss
that belonged in another time of day, or rather, night.

There was nothing playful about the lessons, however.
Over the weekend he wrote grammar exercises she set, and
learnt vocabulary, her selected dictionary of spoken words she
judged should be the most apt for, example, interchange with
his students when he brought them home; it became also a
rather enjoyable exchange of roles, lecturer turned pupil. Jabu
never corrected him in the students' presence, left it to them
to slap their jean-armoured thighs in applause as they could
coach him, throwing in some useful near-obscenities that she
vetoed, sharing laughter. This did not affect his authority as
their lecturer, a kind of authority other than that of her father,
which had done so much in the past for her to be equal to
the present. Surely it was in her Baba's tradition, smuggling
books to her when she was imprisoned without trial, an after-
hours class of headmastership and spiritual duties as an Elder
in the church, that she was furthering her husband's emancipation by giving him the ability to express himself as an
African, not only by a European tongue. Once her father had
spelled out for her to read, by making sequence of the words
underlined in the pages of textbooks he somehow managed to
get to her in detention, another maxim. 'It is unfortunate that
we use the language of the oppressor to speak for our freedom.'
She learnt afterwards those were the words of Gandhi.

Steve was right about the 'Alertwatch' company whose fees
the Suburb subscribed to every month; there would be among
them *impimpis*, black traitors who worked with the apartheid
army. There are not many skills of guerrilla warfare of much
use in the aftermath known as peace. The only aptitude that
might be useful is that for violence, and it has been taken up
by the defeated army's rank and file. Join the present version

of the country's army, but because of your past there's no place for you there—be employed by the new industry, the security companies. You'll have at least familiar guns in your hands with a different licence to use them, not to defend apartheid but to defend private possessions. At Christmas Jabu had the Alertwatch patrol on the list, postman, municipal street cleaners, to whom it was apparently the suburban custom to give a small cash gift; poor devils, what chance did they have of training for anything else, coming from the poorest of the poor who were her people; his people too, God's people. It is not often she shows a remnant of what it must have been to be a pastor's granddaughter, church elder's daughter; he assumed that like him, being a 'Christian' was something of an ethnic label long come unstuck in the only dedication they knew, under that other rubric, justice. But in the chances of change, many labels, *Blankes Alleen* off benches, Whites Only off public toilets, people seemed to be looking for a hand-up to some authority beyond, no, outside the common condition won by revolution, although such other kinds of authority had proved useless in the past. The Dolphin boys were seen in well-pressed pants actually going to the neighbouring church (though Alan and lover still had been turned away from one elsewhere), what need was there of baptism other than splashing benediction in the pool? Some genuflection of thankfulness that the law had recognised their gender. Thank God. Comrades were dispersed among a sometimes unpredictable range of activities and professions. Some were qualified to return to the professions and enterprises they had abandoned for battle camps of bush and desert. There were lawyers and doctors the beginning of whose youthful careers was interrupted for those years, the demand beyond making your way. Most took up the career rather differently than what might have been if the Struggle hadn't taken first place from the child's ambition of what it wanted to be, or precepts social as well as intellectual expected. There were white doctors who chose to treat, along with black doctors the days-long queues in urban squatter camps instead of setting up private practice in city complexes of the latest architectural design. What is Roly doing? Where's Terence these days? Somewhere in industry, perhaps disappeared into big business, one back in the fold, family supermarket chain, another had found his place in a vast mining consortium and—perhaps seen as useful—representing for the times its conscience, he was promoting policies of better living conditions for the black miners as poorly paid as poorly housed in compounds. Some black heroes of the Struggle with the spirit of high political intelligence, leadership, powerful personality, had been seated at once in Mandela's government; some survived into his successor's, others opted for the other power, at last attainable, in the financial institutions of the old days which still own natural resources of the country below ground and the means above to convert them into wealth. But this is all official report language stuff. He and Jabu know another that creates things as they are. The normal life. The one that never was. Among their friends are comrades who are writers and actors. Poetry was written on paper meant to wipe your backside, in the years in prison. From the one everybody in the world knows about, Robben Island, the manuscript of an entire book was smuggled out in the reckless ingenuity that's devised only within circumstances of impossibility as a factor stimulating an unknown faculty in the brain. Men who had within themselves the third sense of entering the identity of other people, places and times relevant to their own—actors who had never been on a stage—performed *Antigone*, known to a reader from a smuggled book among them, in their hour in the prison exercise yard. Meanwhile, during those years in the segregated cities there were blacks and whites who wrote and performed plays which enacted the relationships of the apartheid country in all their racist contortions, boldly and usually getting away with this because there were no theatres in the small white towns, in the black ghettos, the squatter camps, where the general population could be corrupted. For the same reasoning the Censorship Board rarely bothered to give any credence to these plays by forbidding them and closing the performances before colour-mixed audiences in a theatre declared for whites only.

These days Steve and Jabu are invited to rehearsals of the freed talent of writers, actors, singers from whom the opinions of friends are sought, criticism argued. Growing up in the 'location' beside the coal mines Jabulile had never seen a play until she was at the students' Christmas effort at her teachers training college over the border. But her opinion was found worth listening to when one of the comrades' plays reimagined a setting and social arrangements half-lost or half-ignored in the generation of labour herded down mines or in factories instead of themselves herding their cattle, and the generation that has lived by the edicts of Marx, Lenin, Fanon, Guevara instead of tribal custom. The Dolphin Marc put before her the draft of his play, with its version of the dimension of freedom gained. From her half-rural, half-industrial base, as a background to her transformation first as a revolutionary and then school teacher, she seemed able to believe with certainty that *this* custom now wouldn't be followed exactly like *that*, this reaction to a girl refusing to be sold for a bride price to a man she didn't want was likely to be different from the submission of the past; a pastor portrayed might not have been a sellout reporting as God's will a secret ANC meeting of the time in his parish. People who had written out, so to speak, since 1994, inside knowledge of the lives devastated and endured, were publishing in mushroom ventures heroic stories from precolonial legends, appropriating these to their present as Europeans do those of ancient Greece. What the white regime called tribal chiefs now were Traditional Leaders sitting in parliament like any other political party. They too had brought ancient individual authority in languages and territorial fiefdoms to something of a common identity within the powers of government to direct people's lives. Yet—in the bewilderment—paradox of freedom, who would have thought of it—the Traditional Leaders at least offered the support of observances of conduct that had directed life in some certainty; so—the ancestors are still with the people as they were through humiliation, the racist assaults, the wars; there through eternity. And to whom the people are still responsible? A few traditional Leaders had collaborated with apartheid, given status in reserves for blacks known as Bantustans—'Bantu' = people, as in racespeak reference to those areas.

The ex-Bantustan leaders aren't exactly *impimpis* from the past in a modern democracy. People are free to recall themselves as they wish, just as the couple Jabulile, Steve, are revolutionaries become citizens. The Constitution confirms it. The normal life, the one that never was.

There's a hand-delivered envelope, messenger, not post. 'Steve from Jonathan'. —This's come.— She hands it to him with a shoulder lift of curiosity. Inside, a printed card with the celebratory scrolls of some occasion. He reads; then reads aloud not so much to her as to himself. It's an invitation, an invitation to the 'barmitzvah' of a son of his brother. The date, the address of a synagogue. —What is this?— He waves the card.

The amazement surprises Jabu, she takes the question literally. —Isn't it something the Jews do . . .— Jewish cadres might have referred to it when memories of childhood were exchanged to pass the time between tense preoccupations in the bush.

—To make a boy a man. Like you do with ritual circumcision schools, only it doesn't hurt.—

Of course she knows his circumcised penis was done when he was a baby.

—It's a religious ceremony, isn't it?—

—*What is this?* Jonny, Alan and I were snipped at my mother's whim, I suppose, that's all Jonny can claim for the religion, just as our father introduced us to Father Christmas not Jesus on the cross. *What's got into him.*—

—Maybe his wife wants it.— Brenda, the one who embraced her so enthusiastically when she was introduced to the family.

—Why should she, not Jewish, is she. Not so far as I know, I've been away from them so long.— He slides his mobile out of his pocket. —I'm going to ask him what's it all about.—

—No, Stevie no— She's beguiling, her hand on his wrist, there's a mock tussle, always good to grasp one another but he prevails.

Jonathan has an evasive easy answer for his brother who surely knows him well even if different politics meant they were out of touch during the years when Steve disappeared from family life. —I think Ryan is happy with the idea.—

But what, whose? Why shift it onto the child.

—Well . . . we didn't have much idea who we were, when we were kids, did we, Andrew and Pauline didn't seem to think it mattered, then.—

—The human race.—

Oh yes, the Leftist in the family; knows the answer we got wrong. We businessmen golf players—except that the black president plays golf now.

—Whatever. Did we know the difference between our mother and father. I don't remember anyone telling us. Andrew Christian Pauline Jewish, and us . . .—

—Did categories matter.—

—Stevie, there's so much that has, if you're going to talk about categories. Everything you were was decided just like that. It isn't enough to be black or white, finish and *klaar*, the way it was, in the bad old days—you belong somehow to something closer . . . more real, you can, it's possible . . . right.—

Muslim girls, daughters of Indians themselves third- or fourth-generation South African; he sees them on campus, buttock-sculpted pants, asserting breasts, high heels, film-star faces, and heads shrouded to the shoulders in widow's black cloth.

—You'll come.— His brother spoke with assurance.

—Love, you don't have to.— He had told her.

—But of course I'm coming— and then —You don't want me to.— It was not a question but an accusation, were there still situations in his life where she would be considered out of place. (Were there any likely in her life where he might be.)

He gently denied the ridiculous. —Just don't want you to be subject to this kind of thing.—

Jabu consulted Brenda about what to wear; the outfit she'd be expected to by her father elder in his church, on a special occasion in the calendar of worship? He would give the eye of approval, according to the season, to modest summer dresses or skirt, blouse and jacket, Western style, like the three-piece Sunday suit he wore although Archbishop Desmond Tutu in the Anglican Church had introduced traditional African robes in which he even danced down the aisle as part of church services.

—African! Your lovely skirts and those beaded collars.—

—Do you cover your heads?—

—Oh no, your hairdo looks marvellous. The Jews and Africans are such ancient people, they both had their special get-up for women, yours's great, but thank God we won't be likely to have anyone arrive wearing wigs.—

—Women had to wear wigs? Over their hair?—

—Their heads were shaved. I've picked up all about this while Ryan's been at school to the *yeshiva*, that's religious school, like the Muslims' *madressa*.—

She has a maze of pathways round and across her head. You trip over pavement hairdressers in the city but hers is achieved in some fancy salon she goes to. What women will allow to be done to themselves. Fashion; or conformity. What's in fashion's a conformity of some kind? I loved her first with the busy halo of African hair she had. To my hand it was the hair at the place I go into her.

He wears a hat borrowed from Jake, although it turns out there are skull caps laid ready at the entrance to the place of worship they've been given on the invitation instructions to reach. They are led in by a young man who takes his function ceremoniously, hesitating before the rows of seats, indicating the best choice. The synagogue is large, high-ceiling but without the elaborations of a church of such proportions, no graven images, bare of chapels where special favours are asked of this saint or that, like highly qualified doctors specialising in different pardons, benedictions, solutions for various spiritual conditions. It is simple in spacious lack of distraction from the only focus, the curtains behind which there must be something holy hidden, on the far wall above a platform with a discreet pulpit-podium to one side.

Seats are comfortable as those in a luxury cinema, very different she finds them from the benches in her grandfather's and her father's church; Steve doesn't remember how his young backside might have been accommodated accompanying father Andrew on one of his rare obligatory occasions to show up in church, a wedding perhaps, or a funeral. In front of them are books slotted in pockets on the backs of the next row of seats. The woman beside him—he gives a quick glance of polite acknowledgement, but she is passing the time pushing back the cuticles on her fingernails, the man on Jabu's side is praying, just audibly, a white shawl falling round his neck. Jabu's careful not to disturb him by jolting the chair arm and she manages with her usual natural grace to succeed in taking a couple of the books without doing so.

There is pervasive talk, even giggles from young boys apparently corralled to a block of seats across the aisle.

Is this an orthodox or a reform synagogue. The woman is satisfied with the condition of her nails and he can ask her. It's reform. Jabu is turning pages to verify something she's finding in one of the bilingual books, there's movement of her lips—she's trying to mouth Hebrew words, she who speaks at least four languages other than the natal isiZulu he's picked up under her tutelage. If you're black you've had to improvise communication with unilingual whites, she'd probably easily acquire this ancient one, too.

The rabbi welcomes the congregation in Hebrew and with colloquial English, not the tone Jabu's accustomed to in church, whether spoken isiZulu or English, implicit chastening against inattention to the presence of the Lord. His Hebrew is poetry, there's a choir singing in that language, you don't have to be able to read music in order to understand the beauty of it.

Steve has been looking about to see where Jonathan is sitting, if he's not behind the scenes, who knows what the protocol may be for the father in this male ceremony.

Andrew and Pauline—must be here, Jonathan's and his parents, the boy's grandparents. He has passed over the man in robes and a turban-like headgear, fringed prayer shawl, some ecclesiastical functionary among those in the gathering, although standing, not seated, where yes, the parents Andrew and Pauline have been spotted. He glances that way again as if to mark, we're here too, Jabu and I. Family solidarity in the most unlikely circumstances after the years when I had to be removed from the way of life expected for me.

The rabbi or whatever he is: he has the face of Jonathan. He is Jonathan. That's my brother. How could I not have seen. Known him.

Can those stage props have changed him; the sign of change, this one way: his. What was it he said that day, it isn't enough to be black or white, finish and *klaar* the way it was in the bad old days, you belong to something . . . what was it, 'more real'. What's more real than what we are, now! My Jabu is a woman the same as your Brenda is a woman, same rights—must I spell them out. Your Ryan and our Sindiswa are growing up not tattooed White Master/*Swart Meisie* just as the Nazis tattooed numbers on the inmates of concentration camps. Why d'you need that ghetto disguise to make you real?

This Jonathan, the functionaries, the boy, are now grouped on the platform.

Jabu senses beside her that Steve is not aware of the address being given about the significance for the boy to be bar mitzvahed, he's not even hearing the edict taken not only to be faithful to Judaism but to fulfil human responsibilities to everyone, the people and the country. Good sense to hear; she turns to him—and there are his hands splayed palm-down on his thighs. The male gesture of tense reaction she knows in him although she doesn't, this time, know a cause. Her hand like a secret between them goes over his. There is some sort of text reading announced to which the assembly apparently is to respond at points from the pages and lines given in the books supplied. In the church most know the Bible but here at the occasion there is scuffling and consultation of Torah and prayer book among the congregation, which certainly includes Jonathan's business associates of various backgrounds religious or otherwise, some Afrikaners, ambitious brother capitalists no longer the master race. There's one black man among them, must be member of a board; an example of forward-looking recognition of Black Empowerment policy in the second Leninist definition of power, 'first gain the political kingdom then the kingdom of finance'.

She is the only black woman.

Jabu flutters the pages of the right volume and speaks the responses at the right moment in the English version along with the Hebrew of the old man in his fringed prayer shawl. During pauses when nothing seems to be required of respect while there is activity of some sort going on up at the platform, Jonathan's alter ego stands as if awaiting orders, there are men in the same kind of dress and in conventional dark suits coming to put a hand on the shoulder or briefly round the arms of the boy Ryan with instruction, advice or homage, the boy's not seen to do more than nod slow and repeatedly. Brenda leaves her seat and goes up to the official group, comes down again, then once more summoned. There is no word seen to be exchanged between her and the figure of her husband. At some stage there is a rustle of hush in the congregation-cum-audience; a moment has come. The boy walks up to the podium-pulpit with back intently bent, straightens, swallows (you can't see the movement of the Adam's apple from the distance of the seats but everyone knows that brave pause) and delivers his candidacy speech in the English version and in Hebrew for which he has been under tuition for several years. Then comes the other Moment, the revelation by the young hand about to be that of a man, of what is most holy in this house of God, as the revealing of the likeness of the rebel Jew, Jesus, is in the other religion He inspired. The boy takes hold of a cord, the curtains sway on the wall, shake folds and curl back either side with the flourish of a retreating wave. He lifts out the Scroll of The Law. Jabu's half-turned in her seat as if she's about to applaud, but knows better than this secular impulse, in a house of worship.

And that's only the beginning of the spectacle, there are ceremonial embraces up there, it's like a scene from a religion ancient as an archaic Greek frieze, it looks as though some in embrace are going to succumb to the floor. And the solemnity changes key to something different, an order is being made of the rabbi, his cohort of family men and male friends, doctors, lawyers, stockbrokers, businessmen, some transformed by a token enrobement, family women in whatever is their individual best (just as down in the congregation Steve's wife is in hers) with the inducted boy carrying aloft like a trophy the Scroll of The Law on its staff. He leads the parade down from the ceremonial platform and everyone rises, the ignorant taking cue from the conversant, Jabu from the devout old neighbour and Steve from her. The procession is coming slowly down the first aisle, slowly round the second, apparently held back in pauses, by those congregants nearest. As it approaches the row where he and she sit, the woman on his left stands and pushes past their feet to get to the aisle, hampered by the unsteady old man already risen. Jabu, Steve see those who are closest enough to the aisle lean a hand straining to touch in the procession's passing the holy object carried by the celebrant. There is silence except for the stir of feet and clothing.

The held breath is released. The Scroll back hung in place. In a gush the procession breaks, interrupted, disbanded by everyone crowding in with congratulation on the way out the doors, the excited, half-schoolboy-chaffing boys burst from their exclusion to entrap this one of theirs who has just breasted the tape on the finish line of the instruction they shared.

There are strangers who arrest Steve, knew him as a little boy, take the opportunity to recall incidents he hasn't retained; time overlaid. There is a garden to this place of worship and food and drink laid out on decorated tables under the trees. Jabu provides plates for him and herself and keeps up a running commentary to him this looks good, aren't you going to try that, and in friendly asides to others, before the choice. Jonathan has emerged from his robe and headdress, he comes over to his brother it seems to present himself in uniform dark suit and tie. He is carrying two glasses to take up from a tray another to hand to Jabu. Instructs her: Mazeltov! She's congratulating him again—she and Steve were caught up with the family on the way outdoors—and he leans to be kissed cheek by cheek. —So glad you came.—

Is it to confirm to the revolutionary brother that she is today converted. Or that he's not himself conventional, isn't this ritual just concluded, another kind of sign. In reverse? Or is it that he's sexually attracted to her—they shared toys in brotherly compact. Anyway, she's a better guest than Steve, she moves and talks easily among the crowd.

She is the only black woman, yes.

—Who's the black beauty?—

The speaker is waiting with Brenda a turn in the ladies' room. The heavy kosher wine releases polite social inhibitions.

—That's Jonathan's sister-in-law, his brother's wife.—

—How did it happen?—

—Oh they were in the Movement.— Brenda knows the terminology, if her friend doesn't. —In detention here, or over the border somewhere in camps. His family never knew where he was while he was supposed to be at university, between times he got his degree, mysterious guy. Yes, she's lovely; sharp as well.—

—You knew him? The brother. Never mind the racist thing . . . it still must be strange, with a black woman . . . at least at the beginning, no?—

—Oh ask some of the respectable husbands you know!—

The occupants of the two toilets are taking their urinary meditation, whoever they are.

In the female privacy Brenda emerges from the persona the occasion makes of her, traditional wife of traditional Jonathan and traditional mother of the son inducted to manhood.

—I've always wondered. Something else. Not the same but. What's it like, to have that . . . a black cock coming into you. Are they really black or like the inside of their mouths when they laugh, and the palms of their hands, sort of rose-colour, always wanted to know.—

The friend contrives to look as if this confided attraction has not been said, coinciding with an avalanche whoosh behind one of the doors, and the occupant comes out.

Alan was there unnoticed among the seated in the synagogue but not to be missed balancing heaped plate and glass in the style of a partygoer. They meet one another, these other brothers of the one become a real Jewish boy's father, with an unspoken you here too. Alan laughs; it's for himself, he's no longer what's queer in the family—in the dictionary not the sexual gender sense, it's sibling Jonathan who's for some reason deviated from the non-observant but accepted the identity of Christ inherited from their father, given up what may be protection against anti-Semitism that hasn't disappeared with the smoke from Auschwitz. He tweaks one of Jabu's coloured-thread-plaited locks. —My favourite woman.—

—That's not saying much, considering.— Steve's endurance of being there diverted to one of the sharp exchanges that began in boyhood fun against the solemnity of grown-ups.

—Where's Tertius?—

—Jabu sweetie, I didn't know, with what's going on with Jonathan, whether it'd be kosher, as a couple . . .—

—Well you're the one that's read up all the religions—

—Except Marx, Che and Castro, my brother—

—They say the Torah has some good advice, you'd know if God's quoted there, as the Gereformeerde Kerk says the Bible does declaring an abomination?—

Daughter of the other abominated, the sons of Ham, Jabu enjoys family jokes for the occasion.

Steve judges they can decently leave 'Jonathan's farce' and go back home to reality.

They're alone apart, she and he, each, in his brother's family celebration. They have been together in the meaning of so many situations, in that each has chosen resistance, revolution, it isn't one of the conventions that order existence in white suburb or black ghetto. It's a place of encounter in an understanding that hasn't existed before. As with falling in love.

What's he mean by 'farce'? Nothing unusual in reviving a custom. Your people are your people, Baba is my Baba, I still serve him the way of a daughter of our people although I moved on.

Back home to reality, Sindiswa under care of a widowed relative of Jabu's father who has come to live with them; not exactly a nanny employed as in the old order of the whites (a quick denial) but at the request of father to daughter. Some solutions to what she knows are his too many responsibilities to church and extended family. Steve grew up of course in his, Pauline and Andrew's home, where servants were taken for granted as part of the household, black, separately housed in the yard, with what was decided a decent wage considering they were also fed.

He could not have a servant, man, woman, doing what everyone should be doing for himself. In Glengrove he and Jabu washed their clothes and dishes, sucked away their own dirt into the vacuum cleaner. His guilt at the obliging presence of Wethu, specially attentive to him in the subservience owed to males in the Elder's extended family—he had to take out of her hands his shoes she expected to polish—was something he saw Jabu didn't share; he insisted Jabu's distant cousin or whatever she was must be paid. But of course that makes her a servant; in the extended family at the coal-mine village women in her dependent position are sheltered and granted respect but not paid. Jabu hadn't thought of money;

to her, that he did—more than sense of the revolutionary equality, justice; it was a sign of sensitivity, one of the qualities of her man. Wethu occupied what was supposed to be the room for comrades in need of a bed when passing through the city from their dispersed lives—but she told Jabu by way of her tears she couldn't explain even in the language they shared, my child, I want a place, you can fix the window in that shed.

And it was so; she was without their intention, left out when Jabu and Steve animatedly exchanged opinions of what they'd heard, read and seen on the news, and told of what each experienced with whom, achieved or been frustrated by in the working day; Wethu's vocabulary in English didn't include the references and slang understood between them; she was in communication only with the child, or when Jabu remembered to say something that might be of interest to her, in their language.

His isiZulu, taught—passed on—to him by Jabu so that he could speak to his daughter in her other heritage, and in linguistic aspect of intellect as one a little less inferior in his efforts to communicate sociably with his students invited home, who were voluble in up-to-date hip-hop English —this also wasn't isiZulu usage familiar to this woman, Wethu. So he was experiencing in himself: class difference could take over from colour in what's going to be made of freedom.

Steve had the shed of the empty chicken run pulled down and a room with a bathroom built in its space by a friend of Peter Mkize, a construction worker at a white consortium who had taken the chance of setting himself up independently as a builder. The house owner approached through the estate agent had no objection to the improvement of the amenities of his property. Wethu's all-purpose tears again; Steve had gently to return the pressure of his hand to that of hers wringing his in gratitude. May God bless you. May God bless you.

A room in a yard.

It was the year the Holy Father decided to appoint their most progressive teacher, loved by the children, to direct the junior school.

Why did she give up teaching?

It was also the year she completed with high marks the correspondence courses as preliminary study for a degree in law.

Look at this without any quick answer of unquestionable certainty ready to slip off her tongue. There was the attempt at objectivity they had learnt necessary in examining a choice between decisions to be taken in the revolutionary cadres.

What the reasons could be, and these were with them in the times of silence which keep the balance of living together in the tenderly joyous interpenetration of love-making, and the need to be a self. Whatever that identity may be, or in the process of becoming. She was the child of a rural ghetto, daughter of an Elder in a Methodist church, she is the woman—wife, that legal entity—to a man of the pallor of colonialism. Which of these identities, or all, make hers. The books her father had brought her to read, from childhood; their text contained more than messages she was to spell out by stringing disparate underlined words. The reading habit he's nurtured (another identity); while reading as a student she'd smoked good Swazi marijuana but given up that as a cadre with the need of a clear head. One among books she and Steve buy as presents for each other and the bookshelves they'd put up in the house, is by an Indian, Amartya Sen, and these ideas of who you are, made up of the activities, genre of work, skills, shared interests, environments you are placed and place yourself in, are his definition of identity. Multiple in one. That's who you are. It's something her own life, Steve's life, fits. But so far the most definitive self comes from the Struggle. Whatever that means now.

It's not something to talk about even to him. It's not left in the bush camp or the desert or the prison, it's the purpose of being alive; still a comrade. And it's law that confirms or denies it. There's the Constitution to make freedom possible.

So she's going to become a lawyer. He's aware it is not a choice enticed by money although teachers are poorly paid as if they owe a special tithe to the country's development. She'll be somebody's articled clerk for some time, earning peanuts. A kind of pupil herself, again; didn't the devout Elder, her Baba, send her away to get something better than apartheid education, something of freedom, over the border.

Whenever she arrived on a visit to that definition of home as where you come from, no matter home has become some-where quite else, the women looked at the flat stretch of cloth between her hips; and then towards her mother: what was she saying to the daughter about this. All that should be said again and again. When are there going to be more babies? The child she brought to her *magogo*, *gogo*, sisters, brothers, aunts, cousins in the Elder's congregation, was a girl. How could she tell them without offence, those with high bellies and those with round heads and exquisitely tentacled miniature hands at the breast, that she and Steve postponed another child rather than taking the obligation to fecundity, because the nuclear one isn't the only family, its brood the only children. Your time doesn't belong to you exclusively or even foremost to own progeny. The revolution comes first because the sacrifices that were and are its right demand are for your own and all children. That's not a plug from political rhetoric. There's no good breeding future slaves of one kind of regime or another.

Of course Jabu's work influences their postponement of a companion for Sindiswa. With the achievement of her LLB she has been taken in as attorney by one of those new three-name legal practices which are literally up on the board, signs of change, one with an Indian name, another with an African name, among the partners. No denying that her political CV if not her colour was an advantage in the choice out of other applicants, but that's no reflection on the abilities she had to offer. The firm did not deal with divorce cases, the partners kiddingly accusing one another of turning down the most lucrative briefs, but was known as appearing for the defence in property disputes which used to be more or less exclusive to whites, with a few Indians who had acquired business concessions in the urban area where at one period Indians had some undetermined rights. Blacks had none. Now, anyone may own property anywhere—capitalism freed of its chains, Jake says wryly, announcing he and Isa, who always could have had that white right, were buying the house they rented—but inheritance rights were compounded by the remnant of religious or traditional law that had been recognised by the apartheid system, whether just or not. Keep the natives quiet where this doesn't affect anyone else. Among blacks, after the husband's death the wife has to quit their home acquired together; the house was to be passed to his brother. Jabu was Ranveer Singh's assistant in court on one such case, taken up and instructed by a legal aid organisation as a Constitutional rights issue, let alone a humanitarian one. The Justice Centre had briefed a prominent civil rights Senior Counsel, comrade whose patriarchal white face did not match his feared cross-examination techniques. At tea recesses he was centre stage in discourse, an oratory she was too impressed and inexperienced to know an attorney should not interrupt, and her unexpected questions surprised him with their aptness to the relevance of his anecdotes to the case being heard. This young black woman must have grown up as what it meant to be black in that old regime—his big head agitated encouragement at her—the political nuances in such cases, while upholding the breach of law, not to mention (he did) preposterous breach of human dignity, one must know that from the perspective of custom, unwritten laws, by getting the verdict in favour of the complainant you are putting down Constitutional law's feet sacrilegiously on some traditionalists. Black victims again . . . and without them, what sort of national unity? A legalistic-moral system seceded from it? The traditionalists believe freedom includes recognition—no, incorporation of the particular organisation of life that governed their ancestral relationships, their concepts of entitlement, before colonialism and apartheid. Apartheid dead, black president in the cabinet, members of parliament, but their traditional laws are alive. Can we afford to insult for their own just benefit members of the majority population. Answers himself. —Well we're going to win this case.— A wide laugh, everyone joins him. —Law enforcement means taking risks—on principle.—

The other lawyers use his first name, first names all round, she addresses him formally as she has been inducted since childhood in approaching an elder and anyone of obvious rank; the other siblinghood, of comrades, hasn't outmoded that for her even while she's uninhibited as a result of that comradeship. —The majority of the black majority (she underlines the neat significance with drawn breath in tightened nostrils)—I don't think would want to see traditions made law, certainly not when it comes to property. I mean, there was so little we could own that all white people had a right to, who would want to have in the Constitution the right to evict a woman, hand over a woman's home to a collateral—a man, of course.—

It was a diverting contradiction, appreciated by the Senior Counsel and others; that the member of the population from which traditionalists came should speak treason.

At the end of the trial, which indeed the S.C.'s lead won for the defence, as she thanked him for her benefit of having been allowed to be even a small part of it, he said as if he suddenly had his attention tapped by a detail overlooked —You should be at the Justice Centre. Why don't you come along and see the director, I'll have a word with him.—

This man of her father's generation, distanced, distinctive by public achievement, recognised in a marginal note of judgement what was for her the fulfilment of something not to talk about even to comrade, confidant, lover. To come out with a claim as a boast. The purpose of being alert—still as a comrade. The possibility of it. Opportunity.

In her new employment at the Justice Centre Steve lived with her transformation, the growing confidence in the voice, the certainty of gesture, the pleasure of relaxation evident in intervals between concentration on the current work at night preparing précis from notes taken on an advocate's sessions with the attorneys and, soon, appointed to what she was gifted for: speaking to witnesses to assess what could be expected of them in the dock—coaching was the disallowed description. Whatever was mandated in this aspect of her professional responsibilities, she took it as her responsibility to give the nervous, frightened or angry people understanding of the fears even of this kind of interrogation; hadn't she known the other, in a prison cell.

He found Jabu happy; fulfilment, isn't that what 'happiness' is. That he wasn't responsible for this part of it—component— is of no account; he shared it. It was unexpected when she brought up something that did involve him. They had made love. Whatever the daily apartness of the worlds of work, in identity, the illusion of exalting into one leaves an echo in which anything can be broached. —We should have another child.—

Heard.

Hadn't they decided for good reasons on which they also were at one, their purpose wasn't to perpetuate the human race, not even in the advancement the mixture of their distinctive bloods did, there were billions of others just as well equipped to breed, billions of women for whom this honourable task was the best they were equipped for. No condescension, discrimination in this fact. Be fruitful. The father's church said so, probably Jonathan's Torah said so, the eyes of the women at her home village said so.

—Sindiswa needs . . . to be an only child isn't a good thing.—

—Sindiswa gets enough companionship. She's very sociable, school buddies, kids of our neighbours here, in and out.—

—But they have the same mother and father.—

—If you're going to take Silk one day. An advocate with the kind of twenty-four-hour work that means, you know how Bizos and Chaskelson and Moseneke slave but they've had wives to stop the squabbles dry the tears and wipe the bottoms—

Touch of her lip to the crook of his neck, the skin the softest most vulnerable of a man's body, before the sandpaper of shaved beard begins—unless male lovers find the anus the most, how does a woman judge. —You've always done your share with Sindiswa.—

—OK. But all the mother stuff. You'll neglect the work, your mind will be elsewhere, and you'll be guilty, either way, before the children or the accused.—

His hand, shield on her breast as if some avid infant is already sucking her hard-won chosen life out of her. —I don't want you unhappy.—

—I won't be. We're not talking about a brood, five, six. There's Wethu—look how she and Sindiswa get on.—

A member of the extended family is not a nanny.

A woman is mama to all babies.

Jabu's reasons for convincing Steve they should have another child.

Her reason is not the stated one that Sindiswa needs a brother or sister. Neither is it that when back Home the women look at the flat waist where they expect to see a belly; her mother puts forth what in the extended family is taken for granted: your husband wants sons.

Jabu's the one who wants a son. She has produced a reproduction of herself, the female who has to prove her own identities beside the sexual one. If it hadn't been for her father she might never have done it; would never become an advocate (some day). A son doesn't have predetermined by what's between his legs, his function in any extended family, at Home or in that of the world. He's born free. At least in this sense. She wants a son, everything she isn't. It's the Other, to complete the fulfilment of favourable court judgment. Looking to the ambitions Steve has for her —If I'm an advocate I can't be a woman?— That's all she'll say of her reason.

He can only understand it differently. Reversed, as happens in pathways of the maze in which humans meet one another. —It's that a woman *can* be an advocate now!— At least it's understood mutually he doesn't have to specify 'black'.

Nothing is agreed to, as was the decision not to have children after Sindi. When he made love he had within the ecstatic ineffable there was perhaps something he was not, could not be aware of. She was the one who swallowed or didn't—how would he know—a pill in place of God's will some believed made the decision whether or not there was to be life.

Jabu had somewhere read or on Internet consulted learnt that conception of males was more likely in winter than summer (something to do with the body temperature, the semen stored in the testes?) and it must have been when winter came that she had not taken the pill. The son was conceived in the Southern Hemisphere's African winter, and born nine months and three weeks later, in confirmation of the theory she'd accepted on the principle some of the Home women called book-learning.

The delight and power over the future in naming a child. Among comrades there were Fidels and Nelsons and Olivers taking their first steps. But these comrades didn't want to choose for their infant who his heroes must be; he would be growing up in a time when there might be others. Then there's the happy fact that race, colour are a synthesis in their children; African name, European name? The name for the son came from somewhere out of the short list in mind, by looking at him: he was Gary. (Some film-star name?) Jabu was trying it out on herself and Steve: Gary Reed, the G and R, the initials went well together. It was Steve who named the son also for her father: Elias.

How? Why Steve? She laughed, all tears, scooping up the baby. *Elias*. Steve knows her better than she knows herself. The Mkizes, Jake and Isa, the Dolphin boys come to celebrate their son. She carries him in, Wethu in Sunday church dress beside her, and presents: —Gary Elias Reed.—

The Dolphins have brought along guitar and drums, they pluck and pound out Kwaito but also know older African music, and Wethu, although she hasn't taken any of the wine that's going down throats to the baby's future, born in the Suburb won over from the past, she is roused as if summoned to ease forward in a kind of sway-ing genuflection and raise her voice clear of the chatter and laughter. She sings. The scale is low, high, ululating, up to the roof and out through the open terrace, claiming the Suburb. Nothing like it ever came from the choir of the Gereformeerde Kerk, in its day.

This is no alma mater, the university where he had somehow graduated with his industrial chemistry degree while
acquiring the alchemy to sabotage the regime in which higher
education was an exclusive facility. The new student 'body'
was beginning to be many-limbed. Among the white students
whose parents were paying tuition and hostel fees there were
rising numbers of young blacks with confidence in their right
to knowledge that would lift them out of the level of skills,
money, dignity their parents had been dumped at.

The place of higher learning is open. The undenominational
bible (want of a better title for secular faith), the Constitution,
decrees this. But like most decrees it doesn't, can't ensure
what's called 'capacity' to benefit by them. Young men—so
far, fewer women with that nerve half-grown Jabu had had
abundantly—are registered on scholarships or sponsorships
of some kind, there are even white employers who hand out
a bonsella chance these times, to a servant's bright son. The
'bridging classes' Senior Lecturer from the Science Faculty
gives voluntary hours to: a band-aid. He knows it doesn't deal
with the chasm of poor schooling the students claw up from.

The Struggle's not over.

There are still some professors of the past on the faculties
along with the intake of comrades like himself known as the
Left by academics not wishing to question themselves too
exigently whether as an acceptable political category this can
be taken to include, in support of just ends, power stations
that were blown up.

The comrades, the Left or however they're seen, are aware
they have to re-educate themselves somewhat. The immediacy

of uncompromising back-and-forth in the bush, guns and cell walls instead of theses and coffee-vending machines in a faculty room—their kind of blunt confrontation will be misinterpreted by people who haven't known they may be dead in the dirt next day. —If something new is going to be made of the university we'll have to start with what we've got. We have to get on with the old guard on the principle that we don't accept they're guarding the same education any more, doors closed. That we trust they know this.—

—Even if they don't?—

—Even if they don't.—

—Exactly.—

—They should take early retirement—it's late.—

He's stirring his coffee as if repeating the sequence of those words heard. —No, no. Hang on. Most of them are good teachers. Some better than we are. They have the broad, worldly—sophisticated—general knowledge the students need to be given real access to. Grant that. Who's out there to replace them right now.—

Shudula Shoba's Struggle record isn't known, maybe it's enough he rescued himself out of the ghetto to earn a Masters, but he's one of the new appointments at lecturer level, under distinguished professors, novelists and poets. —Mphahlele, Ndebele, Kgositsile.—

He's too new to the faculty to ignore voices over his informing what he ought to know, they're already professors in other universities. —Sharp sharp—but some of the other big names, they're in rural colleges, just one step above high school, wasted there in the backveld.—

—You're going to poach them away from the people?—

The exchange isn't abandoned even as a few establishment professors come in with greetings all round. Coffee-vendor bonhomie. He puts his words into practice at once: —What we've got is with us.— Steve's remark is for professors all, against a clink of cups and the derogatory hiss of the coffee dispenser. —Don't you find our bridging efforts inadequate. Band-aid.—

—Here we go talking end results when we ought to be doing something about the beginning, I've got students in African Studies who don't know how to write, spell in their own language, mother tongue, they have the TV black sitcom vocabulary, that's all.— Lesego Moloi, survivor not only of the Struggle but by the old-time academic favour whereby a black would be hired as an exception by a white university only for that branch of learning, no matter what other post he may qualify for. He lifts and drops the soles of his heavy shoes in accompaniment to his words.

—So what should we be doing? The Convocation of the university doesn't run the education department's schools.— Professor Nielson still wears a suit, shirt and tie as the undergarments of the academic gown although there is a relaxed standard of suitability started with the example of Mandela's tunics. Professor Nielson cannot avoid having the tone of enlightenment dispensed even when not teaching. He's what father Andrew's generation calls a stuffed shirt, the starched shield once required as evening dress. —You're not proposing we lower university entrance standards further. Is that what a university is, not an advancement of knowledge but a descent.—

What Steve's question is—whether a token of coaching in hopes of bringing them up to university standards can achieve recovery from ten years of hopelessly poor schooling.

—We're simply to make the scientists, engineers, economists—you name them—out of its product.—

So what came of it, she wants to know.

What would there be to tell that wasn't an excuse.

Well, it was time for everyone to get back to the lecture halls, seminars. Or those declared hours when students could come to them in the small rooms that have their names on the door, bringing requests disguised as problems. That's what's come of it. Band-aid. He brought it up before Jake, Isa, the Mkizes grilling sausages and chops on a Sunday (as the former inhabitants of the suburb did). Their children inventing wild games, wrestling and tumbling, limbs mingled as those of their parents never could. He thinks he knows what should come of it. But he's telling the comrades, not the academic colleagues. University's Convocation, student organisation—the vice chancellors!—they ought to be demanding meetings with the minister responsible for education in schools. Breaking down his bloody door! It's *our* business. Education can't be lopped off in two, it's a contiguous process, our Moloi in African Studies gets students who can't read and write in command of their own languages, I have some—maths is a foreign language they haven't had the teaching to grasp, just enough, functionally, to scrape through the final school paper.—

—So what are you and your profs doing about the get-together?— Jake mimics an empty hand signalling Isa to offer more bread.

—That's what I said.— Jabu turns her shoulders and breasts, one of her unconscious physical reactions of differing opinion that made her individual to Steve from the beginning of clandestinity. Since way back in Swaziland they had taken it as part of freedom to be gained that they can imply criticism without breaching love.

The same applies to friendship; Peter Mkize takes up from comrade Jake. —Why don't you start it going? Get together lecturers, profs, approach the vice chancellor and have an appointment, whatever, meet the minister up there in the parliament, tell him what he doesn't want to hear.—

The children are asserting their rights, clamouring for ice cream. —It's not time yet.— The mothers clamour in rivalry. Everyone is laughing, biting into the meat that must first be eaten. The choir starts up again, ice cream ice cream.

One of the many things you learn in a liberation movement is take heed of what comrades challenge you in. A week or two after, he began to broach to colleagues, first those already grouped as on the Left, what was the teaching profession's responsibility in the situations of freedom, and then, on the same principle to the old guard, the proposal that there be a discussion whether a delegation of academics should meet with the minister to face the facts of two educational processes that should be one and are not. The discussion took place in the faculty room for an informal start. Opinions were hesitantly if not reluctantly expressed. The coffee machine again resorted to; this sort of meddling academia in government was heard as (of course) in conformation with the Left, citizens of the university unite, that stuff, update variation of an old rallying shibboleth that recruited whites against the *swart gevaar*. But it was one of the Lefties who came up with the irrefutable the minister would put on the table: there is not enough money to fund school education of a standard to pass seamlessly to universities, less than a generation after the end of hundreds of years when resources for education were spent overwhelmingly on the minority of the vast population. —Education. Funds in the exchequer are to be shared with health, housing, transport, everything that is social need. (Doesn't mention Big Brother Defence.) To ask for more?—

It's not time yet, for ice cream.

She listens to his account of the academic meeting while folding clothes Wethu has washed and ironed, and continuing a process, placing his shirts and socks in one pile, Sindiswa's dresses, jeans, Gary Elias's shorts and shirts in others.

Why does he give up.

If you're used to rejection you just go on for what you need, working at it. How could we have got to vote in '94 if we hadn't followed the banned Freedom Charter. How'd I have got to school ahead of my brother and then away from 'Bantu Education' to Swaziland, if my Baba had accepted that at Home females come second, for a black daughter education comes last. Hopeless. Why doesn't he just carry on. If that first lot is left hands-down there will be others in the university and even outside who'll act differently. You only decide it's hopeless if you're used to having everything. If you've been white.

Ashamed to be thinking that. Of him.

Life intervenes. Coincides with the group putting an approach to the minister on the back burner. The time for death of a parent; parents are always older and closer to this than a son realises, the main relationship was in childhood, boyhood. The Struggle brought other fundamental bonds in its place; if it's something for regret. Wasn't there a time once for the good son to have joined the father's cricket club. He's going to be cremated, as stated by him in his will. The son's moment of presentiment . . . Jonathan's not going to turn up with a rabbi? How ignorant of part of your inheritance can you be! Jews are forbidden cremation. Don't worry.

Pauline somehow persuaded their father to have their sons snipped. But seems to have recognised. Andrew's non-observant Christianity. Andrew's will also specifies—no religious service. Several of his friends and business associates are invited or appoint themselves to speak of him before his coffin in the hall of the crematorium, its seating suggesting a place of worship of some kind. Strange for a son to hear his father summed up in eulogy, oratory. Jonathan (no rabbi) as the eldest son speaks for the family.

It's over, people are tentatively about to stir, as Jabu does beside him, but she rises to sing. Unselfconscious, she rises to sing for him, Steve's father. She is in her full African dress as the understanding of the import of the final occasion in life. As the nanny-relative understood it first, at the presentation of a newborn son. No one moves, arrested.

Some potent substance is being generated in his body by the voice. He knows now that his father has left him, has always been within, with him, and is gone. At the last note, there's a susurration of admiration, movement urged by emotion, Jonathan's Brenda is propelled to shackle Jabu's robe in embrace, weeping proudly. She takes Jabu's hand through people making for the doors, as if Jabu is her own production. Brenda's changed the admiration, appreciation of some special tribute, into embarrassment, for some, at their own emotion; if it transcended something, it's true that one of the character-istics of being black is that peasant or lawyer, they certainly can sing.

The years are identified by event not date. The year of the third election in freedom was the year Sindiswa was of an age to have her education considered seriously. He had taken for granted, Pauline and Andrew's son, that when the time came they must have chosen, for him, a school from where they believed he would be prepared at a university for some career. For the Headmaster of the boys' school and Elder of the Methodist Church in the 'location' outside the coal-mine town, seriousness about his daughter's education was a strategy against a social abnormality and—eventually, contriving to have her continue the learning process over the border—a political defiance?

With what anticipation did they sift through the options open to choose a school for Sindiswa after the one she's graduated to from day care. On their principles, she should go to a state school. Those that had been white schools, at last open to all children, were well equipped but deteriorated by lack of funding for maintenance, and teaching standards lowered by overcrowded classrooms.

They could afford to give her something better.

Privilege? Come on; admit it!

He's the one who challenges himself and her; she reacts to this as absurd, a convention craven to dogma even if it's their own. Her Baba didn't betray the black freedom movement in sending his daughter to a training college over a border, the result of which she has qualified to work for the advance of justice!

He hears this as specious, something never to be expected from her. *That* was entirely different, another time.

But now the child. All right. Not to be argued over; the child must have the right to come first, beyond orthodoxy of comrade principles.

A different time.

There is only one time, all time, for principles you live by.

The Senior Counsel who had found a moment to put in a word for her employment at the Justice Centre was a descendant of immigration from a natal country once occupied by others: the Nazi army. He had escaped to a distant mirage Africa as a child with his father. They were poor and without a word of any language but Greek, but they were white. Acceptable. He grew up eking from whatever opportunities he could grasp an education which had culminated in his appearances as defence of the accused in apartheid trials of liberation leaders, at risk of landing up in prison himself, and in the aftermath he is equally preoccupied with the process of justice in unforeseen occurrences of its transgressions in a free country. But he had never forgotten that as a South African—African who had earned that one-word identity—he also was Greek. When he became well enough known, which means recognised in the outside world for his standing in the annals of the legal profession, and was able to raise money among the diaspora Greeks who had either feared or admired him, he brought them into the founding of an open school where Greek would be a compulsory subject along with the usual curriculum. From something rather in the category of the sports and cultural clubs of Italians, Scots, Germans, and the eternal diaspora of Jews, the school had responded to the country's freedom by expanding with the energetic promotion of admission of black children, any mix of colour on the population palette, the only stipulation that they learn

Greek among their other subjects. The privilege of a classical education thrown in.

A fee-paying school. It's not an innovation to deal with illiteracy, but there are a number of bursaries endowed; any child with proven ability could come from a makeshift rural school without toilets or electricity among the shacks.

She should see it for herself; naturally her mentor says it is the right, the only place for a child. But no, a father's responsibility as much as hers, he must come although this child is a girl and back where her mother lived she'd—still, maybe—be last in line for school. Unless she had an exceptional Baba.

So as they had taken up Jake's invitation to look at the house which was their first home together (for him: she might not agree) they went on Senior Counsel's invitation to visit the school. He toured them round classrooms, art studio, music section, library and Internet facilities, swimming pool, sports fields, botanical garden, with a volunteer entourage of eager pupils to whom he turned aside, interrupting his accounts of the values by which the school was directed, to chat and chaff.

Each saw the other was picturing Sindiswa in these settings.

On their terrace that early evening, with the subject, Sindiswa, there, as they had sat alone with her as a baby that evening in Glengrove when the street sky was ripped apart; a decision was made. But this time there was quiet.

Only Gary busy building and then gleefully attacking his Lego fortresses.

It distracted her father's attention from Sindiswa. There was only the caveat from him, in his mind; the school uniforms are too elaborate. —Those sports team blazers, white with braid and gold. Waste of money enriching some outfitter. 'Conspicuous consumption' crap.— He pulls a face at himself in admonition of this pious old tag of political correctness.

The academic indecision to approach the minister, pussy-footing, brought about irritation of frustration which affected all his responses. Even Jabu's constancy irked: —Just call them together again. Don't let them off.— It's her variation of a woman's nagging.

—I put notices on the staff board, I pushed messages under their doors. Three turned up yesterday, no sign of the others.—

—The old profs.—

—Not only . . . but I begin to smell there's this idea—excuse, pretext, who the hell do I think I am?—

She jerks her head at them.

But it's not as irrelevant a question as she dismisses.

—An upstart from 'The Struggle' who doesn't know he's under a different command now?—

She sweeps decisively into cupped hands bits of Gary's plastic building units that have scattered. —Speak to them, one by one, each one. *Khuluma nabo, ngamanye, emanye!*—

—A kick in the butt.— He supplies what he thinks is more or less the meaning of the expletive-sounding one in her own language. It hasn't been part of the coaching she's given him.

Before he could take up the conviction he has of his own strength of character an event on campus, of the campus, not of the faculty room, made a kick in the butt too late. The students commanded possession of the university with an authority that made their previous protests mere tantrums which had been, could be contained in toleration, freedom of expression after all. The organisers—if such spontaneity can be attributed to a Student Council—were far outnumbered by other groups and factions, sects, political and religious, Gay and Lesbian. Gatherings that began before this faculty building and that, the library, the colonial-classical façade of the Great Hall where graduation ceremonies take place, were encompassed, overflowed and became one uproar on a venue generally regarded as too dispersed to demand attention for protests: the sports fields, football, cricket, invaded like the angry spectators who can't be kept off when they reject a referee's decision. The speakers were empty mouthings under the thunder of drummers and bellow in song, jetting as the crush surged; it didn't matter, all knew what their issues were, on placards, T-shirts, home-contrived banners even if some were ancillary GAY BASHING CRIMINAL UNDER THE CONSTITUTION to the overall purpose NO TUITION FEES EDUCATION OUR RIGHT WHAT ABOUT THE BETTER LIFE—election promises hurled back at the other all-powerful referee, the government. Self-destruction that had seen people of their ghettos burn down the scrapheap of living begrudged to them, the ramshackle cinema, the school without books, the clinic without water—this irrational impulse of reality. Trash is vomited from bins, lecterns are crushed like matchboxes, files rifled from the admission offices are danced round as they burn, on the sports fields the goalpost altars of the games the rioters themselves worship, are dragged up, tossed over.

The students who come as friends, familiars of the house, Jabu and the children—Sindiswa has a favourite whom she tells boastfully about her school—they must be among the spore of heads covering the space he looks down upon from his room in the science faculty. It would be unlikely to come across them there, find them in the anonymity that erases all personal features of the crowd. Yet they are some sort of recognition to be claimed; allow him, member of the academic faculty, to go out into it?

He can't see far among the bodies pressed around him. There are white hands among those raised in the stomping, chanting, so he couldn't be so noticeably there, the absorption in purpose is blindly fervent, he knows from political rallies. In the mass you have no direction of your own, he is carried along in a surge towards the main gates of the campus. Outside between the street and the gates, another gathering—a few pausing in curiosity before turning away, others, some black men and women literally throwing their yelling weight about. All cling to gates too wide, tall and strong to shake: they've joined the students' action.

He tries to make a way to other parts of the campus but progress is against powerful currents as urge drives each limb of the great body to join that. He reaches only the science block from where he had set out.

Did any of his academic colleagues to whom he'd been advised to kick arse attempt to be along with the uprising against tuition fees most of their students couldn't pay (so the cell phones worn like ear ornament, who pays for the serial calls). The faculty coffee room may say, factually, the university couldn't exist without tuition fees to supplement the government's inadequate grant; 'funding free education is that government's affair'. No dereliction of the university's responsibility towards students?

Did he have a place down there (he's back up at his window again). Claim it—claim on *him*—because of his part, his decision to get mixed up in providing scientific know-how and ingredients to make bombs, his Jabu, his children gestated in a black womb. There are bonfires signalling here, there, like the Guy Fawkes ones of his childhood commemorating a revolutionary arson he and his siblings had never heard of. One of the bundles of whatever was being fed smoking to the flames was very near the archeological museum where tooled stones are the reminder that young men rioting are the descendants of peoples who had skills before invaders brought others; he had a sudden fear not for himself but for what is an extension of self, the work, research that was in progress in the science faculty. What if they burst into the laboratories where climate change is being studied for solutions that would save their own existence on this planet.

Who the hell does he think he is.

What's the difference between trashing a university that can provide knowledge only for money, and the street gangs who hijack and rob—ah, but *there's* the difference, the hijack brings means to buy, own the advertised products the hijacker doesn't have; there's no gain in ransacking a university.

What if they come. Would he say comrades, it may be justice to let you into the laboratories to break the privilege others have to qualify for such work, tuition at a price your parents and grandparents, great-great-grandparents have earned down the mines, building the roads, digging the earth for the crops of masters.

This opposition within, clashing contradictions, it didn't exist when you were closed away with yourself solitary in detention, and even in the bush tents where between action that seemed the answer then, immediate, which accounted to and for every contesting manifestation of living. There were discussions on what's supposed could be called moral choices taken—made do with?—in the 'situation' of the old regime— everyone would be freed for good (in all senses of the two words) of all evasions once that regime was *finish and klaar*.

Who the hell do you think you are.

The answer is go back down into the body of the throng. But this time someone pressed against him in the strange intimacy of a peristaltic crush, twisted face round. —*Eish!* You Professor Reed from Science!— He's not a professor yet, Senior Lecturer with a thesis to complete, but with this greeting he has a rank in the protest, if far back, in the combined push from the playing fields and the surrounded faculty buildings again to the main gates. There's a backlash in the great body followed by a surge forward as common breath taken: the police are at the gates now the gates have given way, their dogs are barking against hysterical shouts in the theatrical effect of tear gas. Fight your way (as if that were possible) to the front and then, as a white man, the old authority that was the ultimate one, tell the police to lay off the assault? The students are throwing whatever they can pick up at the police, who are mostly black. Through tears and retching coughs they yell insults in many languages as batons strike them. As far as can be made out the leaders of the Student Council who were in the front line have been overcome and arrested, there are police vans swirling sirens in the street, and the other students are being dragged pell-mell random into vans.

Dispersal begins raggedly. Some small groups re-form with attempts at addressing the break-up, the campus is haggard with destruction.

His keys there in his pocket; he gets—escapes?—to the academic staff car park; few cars, no damage done to them—most of the academics have made off as soon as the protest grew. His book-bag and papers are on a table somewhere in his room and the door's left unlocked—irresponsible. There's one of the academics about to open his car. —You're all right? You get caught up in that chaos?—

—Not caught up. I was there.—

Professor of Classics—yes it's Anthony Demster—takes this as a philosophically sophisticated way of dealing with the disturbance.

—What went on at the university—the police—I tried and tried to call you after we heard at the office but you didn't pick up!—

To put it to her; they were so familiar with each other's reactions to the predictable or the unpredictable in their not far-off life on the wrong side of the law.

As customary, she's doing something; she'll continue routinely with some part of her unconscious (what is it—pushing the heads of keys into the clips of a leather holder) while her voice is intense with concern. The Classics Professor: did you get caught up in it. But she knows better than that. As if she knew he would leave his little academic enclave and go down there, among the crowd, who this time happened to be students, some of them his. As she would.

—Wasn't there anyone among the leaders who could direct, I mean the way it was going. So they could be heard . . .—

She's asking; she who sleep-deprived and in imminence of other torture had resisted giving the names of comrades the interrogators wanted of her.

A way now. Meeting in the Great Hall with the vice chancellor principal of faculty and the Students Council in discussion of the matter of tuition fees? —That's the government's affair.—

What would the result have been? Agreement that the Convocation would meet to consider an inquiry into the implications etc. of social responsibility implied by free tuition at university level? Who can pay and who can't. A means test?

—I couldn't even get together a so-called delegation to tell the minister the university's little problem, attempting to teach students who come out of school half-literate. What choice is there for them. *Out* from the lecture halls and our baby-care seminars, to the campus!—

He tells her like a confession only just realised—to himself, that when the swell of bodies landed him back near the science block he ejected himself and went back up to his room, met nobody in the corridors—keeping themselves scarce in their rooms, quit the campus or holed up in the faculty coffee room. But what did he have to feel himself more honest about as he stood again at his window, looking down at what was officially referred to collectively inoffensively as 'The Student Body' and now really was that, a mythological entity of many limbs. So down again, leaving the room open.

—The campus is really badly trashed? What's the sense in that. They have to live with the mess, themselves. No, no what'm I saying, the black cleaners'll have to come on . . .— Jabu still has in her the discipline of the Struggle: you must answer for your own actions . . .

Burnt documents trampled kicked about like dead leaves. A computer (whose from where) lying among broken shrubs. Who knows what, from bins in the women's toilets. As someone offering knowledge, however mingy the access, one who's accepted to be an academic, wouldn't he be against students fouling their nest. If he believes in the purpose of a university existing however inadequate to circumstances it may be. If not, why be there? Teaching in the limitation of what you're able and writing some fucking thesis so that you can pass on something more to those who need it, whose right it is.

Principal, Vice-Chancellor, faculty and representatives of the students were summoned to a meeting where the students succeeded in the university's condemnation of brutal police action and arrests; and the principal and faculty succeeded in condemning the destruction by the students of campus facilities.

Sindiswa was born at a time when the new life of freedom was just three years old, child of change. She was even-tempered and happily responsive to everyone and everything. Her brother, Gary Elias, who had taken his first steps in the security of the suburban house was not, as Steve, while distrustful of fatherly judgements said, 'easy'; would not go further than that. Jabu laughed—this was a naughty boy, as someone might say 'tall for his age'. His primary schooling was at a local school, as Sindiswa's had been before the Greek school, where she was reported by her teachers as top of her class. But the character of naughtiness the boy's mother saw as usual began to be troubling. He punched a classmate, narrowly missing the eye—Steve and Jabu had to visit the parents to apologise. Gary 'borrowed' without her permission Sindiswa's treasures (a conch in which she had been shown you could hear the sea, a carved box one of her Indian friends had given her) and damaged or, as he said, lost them. She was forgiving but hurt; and that seemed to annoy him. Jake told Steve he ought to take the kid along to watch football, the university games, join Jake and his rather older boys, giving him innocent male status. Gary listened to his father's and Jake's explanatory comments of what was happening on the field without reaction: tugged Steve's shirt —When will it finish—

—I'm going to take Gary home over the long weekend.—
    —That's an idea. We'll all enjoy a break.—
    —Stevie, I want to take him to my father. He's experienced with boys, he's been head of that school, how many years . . . I'll talk to my father. It's better if I take him alone.—

There's still—always—something distancing about Jabu's bond with her father. For Steve, who did not know any such unique relation to his, only felt the loss for those few moments when his father was dead. He got up and folded his arms around her back, she turned not to release herself but so that they could kiss, their secular blessing, whatever happened to pass between them.

Jabu and the boy came back late on the Monday, last holiday night, she lively, not tired by the long drive and he bounding, in charge, out of the car with the usual spoils of her natal place, this time avocados and eggs—Gary brought them from my mother's hens himself, she told. Steve cooked a second supper, some of the eggs with leftover meat and he and Sindiswa ate again with her and the boy, praising the taste of the bright golden yolks, Gary unusually talkative telling of the calf he had touched, just born, all wet, and the bird—*inyoni*, Jabu prompts with the Zulu name—that nearly hit the windscreen, these events in the sum of days he'd passed. —You lucky thing— Sindiswa presented him with her admiration.

In bed, before turning out the light above their pillows —Your father, what'd he say.—

—We'll talk tomorrow. *Lala* now, *masilake manje*.—

Tomorrow was a working day, breakfast, Wethu demanding news from home, how-is-Baba-mama-auntie—all right, delivery of the children, routes divided by alternative maps drawn by traffic, Jabu in her car the Greek school, him to Gary's primary before the science faculty, her destination Justice Centre. So it was night again when the children were in bed that there was time for her to tell him her father's thoughts, advice about the naughty boy. The loyalty of her mother love to persist in seeing him as just that despite behaviour gone beyond the happily mischievous.

Boys will be boys. Yes, will be seen, lived with differently in KwaZulu her home (no other home will ever deny its status) than in the suburb of freedom. That's really what there is to hear about.

Whenever she's approaching that way back it's a route inside her as well as a road taken, and it is her father, whose stance imaged above the road. Only when she slows the car for the safety of the children who recognise it, leap alongside calling out Jabulile Gary Elias, *wozani*! to be the first to announce her—does the entire familiarity of the place of origin come to her as if she were pinching peaches from the tree before they were ripe, being pulled along wild tumbling rides on the fruitbox sleds of the boys, sitting with the Church Ladies at their prayer meetings.

Her mother comes to greet her and the grandson in the usual attendant women, everyone embracing her as also a mother and not sparing the grandson, who presses his elbows tight against his body in attempt at evasion.

Her father stands on the red-polished cement steps of the headmaster's European-style house, his stance that is there, imprint in her mind. She moves to him and he down to her in the respect with which the women back off. He and she, father and daughter, embrace, enfold in one another's arms almost like some special wrestle, but do not kiss. She can't remember Baba kissing her even when she was a little girl. He doesn't have to; the way everybody's father husband boyfriend does among comrades in the Suburb. He takes her palm and walks her away into the house after she's made a brief halt for his grandson Gary Elias to be greeted with a grown-up grasp of hands, and to be released among the boys who have already claimed him, always taken up from where previous family visits left off.

Her father leads her to the cabin-of-a-room which is the only completely private space of the house except for the brief use of the combined bathroom-lavatory. Her mother hastens up with some half-reproach half-concern about tea and food, but the exchange with her father's calm ends in his instruction that the grandson be fed and tea be sent to this room for his daughter and himself, Jabu will join the others later.

Until one of the young girls brings a buckling tin tray with tea and two slices of cake (the headmaster has a mobile phone and of course his daughter has told him she was coming over for the long weekend) they exchange the expected: how is everyone, was there too much holiday traffic on the roads. She reminds the headmaster of what he already has been told, his daughter's husband has been appointed Assistant Professor as the result of his thesis on approaches to the transformation of education. Baba tells he believes he has succeeded in getting a Carnegie grant to set up a library and eventually an Internet facility at his school.

This opening somehow establishes his instinct—always intuitive of her—that this isn't just a family visit. She speaks in their language without being aware of it when she is back home, but he as unconsciously often speaks to her in English, perhaps recall of the years when he was preparing her for the standard of the language that would be required when he sent her over the border for the education he was determined she should have. The synthesis of communication: cultural authority of the natal, and the other one taken of right, freed of the colonialism it signified, are an intimacy they have with no one else. Her lover Steve would never, in his valiant efforts to learn isiZulu from her, reach this. Their children: Gary Elias playing games where action not words matter, with cousins in whose blood he has a share, would have the language from them, a second language; never home tongue.

—Baba, about Gary. Gary Elias.—

Before she could go on, her father took moments to look at her, them together on the time-plane for this. —How old is he?— He certainly knew but it was necessary for him to be accurate: if you have spent a lifetime with schoolboys you have learnt that every week, month, is a whole period as a year is in adulthood, not alone the body is budding, changing with awareness of itself. The question of the child's place among others is looking for some form of assertion.

He has a better way of seeing this. —What does he do, in the family.—

—Baba?—

—What I say, my child.—

—We're his parents, we do . . . for them, the children, I hope the right things.— English now, comes as the language. —I mean, we love him . . . show him . . . we are busy with whatever he needs at school, we let him have his friends around welcome, any time. If he gets into trouble he can come to us . . . help sort it out, he doesn't have to become aggressive, Steve's the last man in the world even to slap a naughty child . . . *sesibone udlame sekwanele*. It's difficult to understand how our child could punch another kid in the face—he did it—a close friend thinks we should encourage him to take more interest in sport even though he's still only kicking a ball around, but at a big soccer match he couldn't wait for it to be over. Of course Steve's not a great fan, himself.—

Her father takes his time.

—A boy must have duties. Yes, he must do things for you. Yes. A family can't be together if children have no part in what has to be done every day. When they have these things, obligations (he was speaking in their language but now changed to the particular harsh cadence of English) tasks they don't like too much, these give them the knowing they count for something, they're not just there for what did you say, love.—

It is always clear from her father when the final word has come.

Mothers, sisters and the one brother still left at home, the others, absent husbands, gone to work and live in the cities— they were ready for her. Only the eldest sister, born a year ahead of her, was aware of the sister's difference as the one who had been in prison in the apartheid past; the others placed the difference as her being among the women transformed, in the soaps they watched on TV. When, once or twice, a sister had been invited to visit Johannesburg, the house in the Suburb, she wanted to wander shopping malls as a tourist in a real-life television scene—there was the admired sister's difference, the world to which she belonged; although that house didn't look much like a television set.

Now sitting all together with her among them at home the difference, prison cell or shopping mall, wasn't present; they chattered and laughed in their shared idiom, the latest-born baby was handed to her lap and stared to her encouraging drawnback face with eyes newly able to focus—*Uyabona ukhuti uyaba ngummeli omkhulu!*—exclamation from an aunt or grandmother chipping in, she's seeing you will be a great lawyer. The exaggerated gasping, whooping of people who are happily at ease to be gathered when there are so many part- ings, this sister-daughter long missing from among them for unimagined reasons, prison and marrying a white man. But the oldest aunt or grandmother kept her everted lips down- pressed on either corner in the withdrawn certainty that this is one who can inhabit the future.

—What do you do?— A girl of about twelve, from the look of her breasts, has been mouthing to herself for the courage to speak, nervously remembers respect to add —Mama Jabu, please.—

Her father is there in the background ignoring moves of homage to vacate a chair for him. —If someone is arrested by the police for something he didn't do, mama tells what really happened and why he should not go to jail. She works for justice, that's what's right.—

—And if he did do something bad?— The Zulu language is voluble about transgression: —*Uma enze okubi?*—

Laughing Jabu calls as if across to her father what he might answer. —Then there'll be another lawyer who'll say he didn't do it.— Shall she try to explain the concept of justice Constitution defines, to this child—it would seem like bragging. The small place she's made for herself in the new dispensation (that's what it's called among lawyers)—and isn't it him, he who made it possible for her to do it.

She's carried off to admire the queen-size bed and the paraffin-powered refrigerator-cum-freezer one of the husbands working in the city has had delivered to his wife. (And didn't she herself want just such possessions when Steve and she were moving to the Suburb.)

Her father walked with her to the car, his very presence having made clear to her mother and the extended family all were to respect this, once the exuberant and tearful farewells had been made. Gary Elias was already scuffling with two boys in the back seat.

—Baba . . . I don't usually appear in court, I mean for a complainant. Mostly I prepare witnesses. For cross-examination. It's scary for them, the kind of close questioning, they need to know how to deal—say—

She doesn't need to add, not to incriminate themselves.

—That is just as important.— He's standing by the praise he gave, not something glibly produced to impress children. She turns to cling to him for a moment and his arms in his stiff black jacket are firm around her, with a quick release. A few words over his shoulder to the boys and they tumble out of the car; her boy, as if commanded, takes his place in the front passenger seat. —Wave to Babamkhulu!— as she shifts into gear.

Her father's hand, lifted like a salute.

Time to talk; pack the day aside. Sindi and the boy have been allowed to watch a wildlife documentary DVD, and although in the shared living room, their attention to the screen means isolation from anything, anyone else as the way is for children of their time. (Nothing to be done about it, and at least a nature series is not a channel soapie.) —You were going to tell. What did he say.—

—My father. Well.— Can't take him lightly. —He says he must have—tasks, he called it (old word, italicised, from Baba's childhood among missionaries)—things to do, for us, the family, some of the everyday things. Responsibilities.—

—I don't get it. Responsibilities? Nine years old.— Of course the father's not only a headmaster he's also an Elder in the church, always with the habit, some subject to preach on. But her attachment to Baba is central to her, mustn't be fingered.

—He should have duties. *Kufanele abe nezibopho.* When children have these—even doing things they don't like too much—this means they're important, they know they count for something. They're somebody.—

—You love him, I love him, we love him isn't that what shows how he counts.—

—Do, give something, not just here to be loved.—

Love. Irrelevantly at this moment he knows how he desired her. —Jabu my darling. What could he do for us, empty the kitchen bin instead of me taking it out, wash his shirts in place of Wethu and the washing machine. What 'tasks'—no goat for him to milk here, no chickens to feed here, no wood to fetch.— The sharpness is kindly—not patronising?

Here. There will always be these moments when she is not 'here' with him. And when he's not 'here', wasn't 'here' in the clandestine Glengrove with her, some tug of your outgrown kind.

They made love not war between them that night.

What was still mustered of the academic group eventually did get that appointment to meet the Minister of Education. Couldn't be called a delegation, that would imply representation of the University Convocation. It seems one always keeps the identity of dissident whether as a revolutionary or what's known as a law-abiding citizen taking the right of consultation. That's how they presented themselves, their spokesperson initiator from the Science Faculty falling into line.

The Minister most unfortunately is unable (or has the foresight?) to receive them as he is in talks with a delegation from abroad. They are before a senior member of his department, a heavy finger stuck between the pages of a file, should he pause for recollection of a date, a fact. Lesego Moloi remarked afterwards over something more reviving than a coffee, that one's been dug up as a loyal member of the Party from a *kraal* college somewhere to show that the department's really Africanised.

The Minister's deputy listened with the posture and occasional stir of close attention, to be read as agreement or doubt, then gave the account they knew would come, they could have recited it for him. The redeployment of available finances from the days when ten times more was provided in education subsidy for every white child than for a black child meant that an equal subsidy for all, now, required greater resources than the department's budget allocation from the Department of Finance. The need to fund justice in education in less than one generation in something like five centuries of discrimination (he hawks to clear his throat, turning to pages where there might be a decade fixed by historians when missionaries first transcribed a people's volubility into written symbols)—yes, it's inevitable that resources are inadequate; but the limit the country can afford.

What's the purpose of one of Steve's group bringing up money found for spending on arms when no enemy exists to threaten the country which has the strongest defence forces on the African continent?—that's not the Minister's Department, you're in the wrong building, Bra, take your guys to the Ministry of Defence.

The man assures the Minister's concerns for the consequences, for university teaching, at a time when the continuation of the country's remarkable renaissance (doesn't miss the buzz word) must have engineers, scientists, economists, geologists—he pauses; every one of these academics will add the inclusion of his particular discipline.

—Literacy.— Steve presumes to speak for them. —Nothing of this can come about unless you can raise literacy. In any of the mother tongues the children speak, and English, Afrikaans, the languages of their instruction. The vocabularies used in university subjects are way beyond students, no fault of their own. They run to Internet, quick fix, for words they don't understand, can't spell, not to the dictionaries where all different meanings, contexts, uses of the word are to be discovered.— He doesn't know or care whether it's understood he's using the 'word' in an adapted creational sense, the Word is not God, it's Man, what gives humans the text of thought. The Minister's stand-in does not take offence at bluntness, he puts a politician's hand on this academic's shoulder as the group leaves. He has assured them their openness and trust in coming to the department is the way forward (renaissance-speak again). The department is applying itself intently to changes that will bring about development necessary for the times. —What the fuck does that mean— Lesego, using current limited vocabulary of the pub to which they have retreated. But nobody takes up the irony.

Not long after (there's probably a change of minister in a cabinet reshuffle by then) there is announcement from the Department of Education to mark the esteem of the people for education and the dignity of those in school: the children are now officially designated as and are to be referred to as 'Learners'. The demeaning 'pupil' belongs to the discriminatory past. And what resolves in final examinations from the years of being a Learner is now called 'Outcomes'. Results no longer exist.

The church pool friends are the best of hosts—female guests noting that old conventions in allocation of domestic roles have been discarded in Constitutional normalcy of gay households more completely than in heterosexual ones. Ceddie, the jambalaya cordon bleu, cooks while Guy the apprentice (in the order of sexual relations managed by the commune, as well?) peels and chops, Justin who seems to be the Elder (as Jabu's father in another church) mixes drinks, chattering ice in glasses along with animated indiscretions about the clients in the decorator's business where he works as an interior designer. —I make houses habitable after the architects have cleared out.— That's the way he mockingly describes himself. —Wifey wants a full-length mirror in the bathroom so that she can check the spread of her backside against the kilos on the scale, husband prefers not to see what he's neglecting in favour of the new girl he's picked up among women who're now getting theirs down on boardroom seats.— And he gets his laughs, as he distributes the drinks, for his unprejudiced tolerant gossip: the *kugels*—Jewish sweetmeat term he's picked up for all over-dressed rich women—these days they're also Indian, black, mixed palette of the risen middle class. Politics touched on indirectly with Justin's quips from the underside of progress are not the subject of talk the way they are when Struggle comrades, Steve, Jabu, the Mkizes, Isa and Jake gather alone, belong for ever under that rubric, which needs no tattoo to mark it—although Isa was never a cadre but a fellow travel-ler late-come recruited as Jake's freely chosen wife. At times she's good leaven in their set. That property in her personality isn't necessary in the company of the Dolphin commune and its friends, some of whom are still arriving. Lively anecdotes of where you've been and what you've been up to, holiday trips, the predicted break-up of 'this' relationship and the surprise blooming of 'that'; ambitions in professional activities, Marc's just written a second play and does anyone know a backer for production, he's found amazing, you'd never believe it—such talent—among young black men who wave you into parking bays, no education, can't read a script you have to teach it to them orally—

—Illiterate.— Jake confirms, reminded. —What happened to your call on the ministry?—

Steve asking Marc what his play's about—turns aside: this is for everybody —Haven't you learned the new terminology for your kids?—

—You mean?—

—They are Learners and there will be Outcomes.—

—The ministry have any plans to get them past ABC?—

Steve's shoulders rise and drop. His response is curt. —Euphemisms.—

Jabu is concerned that this exchange means the happy lunch is going to be spoilt for the Dolphins by the preoccupation of Steve and Jake—heavy. She glances at Steve as a mother hushes a child with a certain loving look.

He pauses in dismissal and turns back to Marc and his play. Euphemism. Not a word Jabu would be likely to use.

Not in her vocabulary of what?—her three, four languages he doesn't know, not in the vocabulary her father expanded for her through his reading of books in English smuggled from a library for whites. Everything's been definitive for her, imposed. Her experience. He dismisses again—in himself, the glib judgement. Black is being black that's all, has been; in some circumstances, still is.

The gay commune like every household in the Suburb except Steve and Jabu's, which has a resident relative, deploys a domestic servant called a Helper as a school child is a Learner, but the Dolphins' woman doesn't work over weekends. Isa knows this through her own helper informing her that those men in the church house grant this desirable condition of employment which she doesn't. A word aside to Jabu, and Isa and Jabu insisted they would do the washing-up. Comrades don't exploit their hosts.

Yet a kitchen is like a Ladies' Room in a public place, the secure refuge for confidences—same food-warmed air despite the fan the Dolphins have installed in their conversion of the chancel into the place where (some of) the appetites of the flesh are catered to by the latest models of microwave and blender, and a dishwasher helps with the aftermath of sinful indulgence.

—I've never known them, you know, so close before. They seem just like us, don't they—living here like us in this suburb, keeping house, bothered having to call the plumber because of leaks, paying the monthly fee of security patrol. All the stuff that goes along with being married, domestic, in the end however you started together. Steve and you, Jake— coming in from the cold. No—the heat, *Umkhonto*—I don't count myself in your class, Jake has to stand in for me; well, another way, they've come in from the cold. They're neighbours with the rest of us. We lend each other the lawnmower, soda water when we run out. Comrade bourgeoisie. Oh, by the way, I resent, that's one thing I hold against them, they've hijacked the word. You can't say you had a gay time, you like gay colours, and what about 'gaily', you can't walk gaily along feeling happy—all these have a special meaning these days. Theirs. You can't have that word just for living it up. Having a jol.— Isa was stacking the plates into the machine, word by word.

Both were laughing, because they were doing just that, themselves with these good neighbours.

Jabu put the detergent tablet into its slot and snapped the latch, Isa pressed the right combination of switches. Under the machine's swirling tidal rush that isolated them she was able to speak as if without being heard. —Have you ever had a man do, I mean what they do—to you.—

Jabu runs the palm of one hand down the fist of the folded other, cautious as what she understands Isa has said cannot be what she meant.

There was never a curtained confession box in a Protestant Gereformeerde Kerk, but there can be confession under the leap tide of the dishwasher. Isa places herself before the black box curtain.

—Once I did. I was crazy about the man and he told me, to know everything sex is, can be, do. It was so horrible Jabu— some goo, Vaseline, so he could get into me and it hurt I was ashamed I felt like I wanted to shit he came on his own with-out me. All I could get out of it was the idea of the dirt in that place, my dirt, coming off on him, his thing. How can they do it to each other?— An abrupt gesture—stayed—in the direction of the swimming pool. —And we have the clean soft smooth place specially for them. To take them in.—

Jabu could only move to take Isa's hand as if whatever had happened had only just happened. This woman Isa-and-Jake,

Jake didn't know, would never know? That's certain, the way some things can't be said between a man and a woman: what had been told now. It's a responsibility she didn't want—to have received it.

Isa was asking as if to put finality to the moment in the kitchen —A black man wouldn't do it to a woman.—

A question. Or an affirmation to compensate for all the assertions of blacks' savagery that she had lived among as a white.

Jabu was finding herself as she so seldom had time, was ever challenged within, to be set in the past—going home was done easily now, with a sense of belonging unchanged though experienced in a new self; no estrangement. The way sexuality had been, was still ordered there—and the way it was far from home, Swaziland college, recruitment to detention, bush camp; correspondence courses, Freud included, in Glengrove clandestinity. This kind of order is what she would think of as 'sexual code'. What did she know.

Men. Was there a black man who would do the same thing to a woman. Who is she to say—in her reaction. Claim a superior decency—sensitivity, for blacks?

The two women left the cloister of the kitchen and came among the company mainly of men with Mkize's wife there innocent of what had passed between her comrade sisters in the domesticity for which they were being jokingly lauded.

E verybody goes overseas.

    It's understood that Steve and Jabu have a particular life of their own and are not often involved in the many occasions of celebration which are observed in the Reed clan. But when they do take part (it's Jabu who says it's only right they must) Jonathan seems always to have just returned from a business trip or holiday 'abroad' with his wife. Brenda tells graphically of Trafalgar Square, castles they have seen, Montmartre, Roman tavernas, the Holocaust Museum in Berlin, the beaches in Portugal.

Places Steve and Jabulile have never been. Steve might have once gone on a student tour to Europe if it hadn't meant fiddling while the townships burned in police fire. Only a very few blacks, venerable as scholars or Christians, promoted by the institutions or white benefactors got out of South Africa for reasons acceptable to the powers-that-were for the issue of passports; the others were escaped freedom fighters receiving military training in Moscow, China, Ghana . . . If any of these came from the coal-mine village no one would know of this. Except maybe the schoolmaster Elder. His daughter had got as far as Swaziland and detention in a South African prison; that he knew. She had learnt something of the existence of the outside world by some pictures of it in her father's clandestine store of books secretly coming from and to be returned to the library he had no right to use.

Both she and Steve had seen it all on television, the daily devastation of wars, and the Sistine Chapel. While, of course, his brother Jonathan and eagerly receptive wife had never experienced the inside of a tent in the bush or desert camp where each night you could be spending the last of your existence without ever having had the chance to look elsewhere, at the wonders of the world.

Everybody goes overseas.

With the new millennium came the time they could and did. Justice Centre cooperatively allowed her leave to coincide with the winter vacation at the university, summer in the other hemisphere. As his brother Jonathan was so knowledgeable about airlines and flights and Steve, against her suggestion, wouldn't ask advice, Jabu herself called Brenda, and Brenda delighted, insisted on coming over to give hers. Where exactly was the house again, she's been there once, how long ago—bringing a generous gift of the latest baby equipment when Gary Elias was born—wasn't there some old church where you had to turn . . .

Even though she and Jonny didn't need to skimp it (this was the way she put their resources) she always made it her business to get the best value for a reasonable fare, and of course there were cheaper ones she could also recommend, their daughter and a pal had happily travelled that way. It was a Saturday morning and Steve was at the gym; Jabu offered coffee and the two women talked for the first time outside his clan occasions. —Is your little family complete now?— If Brenda was thinking, though not from the same authority, of the home women's expectation always of more babies—isn't that the African way?—this wasn't patronisingly white, coming from this woman. Quite the reverse. She is eager to be loved by a sister-in-law, the Reed family's black stake in the new dispensation. Steve boyish in brief shorts and with hair flat from a shower walked in just as she was irrepressibly repeating the embrace with which she had waylaid Jabu at his father's funeral. His quiet greeting just as irrepressibly expressed that this was excessive, but when Jabu was released the women were two bells set pealing.

She and he come from an era where the nuclear family was not, could not be, the defining human unit. This young comrade parent or that was in detention, who knew when she, he, would be released, this one had fathered only in the biological sense, he was somewhere in another country learning the tactics of guerilla war or in the strange covert use of that elegantly conventional department of relations between countries, diplomacy to gain support for the overthrow of the regime by means of sanctions if not arms. Children were taken into care by whomever among the comrades was still available to do so, sometimes handed on from one possibility in this family of circumstance to another when the first surrogates were in turn detained or had to flee, take up the Spear from across borders and seas. The conception of family formed from when there was survival necessity, without religious edicts (the Methodist church of Jabu's father, the synagogue for which Steve's mother had declared herself with her insistence on the circumcision ritual for her baby sons) was like a discipline left over from the circumstances of a freedom struggle taken for granted, naturally, so that if a comrade had a career obligation to go abroad for a time, or there was the opportunity for a couple to enjoy a trip overseas, someone from the past would take in the children. Jake and Isa doubled up their children's two bedrooms to add Sindiswa and Gary Elias to the cheerful occupancy of beds, cricket bats, skateboards, figures of space monsters in their boys' quarters; of beauty queens, junk jewellery in the daughter's den.

Where would anyone go, first time out of the African continent—far from Mozambique, Botswana where he had been deployed (never got as far as Ghana, let alone Moscow),

Swaziland where they met and made love for that first time. Now you had a valid passport.

London it was. Of course. England, from where the missionaries had come who founded the school where her father gained along with religious devotion some knowledge of the world with which he had determined she, his daughter, should be armed. Missionaries, who Jabu learnt in her first kind of clandestinity talk with detention cell comrades under lights that stared the continuation of the day's interrogations all night—had come with the Bible in one hand and the gun accompanying them in another, to take the people's country from them. Drew it on maps under a geographical name: South Africa. The continent the shape of a great bunch of grapes dangling towards the South Pole, and the weight of territory at the bottom the country of the isiZulu, Sepedi, isiXhosa, TshiVenda, Sesotho, XiTsonga. The same England where one of these same Englishmen started a campaign that banished the slave trade which had made many of the English rich both as flesh merchants and as owners of sugar fields in other people's countries, where slaves did the work remote from the small island which was England. These contradictions don't seem so unlikely to an African—South African—in a country no longer anyone else's claim, Dutch, English, French for a few years in one region—because the present of freedom has its contradictions. These were in the lives of the people who came to the Justice Centre for redress after employment dismissal, eviction from their homes, traditional or religious customary law against Constitutional law. These were before her every day as an attorney assisting one or other of the advocates who represented the right of citizens to be heard in the country's court.

London not exotic, as arrival would be in China, say, even France, Germany. Descendants of those who lived as subjects of the overlord always know much about him, his habits. Both he and she had been 'brought up' with strong tea brewing in its pot; in Steve's case, also Andrew's bacon and egg breakfasts. London that her father had been taught was the heart of the mother country, the empire ('wider still, and wider, shall thy bounds be set' sung in school choir) of which his coal-mine village was part; London that was the 'home' elders in his father Reed's family referred to when going on a visit, although several generations hadn't been born or lived there. The famous parks legendary for soap-box speakers in tirades against this or that seemed to have fewer, and the shaven Hare Krishna, familiar from their place among black street hawkers on the pavements in Johannesburg, apparently had been succeeded by punks whose designer heads, ear- and nose-rings were reminiscent of ancient tribal distortion/decoration in her ancestry: a sign of one world, unbroken past and present, in contradiction (again) of the conflicts that were tearing life-fabric as a motorbike tore the street at Glengrove Place. But the lovers or would-be lovers—even in a permissive democracy you generally can fondle only so far in public—must be as they've always been. Here, always on the wet grass—Steve's tolerant remark about the climate and stoicism of the British, that brought from Jabu the South African local exclamation that can express empathy rather than judgemental disapproval —Shame!— She ignored the summer rain and chill, wearing her high-heeled sandals. Steve had given her love-presents but never chosen and paid for her clothes; suddenly, here—wanted to buy her 'things'. What? That wasn't the kind of male/female contract between them, theirs, comrades. He bought her a ski jacket, the warmest garment there is, the salesman assured him.

In a different place you become different people. Not that it isn't pleasurable.

They stayed with comrades from home, emigrants who shared an old house in a working-class suburb with a West Indian couple and were looking for something affordable in Kensington (fat hope!) or somewhere else not too upmarket for them. Both couples were doctors, and three worked in the same hospital while the fourth was studying for a further degree in paediatrics at a specialist institution. The London comrades had little leisure, he and she were free as they were glad to be, about, alone. Within the separate circles of their careers, the lawyers, clients, court officials foremost in her consciousness, as was his among students and academics; the demands of children, practical distractions of a household, liens with comrades in the Suburb, they were often preoccupied, whether together alone, or together in company of others. Except for that blessed place, bed.

Here London was a twenty-four-hour exchange of self: theirs. They didn't watch the changing of the guard but did follow others of foreign tourist itinerary, while selective of what was sometimes a discovery, now, of interests each did not know the other had. He wanted to wander through the famous hothouses in the Kew Royal Botanical Gardens, she wanted to catch the last day of an exhibition of Mexican artefacts she'd seen advertised on the posters. They went to the British Museum because they felt they ought; and then spent three hours totally absorbed in all there was to learn, also of how a culture makes itself out of others—the glorious Parthenon frieze that a British ambassador took from Athens and which was displayed under his name as the 'Elgin Marbles'. The National Gallery high on Steve's list; in the Reed home there had been a book of reproductions from the Gallery he took to his room, becoming aware of the mystery of art maybe an answer to adolescent emotional confusion, as later he was to turn to science, and finally political revolution as the rationale for him to understand human existence. Even the private school for whites, to which he had been sent for the privilege-above-privilege beyond state schools for whites, had not taken pupils, as part of education, to art museums; any more than Jabu could have been. And in clandestinity days she was not admitted to the Municipal Art Gallery in Johannesburg; he wouldn't go where she couldn't. What they knew was the work of the black and white artists shown in small galleries that tightroped the fine line between what would pass as surreal licence (not much to do with anything, far as censors knew, eh) and defiance of apartheid law and religious taboo. No black-and-white lovers *sur l'herbe*. No Jesus on the cross other than a blond man whose pierced body is pale. Dark-skinned Saviour: blasphemous. One such happened to be, even greater travesty, painted by a white man, traitor—it was seized from the gallery wall and banned.

The centuries of painters and sculptors which had created the visioning of the world was work neither he nor she had seen other than as reproduction. Quietly not remarked to one another, in the National Gallery it was to each another pair of eyes given. For her, da Vinci. She walked back again to *The Virgin of The Rocks*. Steve stood beside: her experience. She turned at last, to him, as if it were he who had given it to her, it came from his past, which was not only the colonial heritage.

Returning to the entrance foyer of these places is coming to the souvenir shops, bookshops, people struggling into coats for the return—to the city. She bought a postcard of *The Virgin of The Rocks*. Directed to a post office in Trafalgar Square she stamped and mailed, sent it to her father. The Elder in his Protestant church.

He said —Do you think he'd really like the Virgin, she's so Catholic.—

—Aren't you dying for tea? Or coffee. I am.— She was gone, back into the street. Looking this way and that, as if expecting to be hailed. Spied a coffee bar where they sat behind a heat-blurred window and agreed and disagreed, transported, about what had confronted them.

Another day they were at an exhibition of African Art. It was meeting in another place, space in life, someone you know intimately. They had the special animation of pride ethos shared, although here was her ethos, and it was his by adoption—no, earned with formulae and chemicals for explosives while in the paint factory! The Greek gods and warriors in some museums are all aeons dead but the African sculptures that combined without contradiction the abstract of reality, the totality—bone structure of human faces, feet, limbs, the perspectives of features profile, frontal, appearing anywhere in single, the one image which Picasso took for himself from the African vision, they are still being created at home, by people of Africa whose vision it was and is.

Macbeth probably had been chosen of Shakespeare at her Swaziland school because it was thought young Africans would more easily understand this play, it would relate to the tribal chieftains of their own history. When in the London rain he declared 'Let it come down!' he confessed to her amusement he'd played Banquo in his school's production: they must get tickets for the performance at the Globe listed in *Time Out*. She didn't know about the continued existence of Shakespeare's Globe; but that he had been familiar with as living heritage in the English culture from which the Reeds came far back and passed down indiscriminately along with the imperialistic ones the comrades set the Spear against—and there occurs to him, too, from *The Tempest*—he quotes Caliban for her: 'You taught me language, and my profit on it is I know how to curse'—his island's invaders from Europe.

In the Globe they stood in the audience as in Shakespeare's time, in its open auditorium. The endless conversation of English downpour drowned the beautiful delivery of the cast and drenched her; bewilderment at this primitive worship of the Bard's shrine —What's the idea of having people stand out in the rain?—

Their comrade hosts offered as *their* treat a Soho night club: a black singer from home (she's made it in London, a wow) sang with the instrument of her whole body along with the voice, music by Todd Matshikiza, the composer and jazzman from Johannesburg who had died in exile, some other country in Africa. Too wide awake with the beat they lingered together before giving up the evening. In the shared living room the West Indians and their friends had left empty glasses, the shed coats of bananas, and a mat of newspaper sheets, open bottle of wine, as if welcoming, Steve was stretched out on the floor with his head against the base of the sofa between Jabu's feet as she sat. He was playing with the spindle heels of those sandals of hers, scuffed by London streets, as a light late-night context to what he was saying to their comrades —When are you coming back?—

There was a pause. Perhaps the English rain had stopped, outside. A silence when something that shouldn't have been said has been said. A subject the speaker knows is taboo. The woman, Sheila, began —But why?— and the man snatched from her —Why do you think of that, what would the reason—

To go back.

—Home.— Jabu addressed nobody in particular, as one stating the obvious. The two doctors had been avid for details of the mounting number of AIDS infections and deaths in the country they had left. —There's a shortage of doctors.—

—And you two are good ones.— Added, perhaps it was the wine in him that found plain speaking from Steve. —You had your training at our medical schools.— It could be a reproach.

—I believe you've got doctors from Pakistan and even Cuba. It's a choice, where you do your work as a doctor. Your obligation to the patient, the profession . . . it's the same.—

His woman Sheila came to his rescue perhaps to prevent giving away before comrades in this hour of indiscretion released by beat of rhythms and drink, more personal and questionable reasons. Isn't there a right to ambition and professional prestige, after years that these had no claim against dedication to the Struggle. What do you owe; after.

He spoke for himself. —I'm getting skills for the care of babies and children that don't exist at home, no such facilities.—

When they stirred for bed and the usual token goodnight embrace, he hung back to be last beside Steve, and shaking his head to dismiss his woman's loyal justification on his behalf along with his own —I envy you. And Jabu.— The voice the murmur allowed oneself in the dark; he switched off the lights.

They hadn't missed the children. Didn't have to confess or tax one another with this unnaturalness. Those two weeks in London, mother lair of the imperialism they along with their comrades at home saw lingering while the USA was the successor imperialist, were freedom they never had tasted. Free of the discipline of the Struggle, free of the discipline of the Aftermath, the equally absolute necessity to resist, oppose the underside prejudice and injustice persisting, whether with the witnesses she must coach when the Justice Centre is to testify for their defence or whether he must be regarded in the academic establishment as a Leftist troublemaker self-righteously supporting students in their ungrateful demands of the higher education system granted them by a Constitution. Time; to be alive for each other, without other commitment. Is the term for a first ever like that—holiday.

The children. Sindiswa had quickly become a directing personality not the guest of hospitality, she didn't want to hear anything about London—the place the presents came from, yes—unable to tell fast enough in her splendid shrill tumble of words everything said and done in the adventure of Isa and Jake's home. Isa said Sindi was an entertainment she didn't want to part with.

Gary hung back. He had the air of someone nowhere, self-misplaced. If such, an adult state, can be attributed to a child. With that guilt upon them, Steve and Jabu were back in the Suburb and with the exploited coming for redress at the Centre and the students coming from their university, circumstances centuries-long in measure against a two-week desertion.

The rent has been raised; he remarked with a mock sigh to Jake —Your comrades and gays' Suburb's going upmarket.—

—Yes my brother, the bourgeoisie created by the landlord capitalist . . . Well well whatever.— He and Isa had bought their house.

Was it after Steve one month paid the rent again among other obligations, online, that he and Jabu first thought of buying the house. It had made claims of being their home— Gary Elias learnt to walk there, Wethu's quarters evolved out of a chicken shed, grease marks on the wall behind the divan-doubling-as-a-sofa where comrades had leaned their heads, garden progressed under Jabu's hands from initial planting of the Dolphins' welcoming hibiscus plant—ownership wasn't legally justified. Jabu looked up the lease: they could be given three months' notice to evacuate, relocate was the term she used for the clause, if the owner decided to sell the house. Wasn't that rather unlikely. But if the landlord has a relative or a chum, now that there was a shortage of housing and the enclave was indeed going upmarket, it might be sold over their heads. They were able to raise a bond without much difficulty at the bank; both members of a couple in middle-class level of employment, professional. If in his case, the lower financial echelon of the academic; she in the legal one, non-profit making, but could become an attorney in commercial practice any time.

—So we've bought ourselves a house while others including comrades . . . millions are still under tin and cardboard.— Who takes census in squatter camps.

The statement is for both of them. It's also the accusation. They are sitting in the dark on that terrace where the neighbour's tree leans and hides before them a wall defining a limit, this side, of what they've just exclusively acquired.

The tsk tsk tsk of cicadas is in the silence. Where is the difference to be felt between this occupancy of the house as owned property, or living in it, paying for the privilege to some other property owner. Principles are so impractical in the compromise reached of the ideal envisioned when it didn't exist.

—It isn't a big smart place with I don't know how many rooms.— She sounds indulgent of him, as if she were not involved. He thinks too much; didn't used to be like that. In the Struggle you acted, gave yourself orders in response to what came up had to be done, this day, this area of operation.

—Just enough for two kids, the mother and the father. And just one collateral, Wethu. Own that space.— He waves: I know.

—So you're sorry we bought the house.—

He stiffens head back nostrils flared. Doesn't speak.

—Sweetheart— The childish call that was picked up from whites' vocabulary of affection when first she was at the college in Swaziland. —We've lived all over. Why shouldn't we have a small home now, we're not taking it away from somebody else.—

—Well so far as that's concerned you're right, it's a bit late, how do we know whose *kraal* this once was, here where the Tswana were before Mzilikazi came down on them, and then the Boers, and the English.— That's her own history. —You've never seen the remains of those ancient gold—or was it copper—workings, not far from here?—we must show the kids.—

—But how far can we go back. How far are we supposed to . . .—

—Yes, you're right, that's archaeology, anthropology . . . the restitution of land doesn't include the city suburbs, that's for sure . . . aren't we lucky.—

He so often comes out with contradictions of himself that bring her to laughter, it's one of the things that make him unique, her lover.

The gentle laugh draws him in; together under the cicadas rasping their legs to give voice after rain. Jabu comes from the dispossessed, she doesn't have to feel guilty, even of betraying any revolutionary principle that property is theft. Maybe she's right again, that's archaeological too, by now. To live with someone her kind is, for a white, a reassurance that's safely out of reach of analysis. She is. We are. Us.

Personal and public situations have been a synthesis in them since they happened to meet in Swaziland and this doesn't change in freedom. Before the interlude, London, there had been rumours trailing after allegations that arms deals for the country's defence force were 'subject to possible irregularities and offences'. An addition to Steve's collection of euphemisms: these for corruption. Names involved included the brothers Shaik among comrades who were not black. These Shaiks were just unfamiliar names. Of course many people had names other than their own during the Struggle, a resort against identification. Accusations fall protracted thick and thorny hooking one to another. A key finding is that no irregularities could be laid at the door of Mandela's successor President Thabo Mbeki and ministers: the National Prosecuting Authority had issued more than a hundred summonses obtained statements from witnesses, numerous documents, searched premises in France, Mauritius as well as conducting raids in South Africa—a French company in the Thomson-CSF group with a German frigate consortium were contractors for the arms deals.

These become part of daily chronicle when the circle of the Suburb rounds.. Peter Mkize bitterly despondent. —Who'd believe it. This what we fought for? Tell me? This is why we were burned and chucked in the Komati River?— Everybody understands his authority to say this.

Translate every statement as if it were in a foreign language: a Shaik is go-between of the arms dealers, whom he claimed gave their bribes to Zuma.

Steve feels for and with Peter Mkize the shamefulness of the human race, not personal, worse than that. —Why do we expect to be different. Mexico after their revolutions. Russia after *the* revolution, and after the end of the Soviet Union, revolutionised this time by capitalism.—

Marc is the one among the Dolphins who is passionate about justice beyond discrimination against men and women who don't fit emotional conventions. —The fat cats are always with us. Just have to get on with it. *Ubuntu!*—

—We must expect—we must be different! What are you all saying? *Ubuntu*—you know what that is? Do you? What is happening to it, why it comes to mean that because those comrades were in the Struggle they can drive their Mercedes and buy palaces for their wives with bribe millions from foreign crooks! Sell us out! How can you take it like that!— Jabu's whole body restless with outrage.

Who can respond.

Jake will make an effort; she's got guts, that woman of Steve's. —Can somebody tell us? One of us *say*? Shit. *Ubuntu*—we're all one, I am you, you are me! What power do we have. We thought we would have, that's what getting rid of apartheid and all the props meant. International finance cartels neo-colonialism call it what you like. The arms trade. Bribes are its accounting system. Crooking the books for customers, with money in exchange for tenders. This isn't selling pizzas across the counter! So come on, what can ordinary guys like us ex-combatants do? It's the Shaiks hand in pocket with the Zumas who inherit the earth in dollars sterling euros, whatever the currency up for the deal.—

Well, it's not a response.

It's too feeble to say what some are thinking: wait for the next election and the next. And according to what has come out of this meeting of minds: there will be a change of personnel, maybe, but the same world accounting system, Left or Right.

She went home, that unchanging destination, to the Methodist Church Elder's, headmaster's village, to KwaZulu at intervals as unthinking as change of season. It's not expected, perhaps not even particularly wanted, that her husband would always come, with the exception of a Christmas visit or a funeral—there respect was obligatory whereas weddings were more women's affair. Sindiswa was entering the phase when school friends were closer than family, and usually elected to spend time with them instead. But Gary Elias jumped into the car beside his mother in eager anticipation of the enthusiasm with which he would be received by boys who seemed all to be his cousins or at least in some way part of him. Jabu was pleased because she wanted her father, the man who could read the being of male children, to cast an eye over him, his development, from time to time. If grandfatherly it was dispassionate, professional, experience; Steve, though an educationalist, one must admit knew more about young adults the university age, his son he saw relived as in his own boyhood which was happy.

The behaviour of rejection—in his situation necessary because of the imprint of his white hands conceived in privilege—had come only with adolescence. Gary Elias would not have to 'grow out of' a false situation into the real; he was born into reality.

Her father had called to invite her son to spend Easter school holidays at the KwaZulu family complex of which by his mother's birth he was a member. —Baba, but wouldn't it be better in the winter holidays, you'll be so busy with the church over Easter.—

He dismissed delay with his old adage from a school primer. —No time like the present.—

She takes it that in her father's wisdom he's judged the boy is ready to bring ceremonies of the two experiences of living, which are his heritage, together in full self-confidence.

So she's sitting again in her father's cubby-hole of privacy: the perfectly refolded and stacked newspapers—of course her Baba's an assiduous follower of what is evolving of the country's freedom to which he can allow he took his part, risked to direct his daughter. But they are too engaged by her father with the decision whether Gary Elias will sleep in Baba's house or stay with one of his mother's brothers who has boys around the same age—to speak of what her father must have read in those papers. Jacob Zuma, the Mtowethu Zulu who before he attained the second highest position in government, Deputy President to President Mbeki, was Umpathí Wesigungu Sakwazulu-Natal, the KwaZulu head of Executive Council, these days is suspected of collusion in bribery for arms deals.

She has delivered Gary Elias to Baba.

Driving back to the city, home and Suburb where arms are the subject of speculation and questioning preoccupation between comrades—herself among them; like a tap on the shoulder: I didn't ask. My father. What he makes of this. The Brother Zulu was one of the old Freedom Fighters out there among the best, close to Mbeki, he served his years on Robben Island. What this means. In the present.

The talent-spotting eminence, Senior Counsel who in her first years at the Justice Centre moved on appointed as a judge, had not been mistaken in casually recognising her potential. Her quick capability in providing preparatory work for the Centre's advocates became noticed in court and she was several times approached by lawyers from commercial firms whether perhaps she was available part-time to take on Assistant Defence in one of their Common Law cases. Whether this was influenced by the fact that she was black as well as a woman would show the adherence of the firm, Abdillah Mohamed, Brian McFarlane & Partners or Cohen, Hafferjee, Viljoen & Partners, to standards of transformation of the legal profession from whites only status, was of no account so long as it was being put into practice. What was of account was that the Justice Centre, knowing it was conviction to defend the exploited that kept this bright and conscientious attorney from going into commercial practice, gave her leave to take part in private legal work now and then. The earnings at a Constitutional Rights organisation are a matter of commitment in comparison with what a lawyer can earn in commercial practice.

She might have stayed on at the firm where she was articled after she abandoned teaching at the Catholic Fathers' School; just when he left the paint business and went into education. Hers would have been a choice of money over what had decided her concept of being alive since her recruitment to freedom struggle, the induction through detention in a prison. As generations of uncles and brothers from Baba's extended family had been imprisoned for walking the streets of the city without the passbook in their pocket. But the choice—chance—now to engage as a lawyer honestly enough, without depriving the Justice Centre or herself of dedication, meant some resources to meet the expenses, mouths gaping for money, of the nuclear family life in the Suburb. Steve and back-up Peter Mkize, who had once been a motor mechanic before *Umkhonto we sizwe* (and proved a usefully skilled cadre in the transport vehicle deficiencies of a guerrilla army) decided that her car was a write-off dangerously unreliable and selected for her to buy one that had safety features, fancy locks, she couldn't be expected to think she'd have need of, was more pricey than she thought right for her limit of acquisition. But school fees were raised—that should be, she and Steve agreed if teachers are to be paid adequately in private schools even while those in state schools must be supported in their demands against miserable reward as if they were the least important factors in a 'developing country', United Nations-speak for one with no man's land between the heights of the rich and the poverty swamps.

Education. That's Steve's department isn't it, in the partnership of ideals with love and sexual fulfilment and the pledge of children, which is the mystery called marriage. There's rock beneath their feet, below the different work each does; their common beliefs. He waves her off to test-drive with all this between them in his smiling confidence and in her recognition of his supervision for her safety. What is love? You learn only as you go along. It's not what overwhelmed at the beginning . . . Any more than you would have thought of hijacking (everyday on the roads now) as part of freedom; but you should've because there could be consequences of freedom not succeeding—not possible to in less than one generation? Not accepting the revolutionary ways and means to achieve the closure, historically vast as Space itself, between the rich and poor in human span as opposed to eternity.

He knows. She's said it fondly many times, he thinks too much. Better just get on with it. His thesis has been published in a scientific journal. He's still the Lefty in the Faculty— yes Leftover from the Struggle in his attitudes towards the orientation of the university. Always arranging seminars interdisciplinary on this aspect or that, the relation of academics to students, some process of new learning for both; while some white academics have spent half a lifetime in research of one nature or another, both as students and in honoured posts at universities abroad in the world, École Normale, Universität Hamburg, Institute of Advanced Studies Boston, St John's Oxford, Japan, God knows where else students haven't heard of. Assistant Professor Reed and his Comrade coterie are surely encouraged by the appointment of a professor from another country on the African continent to the Chair of Economics—some sort of tentative towards recognising cultural interdependence not as customarily defined with Europe and the USA. The economist, with his Oxford degrees and accent, was in academic rank more on that of the old guard round coffee, even though in elaborate West African dress and embroidered cap. He warmed his manner of speech with expressions, slipped into locutions from his own people's usage, and drank with the Steve coterie, initiated to the bar where they met. At Steve's house he was jauntily delighted to find the man had a black wife—apparently the sexual mores if not the taboos of the past in this country were still in his mind. He immediately started addressing Jabu in his own African tongue as if somehow she must understand; a verbal embrace just between the two of them. It was a compliment to her. She looked round to the others crowded on the tiny terrace, the place of welcome, as if someone did, could understand—there was a burst of laughter from Peter Mkize —He's making a praise song, how beautiful you are, your eyes, your—

—Don't let's go into details any further.— It was one of the Dolphins, cupping his palms and giving a curving thrust of the pectorals.

—How'd you know what he was saying—

—I don't, we know she's a beauty, don't we, she's got features.—

The brother from another part of the continent lowered his eyes on himself and moved his fine head in confirmation or sophisticated contrition. Everyone agreed he was an acquisition to the university; congratulatory, as if Steve had had something to do with the appointment. But it was most probable that it was through Professor Nduka that students from countries on the African continent were accepted for registration at the university; they can afford to pay the fees or are protégés of some international foundation that does, unlike the country's own youth, who do not have enough either of money or scholarships; 'the university is open to all', Steve mouths the quote to Jabu. She will be thinking even if she doesn't say as she did before, What are you going to do about it. Act. Act. He and the others of the group at the university who are again questioned: How do you promote the integrated culture of the institution in its identity as African with appointment of a Nigerian as head of a department—and march in protest with the men and women of our people who can't afford to pay for a place in higher education.

If some churches still outcast homosexuals the theatre celebrated the opening night of Marc's play, at last, having been rewritten by him in its successive versions, to his satisfaction. Like Jabu's Baba, Marc has his philosophical clip to serve all circumstances: Tell it like it is.

The Developed World has been used to this probably since the Oscar Wilde trial (although he only said he had nothing to declare but his genius—not that he had nothing to declare but his love that dare not speak its name), but in the Developing World homosexuality has been a titillating subject for insinuating patter by stand-up comedians in sleazy night clubs, not a theme for the theatre.

Jabu is at the opening with one of the lawyers for whom she is what she calls 'on loan' from the Justice Centre in a child custody case; Steve was to be at a dinner for a visiting scientist that night. The play, which Steve and Jabu had been elected to read as a duty of their objectivity as well as privilege in its early versions, is very different in the dimension of performance, real voices and bodies. Live, it is seen to shirk the temptation of reverse claims, superiority above heterosexual relationships; if there are no wife-beatings and female ball-busting emasculation in this other sexual love relation, there is jealousy, betrayal and—a characteristic or irreverent teasing laughter, at one another, over all.

There was no interval so after the end the audience lingered in the foyer and bar to talk about the play and the full-frontal style of performance. Jabu felt a gentle tweak at one of her piled-up locks—Alan is there, behind her.

—Have you ditched my brother, who's the guy?—

She's worldly enough now to answer in kind. —Why should I do such a thing, a man from a family as distinguished as you Reeds.— She introduces him to her lawyer colleague. Like the temptation to mention a present malady to a doctor one meets, for a free consultation, Alan takes the opportunity to interrupt enthusiastic exchanges about the performance, in the spirit of Marc's clip. —D'you think gay marriage is going to be legalised? What's the talk among you male—and female— members of the profession.— An intimate cosy tip of the head acknowledges Jabu as among them.

—I should say it's inevitable, but who can predict how soon.—

—Sooner or later, then.— That's all the information you get for free: the unspoken, Alan feels he shares in amusement with Jabu. He won't embarrass her by harassing the lawyer.

The performance perhaps creates a certain atmosphere along with the air-conditioning that allows frankness and wit. She asks playfully —You thinking of getting married?—

Alan gives her a little—hush there—hug.

Home, just past the church that usually exudes light and the latest digital recording, dark and silent, the pool in reflected streetlight the only open eye.

Steve is already in bed, arrived before her. He wants to hear all that he's missed. She has questions that come to her, she wants to ask—sits on the bed pushing his book out of the way and they talk as if she were an animated guest walked in.

—I can't explain—it hit so hard, I don't think I was the only one who saw how there're ways we don't even know we show prejudice, hurt them, maybe friends, our friends—comrades . . . our own. The pool was shiny when I passed, just now . . . And how they laugh at everything that happens to them. It was so funny, the play. I didn't realise how they do this, when we read it.—

—Laugh at themselves.—

—Yes! At themselves.—

—Look, if you can do it you're safe from what others say about you, your jokes quash their jeers, you poke fun at yourself and make a tough hide of it, the disgust and disdain just blunt themselves against it.—

Later when she had shed the evening experience along with her clothes and was in bed, the place in life each shared with nobody else. —If your people— Somehow this was not an attribution of separateness that was ever used by them, neither in naming his mother Pauline, Andrew, Alan, Jonathan, Brenda—the Reeds—nor her father's gathering of Gumede collaterals, the broods black and white recalled in their familial clan relationships. —If blacks sometimes could do the same . . . Now that the old law is on the rubbish heap. Take up the small arms, you get what I mean, instead of the cowhide shields the waving *assegais*, the traditional show of identity, dignity against the white crap that's still thrown at them— But at once he catches himself out. A correcting groan. —How can anyone compare a situation where you and your people have been used as a blank to be filled in with another people's notion of what a human being is. Compare with the ridiculous—who should give a damn about who does which with what and to whom. In bed.—

She is down-mouthed smiling at her Steve, he doesn't see, in their dark. He didn't say 'who should give a fuck about'.

As each practised the professions they might perhaps not have chosen if different youthful ambitions had not been put on hold by the Struggle, and in the aftermath freedom, overcome by necessities of private living, they often had obligations outside daily working schedules, hours each spent without the other. Hers, representing real advancement of what was better than ambition: fulfilment of her place in that basis of what's called the New Dispensation, the law; his without the sense of common action in an alternative to the old confines of education, hers alternative to the defence of justice confined to those who can afford legal representation. She was embattled in the accepted opposition between prosecution and defence in court, but she's at one with the colleagues, at her level the attorneys, and the advocates whom they serve, as she was among comrades in the Struggle. Even if most of the lawyers in the commercial firm she was 'lent' to had been fellow travellers onlooking from home, all are committed to justice now. In the laboratory, in his seminars, he served his academic purpose of imparting knowledge and skills; when the information notice that he was available to students in his room brought timid bewildered ones or cocky aggressive ones to his door, and the bridging classes which he and what remained of his like-minded academics persisted with the band-aid to school education he gave his obstinate best effort and encouragement. But in the faculty room he was in a coterie of the present among the structures of the past, fuming inwardly against the coffee machine's mantra, the rites of scholarly self-esteem rising in fragrant steam. There were scientific conferences he attended to educate himself, faculty dinners for visiting research scholars he was invited to on the strength of his thesis being accepted by the university—the Vice Chancellor's speech-making pride in the Department of Science, its choice for association by scientists prominent in astrophysics and the twenty-first century conception of the nature of the universe.

As well as formal gatherings of the legal profession, Jabu had restaurant lunch quite often with this or that partner of one of the commercial legal practices she happened to be working for temporarily. She would put her hand on her stomach that evening, not wanting to eat again when she sat at the table with the meal she and Wethu had put together to feed the children and Steve, his lunch having been a snack in a fast-food chain favoured by his students.

At her pauses in the day she and table companions would be occupied in shop talk, analysis of what had taken place in court; he and his students, along with their pizza, argued over how the university was or was not meeting their expectations.

As the muscular image of a professional sports player develops a certain conformation so Jabu's image went through certain changes. Though her hair was the African crown of braided patterns and locks that was the general assertion of traditional African aesthetics reinstated in the free woman, she has as if unnoticed by herself begun to adopt the other traditional convention of female freedom, the informal but well-cut pants and jackets of professional men. This was an outward expression of something . . . an impression she had managed or been given a synthesis between the working relevance of the past and the present; which Steve had not.

Return from the daily separation of preoccupations is not only to the children as the core of the personal living state. It's to the Suburb; it was with Jake, Isa, the Mkizes and other comrades who renewed contact that there was in place, space claimed to consider, with confidence of mutual experience and understanding, what they had envisaged to be achieved. What was happening in the country. Even the occupants of the old Gereformeerde Kerk that would have consigned their kind to condemnation were interested in the secular concern with the aftermath of the struggle for freedom in which they hadn't taken active part, although some of their orientation, white and black, had been revolutionaries, comrades in prison and in the bush. The playwright Marc, probably researching for certain aspects of a new play in mind, brought dramatic first-hand accounts about what was not being done about the degradation of black workers existing in conditions worse than the 'white farmer keeps his pigs'—it was Marc who confronted the Dolphins to see beyond the particular discrimination against themselves. Sunday's permanent invitation for Jake, Isa, the Mkizes, Jabu, Steve and everyone's kids to come to the pool became socially political amid the cult repartee and affectionate dunkings of the commune.

These—Suburb family occasions, public rather than private, were in a sense, guarded. While decisions taken by the government that affected everyone, taxes, health insurance, crime, were talked about with criticism of cabinet ministers and ridicule mimicry of some politicians livened the exchanges, laughter all round, there were aspects of these matters Jake, Isa, the Mkizes, Jabu, Steve, did not speak of. Did not offer, as if by political vows like Masonic vows. When they were alone together in the house of this one or that, the same matters were under a light different from that reflected by the pool.

Kinship of prison and bush between the comrades, tentacle within, this was a meaning of their lives that could not be erased. They had known rivalry for esteem, nose-picking habits, farts, hard to tolerate cheek-by-jowl in the tent and the cell, jealous sexual tensions when there were women comrades among them, all the human shortcomings, faults and passions; but outreached, outdistanced by the Struggle. Alone together now they could remark on veniality from inside, informative experience, signs it was always there, in this high government official, the cut-throat determination of this Under Minister to oust that Minister, the question why so-and-so, whose pathetic lack of capabilities comrades all knew too well, had been given the leg-up in a ministry while so-and-such, comrade of brains and integrity, seemed to be sidelined onto some minor committee chair.

These were not facts and doubts for Sunday morning gossip.

But the family of the same Shaik was continuing to appear in the newspapers in connection with the arms deals. The first democratic government had formed a Department of Defence Strategic Arms Acquisition Programme, on the principle that the country needed to strengthen its defence booty inherited in defeat of the apartheid army's force. Corvettes, submarines, utility and marine helicopters, fighter trainers and advanced fighter aircraft went out for tender in the world with the proviso that foreign arms manufacturers promise to invest in the country and create employment. The Shaik name—family of brothers, Shabir, Yunus known as Chippy, Mo—is a front-page staple in the news since the delivery of arms under contract has been in progress for more than five years. There had been something called an Audit Steering Committee, and then the government signed this Arms Deal as a necessary expenditure of billions. A Shaik was a member of the steering committee.

—Who the hell is Chippy Shaik, anyway?—

—Here it is, you've just read, 'Director of procurement in the Defence Force' when the 'irregularities' in contracts to sub-contractors now under investigation were awarded. No—but as cadre in *Umkhonto*. What *was* he.— Jake answering himself with the grimace of culpable lapsed memory.

There were so many levels of activity in the Movement (that other euphemism, this one for the Struggle). Some would have been familiar with the deployment, whatever, of Shaik, but along with Jake, Steve and Jabu weren't.

Trust Peter Mkize. —Doesn't matter. Shaik turns out now, eh, to be financial adviser of our Deputy President Jacob Zuma. You've seen what's come from the Auditor General's report, the cost of the deal in billions far higher than the government's figure and nobody can say what the final costs might be—why? Something like 'industrial offsets'. *Eish!*—

Steve knows what everybody in the outside world takes for granted. —The arms trade is the dirtiest of them all. 'Industrial offsets'—that'll be investments and trade opportunities that tender sinners promise to advance for the good of the country. Arms dealers know they can forget about these obligations. Their bribes to ministers?—government officials who decide tender awards.—

Jake snatches from him like a flag —That's sufficient contribution to development of the country!—

The complex Shaik kin keeps being unravelled. —Zuma's financial adviser's brother Shabir got the arms deal contract although it was twice the price of another tender, of equal standard—

—Whose pocket took in the bribes— The refrain.

—If the deal ever does come to court we might—

—Zuma as President elect—as if the President will ever—

There's a lawyer among them. —He was arraigned. And he appeared in court on another charge—of rape.— She was present when he did, and was declared not guilty.

The Suburb comrades follow the beginning of what is apparently an era in the aftermath of revolution attained.

—With apartheid we were the pariah of the world, with freedom we become what we never were, we're part of the democratic world. Corruption doesn't disqualify. It's everywhere.— That's Steve.

Jabu is withdrawn as if among strangers.

He interprets, from her manner of response lately to ordinary happenings: angry when a pot of food she's not checked soon enough threatens to have dried away the gravy, chastising herself by tugging at her scalp with recalcitrant braids when she's at the mirror in the morning, and at her self-accused carelessness at letting her car run out of petrol so that a colleague had to fetch a can from a service station before she could drive home from the Centre. At times when they are alone together she will get up abruptly, a gesture of rejection of some TV commentator, leave the room; on other occasions she will be so eye-to-eye with the image and so tense against what is being said she ignores what she is usually alert to against all other registers of her attention, conversation, music—the racket of some trouble between Sindi and Gary Elias. He sees, feels approaching, pressing upon him like her flesh against him in their intimacy, that Jabu is affronted and disturbed, beyond his own reaction.

She does not say much when he looks up from the newspaper —D'you see this—'Zuma allegedly solicited a 500,000 a year bribe' from the French company that won the contract to supply some equipment for corvettes. Shabir Shaik's company was the French's black empowerment partner—

—Why do we do what the whites do in their countries. What business is it of ours. We aren't their black colonies any more.—

He noted but did not misunderstand the juxtaposition in opposition, whites and blacks; 'we' excluding him, her man, from its solidarity identity. Jabu is shamed by the betrayal of blacks, of whom she is one, by themselves; although racism is no part of her life, finally proven by the existence of her own two children?

Gary Elias's periods of the year spent with his grandfather are regular, pleasures not outgrown as his activities and interests at home in the city, school and Suburb grow. At least once among the school holiday visits his dad came along with his mother to deliver him to the village and pay his own respects: husband of the daughter not only of the Elder of the Methodist Church and headmaster of the school, but of the family commune. While he drove Jabu mentioned in undertone, they wouldn't bring up the subject of Zuma during the visit. Her father had known Zuma well, was associated with him way back while he was MEC for Economic Affairs and Tourism in the KwaZulu Natal provincial government.

Steve had thought the arms deal was exactly the subject to engage, of interest to everyone in the village. Her father who always directed the conversation among those who gathered with him, wife and extended family in welcome, did not mention it, and authority emanating from him as naturally as he breathed, no one did. There was much else to exchange. Two lively cousins Gary's age were urged to tell about the science laboratory equipment that had been donated to the headmaster's school by some Norwegian foundation—this news produced in recognition of Steve as a man of science, must be a professor. —The Education Minister was here himself with the Norwegian Ambassador, you have met the Education Minister, Jabulile?— No limits to the level of achievements won for this daughter he had somehow instructed even when she was in prison. Everyone, including the survivor of Jabu's two grandmothers, carried in respect tenderly to a chair, went to see Gary Elias playing goalkeeper with the style of his

triumphs in the junior team at school. The comrade's advice
has been right, the boy was no longer a reluctant spectator of
sport—Jabu exchanged a look away from the leaping catch
of the ball, at Steve, in their acknowledgement. He spoke his
acquired isiZulu and those around celebrated in applause for
both him and his son. At a signal from Jabu's mother food was
carried in a procession of pots and bowls and there was bottled
beer as well as a calabash of home brew her father had learnt
was much to Steve's liking.

These visits passing the grandson from one home to what is
another have coaxed his son out of his temperament of withdrawal into open security, a belonging that before existed
only in his blood. A child's secret example of Tutu's truth and
reconciliation?

And the timing of this visit seemed to have brought assurance to Jabu, she chattered all the way back to the city, the
Suburb. She was recounting stories, events from her childhood
in the place in the world they had just left; what, so young,
she hadn't recognised as rivalries between the Elder's pious
congregation, the in-house power struggles with the heavy
presence of the relatives in their thatched annexes, the skill
with which she'd understood later, her mother managed not
to be totally extinguished by her father; while this daughter
belonged—chose to be—only to him.

If the question of Jacob Zuma's relationship with Shabir Shaik
didn't surface at her father's house, it is raised where politics
are also sidled round tactfully by Jonathan and Brenda, out of
respect for commitments they don't share with the combination of Steve and his wife, though they had warmed to and
always welcome her personally. On the Reed mother's eight-
ieth birthday, a party is in progress at Jonathan's house. It
is Jabu who's given time and thought to with what present

Steve should honour his mother on what would be recognised with ancestral respect in the church Elder's community. Someone addresses in kindly attention as to one who would be concerned —What's going to be done about this corruption stuff that's coming out. How serious is it—or just infighting, like all governments?—

Jonathan doesn't wait for response from Jabu. —People are confused about the sound of the name. *Shabir*—thank God he isn't a Jew.—

He has to keep on reminding, telling himself. The arms trade, dirtiest in the world. The true cliché. There was no impulse, it was back then, no time to face this when *Umkhonto* had to lay hands on arms wherever and from whom they would come. Not the democratic powers of the Western world; these were busy stocking up the armories of apartheid, military and financial.

—So what d'you do.—

You knew what it was you had to do in the bush.

He answers himself, in new derogatory voice: Get together a delegation. Yes? This isn't your troubles in the lecture halls at a university behind its security gates, my Bra. And we aren't in your camp in Angola, ready for our Cuban comrades to fight beside us. Mustn't apply the code, the morals of the Struggle, as adjusted to the tongue-twisted Peace-and-Freedom.

From Peter Mkize, Jabu and Jake the question, statement— whatever it is—comes outspoken. So what d'you do.

And answers himself again because no one else wants to, or knows. —You join the chorus from the opposition holier-than-thou, slam for your own upright benefit the corruption in the government, corruption by the ANC.—

Peter speaks as if constrained to betray under interrogation. —Zuma was our Chief of Intelligence in the bush.—

—And ten years on the Island!— Jabu keeps the calendar of armed resistance.

Heroism has an imperialistic halo, not to be invoked for individuals when every cadre was dedicated to whatever the Struggle demanded; in responsibility, stoicism, suffering.

Jake brings knuckles down on the table, crushing something.
—How's it possible to believe these same comrade leaders
have forgotten what they were, what they fought through—in
exchange for freedom as bribes, freedom as money.—

Perhaps it was the very same October evening that it was
happening?

Not only the *ware* Boer suburb has transformed in accordance with political correctness as an expression of justice. The
suburb of fine houses, many with fake features of the various
Old Countries from which the owners came, that had been in
well-off white ownership has also undergone invasion, if not
transformation. Where the white inhabitants, some second or
third generation in possession, have sold the family home for
security reasons and bought an apartment in a gated complex
supposedly quarantined from burglary and assaults, or left the
country to live out of rule of a black majority government, there
is no longer any law to prevent any black who can afford such a
stately home from acquiring it. One block away from the house
where Steve grew up, past which he rode first on his tricycle,
later bicycle, the Deputy President Jacob Zuma had chosen to
buy, and lived in flittingly from time to time, a house among
his other homes about the country. During the week when
the now ex-Deputy President Zuma, dismissed from his cabinet post by President Thabo Mbeki as the consequence of his
financial adviser Shaik declaring in court Zuma received bribes
from a French arms dealer, Zuma was in his house neighbouring
Steve's old home. A young woman, daughter of a comrade with
whom Zuma had shared ten years on Robben Island, and who
in respectful African custom addresses him as *malume*, uncle,
asked or was invited to spend Saturday night after a party in the
house. A confused story: both probably lying, they had intercourse—the only admitted fact. She laid a charge she had been

raped. He, in *this* trial that did come to court after postponement from December to April, said there was consensual sex. Zuma headed the 'Moral Regeneration Movement', a government initiative on prevention and treatment of HIV and AIDS. He admits he knew the woman was HIV-positive, he had no condom; he took a shower afterwards as this was, he said, postcoital cautionary prevention of infection. If not in so many words, a gift to the press. A cartoonist created a crown for the man that would surely ever after be his royal image: a plume in the form of a shower sprinkling over his head.

This is the subject of gleeful uproar in the Suburb round the church pool. The Dolphins rejoice in this other example of double moral standards, for both arms and sex deals. A man who had held the second highest position of power in the land, Deputy President, apparently committed to fight HIV and AIDS, tells the male population a good soap-and-shower on the penis, after, is all you need, no antiretrovirals necessary.

Jake can't resist. —And if you do find you've caught the incurable clap, you just put yourself on a diet of beetroot, garlic and wild spinach—if you can find that traditional veg at the supermarket.—

Everyone laughing again at what's become colloquially the priceless synonym of absurdity, the nature cure advised by the Minister of Health in her rejection of antiretrovirals. That other trial, the arms deal corruption, has been indeed referred again (it will go away) in legal complications of irregularities. Jabu is best able to explain, passing on the enlightenment from the access of her own intelligence to expert legal minds.

Marc dives into the pool and comes up exploding water and laughing, shaking a shower from his fashionably shaven head. —What a fantastic plot! What a cast! If only I could— The playwright seizing on a new twist to a marvellous plot.

She sits in the court with the onlooker crowd on the day when Jacob Gedleyihlekisa Zuma is cross-examined about how intercourse came about if it was not intentioned by him and he answered that in view of the affectionate good-night exchanges between Uncle and a friend's daughter (her provocative scanty attire already described to the court) it was traditionally incumbent in Zulu culture for a Zulu man to satisfy a woman who showed she was sexually aroused. 'You cannot just leave a woman if she is in that state.'

It is illegal to make public the name of a woman who has laid a rape charge. To protect her anonymity this woman is known in court and to the media as Kwezi, 'Morning Star'.

Outside the court Jabu, a woman among black women, made her way past those shouting their message. —Burn the bitch!— The image, photographs of Morning Star, are in flames.

The ex-Deputy President is found not guilty in his rape trial.

Marriage. A common identity. Is that what it is. What it stands for, leave the takens, the sexual implication out of it, the biological, even the legal, the mutual health insurance, tax benefits et al. These are Sunday church swimming pool subjects aired, argued over, kindly jested about to the comrade Dolphins by the Straight in the company. —So you want the right to get divorced?—

Whether by words avowed in church, mosque, synagogue, temple, in a magistrates' court or in love vows privately coupling two of the same sex—marriage: it's a term for a common identity encircling all the individual difference between two human beings. But mustn't assume the differences are not there, the other identities: mustn't presume they are like elements in a laboratory that combine to produce one substance to create decorative endurance or an explosion, according to the imperative at the time. He and she share political dismay at the Zuma 'affair'—in both senses of the word, in this instance—the arms deal corruption charge that may never come to court is the other. She's a lawyer identified within a resource for justice. He has an identity as a teacher, for him the designation 'academic' is a social class distinction; both lower and upper levels of learning alike are served by teachers. If a hero comrade turns out to have sexual morals as feet of clay, at least the university is showing signs of transforming into what he believes such an institution should be in the need of the present. He was an industrial chemist in a paint factory clandestinely producing formulae for making bombs, he was a cadre (these terms seem too Stalinist post 1994?) in a liberation army, he has now yet another identity in the synthesis of self. What's called in psychological jargon job satisfaction's a distraction from political disillusion. He's able to come home to tell how some of the students who attend band-aid coaching are turning out to have the determination, the unbeatable guts comrades had to summon in *Umkhonto* situations—discover in themselves what uninspiring schooling had stifled. An ability to concentrate, question, an urge to use that over-aweing tomb, the library, as well as quick-fix Internet, educate yourself in innate fascination of discovering the apparently limitless reach of that mystery concealed from your own mind. Some are opening to a vocabulary of ideas as well as words beyond *so how's it, cool*. This he could exploit for them by persuading scientists from nuclear research, virology, particle physics, to condescend to brief seminars where the 'underprivileged' were bold enough to ask questions that showed they had some perceptions of the ecosphere not confined to the romantic monsters of space-busters. They are given the revelation of Grid, learning a scientist named Wilczek's concept of stuff that exists in what is regarded as space, emptiness. So it's not a void? There atoms and nuclei are held together by forces acting between all the pairs of particles that they contain. It's a highly structured, powerful medium whose activity moulds the world where their eyes see nothing. Wonder . . .

She was glad for them, for him, in the way of someone who has always had such expectations of someone like him. The idea that she might sit in on one of these sessions somehow didn't come off. Peter and Jake were elated at the participation of the band-aid students when invited to an exchange between them and a visiting luminary.

Jabu had asked—would he manage care of the children, meals and all that, if she went to KwaZulu for the weekend, taking Wethu with her, Wethu hadn't been home lately, a visit was due.

Could he manage! He laughed, butting her cheek with his. —The kids'll have a ball, undisciplined, and I can get takeout I'm sure from the Dolphins' jambalaya.— He knew what she did not say: she needed to be with her father in what must be to him the betrayal of the amaZulu, the people, disgraced by the behaviour of one who had been MEC for Economic Affairs and Tourism in their provincial government; one with whom the church Elder and headmaster had grown to be inducted to manhood by the killing of a bull by bare hands.

All the way with her attention an automatic pilot performing the functions of driving she was rehearsing what she would say. What she would say, best. What would invoke naturally with respect, the particular relation between them, the only way to speak. Wethu beside her was not so much uncommunicative as in the same state—there and not there—but with a different absence, already taking the paths from clay-smeared house to house, seeing from behind door to door the brothers, sisters, the old and new born of the collaterals from which she came. So neither felt any awkwardness in their silence.

—We're nearly home.— And Wethu's composure half-woke to her habitually tired smile along with some low sound of assent, as if every huddle of trees, wave of sugar cane under the wind was landmark of a personal map. Only when there was a roadside store or an old church surviving in childhood memory the experiences by which she had left behind the images, Jabu saw that there was no longer time to prepare herself for sharing her Baba's troubled self as somehow nobody else could.

As she took the turn to the village: a big poster of Jacob Zuma grinning lopsidedly as it had lurched loose from a fence pole.

Must be relic of a meeting of some sort: before.

The dirt road to the house passed the headmaster's school, there were boys leaping, crouching about in a football game where Gary Elias had played. It was as if walking not driving, step by step, the final road that was drawing her to his presence, Baba.

*   *   *

She has told her mother on landline, she's coming; he never answers that phone, it's for the convenience of the women, he has his mobile. That way it wasn't needed she would have to guard herself against giving away her purpose, demeaning it by the conventional means of overcoming distance. Her mother quite naturally assumed it was the daughterly duty to all women of the extended family that obliged her daughter to consider it time Wethu had a visit to take up liens from home. So a group gathered round Wethu in cheerful welcome, some then furtively drawing back to eye the changes in dress that on each return marked their sister a city woman, and the mother's arms claimed her own daughter. Baba was there apart, as always in his contrasting calm, the stance special for her, ready for her. The hands of each went out to clasp and hold the hands of the other, he drew her to him without her breasts and his body meeting.

They exchanged the usual: how was the road, not too busy, yes, the children are fine, Steve in charge. —We were expecting you next month, with Gary Elias.— The handover for the school holidays. —Oh of course we're coming then, everyone.— Baba must need all the support he can get, grief comes not only from death, but the debilitating anger of shock. She felt anger in him, the tightened grasp on her hands, and the impatient lower of his eyes as they sat through the serving of tea and cake, even a bowl of potato chips from the store (her mother thinking Gary Elias might have been along). Wethu was another being, here; but it wasn't the time or purpose to observe and feel troubled at having isolated the woman from belonging. Her father put down his cup and stood up, his signal everyone accepts every time she comes home. Father and daughter left the veranda gathering unremarked.

The passage to his cubby-hole study where at her beginning so long ago he had told her she was going to school before her brother Bongani—she had gulped a yell and laughed tears. She felt something now, a strength of him, Baba—she didn't have for (her others) Steven, Sindiswa, Gary Elias.

On the door to his privacy there is the same poster that was hanging on the fence pole.

Amazed disbelief. Collisions of fast-rapping heart—her father such a man, so distinct from anyone else in his dealing with ambiguities self-contradictions which are yes or no to others. The remarkable headmaster; the Elder.

Some Christian faith that this man grinning on his front teeth gap must be saved, in the way of the church. Something they term a lost soul. An image set up for redemption? An Elder could believe that. It has been her—what—shame, regret, guilt that although she has been part of the Elder's congregation since she was old enough to be in church on her mother's back and she still believes in the first revolutionary, the Lord Jesus and the ultimate Father, God, she never depended on Him when she was in detention, in a bush camp, there was that other faith, the only one, Freedom. She can't understand: but is Zuma set up, to be saved.

She comes in and performs the action, pulling out one of the two hard chairs for herself as is expected. He's walked round the side of his desk and is seated in the chair with pressure-sagged leather arms that belonged, she knows, to his father the minister of the Methodist Church.

It is usual when they are at last alone together that she waits for him to begin their time to talk.

He sits straight-backed, opens and then closes his lips, once, and looks to her. As if he can't find the words.

They come bursting from her. —I've been thinking of you, all the time, Baba, I couldn't talk on the phone, I was in the court and I heard him, I heard it all. He said it himself. And when I left, the women outside shouted terrible things. She must be burned. The women shouting that—

He hears something different. —The papers attack him like wild animals. They are out to tear him to pieces, that's all. It doesn't matter the court, the judges found him not guilty, the lies of that woman—

—Baba—

—I'm saying what we can see, what we know.—

—What we know. Baba what is it we know.—

—Mbeki and his people he gives the important posts, they'll do everything, anything to stop Jacob Gedleyihlekisa Zuma from being president next time.—

—Zuma.— She says it to make it real.

He pronounces across this as confirmation of everything he is expounding, feeling, and that she must be experiencing with him. They are speaking in the language, Zuma's tongue they possess with Zuma: their own. Father and daughter have always shared perceptions, hers from maturity instinctively received, his from the time-step ahead of the young, received by him. His daughter. *Zuma.* When she says *Zuma.* It's the affirmation of all he has said, is saying for them both. It would not be necessary to speak of it at all between them, what they feel, the vice of appalment clamped inside them, the spoken cadence is only to put it out to the air like the blast-wail of the raging women outside the court.

She is saying again, again, *what she heard in the court* before the judge, the lawyers, the people she sat among, anyone will tell this was what they heard, she's heard, the young woman was his comrade's daughter, he had been ten years on the Island in prison with the woman's father, he knew she was sick—

Baba listens to her patiently; almost recognisably. The Bible Constitution, its laws that command human behaviour in which (yes) he is satisfied she has had the opportunity to become learned, cannot deal with this matter of spiritual morality. Of course she doesn't know the stricken souls of men, she can't believe what indeed she does know *now*, that power ravages the soul and a brother, Mbeki (she'd call *Umkhonto* comrade) takes it in fist to strike brother out of its way.

She cannot speak to her father about the other proud statement to the court—a Zulu man 'cannot just leave a woman if she is in that state'. That it is traditional in Zulu culture for a Zulu man to satisfy a woman who shows she is sexually aroused.

Share politics, yes, even passionate disagreement, disruption in the confidence between them neither shares with anyone else quite the same way. But the matter of sexuality. No.

The evening passes somehow in the company of her mother among the lively women. As customary, it was their turn to have a share of her time back with them; she becomes more and more desperately aware of the need to take herself and her mobile into a corner somewhere in that family home where there is no privacy except Baba's, or the lavatory; call Steve. To say—what. The landline is continually occupied; the children taking a holiday at least from one parent's surveillance to chatter with friends without using up cell-phone batteries, and Steve's mobile responded with the message (recorded on his request in her voice because he likes it so much) that he was not available but would call back. Later she slipped out into the dark and against the live voices and contests of radios between rap, gospel and kwaito coming from earth-wall houses, the running, brushing past of children's games, found Steve's voice.

—I'll be coming home tomorrow not Sunday.—

—Poor darling, is it hard going, he's in a state of shock to put it mildly, I can imagine.—

She isn't in tears but her voice has the heightened register of that level. —Yes but it's not that—what we—he's up in anger, it is all a plot to keep Zuma out of becoming president. He's—he's like stone, furious on behalf of Zuma.—

—Not *at* Zuma? Disgusted?—

—No no, the papers, the woman. It's lies, all a plot.—

—But you've told him. You were there—

—I told him— and she silences herself— I want to come home—

—I wish I could fetch you right now.—

These are better than love words.

Wethu is not to be deprived of half her visit as someone will be going back to work in the city on Sunday night and would transport her.

Alone in the car rehearses not as she had on the drive to her other, KwaZulu home what she was going to say to her Baba sharing with him the disgrace, the betrayal of the amaZulu by Jacob Zuma: but the recall of the small private place, the hour between her father and her while he turned betrayal around. Completely: to represent people named and unnamed who were not that giant body naked power, but power fully garbed with lies and scurrilous scenarios—woman paid to cry rape—disgrace and destroy the great man who is president elect.

Burn the bitch. Hadn't spoken of it to her although he said he had read all accounts of the trial and events around it. Does the devout Christian, son of the pastor and himself an Elder in his community church allow a call that a woman be burned as some sort of heretic to the faith of power, as heretics of the Christian faith were burned in the Crusades.

Something else she hadn't wanted to come to surface with the threading of the road back beneath her. Just as respectfully she couldn't speak before her father of sexuality, out of his respect for her, his daughter, in her choice of a man—white— as husband and father of her children, he couldn't say what else he had read: there are whites who own the newspapers, behind tactics to smear Zuma, along with his black political rivals for power. Is it possible that her father who gained for her as a child the rightful chances wrested from within white race privilege, could somehow, facing her yesterday see her, his private revolutionary creation, as part of the whites who fear and want to destroy Zuma.

And she will never be able to tell Steve this that has come to her on the road home to the Suburb where she belongs, has chosen.

Parallels in life reduce the obsessive impact of one when they suddenly meet. While she was driving back to the Suburb Jake was leaving it early in the morning to pick up an old comrade visiting downtown. At a traffic light as he fumbled for small change to give a beggar at his window two men thrust this accomplice aside and one held the hard cold snout of a gun at his head. His car is an automatic, a foot free, he accelerated to throw them off and as the gunman lost his balance the gun slid from ear to neck, the man's reaction was to fire. The bullet broke a vertebra, the men snatched the keys from the ignition, pushed the slumped driver to the passenger seat and drove to a deserted building site where they dumped him among the rubble, disappeared with the car.

She arrived to find Jake's children over in the house, the viva- cious, talkative Isa with the drained face of someone standing at a grave; Jake had just been discovered by vagrants who led a policeman to the dead man they'd found in the place that was their shelter. But Jake wasn't dead; an ambulance had taken him to hospital and surgeons were assessing the damage. The stunned, stunted language Isa used as if someone were totting up a bill. Steve had met Jabu in their doorway, her embrace unable to be returned; he was about to drive Isa to the hospital although Jake was in the operating theatre, she couldn't hope to see for herself, believe he was alive. What else can one do for her. Steve. He has no answer, only a deep breath with his mouth forgotten, half open.

What to do for her, Jabu: to be with the children, feed the children, apparently they had been told Jake had an accident, car pile-up, but wasn't really badly hurt. Although disbelief was in the turning away of the eldest son; how could he not know differently from evidence of the stranger his mother had become. He is the one Jabu told the truth, when Steve called from the hospital, the bullet has been removed; she hoped this was heard by the boy as that his father was *alive*.

Steve stayed beside Isa hours at the hospital. He saw she had to witness Jake out of that theatre anteroom of life and death, recognisable as himself in a bed in an intensive care ward, although not conscious, and detained by a straitjacket collar of plaster and bandages; either arm in a sling, the rest of him under shroud of sheets.

What to do was to make a meal for the two on their return, persuade Isa she was hungry although she didn't know it. She first refused the panacea, a vodka or wine—Steve and Jabu didn't have whisky in their house (Jake and Isa's tipple). Then when Jabu brought in a plate of spaghetti and some bottled tomato and basil sauce she'd found, Isa helped herself to wine with some unconscious instinct of her usual resilience available. Jabu said she would spend the night with her. —Oh I know you would, I know— Comrade: that remains more than a friend. —You mustn't . . . I'll take one of the kids in bed with me . . . don't worry. I'm not alone.— The Reeds would drive the children to their schools on Monday morning along with the Reed children, that's understood.

Steve walks Isa and children to their house as if it were not the familiar two blocks around the corner.

Gary Elias was 'sleeping over' at a school friend's. Sindiswa has begun menstruating this year already and the change in her body, barely any sign of breasts yet, has taken her out of the security of happy childhood—and it was one, from the time she lay kicking on the balcony, Glengrove Place, and the motorcycle tore up the sky like a sheet of paper—to an inkling in herself of the happenings adults have to find the way, what to do about, instead of having this done for them by parents. She is a reader and Jake—Jake's the one who lends her books he thinks she will like, enter into the imagination he senses there in her, not books she ought to read (as Steve sometime presses on her). The young shouldn't be exposed to the horror of violence coming so close, although it is round them in this city, this country, the world they know at the remove of its mirror TV screen entertainment; Isa has thought it best now to tell all the children, her own and the Reeds, of the kind of injury Jake has and that he was hijacked.

As they prepare to go to bed, in the absence of Wethu, Steve, Jabu, Sindiswa washing the day's dishes, Sindi breaks in. —Everything's tied, I mean, to your spine, I've seen it on a chart . . . will his legs and arms work if it's broken some-where . . . ?— Her father's in the science department at the university, he will say,

—I don't know enough about the intricate nerves in the spinal column—I'll talk to the medical school professor on Monday. Maybe if the fracture is at the neck this will affect mainly the upper part of the body.— And although she's almost grown-up, he doesn't add, the brain.

Jake spent weeks in hospital and finally in rehabilitation before he regained memory, spoke—could use his hands; walk. Sympathy bored Jake, family had to show love by other means (his younger son did a wicked cartoon of his father as a puppet, nurses pulling him about). Comrades were expected to know, however terrible, unforgivable the attack on him had been: —My turn.— Wryly with the twitch of grimace smile; the comrade knew he, Jake, sees that bullet in his column of life was return fire, *eish!* For all the bullets that killed, yes, the always-cited times, 1976, the '50s, '60s, '80s, the Trek way back in 1820, how limit the past?—and the shortfall in delivery of fought-for promises by freedom. Peter Mkize present at the bedside of Jake in hospital visiting hour, his brother hacked up among the meat for the apartheid army men's *braai*, thrown into the river.

During the weeks that Jake is absent there is something that couldn't have been expected. Among Jake's *Umkhonto* comrades there was uneasy talk that someone among them ought to be with Isa, but it seemed no one could shelve other, their peacetime personal attachments, for an indeterminate time. A veterans' association was approached to ask if there was not some woman who'd been a cadre, a woman like herself, who could stay with Jake's wife in support for a while; no one found.

It was a Dolphin. Marc the theatre-man, playwright, who unannounced moved in with Isa and the children. Not cross-dressed, a woman like herself. A human like herself. A man from the church swimming pool. Sunday mornings.

At the night-table on Steve's side of the bed Steve lay with his mobile, that other form of communication, a book he'd just been given by its translator, Lesego from African Studies. A book of African fables IZINGANEKWANE-IZINTSOMI, with the kinds of truth fable carries. The quaint mode of understanding stays with him in his closing down to sleep. The Dolphin and Isa. This is another fable; out of the violence, some way the country is supposed to be, now, somehow come about. You don't have to be a cadre of *Umkhonto* to be a comrade. A new identity in what's called freedom.

Professor Goldstein, head of Faculty, is over-occupied with vital financial problems, equipment replacement and what some of his staff feel is their work overload, to accept an academic invitation he would wish to, abroad. Assistant Professor Steve Reed has been chosen by the department to attend a conference on the presence of toxins in industrial production, domestic products, the food industry, cosmetics, as part of a series of international environmental studies. He was unbelieving; surprised that he was to be the delegate: Jabu surprised that he thought so little of himself. —Of course it's you, it's up your street, and look at all the extra work you take on for the students, the university—who else in the department—

She sees the appointment from his and her political mindset: the opportunities of students to have him bring back to them advances in their right to contemporary knowledge.

But this is a scientific conference not one concerned with social justice . . . except, it can be supposed, elimination of toxins from unaware inhalation, ingestion, is some wider form of the mantra justice for all . . .

He has the address of the London hotel where the delegates will be living and gets himself delivered by a taxi from Heathrow. The programme brochure for delegates asks that they call the host organisation on arrival. The foyer is lively with other arrivals introducing themselves to one another or greeting acquaintances with exclamations as if these had come from Mars rather than the distance of some past conference; he doesn't know anyone in this batch, wouldn't know with whom to begin introducing himself, and takes his key card for an assigned room. The receptionist addressed him from a checklist of reservations as Professor, well, Assistant Prof. is rather a mouthful but plain Mr probably doesn't do for conference protocol.

He dumps his bag on the bed: a double, as giving the message that two inhabitants were expected. Hotel rooms like detention cells are so accustomed to a succession of occupants that they have their special air of belonging to no one, ready for anything that might occur along an experience of many kinds. People have made love in them, fought in them, died in them. He took out a folder of newspaper cuttings he'd thought might be useful but too messy for his briefcase and tossed the few clothes he'd provided himself with on the bow-legged chair. The style of this cell is a disguise, old English, nice enough. What's next is to follow the instruction to report himself to a Doctor Lindsey Wilson at the institute's headquarters. —Your name please.— —Steven Reed.— The usual interval for connection then a woman's voice, young voice, high-English, confidently casual —Professor Steven Reed, you are here, already in the hotel, welcome.—

—Thank you. I'm supposed to speak to Doctor Lindsey Wilson—

—I am Lindsay Wilson.— Laughing.

—Sorry, I thought a man—

—And sorry to disappoint you—

—The name—

—Oh I know, but it's also a girl's name, just a slight difference in the spelling.—

They are both laughing at him. —I didn't know the difference.—

Where I come from.

The customary exchanges about the flight, long but OK comfortable, yes, the hotel all right?—and there's to be transport for the delegates to the welcoming drinks gathering at the time in the programme, see you then.

She is as she sounded, this female Lindsay. Between the instructions to men mostly older than him, and the few women of generations who have followed Marie Curie's break-through into the profession of science, she is the facilitator, a type of straight slippery-haired blonde that is the icon of the present's aesthetic for their sex. Many have that ideal of a fall of yellow silk that is down this one's back. In the crowd even *he* finds himself with someone he's met before, Professor Alvaro from Cuba who once had been brought to South Africa by the Cuban Embassy with a visiting cultural group from Havana: comrade. Not here as comrades but in another identity, despite their special greeting embrace of recognition in a place where handshakes and token slaps on the back are the ritual.

She, the woman official who introduced him, as were others to the director of the Institute, chairman of the conference; what her position was, not clear. As this is the host country the welcoming entourage is British, with all the vocal variations of that identity, Scots, Irish, some accents class rather than territorial in origin. Among the French, German, Ukrainian and far-flung delegates his Kitchen isiZulu wasn't much use. But everyone had more than Kitchen English—even us Americans, disarmingly quipped one of them, and all had the vocabulary of their related branch of science to supplement with its jargon in Latin and Greek a more general colloquial understanding across disciplines. Whatever she might be at the Institute, the young woman was to be heard clear as running water talking to an Italian in his own language and then her cadence coming from another part of the bar, to a trio of French, in theirs. He and Alvaro instinctively resisted getting together aside, after so long. Having been introduced as from Africa, he was approached and drawn into questions not restricted to any territory of the continent, while he was conscious of his own particular identity. Well, again, this's not a political get-together. Yet this enclave standing and sitting about in the curve of a worn cushioned area turns to talk about AIDS.

From South Africa? One of them challenges the apocryphal spinach, garlic and beetroot cure. The Minister of Health's made us the laughing stock of the world; laughter can be an expression of being appalled, he's laughing with them: cuts off—reproach to himself—and confirms, his country has the highest number of infected population in the world.

—Who has discovered the virus—the cause—where from?—

Someone gives a token snort —Not in the field of discussion tomorrow.—

—It's supposed to have first occurred in Africa, yes, people eating monkeys.—

—How were the monkeys host to the virus?— A delegate with a shaved head (unlikely to be to disguise a circle of bald pate, he's young) and a beard that may be signal of strong sexuality to attract women and or men.

—That's out of date.— Cast away by someone's tipped hand.

Because it was racist—if only blacks eat monkeys maybe because they had nothing else. But he doesn't produce his inevitable reaction.

The bold image of manhood potency speaks with underlying reproach at the casual dismissal of a subject by a gathering of scientists, lack of the compulsion of inquiry that is science. His question isn't irrelevant to a conference on the presence of toxins in industrial production, domestic products, the food industry: —What did the monkeys eat.—

Dismissal, a professor's second chin wobbles. —They're omnivorous from what I've seen with my kids at the zoo.—

—Omnivorous. What did they ingest in that diet spectrum, what did they inhale as mines, coal, gold, producing waste dumps from the underground elements, invaded their habitat. The environment.—

Others in the academic discourse habit must introduce their ranges of knowledge. —Oh that's all known since way back, silicosis—

Just as this is getting to be contentious the way you'd expect, the Lindsay woman flashes interruption —Look, there isn't a dinner tonight, that's after the opening tomorrow, but some of us could go to a restaurant if you don't fancy eating at the hotel.— It clearly isn't a general invitation but perhaps would interest this small enclave apparently getting on animatedly.

She's chosen the bistro, as a Londoner habituée. The group was along with her, it would have looked unappreciative of hospitality to have dropped out on some obvious-sounding excuse of a previous arrangement—they've hardly arrived. She patted the shaven-head bearded contestant to the seat at her side, a kind of recognition, and then looking round passingly over the others, randomly nodded upon anyone to take the table seat at her other side—it happened to be him, Steve. She was cosily warming to both, as if they were children strangers to her adult self and each other at a birthday party. —It's a bit of a joint, but the food's not as bad as 'intercontinental' suggests, I don't want any complaints from Dr Milano that the osso buco is tough and Professor Jacquard turning up his nose at the hollandaise on the asperges.— It turns out that she's the Conference Chairman's Personal Assistant. She gives this information with upper case initials mouthing formality.

—What a relief, I thought you were his wife.—

The mood lifted by Dr Milano as if the waiter had then drawn the cork from the bottle of Antinori. How happily ridiculous! Probably in her thirties, she could more likely have been his daughter.

—Why the relief—

—Taste the wine, someone—you, Dr Sommerfelt, no one trusts a woman to decide whether it's what it should be—

—Why?—because it means we don't have to watch our tongues with the danger of indiscretions coming to our chairman in pillow talk.—

—Let's not talk shop, anyway. Serious for five days of sessions that's enough, come tomorrow.—

The volume rises, anecdotal. A nuclear physicist from Texas tells the colleague from Norway his adventure in the fjords last summer. The Mexican virologist discovers a fellow bird-watcher in a German from Stuttgart —You know, Herr Doktor,— —I'm Gerhardt, please— —Oh thank you, this is Carlos—in my country people like to eat the birds but I like to be with them, look at the beauty of the world that is in the conformation, structure of bone and nerve in the movements on the ground—not only up there, the first astronauts—

Someone is vague about which of the Africas he comes from: —You're at Makerere, I was once offered a sabbatical in Kenya but unfortunately . . .—

—South Africa—no, no doesn't matter.—

After the rapid apologies habitual to an educated upper-class Englishman Dr Thomlinson tells a confession that he heads the department of the university where he actually graduated 'donkey's years ago'. —What about you? You study here or in your own country? Is it where you teach now? I feel I'm the stick-in-the-mud academic curiosity.—

—Then I'm another one.—

—Oh so you're back in the same science department that produced you.— Glass raised to this shared status.

—Not exactly. There were interruptions.— Raising his glass perhaps to these, the wine is not the stuff passed round at Sunday swimming pool and it's so instructive to the tongue and wakening, down the gullet that he's thinking back to what he won't relate, what it's releasing; the absences in the camps and the other kind, Detention. Has no place in the objectivity of science, its history is of discoveries not battles in the bush.

Dr Thomlinson stretches to fill their glasses, to hell with the Pakistani waiter's sense of protocol. —So you were the bad boy playing hookey.—

His glass meets the neck of the bottle halfway; each is laughing at a different reference of the amiable remark. For Thomlinson it will be having missed lectures after a thick night, student skipping Monday classes, gone beyond the youthful Sunday limit of an amorous weekend.

He couldn't have an exchange with the bearded guy, lean either behind Lindsay Wilson's back or across her breasts, although he would have liked to take further the monkey diet theory with him. She did throw-away rather than address him—We ought to do a Mad Hatter's tea party, but then didn't suggest this move to the rest of the table. A woman opposite him (maybe old but partly reconstructed by a branch of science) took the salt cellar from him, meeting his eyes widely, hers held not in a frame of glasses but of outlining blue and green cosmetics. —I know it may be toxic but I have a craving for this stuff, this Neapolitan's rather tasteless.— It was the opening of a conversation at the pace of savour and swallow, carry on with what was being said, take another mouthful. She was eloquent over any attempt, accepted as useless, of the man beside her to add an opinion or make a comment. Had to guess what it might have been from the phrase or two not overridden; she would tilt her head in her neighbour's direction now and then, and use what must be an intimately abbreviated

'Malcolm' to indicate he agreed or (second's pause, lift of the shoulders) he would be privately disagreeing. Who—which—was the delegate and who—which—was the consort, gender identity couldn't decide. The subject the woman set with the opening command of the salt cellar was effectiveness or otherwise of conferences. Were they a process, or an end in themselves. Was there ever a *practice* that the intention, the duly passed, minuted, published record of proceedings was complied with, that anything was actually being carried out. Significantly. That all a conference accomplished, arrived at, was simply the agenda for the next conference. And the next.

The man beside her at last got in his word. —Don't come unless you're going to be the capacity. Not words.—

She was talking again. He said under her bel canto and hoped the man would hear —This's my first in the big world. I'll have to remember.—

Not much to be expected of the day of arrival; Lindsay Wilson directed who would go with whom in the cars back to the hotel. He and the Beard were led out of the confusion to her car. But apparently the man—had his name now, drawn from him by others at the table, Adrian Bates—was not living along with the other delegates. Himself—he was dropped off at the hotel entrance even received an absent goodnight from the Beard, and an obligatory welcoming 'Sleep tight, I'm sure you need it' from the Lindsay Wilson who'd turned out not to be a man. She drove off with her duty to deliver the other man to wherever it was he was privileged to be lodged.

This was a London not the London he and Jabu had excitedly mapped together, famous landmark to landmark, Hyde Park (detour to the Centre for The Arts of Africa), the British Museum, da Vinci's *Virgin of The Rocks* where Jabu had that other kind of religious experience which can come from a work of art and had bought the image of the experience as a postcard to send to her father, Elder in a KwaZulu Methodist Church. When they had stayed with immigrant comrades in a working-class district and he who had never chosen and paid for her clothes, apologised for the cold and wet, as if it were somehow a fault of his side of the old British colonial colour distinction, and bought her a ski jacket, the warmest one there was, the salesman assured.

There was no obligation now, this time, to see the sights. In leisure between sessions of conference, for most delegates to leave behind concentration was the object; no doubt a few of the old scholarly and the avid young attaching themselves for the benefit or favour they might catch, tocsin of ambition, sat on in one of the rooms at the Institute to continue some discussion beyond the time allotted. Alvaro wanted Spanish food if there were no genuine Cuban place anyone knew of and he and the comrade from Africa followed directions gained from the Cuban Embassy to an address, on foot, because Alvaro had been ordered by a doctor to take at least a three-kilometre walk a day (what's that in old English miles) —You know Cuba we have the best doctors, you know that? If ever you get ill—serious ill, you come to us.—

—What he didn't tell you, comrade, if you stuff so many helpings of paella you'll cancel the effect of the English miles.—

There's a light-hearted take-off from the morning's proceedings when the delegate from a South African university had given his maiden dissertation on the level of laboratory research into the possible and in some instances proven presence of toxic substances in food as defined by the conference.

This had been taken even more broadly: whether the addition of chemicals to boost growth and the nourishment content of crops did not introduce toxic elements, and whether phosphates added to some wines did not represent the same risks at table. A Canadian delegate responded—this was a rather journalistic approach, prompted by the commercial interests of farmers who didn't want the expense of buying new enhanced-variety seed each year essential for enlarging food crops in a world of hunger, and as for the second count . . . the agitprop of crusaders against the pleasure of imbibing alcohol.

There was laughter of the modest-superior kind from those who share that pleasure. Although good-natured, the charge—journalistic—made him feel his inexperience of the cut-and-thrust of these world conferences along with their necessity for the new salvation, Development, that has to take into consideration the ideas of a continent which had been regarded as only a ward in need of tutoring, before? With the exception of its Robert Broom, Leakey, Phillip Tobias . . . Those out there, down there, who brought to the surface knowledge of what we all *were*: in the process of becoming human. Whatever it is that we've become, now. Evolution a process of freedom? From whatever restricts your being? What part had *Umkhonto* had in the late getting up off the ground on your own two feet: never thought of that in quite this way before, taken the recognition in quite this train. Had to leave what's politically taken for granted in order to see it not confined, contained by the Overcome: the Struggle a scientific process of existence. After a day of being received in groups at various scientific institutes the Canadian professor made the suggestion they might get together with a couple of others apparently thought well of and compatible, and do what—oh, go to some night-spot, we are in London after all, it's more than a smelly laboratory. This from a man of age to be guessed at, his lips full and chapped, a little crease lengthwise under each lower lid suggesting he was always inwardly amused while intellectually focused. The casual approach, turning to Steve, was a way of assuring whoever this fellow was, academic from Africa whom nobody knew, so no reputation could be offended. —D'you think Steinman would like to be along? Professor Domanski—or maybe Jeff Taylor, and we don't want to be all male, have you spoken at all to Sarah Westling from Gothenburg, and of course—Lindsay, she's taken such good care of us, Dr Salim, no . . . that wife . . .—

He had no particular names to come up with. —Sounds fine . . . I'm on.— They set off raggedly assembled, late, everyone having had other obligations before; he took time to call home; Jabu would want to hear his version of how his 'dissertation' went down (he'd read it to her, tried it out after the department's secretary word-processed it cleanly). Sindi picked up, Jabu was out. He said tell her not to call, I'll call later.

The Toronto professor had hired a car for the period of the conference —Learn my way about what my grandparents called it, The Mother City. If I lose my Chair of Environmental Studies I can become a London taxi driver, famous guild, now consisting of foreigners like myself, Russians, Africans, Israelis, Pakistanis.—

Professor Domanski was fellow passenger on what they told the Canadian was his first cab call. A lot of wine was downed without any quips about additives, he was at a table beside the Swedish professor who expressed herself in the manner of an actress projecting the drama of her role, dark eyes inescapable, she knew the need to explain them —I'm half-Lapp on my father's side that's why I look a fake Swede—

—Well then I'm a fake African, not black.— But not the time or mood to exchange confidences, tell appropriately to the woman from surely the least racist country in the world that his wife is the real thing: Jabu. They talked occupational social shop for a while, she had taught in America and a semester as a biologist in Ghana. The people—they remember the time when South Africans were there from the liberation army, training—the name of The Spear of The Nation, wonderful— But it also wasn't the time, place to take up her eagerness to press him: what is it really like living in your country now, tell me about how it is, people are with each other after so long *apart*? How without Mandela—what about the new one—

There is good music, a group of musicians' instrumental individuality, also wearing outfits to express this, Indian punk, African, retro-skinhead?—cross-dressing not only gender style. They're giving everyone—Domanski who had his dancing days many years behind him, French Desmoines looking so much in his own habitué night-club atmosphere—each dancer their rhythm, from current kwaito to jazzed-up twenties tango, whether a memory from blackout partying under Nazi bombs to a recall of last week's secret farewell with the lover that students would never have credited their professor had. Professor Sarah Westling's eager questioning about Jacob Zuma (she'd read the scandals, rape and arms deal)—to have at this point place him prancing, knee-after-knee flying up summoned by drums—couldn't he now offer the other one, Thabo Mbeki—read of him?

Lindsay Wilson is standing; couldn't see her profile for the fall of her hair that had its own illumination (natural or chemically produced by some toxic substance) in the dim lighting—he must be drunk on this wine to be joking so nastily, even to himself. Suddenly she and the Beard are dancing. The single conformation that is the body of two dancers if they're good ones is hidden and revealed, hidden and revealed by the interleaving bodies of others. Of course the convict-shaven-skull macho's a good dancer, what else.

She's enjoying herself, she even catches his eye for an instant, or was it Sarah Westling's this was meant for, and him just caught in the swift path of it, her professional attention to keep the spirit of the delegates equally shared, whatever the context. When she sat down again —Everyone all right for wine?— Although the party was the Canadian's initiative and it was understood the bill would be contributed to by all, she was the organising presence. Domanski danced with her, there was a lot of laughter as a kind of argument, he demonstrating, twirling her wildly.

The Beard was dancing with the Swede; Lindsay Wilson descended with a flap of arms into the vacant chair, there was the rise and fall as if she were breathing on him.

He poured a glass of water. She gulped, choked, recovered herself as he rescued the glass and she took it back domestically as a child from an interfering adult. —It's like wrestling with my dog, big Irish setter, who's going to collapse and go racing round the grass first. These Poles.— —I thought you were having a good time.— —Of course! But it seems I'm off form. Haven't been dancing lately.— —Too busy over us.— She has her breath taken back to herself. —Oh new people, that's what I like. You have to have a change from your friends although you love them, some spice, must meet people—in different places, different kinds, the relationships, the climate, everything . . .—

—Where?—

—Where . . . well, skiing in Italy, same station I went to learn, as a child. And Jamaica—have you ever been? And places I've still to go to. But people coming here, instead, coming from those countries, new people. It's not trouble . . .—

—And the immigrants?— But she's seeing conference arrivals, people who have 'fields' of chosen interest not the immigrants from Pakistan, Somalia, Iraq and Eastern Europe who like invasive plants seem to have become part of the indigenous bramble of manual workers in this country. Her quick wit —We moved in on them all right, now they've moved in on us.— Someone in charge of her life. You don't always have to talk politics to be acquainted.

—Are you recovered?—

She stood up smiling as if asked if she wanted to dance. They talked while they danced, about—of all things—schooldays. It is accepted that like her he had been to some family traditional private school for boys as she had for girls. That was her segregation. Her innocence, ignorance: he found himself sharing, telling bizarre school adventures in deluding authority which lay forgotten on some shelf of discards in the canon of what had followed as adventure in the real life: as comrade.

—I've one friend who's survived so far as I'm concerned from the dorm bosom pals, but I don't go to reunions, do you, what's there to reunion about?— It's as if this stranger is telling him he doesn't have to sit at Reed family Sunday lunches though Jabu makes him guilty of excuses. Exoneration come lightly from this chance proximity—the dancing isn't an embrace but a kind of stalking, in the style the music demands at this moment.

—What are your plans for the weekend?— The conference programme lists a break from working sessions; it's spring, there are several diversions, cultural trips offered for those who don't have friends they might want to take the opportunity to visit. —Have you signed up? Of course it means the same company, extension of sessions.—

In agreement about that condition. —I thought I'd see the friends I stayed with my other time in London, I must call—if they're going to be around. And maybe do some reading in the institute library, there're issues coming up on Monday I don't think I'm prepared for—equal to . . . among the great minds. I want to be sure of the questions I'll take up, ask—

—You're so conscientious.— Unserious, a tilt of the head. —If the friends aren't around, you could come to our place in Norfolk if you like. It's horsey, my brother has his retired show jumper, and a pony for his kids. My mother and father keep open house when they're down there weekends. I could take a couple of you, welcome.—

Our place. Husband and family. He hasn't met the husband who probably has preoccupations of his own, free of any obligation to socialise with the conference. —Thank you, it's really more than you should have to think of for delegates— I'll get hold of my friends and find out if they're going to be in London. If not, well, thanks.— —Jeremy'll let you borrow his old nag, d'you ride?—

She didn't wait for an assurance, the bossa nova had suddenly ceased just as they were about to pass the party's table again, and he was commandeered by the Canadian while a singer with the elusive features of some Far Eastern origin caressed the microphone, cooing a pure voice in contrast to the phallic suggestion. —The cabby's ready to take you back when you've had enough.— But Canada signalled for another bottle of wine and settled to reminiscences about colleagues, some from South Africa, Nobel Prize names in medicine, physics, was this one—didactic, but with such a critical mind—was he still alive, no, hadn't he emigrated to some nuclear research project in Germany—we were cocky youngsters together years ago, Einsteins all, in our opinion.—

Except for the courteously gentle Phillip Tobias, whose inspiring lectures he had sat in on although the origin of hominids was not the area of his interrupted studies in chemistry, he knew the other great—all that matters—only by their works—some quoted in the doctoral thesis that earned him Assistant Professorship.

—Of course. You're not old enough . . . you were in short pants, time of my student days— Flattery rather than condescension. And his student days; flunked out. On the run, in Swaziland; or in Detention Block D. Along with the wine, take the flattery as a woman would, glad to be looking less than her age.

The Canadian paid the bill with his credit card and everyone contributed their share, or if there was the muddle that they didn't have the right notes for the amount, vociferously in exaggerated decorum—nobody was drunk but nobody was sober—assuring they'd settle tomorrow. All parted for the 'cab' and other cars that brought them, a kiss in the air grazing either cheek, given men and woman alike by their caretaker (the charming sense of the word) but she didn't leave with them. From the door, straggling, yawning in the urge to be gone; she was to be seen, back within the music, Lindsay Wilson and the Beard, dancing.

In the morning: hadn't called last night.

But at what an hour it would have been. The ringing jangling beside Jabu in the deepest cycle of sleep.

When he reaches her early in the morning Jabu is given a rundown of the evening's scholarly entertainment with the relish of gossip between them—she's in a rush and an account of the serious proceedings so far, although she's eager for his impressions, will have to wait.

That day the sessions' range branched off, burrowed, dived in on trail of toxins beyond domestic examples, the food industry, cosmetics. —Industrial products—a loose term that hardly covers the pervasive products of nuclear power stations.— A delegate who so far had been withdrawn in perfect attention of others, stood up with his microphone and had to pause, applauded: he must be someone unapproachable in his, this field. Ignoring the accolade the man spoke with distant eloquence. —We are all afraid of extinction. That is what the nuclear threat is, to most people. The nuclear threat that is not the Big Bang is one that kills slowly. The state of world data, our information, let alone fully examined and assessed knowledge of the nuclear threat that is not a Big Bang, is incomplete and perhaps never will be. This symposium is an opportunity—obligation—to hear from our colleagues from many regions of the planet which compromise our engulfing environment, anything in the experience of their own country which will add to the data.—

From the apocalyptic to nuclear detritus shit. There's a murmur: all there in their books, but the famous speaker catches it. —We're here to make what's dispersed cogent.— The Chair professor of the sessions smiles in acquiescence and lifts curved open hands of a familiar deity.

Several stirrings, someone gets to rise first and tells of the endangered plant species in her part of the environment, 'engulfing' has a literal rather than a conceptual association there (an acknowledging grunt from her neighbouring professor) with nuclear waste pollution of water stunting the growth of plants and crops.

Water becomes the element that engages. (It's represented here iced, in plastic bottles all along the conference table.) An English professor: —Chernobyl suffocated, the prevailing awareness of nuclear effluent is what you breathe, not what you may ingest, swallow.— A gesture to the delegate who comes from the habitat where crocodiles die in polluted rivers, that chain of life being broken.

He doesn't have to compose what he tells, as he did with his maiden slot of presentation; the facts are ready to mind. He can tell: a nuclear power plant near the coast, yet another in the drive for development of industry, will produce a huge thermal discharge of scorching water from condenser cooling which will alter the sea temperature, destroying kelp. Chemicals and biocides used to treat the nuclear plant's piping will put this thermal and toxic discharge into the marine environment killing larval fish—a massive trauma will disturb the seasonal migration of whales.

He's taken up the demand in habit from way back in the Struggle of responding to what is expected of him in discipline of a given situation.

In the foyer after the session ends he is jostled by further questions, is hearing comparisons with the state of nature in this one's group of islands, and that, interjections of the capability or not, of climate to alleviate conditions, Lindsay Wilson has looked in, her duty to the institute to monitor activity, and finding herself near him half-turns to confirm casually —You'll be ready round two on Saturday afternoon?—

She's right.

He hasn't called the friends of the other stay in London.

That gesture of the turned head caught peripherally in the foyer gathering: the parents keep open house, she and her little contingent. If it was spring in the Northern Hemisphere it was cold (in his experience, of African seasons) as he was delivered out of the hotel by the revolving doors. He hunched in the corduroy jacket that was his all-season protection at home.

Her car was drawn up, she waved him to it with the bright bobbles of her woollen cap beckoning. The car was empty. No one else from the hotel followed or was waited for, apparently. She didn't pause. Snapped her seatbelt.

—Domanski's cried off. I think he's found some long-lost love he thought had left for Peru or somewhere years ago. So many among you—the delegates, belong to some country other than the one they live or have done their work in.—

—Yes, that's been the benefit of wars and revolutions, at least for those countries.—

She laughs at the off-beat idea, in a country that won all its wars. Since how many centuries? Invasions? The Vikings? No one had to flee to somewhere else. Except to establish England far and wide.

There is an attitude in walking when the body knows the direction, the muscles and nerves tuned towards it. Same thing with driving, there's a delicate known objective in the handling of the vehicle. Is she headed for the right street where she's to pick up the Beard. But the impulses that subconsciously control the handling of the car are directed out of the lefts and rights of neighbouring streets, she's turning to a highway. The Beard is not waiting at some host's house. Nothing said but that's evident.

She gossips playfully about the delegates in the way natural between people who are of the same generation—well he's a bit older than she is but they're of the same era, in the same relation to the ageing, some really old academics at the conference. This one wants an exercise bicycle in his room although, poor old dear, he stumps along on a stick, that one wants an appointment at a special audio clinic for tests on his hearing aid he's told are unique. —I'm a bit like an up-grade air hostess, nurse, attendant, if I don't serve the food I take instructions about it. And not only from the old ones—Adrian Bates must have only a soy-based diet—imagine the chef's face when I arrange that.—

It would be tempting to confirm it makes him an exceptional dancer, doesn't it.

The countryside is coming to life, the magnificent trees shivering new leaves and some pools of rain have the stillness of melted ice. —At our place it's what we call mild in England. No longer spring runny-nose.— She takes a detour through a cathedral city to make the journey cultural. Its stone grey is a statement of splendid authority disguising itself as beauty. —No wonder you Brits conquered half the world.—

—Are you religious?—

—Religions cause too much conflict.—

The subject doesn't have to be heavy. —I'm a divorced Catholic, lapsed. Think that's all right, with God.—

She's someone who doesn't find questions intrusive; free of ever having had anything threatening, to hide from—what an easy pleasure to be with. What's called: relaxed. Cool.

—Have you always, I mean only, done this sort of public relations work, conferences, academic stuff?—

—I've tried a few—what, occupations. After university.—

—What's your degree? Let me guess. Social studies. Languages. I heard you in Italian, French.—

—Wrong. BSc. I'm one of you, but as I've said, it was the wrong choice, I'm interested in *us*—people. Yet it looks good on my CV for the head of the faculty to have as public relations woman someone who's an initiate, at least. It won't be my lifelong career, that's for sure.—

—What d'you plan will be.— Wrong verb, her head lifts back briefly as she drives, she's not one who plans or has forces incumbent. —I've run a resort club for deep-sea diving in the Bahamas.—

—How would you have learnt to bring that off!—

—With someone else, it was a sweat in more ways than one, the heat, the catering and the risk that a careless client mightn't surface on occasion, but it was fun. Until the cash . . . and other things ran out. I've had a year with the British Council in France . . .— And as if he had given an expected response —Oh and now, there's a chance I could go with a trade commission to China.—

—So you're taking a Chinese phrase book home for the weekend.—

—You've hit upon a good idea, I should have one. All I've done is eat more often in Chinese restaurants and tried out on the waiters my stabs at pronouncing the names of the dishes. They don't laugh, they seriously instruct me.—

There was no sense of obligation to keep a conversation going, and short silences interspersed while he followed the fields, the villages no longer the children's toys expected but the supermarket beside the pub, and she was at ease in some aspect of her present, which happens to be that of driving her car, activity as unthinking as breathing.

—You've always taught? In a university. You were sure of what you wanted.—

—I was in a paint factory. An industrial chemist, safe place for me at the time.—

She, beside him, will take this to mean earn his bread, any one way or another, while young, free, undecided. Don't spoil this pleasant ride with a somehow compatible stranger, the whole spiel. She doesn't couldn't suspect; she knows him as a conference delegate who went to the same kind of school, English formula, to shed naturally—for adulthood, as she had. That what?—abstraction, Nazism, Fascism, *apartheid*, history she maybe once demonstrated against in Trafalgar Square, she had the choice; and now she has no choice but to accept without fuss there is some danger she might be blown up banally in that other Underground, the tube train, by an unknown from al-Qaeda. An unknown among the immigrants she surely meets in her present career as go-between for the democratic institute and society. Don't open the car to all that. There's just the fresh nostril-widening of breath coming in by the driver's window lowered.

She's telling him that she really wants a cottage, some little place she can fix up, of her own, although she loves the family-free-for-all she can always take friends to. A cottage nearer the city so she could even come down during the week for a night. But it doesn't make sense, she supposes, while she's going to be away, sometimes a post for several years—

When a flash sears across the road a leaping dark thing hare or dog and her voice become the mad swerve of her left hand over the steering wheel the speeding car heaves he grabs the arc of her arm to correct violent imbalance and she rights in a skid—whatever the creature was it's escaped, her left palm falls rigid spread-fingered on his thigh as the speed shudders madly and her sane right hand gains control of the wheel. Drawing back his arm, his hand rests a moment on the hand on his thigh as on flesh that has taken a blow. Then she's in charge, she doesn't stifle the engine, stop the car, she drives them slowly out of the zigzag the tyres have ploughed.

—You didn't touch it. It's unhurt. I saw.— The assurance. Neither suggested they should have got out to make certain. It was true he saw it disappear into a thicket of bushes. —I don't think it was a squirrel— was all she said. Are squirrels special, to her, among wild creatures.

As her car came to itself again, she cried out and turned to him with a twitching grimace —I apologise. I think you need a coffee, shall we stop at a village. Get ourselves together? We're near now, about half an hour to go.—

—You handled it well, I'm the one to apologise for grabbing your arm like that, it must be bruised.—

—I'll tell you after I'm in the bath, too much sleeve to roll up now. We were both pretty cool.—

They had coffee anyway at a rural stall, served by what the stranger would appreciate in the English countryside, a bright-faced old man with an accent of some region he hadn't heard before; that one other time in England. There was a parrot in a cage, nibbling his bars at them. She spoke to it, Hi there Polly two cappuccinos please, and it cursed back in a hoarse invective learnt from some drunk —Shut yer fucking trap fucker FUCK-EER LOS LOS GET LOS— curses certainly lost in their buoyant laughter. All part of the incident on their way. It passed with the early dusk.

In light from the windows an old farmhouse appeared leaned against by two great bent trees he thought must be old oaks— Not so old—she discarded sentiment—my great-grandfather decided to try farming when he came back from that First World War with lungs messed up in a gas attack. My grandfather preferred the stock exchange and that was a good thing for the rest of us. It's never been farmed since. Most of the land was sold off, of course.—

Seen for the first time as if come upon an unfurled painting, an orchard of some kind, a line of trees curving beyond a field where two horses switched tails in the company of (by comparison) an awkward donkey, the tree-line imagined as probably covering a stream; the house not thatched but with rural solidity enlivened by some obvious additions. There were three cars and a station wagon at homely angles on the grass, where shadow children in the light from the house darted between them after a ball.

—Ah, full house tonight.— She, recognising vehicles and children. Apparently it was customary no one, including herself, was expected to call that they were going to be there for the weekend. But he felt rather intrusive, just turning up with her, open house full house. —Is it all right?— She gave a call of mock surprise —Of course!—

His tote bag and her stack of whatever her kit was for the country were left in the car. Everyone was already around food and drink in a wide echoing room with a fire being fed rough logs in fooling competition by two teenage boys and a girl in sheepskin boots. He was taken by the hand to have it presented to a heavy man, evidently her brother, blond as the strands so restless this way and that over her forehead and cheeks due to what happened on the road; so the water-blondness was shared, not chemical. The brother Jeremy took the hand and then grasped its forearm male-welcomely (not the black double-shake, *eish*), although he didn't seem to give much attention to registering the name of the one changing weekend cast she brought to open house. —The parents aren't down— she asked.

The brother was the host, then. —Help yourself before everything's gone—this family's a ravenous lot. Wine's there, beer if you'd rather. My sister's always for Guinness, she knows where to find it.— Women came over from the long table of food. I'm Tracy . . . Ivy, Isabel. I'm this girl Lindsay's Ugly Sister (a beauty); a small girl with her mother's lipstick a purple scar on her mouth insisted, Who're you . . . *Steve*, thanks . . . Steve Steve Steve, repeated in the parrot's cadence.

It could be heard from his South African accent that although he wasn't one of her foreigner friends (Domanski's cried off, yes) he was some variety of colonial. —You here from Australia, mate?— Oh . . . this one or that among the men had a son or a cousin in South Africa, communications or was it automation, Cape Town. A young one dismissed the Square connection: his brother was down there with the

Liverpool rugby team. A grey-locks woman with the presence of some other kind of achievement found herself beside him as he topped up his wine glass, there must have been something about him suggesting her supposition: Does he know the work of the artist from his country, Karel Nel, who recently had an exhibition in London, Cork Street, an extraordinary talent, astrophysics in art. He'd never met the painter but Jake had taken Jabu and him to an exhibition of the work at home. Among the jet and fall of voices, the mood stir of people enjoying food together, there was the momentary link of particular experience, an artist's vision, between strangers.

He was free of any 'taking care' of him by the one who'd brought him along with her, made at ease by another family accustomed, as in the Suburb, to additions of passing company. She was keeping up with this one's news and that one's questions about what she was up to; he caught snatches of her description of the array of conference delegates between gleeful interjections this encouraged. But once she came over—as she would drop in according to her duty to check all going well with the needs at conference sessions—and saw that he was helping himself to ham, pickles, roast beef, store-boxed quiche, and engaged with Jeremy's account of a weird burglary at his London house where only sports equipment, his golf clubs, tennis racquets, son's sailing gear had been taken. —Thieves rather specialised according to the pawn shop demand, these days. Tracy suspects an inside job facilitated by the man who comes to clean the windows, the nice chap she makes coffee for as soon as he arrives . . .— Someone's son with a single earring and a tattoo like a secondary venous system on the back of his hand (familiar insignia of white students at home, earrings are not discriminatory, but tattoos don't show up well on black skin) wants to know if there is good deep-sea diving there, South Africa.

South Africa.

He takes the chance to slip out of the company to find quiet where he can use his mobile. A passage past clamorous timpani of utensils and voices in a kitchen and farther on avoiding an open bedroom where a woman was admonishing a child in the special goodnight register, came upon another open door, a small room evidently the nook of someone who had to keep in touch with principals in the city—there were computers, calendars with circled dates under logos of insurance brokers, industrial companies. The call to the Suburb: summoning as if inside him. Jabu's voice, no distance. —Jabu, hi you can't imagine where I'm speaking from, darling, an old English farmhouse used as a weekend place, everybody, family African-style almost—but of course no one actually lives here.— —Oh lovely. How'd you come to get there— —The conference has a break Saturday Sunday, there are excursions, invitations, this's the family of the director's Girl Friday, public relations, she has to make arrangements for us all. She invited a couple of us but the other one didn't show up. For once it isn't raining in England, but of course I haven't had a chance to walk around yet, there're horses, I could go riding if I knew how . . . tell Gary I'm told the children have a donkey to ride, wouldn't he love that— —I won't tell him, he'll be cross because he's not there with you! Anyway he's got his pal to sleep over . . . but Stevie did you see . . . a farmer's shot a man he saw on his mealie field, he says he thought it was a baboon— She doesn't have to say white farmer (who else). —Justice Centre's taking up proceed-ings for the man's family, he was a worker on another farm coming to see a friend.— —Oh my God (though since the days of being taken to church dutifully by his father he hasn't believed there is One) I see only English papers, they wouldn't be reporting that, too many big horror stories, Congo, Sudan, Iraq. I'll go to the Embassy next week, must read our papers.—

She's to be on the Centre's team?—but as he begins to ask there's a scuffle on the line and Gary Elias's boasting —Dad, I came first in the Junior Marathon, we swam we biked we ran three kilometres— then Jabu called Sindiswa to take her turn.

—Weren't you supposed to be back?— Of course Sindi's so absorbed in her adolescent life it doesn't much matter when it was he went away and when he was due home; it's the beginning of a healthy independency Jabu didn't remember—not with Baba. She doesn't get the mobile back, it's understood they'll talk again without these interruptions of claims on him. —Love to you all.— and under contesting voices, for Jabu. —Home soon.—

And back in the present, the lively company, two old men in Fair Isle sweaters are arguing about the failure of some investment pending on the stock exchange (there's nothing rural about that stock) while Jeremy has turned—his wife Tracy's remarks affectionately, derisively 'fantasising'—to talk about restocking what's left of the old farm with a few cattle. —Stick to your horses.— Everyone helps to clear dishes and wine bottles, including the guest brought by the young woman they call Lyn. As goodnights are being noisily exchanged she waylays her brother. —What's available?— His eyes swerve left to right as he hunches. —It'll have to be the mill, everyone's kids are so grown-up these days, they can't bed down with mama and papa. Rooms chockablock.— —Are there blankets and so on?— —Well of course. Always. Beds made up. As far as I know.—

The mill. What mill. The purpose of a mill, the idea of a mill as a room for a night. She embraced all round here and there delayed to hear something shielded by the swung blind of her hair, and animated with private intimacies, she called, Come! The summons was to her car, they were to get in and drive to this mill. Only the headlights a monster's eyes in the

dark away from the lit farmhouse, a path crackling across stubble and then the monster's sight discovering a shelter, small
beside a shining—path? Stream. Must be a continuation of
what he thought must be hung over by the curve of trees he'd
made out in the dusk on arrival. He has no responsibility for
anything; pleasurably tired, fed and wined. She's in charge.
The car's eyes guide to a door, she shoves, it opens and her
fingers find the switch, a room comes to life but there isn't a
moment for impression of what's there, they are bent into the
car to retrieve their bundles, she kills the car's gaze, they bang
its door shut and she enters the room for him, with him. She
had expected his surprise, his questioning pause, pleasing to
them both.

—It's really a mill? Watermill?—

The bundles are dumped.

—It was; once. Like everything else around this place. No
one knows when it was last working. Tomorrow you'll see the
wheel. Pity it's not yet summer, too bloody cold to skinny-
dip. The stream's so clean, I love to sleep here, good thing
there's no room at the inn.—

It *is* just a room. Camping out: there are two beds as you'd
have sleeping bags in a tent.

—But electricity, it surely can't be coming all the way from
the inn.— This is word-sparring fun.

—There's a generator on, we can have a heater right away.
Oh and you don't have to go out in the dark, that little flap
door has a loo behind it.—

—You think of everything. But you didn't tell me this
invitation was going to be an adventure in the wilds of
England.—

She pulls an electric heater from under the only other piece
of furniture beside beds, a table with a faience flower-patterned
basin and matching jug, the kind you see in antique shops. At

least she fumbles something: the connection of the heater, and he justifies his skilled male presence.

She emptied her hold-all upside down over a bed. So that's hers.

He opens the tote bag and looks at what there is to take out. Pyjama shorts. He never wears a top. Perhaps he'll just doss down as he is. She sweeps an arm in a bow to the flap door, he returns the gesture as she scoops some things from her stash and goes through the flap, there's the sound of teeth-brushing and a brief rustling pause before she comes out in some sort of bunny-rabbit pyjama suit drawn in round each ankle on bare feet, curling up her toes against the cement floor. —Miracle. There are actually a couple of towels in there.—

In a space where he can hardly turn about himself there are indeed stowed as if in a packing case a toilet bowl, a tank and a shower over a drainage hole, hooked-up towels and a jug half-full of water that as he cups a handful to rinse his brushed teeth doesn't taste like tap water, he fancies it comes from the mill stream. In his occupancy there's the rush of the toilet after he's peed; she evidently hadn't had the need, hardly one to be shy of the natural, or maybe knowing the mill she's taken the opportunity up at the house. Women are more private about body functions; they were even in the bush under fire.

She's not in bed. She's frustratedly turning over the spread contents of her hold-all. —I lose track of time, here.— He's come out with his shirt loose over the lower part of him, the inadequate shorts, no fly, just pull up—they aren't encountering each other at a swimming pool.

—Could kick myself—I'd forgotten way out of my mind I'd promised Professor Jacquard I'd postpone his TV interview.—

—You want to SMS him?— If she's left her mobile where he saw it in the car, his is in his tote bag.

This Lindsay is someone quick to take charge of herself: she's let herself down rather than Jacquard. So she's become another persona. Someone other. —No. No, he'll be furious woken up what is it midnight, oh bloody hell, so he won't turn up at the studio there'll be a big fuss my pal the producer won't have Jacquard's mobile number so he can't reach him in the bus to Stonehenge or whichever tour it is Jacquard's taken.—

Someone other: in this, the time of here. She lobs the mobile at him, passed on, all in one contiguity it's back in the tote bag—they are laughing at the dismissal of her conscience and, standing, they confirm this compact, her arms around his shoulders, his arms caught below must go down the slope of her back to her waist. The bunny fleece of cloth suggests a bedtime story, Sindiswa used to feel like this a few years ago. But the bodies of a man and a woman are magnets. She meets the length of his and while they are bending a little back and forward together in the laughter of her release, he feels the rising opportunistic penis. She might pull away. She presses closer. The lips this way and that, caressing, then what is always the real discovery, his tongue in that cave that is the mouth, entry permission gained there to the cave of wild pleasure between the legs.

It was simple. She zipped herself out of the bunny in one movement lifting this foot and that to free herself. He steadied her with one hand and began with the other to free himself of the shirt. He shed shorts last; she held gently, a moment, himself declared there, no foreskin shield. Which bed? Of course she decided, it was the other one, apparently allotted to him, she had not entered hers able to invite him. Before making himself welcome inside her he gave attention to, seemed fascinated by the pink nipples of her breasts, licked round them, took them into his mouth pursed over them, traced their aureoles. She murmured, so you like pink ones (some other lover must have remarked them). His tongue was not for talking at this time.

Who was the appallingly exciting lover, he or she, in a generous rivalry. When she innovated that, he found himself innovating this, unimagined. The invasions of passion were a labyrinth where she took in not just what her body was formed to receive, but also the erotic capacity that had ever been secretly inside him. He was, also; someone other.

They slept almost even as he slowly slipped out of her, their bodies finding a situation each on hipside, facing one another as if the narrow space of the bed was the embrace. Just before first light—must have been, the spring light rises not too late in the northern hemisphere to make up for the long dark winter—he wakened and in the silence caught the sound of the stream. Soon perhaps it reached her, she stirred, her eyes still closed and felt for his presence. Out of sleep they made love again.

She got up first. You can't say to a stranger, come back to bed, let's lie a little, the day among others, hasn't begun. She shook her hands through that flung illumination of hair like a gust of wind. —It's going to be a beautiful day for you, I've arranged it with the sun.— Smiling and bending, knees together in nakedness to gather their discarded clothing, tidying up.

Her neat buttocks and the ride of hips as she went to the shower . . . a happy gasping, the water must be cold despite the generator.

She came out with the towel secured round her tight under the armpit; nakedness now withdrawn from him. —Boarding school, remember 'cold showers are good for you' . . .— Smiling Brrrr . . .

It's one among the definitely middle-class experiences she knows they have in common. —Breakfast's the moveable feast.

Everyone just goes to the kitchen and fixes their own, how hungry are you? There used to be a gem that came up from the village her scrambled made with eggs laid by her own hens was fabulous, famous, but that cordon bleu's on pension now. Only don't ask for kippers, Tracy or somebody brings them, I can't stomach the smell—

He wants to go up and give the kiss on the forehead but the mood she's set makes it unnecessary.

If the sun was shining to order there must have been rain overnight, even after the bracing of the shower the outside world returned to tense him in his meagre shelter of a shirt; but why fuss to go back to his jacket. She, wearing the cap with bobbles that held in brief disguise the waterfall hair, took it for granted they'd take the walk to the house, not the car. They paused as she's said, for him to see the mill wheel first; the old wheel hanging idle like a vacant glance above the stream it was meant to harness.

—Come let's go.— She swerved and ran across the stubble for him to catch up with her, so now the chill was another kind of physical exhilaration beside her. In the comfortably scented kitchen—burned toast, coffee—there was only a miauling cat. Someone had already breakfasted and others must still be in bed. She assembled everything, he amusingly contrite that he couldn't cook. —Don't suppose you have to.— But it might just as well have been the crisp, playful feminist remark, females usually do the cooking, as a reference to a wife. She talked to the cat (whom she called tomcat) the way she had familiarly addressed the parrot, and the cat took up the conversation as if they long understood one another. The other male at least had the attention of being given tomatoes with instruction to halve for frying. —I have my tiger tabby, I couldn't live without him and my dog.— As occurred: —You have children?— —Two. A boy. A girl of fourteen.— It changes nothing. A pubescent girl, a woman like herself. As if he said this aloud to her.

—A boy? Does he look like you?— But it's not an enquiry it's a recognition of how he looks, the conference delegate, in her eyes.

He's not going to ask—does she have a child, by divorce.

What was between them has nothing to do with anything. No relation to others, private and public commitment, loyalties. He takes the board with the precariously wobbling tomatoes to her pan. Now the kiss-touch just a moment on the forehead, the informality appropriately exchanged by delegates at the end of the Canadian's night-club party.

Jeremy appeared robed in an elegant tartan dressing gown. He shared the breakfast while planning the day for his sister's guest in sibling argument with her, interrupted by her indignation when he put the cat out in the protest at its part in the conversation. She at once brought the creature in again.

They would go down to the horses if that would interest their friend (Steve? yes, name come to him) . . . a stomp round the farm maybe, and there's always the general idea of ending up at the village pub if the sun stays out.—

—It will, it will, I've guaranteed it.—

As they left the kitchen, the arrangement to meet in half an hour. —Hang on, Lyn, the man can't be outdoors early, like that, what's the matter with you, he comes from Africa.— He disappeared into the passage and came back with an army officer's jacket. —Not Savile Row, someone in the second oldest profession must have left it here years ago, but it'll keep off pneumonia.—

She couldn't have imagined why he laughed, head back in disbelief at himself donning a regular army's uniform, he, on the run from such, apartheid version, Angola, Namibia. In the striding pace the brother and sister kept round the parameters of the farm warming him up, he got himself free of it, lugged along over his arm. Jeremy in jodhpurs had his saddle with him, she held his horse's stirrup and he flung his heavy body to mount, the movement was all grace, the man and horse first trotting then balancing in arc-leap over a series of tree-trunk obstacles. She brought the children's donkey to be introduced, Eeyore—and had a foot race against one of the children bare-back on it, which the reluctant donkey unexpectedly won.

The pub had well-worn benches and warped tables outside, and flower boxes with cigarette stubs among the tulips putting out tongue-tips of bloom, but no one convivial there; inside the people apparently from the village—Jeremy greeted, waylaid with an elbow. —Ron takes care of the horses for me during the week— —And the donkey— —Yes it's a come-down for him in retirement, after being riding master at a posh country club.— —It's not me it's a come-down for, it's the horses, stabled with that low type.— But the pub also caters for wealthy patrons from their country houses; there were oysters as well as pork and the cook's 'famous steak and kidney pie' chalked on the Sunday lunch board. Tracy recommended pork roast rather than the pie. The barman-pub owner's patter was a conductor of voices, orders, wine bottles, spluttering beers drawn, in familiarity with Londoners and locals. Alert to a new face:—Whyn't you trying my Margie's steak and kidney, you won't get anything to touch it in London or whatever.— And so the stranger changes his order.

The friendliness of these Sunday people makes coming about of any kind of unexpected contact that has happened in context unexceptional. A loop of that shimmery hair falls to be brushed out of the way of her busy mouth as she's eating beside him as it did softly on his body. Someone of the farm-house group has the Sunday papers and sections are sailed from hand to hand . . . there are financial deals, clashes between the Palestinians and Israelis, meetings of the UN Security Council—all distant from this day as what is not reported from South Africa. She ordered a good Chianti to follow the Guinness and her telling some of the others about the subject of the conference was lively interrupted by the delegate she had produced for them. —I'm all primed to bring up the question of tocsins in Guinness and Italian red.— Jeremy happened to lean past him to attract the attention of the showman proprietor. —Not too rustic for you? Enjoying yourself?— —Very much, thank you . . .— Everyone at what once was a farmhouse is accustomed to the variety of passing individuals who must somehow be important to her work.

It wasn't the Beard. It was him.

The Sunday lunch lingered until half the afternoon was gone, people drifting from one knot to another as they caught some snatch of conversation that attracted their contribution or took the opportunity to talk to someone they hadn't had a chance to catch up with in the city. Snatches of banking vocabulary, golf dialect, disagreement over whether Pavarotti was not as great as some other singer in opera just heard, the lowered voices of what must be a pair of doctors, comparing the properties of new drugs, not for laymen to overhear.

Now the family was returning to the farmhouse, the locals off to the village. Making for the mill there was quiet before the spectacle of an early sunset's rictus on a sky's spring face— she was right in her guaranteed sun for him. They didn't talk much, conscious of the presence of each other. At the mill the stream already half in shadow had an eyelid lifted on its colours of the sunset. She stopped, turned on him, at the door, a deep breath held a moment and expelled briskly in consideration. —Do you need to go back. Tonight? Those notes, facts to work on—you said. If you like, don't mind getting up before the crack of dawn we could go very early in the morning. Be in time.— Of course she's calculated the traffic, the exact hour the session's due to begin, no one more easily efficient about the conference programme than she.

A complicit smile at himself. —I didn't get to the library anyway. I'll listen big-eared to the others and take a chance on my ad-lib questions, I'm there to learn from my pundit superiors.— Before she can speak he's adding —I'm serious about that.— After all, she does represent, this woman facing him in changing light, the academic trust by which he is there.

She opens the door with a thump and they are inside, the decision made: leave in the morning! It's the pact they didn't know about, they've come to each other and they kiss deeply for what is not time as seconds a watch records. There is no consideration from either that they'll go up to the house, the lunch was too ample to want to eat again. With everyone else. The room is chilly and they undress one another in the game of desire, mock shivers between the distraction of the warmth in mouths. She dives quickly away into what was his allotted bed and he throws the borrowed army jacket over the blankets where her feet peak, before going to her.

Familiar—and utterly unfamiliar—inside her just as new as the first time ever; rediscovery. But the wildness between them was the same, an innate character in each. As if they were entranced not differently as a man and a woman but were a single sensuousness.

So it's Monday. Monday: they were parted by their showers and getting dressed, he stood hearing the stream, feeling a reluctance, incongruity in emerging to the breakfast company of the extended family who also might have decided to stay overnight and leave early, whatever their reasons. —We're going by the house? Say (for him, guest to hosts) goodbye.—

She shrugged her nose to a little wrinkle. —Not necessary.—

They left behind what couldn't even be seen of the family house on a misty morning, driving by headlights as they had found the mill the night of arrival.

She talked of the conference programme for the few days ahead, how she'd tried to suggest that as the working focus was (sweep of a hand off the wheel) science in its present 'broader contexts' there ought to have been a night at a theatre, a concert, maybe a sports fan among the professors would have gone for the phenomenon of a night football match—she and he tried to guess who that might be—night clubs were part of the subject of environment, of course, but those were left to the delegates themselves to programme . . . She looked at her watch, must have made some quick calculation; changed the route back to London (—We certainly are making good time—) to show him an abbey she said was perhaps her favourite building in the world, so far. And his—so far?— Admitting he had not been much of a tourist, so far.

—But don't worry you're on the conference circuit, it takes great minds to many countries, places in the world, even space is coming closer.—

—This is my first and I'm only here because the head of department had too much else to do.—

Such confessions are disarming, somehow unserious and must be denied by one who doesn't know the circumstances. —That can't be.— She's laughing and her hand again leaves the wheel, hesitates as if going to rest a moment on his thigh as it did after the shock of avoiding an animal on the road; but it's back at the wheel.

What was between them had nothing to do with consistency in life. A reality outside reality. Just real in itself.

Back alone, received by the documentation loose in his

delegate's London hotel room, the officer's army jacket (forgotten to be returned) lying on the bed.

A reality. Perhaps that which sexual love should be.

Or was it a snatch of the alternative, what life might have been if there hadn't been the Struggle, if he had been produced only by the private whites-only school, its greensward a Mother Country import, and grown up to a money-making profession, the corporates.

Final days of the conference brought some resolutions for dedication to the moral obligations of science, which cannot be solved even by the inconceivable possibilities of the twenty-first-century laboratory research into saving the environment of planet earth. Only if world governments provide money and means for the capability of the dedicated scientists, would that come about. The ultimate reality, survival.

That he could carry back to Africa with him.

He could take that result of deliberation in his personal baggage.

Lindsay Wilson managed the supervision of the delegates to the end, likeable, informally dignified, amusingly charming with even the most demanding of them. He, with an instinct for deceit he wouldn't have known he had (the lies you told under interrogation to save comrades and yourself have nothing to do with this), kept the general appreciative manner towards her, like everyone else. Except the Beard, Adrian Bates. He took a seat next to the public relations officer at meals, and he was the one who brought a drink from the bar to her where she was engaged with other delegates at interval when she had succeeded in convincing the Director that they should be indulged with going to hear the Royal Philharmonic under the baton of Zubin Mehta. The Beard of course didn't live at the hotel. Lindsay Wilson had taken him on to lodge somewhere else, when on their arrival she delivered the other delegate in her care at the hotel entrance. The Beard hadn't been included in weekend hospitality at the family farmhouse. Yet the familiarity in his attendance on her now would seem a continuation.

Thoughts arising in context that there'd never been place or attention for.

What happened—what there undeniably had been—was—between himself and this woman whose blond veil dropped over his face and his penis—was simply a private ease, not known to those encountering them. A continuation. When they heard each other's casual voice or the focus of eyes accidentally met. He learnt this from her.

Farewells were hearty among some in the gorilla embrace of coat arms, email and telephone numbers exchanged, many cards handed out like men with something to sell. A number had special requests and went with her one after another to her office to give or note information for follow-up. He had no pretext. As the transport for the airport arrived, she made her usual efficient lift of the shining beacon of her head to summon attention —Professor Reed, I have photostats of those papers you wanted from the library— and went ahead of him into the office. As if remembering, in the haste, her manners, she stepped back for him to pass her, and as if again of itself in haste, the door swung closed behind him. The static of voices and shifting of feet outside was vacuumed into the bus. She signalled dropping her eyelids a moment and firming her lips: the transport wouldn't leave without him. They went to each other and kissed as in embrace in the mill. Those were their cards exchanged. They left the office separately, she first. From among two other late-coming delegates, one of them Domanski, she beckoned him to mount the panting bus.

As Domanski bounced down beside him entangled in briefcase, shopping bags, rolled newspapers, she was out there. Her waving arm was for everyone.

The homecoming at the airport is a welcoming combined embrace.

Gary Elias, Sindiswa, Jabu, in hugging chorus about him, Sindi and Jabu women sharing his cheeks, the boy hung somewhere around his body. It was Sunday so everyone was there, of which he could at once make it an outing by taking all to the children's choice of one of the airport coffee and pizza dens instead of going straight home.

The house in the Suburb claimed him, didn't look any different. Why feel it should have. Jabu with the natural alertness that had developed into lawyerly analytical attention had questions on some of the subjects of the conference that had interested her when she had seen the scope outlined on his invitation. Water pollution, in both rural and urban areas, was becoming the cause of litigation in the human rights cases taken up by the Justice Centre. What was the name of the man who's spoken with such knowledge about the sea, not only rivers—there's still debate, here at the Cape, about the whales every now and then beached and dying—where could he be contacted? She knew one of her colleagues would want to, it'd be useful.

She was taking his underwear and his shirts from him as he unpacked clothes and the papers doubled in bulk from those he'd set out with. But she abandoned what was intended for the washing machine, at the sight of the papers, and carried off a few at a glance, to ask —What's this about monkeys and AIDS come up again?— So he made her laugh with a description over whether it was toxins in food which originated in the primate family the mysterious disease we call AIDS, when a trendy young professor (he did not name the Beard) proposed the theory. Someone then pressing to know more precisely the diet, what did they eat. And another professor in a way of dismissing the whole thesis as if remarking on something everyone must have experienced for himself —Omnivorous. From what I see when I take my children to the zoo.—

Sindi and Gary went about their own preoccupations. Sindi to the secrecy that was her own small room from which there came always, regular as a muezzin's cry from a mosque, the adolescent beat of whichever pop group in favour with her friends, Gary to clean his bicycle companionably in the garden where Wethu was entertaining some of hers. Not spring yet in the Southern Hemisphere, no one goes off to swim at the Dolphins' pool. The Sunday papers whose pages he and Jabu exchange, as they always do, have nothing further of something he heard from her on the phone last Sunday. She gives him whatever facts have come up in the meantime about the white farmer who shot dead his servant's son he says he thought was a baboon. It's an odd connection, grim, with the story of the omnivorous monkeys. The father says he was only protecting himself against a marauding primate come to eat his maize.

Wethu didn't sit as a family collateral at the family supper table—although she isn't a servant she takes Sundays off as servants in white people's houses do. But however she conceives her relationship in the home of a child of the Elder in her village church, her kinsman, it includes coming by to say goodnight although it's Sunday and she's spent the day apart, attending church (not the one that the people in this place, shame on them—God will punish—make into a swimming bath) and inviting friends to be with her in the garden she shares with the family of the Elder's daughter. A clan daughter is a daughter to her as the daughter's man and children therefore are family. She has no inhibition about going to Sindi, who is back in her room immediately after supper, Wethu is an exception in being welcome—nosey Gary Elias has to be kept out. There is a high happy duo of voices from in there, above the music, and Wethu emerges hugging her arms with delight—That Sindi!— She turns the light of it on Jabu and Steve. —And how were you in England, my, my that must be a wonderful time, London, and I'll never see—did you take some pictures?—

—*Eish!* I forgot my camera!— But she closes one eye, at him, she knows he's fibbing, joking because he's let her down.

And Jabu joins her kin, both in chorus —Next time. He was working with many important people, Sisi, I'm sure they were on TV . . . not our TV.—

Didn't send Wethu a promised postcard, should have thought of it. Buckingham Palace not that spring countryside.

Jabu sees jet-lag weariness she herself felt on return from the first, their trip, to London. It goes without saying it's early to bed. Her palm between his shoulderblades after Gary has been hugged and sent off and Sindi called to be kissed. Fresh short-pant pyjamas laid out on the wide bed. She's gone to take her bath, she'll run the tub after, right mixture of hot and cold for him, the way he likes it. He goes in to brush his teeth while she lies there; all the time since Swaziland, the sheen of water on her soft brown shapes.

The nipples are dark berries.

They kissed as this bed returned to recognised, but neither of them would distinguish which of them would not proceed to lovemaking: just her bent arm doubled against his chest, his arm enlaced across her.

He knows—knew—he is attractive to women—that either comes at adolescence or doesn't, and not always implying

189

conventional good looks (although they seem to find he's not short of some). While a student he had a few—could hardly call 'affairs' the fancy term of the white middle class—and the brief interludes in time of the Struggle, snatched, smuggled for relief and about pleasure out of the many different deprivations commitment to the Struggle implied. That faith made even the man or woman's children come second. Freedom demands everything. The price, none of these hasty asides had anything beyond the moments, at best a gift—occasionally not without tenderness—the quick fuck, as it's known. But all before. Once he had 'slept with'—another of the polite euphemisms for the indescribable act, from the exaltation of ecstasy to the desecration of rape—once he had made love in Swaziland with the newly recruited comrade just out of teacher's training class, it was unlikely there were any beckons of passing attraction followed. She taking him in, to her, he entering her, body and being, out of reach of all differences perceived in them by others' categories, both wanting answers to the same questions in the circumstances decreed of their existence—even got themselves married as their particular symbol of the meaning of this state—he had not made love to any other woman.

What brought us together, the Struggle.

That was the attraction?

Looking for reasons for the mill.

And she, Jabu, 'his Jabu'—that's seeing her as an attachment, never mind her independent effectiveness in the world, the time and place they live in. There come random—never thought of, the lunches with a lawyer in successful private practice, very different from her new kind of comrades at the Justice Centre. Has there been one time. Once. Something that wasn't lunch. A passing 'in-house' affair. An unmarked hour that has nothing to do with her constant life.

So. Looking for justifications?

There is some other way. Come out with it. He must tell her what happened at the conference, not the findings of discussions that she was eager to have him relate. Quash. Erase this convenient speculation under the heel of frankness, tell her, Jabu, about the mill. Rehearsing how to say it.

Ah *that* the final indulgence! She's oblivious, make her hurt and unhappy, who can take the sounding in her of what she would make of it—a reflection on herself, what she might fail to be for him?

The moment came; and went—in what would have been the moment for it Jabu is voluble with—Then a row broke out just in front of the doors, some shopkeeper and the men coming from the church, he was shouting they'd left their blankets and dirt outside his place, spoiling the business, it was awful . . . I was right there . . . you've got to see what it's like, when are you free this week . . .—

She is speaking where, in what, they are together, the present. The compassion of a Protestant church (denomination of her Baba) not evidenced by the Catholics, the Jews, the Muslims in their religious establishments, had sheltered refugee immigrants from countries in conflict around this one's borders since the influx started, Christianity appropriate to the circumstances of the times. But now it was becoming a disruption of the city, intrusion, invasion of rightful tax-paying citizens, a threat to business and health. The church turned dormitory flowed over to the pavement where people slept like corpses under any old shroud on scavenged cardboard.

Into this form of reality she drove him. The street they reached didn't look like the familiar fast-paced city, the displacement of functions was the home stage-set struck.

There were the magistrates' courts, fine contemporary architectural expressions of the dignity of the law, human rights. There was the red-brick dignity of the old Methodist Church. The entrance façade of the Magistrates' Courts ignored, obscured by a clutter of occupant people, their makeshift shelters dismantled by the police, piled up like bedclothes to be used again, not trash to be removed. Some men and women, tripped over where they squatted on flagstone surrounded by children wanting a share of takeaway food adults held—these men and women were the fortunate who found small change, washing a car somewhere or begging (the nature of Jabu's work keeps her up to date with how the destitute exist). Others came by carrying their tin plates of food doled out in the church. They pass him without seeing him seeing them: he doesn't exist. Jabu greets them in her language, for her and for him *Sanibonani bafowethu nondade!* When this is acknowledged in the tongue of a neighbouring country she understands, she speaks again, using their language. He is the Stranger.

What are we doing gawping like tourists at these people from Congo, Zimbabwe, their share of Africa. Even though she has some legitimacy and he associated with her through her words, her black skin.

They ought to go into the church, greet the pastor, she's the daughter of an Elder in the same House of God even if not observant. They've seen the pastor many times in the newspapers—a white man, once he was in a scandal of some sort the press won't forget, true or false. Who can put on the moral scale the weights of right and wrong, lies and truth when these people are left without shelter by himself, the *Umkhonto* cadre, and this pastor keeps them alive for conceivable time when there will be peace for them to go home to whichever country it was where they had to leave their lives behind. But the uncountable numbers of this church's different kind of congregation mean that it has to have some of the formalities of a business institution, now. There are a couple of the church's representatives (marshals? Or plain-clothes police taken over) who question, first addressing the white intruder. He has an appointment with the pastor? What organisation does he come from? Is he from a newspaper? There must be a list of people seen as of ill intent, he might be one of the street's shopkeepers.

He cannot enter the church.

She, a woman and black like themselves, is ignored; their manner is flirtatiously dismissive when she surprisingly speaks up for herself, in the way of asserting a right of common law, there is also the law of God's house: you can't refuse to let a Christian into her church. They are sceptical, appreciative of what they take in the tone of sexual banter, but won't let her in, either.

It's not in the nature of comrades' experience to give way to discouragement of what they believe they ought to do. —What is the pastor's mobile number. Please give it. He'll see us.— She is speaking in English now. Pulling rank, an educated Sister, she thinks she knows the high-up people to get her in anywhere she wants. The man grins and twists his shoulders before her, doesn't need to say it; no.

What is unexpected is that there is—impossible—an atmosphere of some sort of home in the organised squalor of this place. A suckling at a mother's bare breast where she sits cross-legged on a bit of blanket and looks so young—how's a man to judge—it might have been born while she took shelter in the pastor's church. There's an old man rolling cigarettes out of torn bits of newspaper filled with tobacco he's taking from a small pile of stubs, there are fag-ends drifted like leaves to the gutters. Step round the woman who has seen the opportunity to count on women's desire to look good in the current city style although they are not of the city, and set herself up in business: a client sits on a box having a pattern woven more elaborate than the one Jabu used to wear, composed of the hair on the head with devices, from a spread of combs, clasps, and what look like rat-tails. There's refusal to accept the denial of ordinary small pursuits.

He and she are the foreigners here. Even she. Black skin isn't enough. She turns down an exit from this scene of someone else's claimed territory which opens suddenly on a street where a wide passageway, sign declares 'Boulevard', of closed elegant shops has become the homeless's version of a walkway supermarket. Takeover. Two young men dance bangles of cell-phone batteries for sale before him. Second-third-hand frayed jeans with the natural injuries of hardship which some white students in his classes reproduce on their jeans as the sign that they're not squares, are splay-legged in paving display with crumpled dashikis and dresses reminiscing on the shapes of their previous wearers, baby clothes that have survived generations.

Everybody's trying to sell something. The importuning cheerful refugees turned traders know only too well this man and woman wouldn't ever need. There's a special kind of animation when you've got nothing left to lose?

Back in the territory of the Suburb, he describes this before Jake, Isa, Marc, Peter Mkize who's come to pick up his son from an afternoon of tackle technique practice with Gary Elias. Isa clucks her tongue, stops herself, then —You've read how people in concentration camps made instruments out of rubbish, played music, there were even stand-up comics, with the gas ovens there waiting.—

—It's not the same.— Jabu will never let pass examples of brutality committed by Europeans as some part of the human condition blacks must inevitably share in their attitudes between themselves, Africans, just as they've taken to computers, Internet, Facebook, Twitter. What the whites did to one another—even if it produced among the inmates of the Holocaust, as she's just seen in the people outcast by conditions in their own African countries and in this one of refugees—a dire spirit. Nothing to lose.

—Of course it's not the same! In the Holocaust you died in gas ovens. Finished and *klaar*. You died because you were Jews. People here come from Zimbabwe where you can die slowly, because your brothers take everything from you, that's the Mugabe way, for themselves.—

—And their other brothers here in Africa?—

—Cousins, not same-mother-same-father—

—All r-right! The same blood of Africa . . .—

Here it comes again—the charge that can't be ducked, held off.

—*Eish!* Of course, what's it with you from *Umkhonto*, why don't you *veterans* do something for these brothers who let us operate from their countries in the Struggle?—

—So no good just talking. What do you suggest we can do, my brother. Go to the church and invite them home with us? You ready to share this room?—

The Dolphin Marc has become a comrade, beyond the pool gatherings where the Suburb bond is simply neighbourly, since he is the one among the local inhabitants who moved in to take care of Isa and the family when Jake was in hospital after the hijack attack. It is he who this week leads them to what he's come across when hopefully visiting a backer for one of his plays, living in a townhouse complex (upmarket he classed it), walled and with guards at electronic gates.

Purple bougainvillea luxuriating over a wall and a uniformed man sat in a summerhouse version of guardhouse chattering to himself on a mobile. The street a wide well-maintained one.

On its opposite side there was a confusion of coiled razor wire rising and sagging along a stretch of open land whose limit couldn't be made out, where haphazardly some sort of organised shelter had dumped itself, a small brick outhouse left over from whatever had been built there, overcome by makeshift of board, plastic sheets, planks, old rugs, like something organic, a wild creeper grown out of the dust.

What was once a gate hung collapsed in the fanged security of this fence. —Ever since I came here I've been thinking, what the hell was this, squatters? Here?— He's been answered now by one of the guards of the residential complex: people from Zimbabwe who were living in Alex township. Our people got fed up with them, taking our houses, taking the jobs in town, there was big trouble.

Read about the violence, the killings unlike murder for money; survival is something else. This is the flood of pavement overflow from the Methodist Church. Here, nobody stops you from going in. The men inside don't pay any attention to the visiting intruders, white men some authority again, inspectors come to harass. The black woman—if she's come to give something to the women—there are no women living here. Perhaps the wives are sheltering somewhere else, the only other ones who fulfil a man's need get in with the dark at night.

The intruders come up to tents where a man is washing clothes in a bucket, pants and shirts sag to dry on the tent ropes. A weary beached Volkswagen is the source of the cavorting heard over the radio; but this raises nothing of the lively assertion that is in the homeless supermarket in town.—*Dumela*, hullo—their approach is taken up by one among the men bent under the bonnet of the car, apparently giving advice about what's to be done there, another standing as if in defence at the lifted flap of a tent. The responsive one speaks confident English —when Mugabe became president in British Rhodesia become Zimbabwe, ex-teacher himself the first thing he did was scrap the colonial education system and establish a general standard of literacy and numeracy higher than that in post-apartheid South Africa. He's telling: all people here—we have been told get out of this place at the end of the month. —Go back! Back! There's nothing there in Zimbabwe. No school. No hospital when you get sick. The money is paper you can't even buy a loaf of bread. I'll rather go back to Alex, I don't care.—

A truck stumbles through the gate and makes for the brick outhouse. While the informant keeps talking—his wife and children are there in the old apartheid Alexandra, someone is hiding them. Him? He has a job, he's been two years an assistant electrician in a construction firm—men are coming slowly from the direction of the truck each holding before them carefully balanced a tin bowl, same as the church ones. It's the Salvation Army truck that has brought a meal. —Yes, every day.— The man does not leave with the others, their heads lifted from under the car hood, the bucket of soapy water flung out and its owner drying his hands against the legs of his pants. He takes from a bag hooked to his belt a Kentucky Fried Chicken takeaway; he has this job someone else covets, even if his room in a house shared with Zim brothers was burned down, he had to carry the kids through fire—he has money, to eat.

From the tin bowls brought back there is being scraped up to mouths a small mound of stiff pap, a hunk of bread and what might be a slice of cabbage.

They don't like to intrude further but it's obvious it has been sensed, the whites and the woman who has shown herself to be a sister—she even speaks their language—are not eviction officials. Then let them be the exception for whatever the reason, to the other side of the street where the ones behind the walls have got city bosses to give the police order—the people of Zimbabwe, out!

An escort of several along with the informant, names have been exchanged, takes the visitors down the irregular order of tents and here and there occupants come out as if to exchange mutual curiosity, and a few words. How long have you been in this place. (It's not taken as 'in this country'.) We've stayed in this place more months than three. Where will you go. They say we must go home to Zimbabwe, there's nothing . . .

In most tents no privacy to respect in 'this place'; that's stripped along with everything else—inside the ground is taken up like flooring by what once might have been uniform bright-coloured mattresses that must have been donated by some international refugee agency along with the tents?

The academic will find out, he's an instinctive researcher. The playwright, man of theatre props used to reveal characters, will see flotsam of individual identities in the few objects, possessions from personal life, a pair of fashionable pointed-toe shoes, a magazine photograph of a naked woman in jackknifed erotic position tacked up on the sack wall; some sort of certificate in a plastic folder; on wire hangers shirts in stripes, checks or Afro-design, the signature of the tent's occupant or the donor of the hand-me-down. And of course there are in these tents the displaced's, the outcast's remaining connection, proof of existence in the world, the cell phones.

Spared nothing. They don't go near, but here are the toilets, single booths in their escaped trickles of pee. The marquee signposted ABLUTION BLOCK—it's closed. No water. That's why the man was washing clothes in a bucket—there's water to draw from some of the single taps standing here and there between the tents. Dumps are not trash but stored households with the leg of a chair poking up, periscope of a life.

Leave it all behind. At least, faced.

You've seen it all.

But stepping round the collapsed gate to the street: they haven't.

She clutches his hand on one side, the Dolphin's on the other, the difference in relation to lover, to neighbour, of no account in what all three are seeing in the street. Curving figures-of-eight displaying mock collisions skilfully avoided, there are white boys on bicycles in the gentlemanly uniforms of the most expensive private school, and have parents who can afford it. They are being joined, happily zigzag, by fellow pupils in the same garb, riding out of the town-house complex gates opened for them with greetings from the guard.

They are black schoolboys. The sons of a new middle class.

They are innocent; their parents are tenants white and black of the upmarket garden complex whose residents' association must have declared the presence of homeless people is a danger, a health hazard to residents of the suburb. A devaluation of their property in the housing market. They have succeeded in getting eviction ordered, across the street.

Couldn't have afforded that school anyway! But he had thought . . . remarked to her when they went to consider a very different one, that first time, the school outfit there was a bit too showy. A triviality. As it turned out we couldn't have expected to find anything else as close to what we want, a democratic education.

If there was a refugee camp just over the road from Aristotle School, and the boys showed off on their mountain bikes in their school uniforms——?

What is he coming to; always expecting another aspect from her, this began for them long ago in Swaziland. She knows what he's saying for himself and for her.

—No—it's not the same, you can't say that, you have to look at what would have happened before. The boys from the camp and the boys from the school have played soccer together, the school invited the boys over to the grounds, the swimming pool . . .—

—Liberal cop-out! You don't change the lives of rejects, you just make for them a few hours more bearable—

—Yes. Yes you do. Or you don't even do that for them while they're waiting for the new justice, globalisation, African Union—whatsit—to award their claim—

—'Award'. An award, that's also a handout, given to you by somebody else.—

But Jabu is a lawyer, she uses the term objectively as it signifies in court, the wronged have a right to what they are wrongfully deprived of. What she knows, he doesn't, is what a single recognition—a librarian secretly lending a man books from a library he's barred to use—means in the man's life and by consequence that of his daughter.

The contradictions to deal with right on your own door-step. At present. Schools, microcosms of worlds. Gary Elias is campaigning, in the freedom to express themselves Jabu and Steve expect of their children, to leave that school chosen for him, Aristotle, where they've seen him develop well, out of his withdrawn nature. That was congenital? Or their fault, something in their nature? The instinct to regard children within the deepest relation they themselves have known along with the sexual intimacy out of which these children have come: regarding them as comrades. Withdrawn. Something in the genes? Sindi has the same ample DNA, of Pauline and Andrew Reed, back to the mating of different bloods during the Crusades, the English who were Shakespeare's Globe audiences, the nineteenth-century diaspora Czarist Jews, back to the tribal wars of Chaka and Mzilikazi and the Christianised pastors, the ancient African and colonialised line of Elias Siphiwe Gumede, Elder, Headmaster. Sindi at Aristotle School throws her arms round the world she's born to.

Gary Elias is choosing for himself the boys' school in a suburb and of the time when he, Steve, went to school, upmarket (that current social identity tag) and gender segregated. He wants that boys' school, a former white school, because his best friend, Peter Mkize's son Njabulo, is a pupil there. Of course the school is non-racial now, Mkize's son wouldn't otherwise have been accepted and neither would Gary Elias be, coloured by his mother's blood. Gary Elias had not been unhappy at the school, Aristotle, that was everything a school should be; proof of that in the opening of his personality to be seen. But the explanation, also to be seen, was that he was in that intense state of bonding friendship with Njabulo that happens in childhood and is strongest, against family bonds, until adolescent stirrings in the testes take over in turn. Sindiswa affronted by lack of loyalty to their school, attacked, to dissuade him; but she was a sister . . . his parents—so many selves to be responsible to as individuals—went to Peter and his wife, a 'mixed couple' in another recipe, Peter Jabu's brother Zulu, Blessing Khosa, to be informed about Njabulo's school. The comrades were reassuring, their son was getting a good education and—they're frank—no trouble with the white boys, everyone gets along together.

There was to be an interview with the headmaster.

—Is he black, we didn't ask Peter.—

—Does it matter, the headmaster at Aristotle's not.—

She's amused, as a reproach to the question.

The uniform and badges for the school are bought, his Assistant Professor father takes him to his first term, first day, he's tactfully insinuated that it shouldn't be a mother who would; and from then on the Mkizes will transport Gary along with their Njabulo.

For Gary Elias, it can be seen at breakfast, these mornings now are joyous rendezvous.

What would her Baba—headmaster—think of the move.

Her open face is of one who hasn't yet given a thought to this, but they have a past, she and her father, and what he would declare, matters.

—I don't know what he felt about Aristotle. He'd only want to know if the standard of teaching is high. The rest— her fingers are interleaved and the thumbs open widely the cup of palms —he expects of us. You and me . . .— She makes clear as if in formal terms unfamiliar to them —The father and the mother.—

It is actual that the boy's expanding experience, the first weeks in a new all-male environment on his own decision, a venture out of the adult determinations of childhood, is overwhelmed for them by distortion all around the country of the standard human behaviour it set for itself against that of its deadly past. In the area where most blacks and shades-of-black (blend of Sindiswa and Gary Elias) still live although if they could afford the politician's better life for all they could live wherever they liked, the refugee immigrants have moved in where because of their colour they won't be noticed in the mass. There're African Brothers who crowd the already insufferably packed shacks, draw the tap water that is hardly enough for the local community. White: unless you stick your nose into places like the precinct of the Methodist Church and the squatters on the wrong side of the road, you don't have to be particularly aware of this invasion except for being importuned at suburban shopping malls by more and more beggars' outstretched hands. In the townships and shacks the presence of refugees— uncounted, who knows, getting in illegally over the vast borders impossible to control, the river some swim across in low water season. Unlike rate-paying property owners of fine houses the poor in their squatter camps have no hope of an official order ridding themselves of the invaders.

No authority but what they can lay their hands on: knives, axes, their resident gangs' stolen guns; fire. Some Somalis fled from their country's particular conflict bring with them their trading instincts and have set up stores which are torched with the new traditional weapons of South Africa resorted to during the Struggle, burning tyres.

And the invaders are fighting back.

In band-aid bridging classes, academic subjects give way to the Science Faculty Assistant Professor's volunteer lecturers' and their students' uneasy preoccupation, via the remove of television, with the wilderness violence beyond the campus. Lesego Moloi from African Studies in the Faculty of Humanities: the refugees—They're not The Brothers now, they are The Foreigners.—

When she hears what's been said at the university she doesn't this time ask again, what are they going to do about it. The teachers, the students.

What are the Comrades going to, can do about it, the cadres of *Umkhonto* (can you ever be an ex-cadre?)

Done what *they had to do*: in the Struggle, and have no say, unless they are city councillors or sitting in parliament, in the conduct of the free country. Cadres that's us: Peter Mkize, Jake and all the other comrades, we companeros of the Suburb. Marc, round the any-colour, any-race, any-sex swimming pool reads aloud from the weekend papers.

—Xenophobia—the whole country's xenophobic . . . I don't know if you can just talk it off like that—

—Well, what else—

Jake signalling: —Peter, xenophobia, African hating African?—

She is accustomed to precision. Jabu breaks in —Is everyone sure what they mean.—

—Well never mind, everyone's using it as what's happening. Xenophobia. Same as anti-Semitic, anti-Muslim—can you come up with something else.—

Back at home Jabu and Wethu cook lunch together, he's come to the kitchen to put beer in the fridge.

Wethu is stirring a sauce over a gas flame and conducting her own pulpit vehemence with gestures of the lifted wooden spoon scattering drips. She breaks from isiZulu to English, fluent with colloquialisms she's picked up in the city, to include him in her congregation. —That rubbish, they must *voetsak* back to Mugabe, they are only here, come from that place to steal take our bags in the street, and shame, shame, look what they do to Mr Jake, they wanted to kill him to get his car, it's only God's will he's still alive to see his children grow up, he can't walk quite right, I see him there in the road, *eish!* They tell lies why they come here, the young ones are just *tsotsis*, *Wonke umuntu makahlale ezweni lakhe alilungise!* Everybody must stay at their country to make it right, not run away, we never ran away, we stayed in KwaZulu even while the Boers the whites at the coal mine were paying our men nothing not even for the children school, and getting sick, sick from down in the mines, we stayed we were strong for the country to come right—If those people don't get out, we must chase them—

Someone who studied by correspondence before the era of Internet, Jabu has her store of reference books (in her father's example). They stand on what is supposed to be the desk in the bedroom but has no space clear for anyone to work at, his dictionaries crowd it.

'Xenos. Indicates the presence of a reference to that which is strange, foreign, different. From Greek, Xenos, stranger.'

'Xenophobic. Characterised by fear of foreign persons or things.'

'Xenophobia. Intense or irrational dislike of people from other countries.' That's the only one in three dictionaries which in its concision has relevance? But the refugees are not invaders from some other continent, the Portuguese, the Dutch, the British all over again. They are the continent, African people, taking collective place in the entire world that's in process of its makeover.

African unity. *Eish!*

She's looked in to call him, food is on the table.

—What are you doing, forgotten how to spell, my professor.—

—This 'xenophobia' . . .—

—I can spell it for you.— She smiles. She sees there's something on his mind but this isn't the time for them to talk alone. Lunch must be eat-and-run, Sindi must be driven to Aristotle, there's a dress rehearsal of a school play, Sindiswa is Antigone, the standby of heroism invoked anytime, anywhere, that comrades performed in Robben Island prison. For Sindi, it's the Aristotle adaptation of a plot to recent African history.

Jabu's gone with her daughter to watch the rehearsal and Gary Elias—where's the son—oh over at the Mkizes'. The looped circles of living.

The bed's there; kick off your shoes and stretch out. The pillow has the scent of her, different from perfume, she's present. Take it up; xenophobia. All of us mouthing for what's happening, a condition we're in, epidemic.

Isn't it taking the way out, a denial, the country usefully finding diagnosis that doesn't admit the facts, the truth (but let's avoid grand absolutes), the reality.

The blacks-of-all-shades, South Africans at home in the townships and the shacks they've somehow put together; they don't disown discard attack and set fire to their brother Africans as if they were foreigners: in last resort against their own condition they are desperately defending the means, scraps of substance, their own survival. No roofs that don't leak rain and cold, no electricity, no privacy even to shit, no roads to clinics run out of medicine, few jobs for too many endless seekers—this is what they *have*, theirs, those with *nothing* are moving in to compete for it.

That's the cause of what's happening. Not 'irrational fear or dislike of the Xenos, strange, foreign or different'. Familiar, African, black-like-me. She's still there in him even if she's with Sindi's mythical transformation, Antigone demanding an updated version, the time of the Struggle, the return of her brother's body from Robben Island. If you know one another intimately enough, mind as well as body, you can talk with the other, her, when she is absent. She's ready to see, admit his explanation, everyone's been letting themselves off the hook with the distancing of a catch-all term.

Himself. Within this reality he's not achieving, won't be achieving anything . . . get out. Get out! What will Sindiswa and Gary Elias's life be. Get out.

And how about Elias Siphiwe Gumede's Zulu people, her people—same village, same people who attack each other as tribalist traditionalist against African nationalist ANC . . . while one side isn't a threat to the livelihood of the other in KwaZulu. Well, that's political rivalry, that's about power. Refugees don't have any. The mobile is felt rather than heard against his thigh. Shift in the bed and draw in the stomach muscles to reach this intruder out of pants pocket.

Jonathan. Now it's Jonathan. So far from in mind. His brother who always prefaces what he's calling about by a litany of family exchanges, how you all are, how we are, what this one is doing, where that one is right now. And why feel impatient, this is the way communication out of absence of current contact is shown; as Jonathan calls me Stevie, we're kids wrestling together on the grass.

Well, mother is selling the old home and going to move to somewhere around Cape Town, it's not decided yet, Jonathan is looking into the apartment question, she's had enough of the security situation, a break-in two houses away, I don't suppose she told you, you know our independent Pauline.

But the purpose of the call is that the boy whose ritual ceremony of entry to manhood was attended by Jabu and Stevie, is now ready for postgraduate studies in engineering. Jonathan and Brenda want him to go overseas; what country, which university would the academic in the family recommend they choose, approach for admission. Brenda depends on good advice from Stevie, the one in the family whose opinion she trusts. And such an admirer of everything Jabu achieves, she's really attached to her—she feels Jabu will understand her caution.

Engineering: it's a science but it is not that of the faculty to which the man from whom they seek advice—and probably imagined influence through academic connections—belongs.

The boy did his undergraduate degree in Cape Town, doesn't Stevie have a colleague there, who might be useful?

Again, not in engineering. But he'll certainly speak to one of the professors in engineering at his own university and hope to come back with information. In the meantime able to say with genuine impulse, for himself —It's good to hear he wants to be a highly qualified engineer—there's a shortage in our country—we need him.—

His brother concludes the statement —And with that kind of qualification you can make your way in another country.— Jonathan perhaps is speaking of a decision.

Months gone by. Now Jabu has been to another school rehearsal with Sindi, they are in the flush of enthusiasm flood-lighting the room as if both are proud schoolmates. Jabu practitioner of the objective letter of the law is that other kind of comrade, that of her children, which he isn't, doesn't manage to be, even with the one of his own gender, Gary Elias. —Sindi's so *good*. I'd never have had any idea she'd understand Antigone so well, she does, she *does*, you have to hear her—and the school of course, the literature teacher and the athletics coach he's also in the arts dance group, they direct together.—

The girl is laughter-gasping, can't contain the praise, the pleasure of her mother.

—What'd you and Gary get up to? He hasn't been sitting at the TV has he?—

—Could be . . . he's at the Mkizes.—

—He should have been with us to see his sister—and there's the boy playing Creon, must have known him.—

But Gary Elias would feel unwelcome, self-outcast, self-reject, appearing in the school he's insulted by leaving.

At this period in the emerging version of herself Sindiswa is wearing dreadlocks like the ones remembered she, Jabu, had appeared in, first, instead of her Afro bush, and that he had regretted. They flung defiance about Antigone's face (not as beautiful as her mother, diluted by Reed strain) as she offers—

'Never, had I been a mother of children, or if a husband had been mouldering in death, would I have taken this task upon me in the city's despite. What law, ye ask, is my warrant for that word? The husband lost, another might have been found, and child from another, to replace the first-born, but father and mother hidden with Hades, no brother's life could ever bloom for me again . . .'

Squeezes eyelids a moment at a hitch in the sequence.

'. . . And what law of heaven have I transgressed? Why should I look to the gods any more . . . when I have suffered my doom I shall come to know my sin; but if the sin is with my judges, I could wish them no fuller measure of evil than they, on their part, mete wrongfully to me . . .'

If her father didn't go to a Greek school she doesn't think he might know. —Antigone's brother Polynices is killed and left to rot by the cruel king Creon when he's involved in a kind of revolution, Antigone's buried him, that's forbidden, so she'll have to die . . .— Oh the plot's much more complicated than that but her mother and father were in the fight against apartheid so they'll . . .

Feels Jabu's watching him, not the performance; as if she has learnt the role for herself. Reminding of those among them who never knew if the comrades were buried and had hoped some confessions to the Truth Commission might have meant

they could find and claim what is left of each other. Exactly.
—Go and fetch your brother now, Sindi, it's time he came
home—and tell Blessing and Peter, we'd like to see them.—
She wants the Mkizes to have a chance to be warmed by the
glow of Antigone inside Sindi, the girl they know with their
own young in shared childhood of the Suburb . . . and Marc,
Marc must see a rehearsal, he'll be so amazed . . . the adaptation attempt, he'll be able to give some tips to the cast.

What's the word—simultaneity. While the school was
dramatising justice for the children to understand as the
condition for them to pursue living their future in this country, Jonathan was telling of the success of the plan of another,
to leave, quit.

—Jonathan called, the son Ryan, he's going to emigrate.
He's accepted at the university my Cape Town man suggested
. . . Lucky boy.—

—Going to study, you mean. That's not emigration.—

—But you know. It was the idea? He'll be qualified to join
a firm, the UK, the USA.—

The footfalls and voices of son and daughter arguing their
way in, Gary Elias already calling —Wha'd' you want me
for?— and to his mother *Ilantshiekhaya kwaNjabula beye
mnandi impala!* Lunch was lovely, Njabulo's place, his uncle's
there from home, he brings greeting and stuff for you from
Baba, Sindi's been *showing off* reciting something, why'd you
send *her, Umthumeleni!*—

W hat are you doing about it.
  Again.

This time the country's share of the world's refugees sleeping in doorways and fouling neighbourhoods; it's climate change like the carbon monoxide that is everywhere, it's the atmosphere, in greater or lesser degree. Just keep breathing. What can universities do but study, research the phenomenon in the Department of Social Science, Politics, History, Humanitarian Studies—the law of human rights eternal above its distortions in the codes of differing countries, societies, circumstances. A seminar in the appropriate department, which a good number of lecturers from other faculties attend, addressed by the Nigerian Vice Chancellor Principal with the firm intellectual decorum broken only here and there by a slip, emotional anger in the African phrasing of his voice.

And a lunchtime meeting of students and some faculty members in a half-filled hall.

Again. Persuaded by students from the bridging classes now become voluntary coaching also for those in their second year, he's one of the academics sitting at a table, each tapping a microphone like the clearing of a throat before giving a view on the subject. Xenophobia. That's the identification, one word, on the Students Council posters hung on the railings outside. Is he the only one among the Professors Jean McDonald of economics, Lesego, African Studies, and the two elected final-year undergraduates, who will question it as glib.

In the audience the students sprawl attentively, there's a girl in a chador gracefully upright in the front row and a male at the far end eating from a takeaway, it's democratically correct, the people must not go hungry. He can't point this out (tempting)—there'd be laughter making a spectacle of their fellow student—the simple presence of a basic need being followed inappropriately is an example of that need as what's being evaded under the poster rubric.

—'Xenophobia'—it's our distancing from the fact that our people right here in our own country, at home (his hand unconsciously knotting itself, a fist) an existence as refugees from our economy, unemployed, unhoused, surviving by ingenuities of begging, waving cars into parking space for the small change (all of us who have cars drop this handout), standing at traffic lights with packets of fruit to sell through driver's windows, if you're female standing with a baby or one that can propel itself playing in the gutter. It's easy—to call them, our own people xenophobic when they resort to violence to defend the only space, the only means of survival against competitors for this *almost nothing*. It's not hatred of foreigners. The name for the violence is xenophobia?—

There's some sort of applause, the confusion of palms smacking together, a couple of feet whose impact with the floor is muffled because the obese soles of canvas sports shoes don't have the force of leather, contesting voices are thrown like paper darts. Jean McDonald is informally chairperson. She takes full advantage of her microphone. —You are pointing out the fact that we are not succeeding in meeting the rights of disadvantaged citizens of our own country—if we can't do that, haven't the resources or the will, government policy, how do we deal with the refugees, who are a threat to even the level of that state—of deprivation.—

—Capitalism! Keeps out people producing wealth for whites just like in apartheid—

—The West backs black dictators whose oppression leads to the wars—people have to get out or die—

—And the black fat cats? Here? They're not living it high style while the Home Boys dig for the platinum, gold, bring dividends, seats on boards, capitalist BEE—

—Crap! What are we talking about? So—these people are Africans? Crap. They come from other countries, languages, cultures, they are foreigners.—

—Not foreign? Exceptions because they're black?—

A white girl whose rising breasts jiggle emphasis. —African Union. There's a European Union, and plenty of prejudice in England when immigrants come in and take jobs, the trade unions—

—Not if they'll do the stuff the British don't want to, plumbers are all from Poland—

Professor McDonald lets the students take over. Freedom of speech even if this means there'll be no coherent resolution to be issued for the university press. But Professor Lesego Moloi jerks back his chair and rises, mike a staff in his hand. He summons with it a student, black, who has a poster open across his knees. The student turns his head looking for friends to tell him what is expected of him. You're not to be ordered about, university isn't a school, but this professor is a Brother, this is a different kind of authority. He gets up and does what appears is wanted, he's taking the poster to the edge of the proscenium and Lesego is there to have it held out to him. Professor Lesego Moloi's regained the table but stands in front of his colleague academics with his back to the restless hall, he's writing in hard strokes on the poster laid out on the table. He turns. The poster is presented, with him. A thick marker pen has crossed out XENOPHOBIA the poster reads in giant strides POVERTY.

It's not an answer: what are you going to do about it. The meagre spoils people are killing for. But the blunt confrontation changed the uneasy quarrelsome mood of the students to real attention, wanting to hear seriously what those among them who should have some qualification, by their particular courses of study—Social Science, Economics, Politics and History—had to say about the condition many came from in their own family background, and for which they were acquiring theories of 'schools of thought' from the professors who now are exchanging with them convictions about the state of the country as if on an equal level of democratic responsibility for it.

This lunch hour get-together not only re-baptised the refugees as an identity, but broke the focus wide to that of the Outer Space on Earth, which separated the poor from what constitutes the rich—a range, factory worker from the new or old-time multi-millionaire in the promised delivery of our slogan a better life for all. Somehow there's the slow move, wake-up. That meeting. And the ecosphere seminar. The group of students from environmental studies, they're taking field trips to see for themselves what they're learning about, the draining, deconstruction of wet lands for mining explorations. —He's telling her all this, and without demeaning it, grins.— Yesterday on the landing between stairs there was something like the ice-cream cart that's pushed by a man in the street, sort of ice-box on wheels. Trashing the campus on principle, rioting on the issue of student grants, OK, that's one thing, but bowling at gutters or chucking into shrubs what's left of your pizza—the conservation group students and staff, have put this—thing—where you're ashamed not to drop your junk on the way to class.—

Jabu's been offered a position by one of the three-name partnerships of commercial legal practice for whom the Justice Centre had generously allowed her to undertake work from time to time. Her keen intelligence of legal process in present circumstances has been noticed; or the firm wanted to strengthen its image with the appointment of a black female attorney, gender equity in addition to its non-racial one. He might have thought that in private resentment—anyone not simply recognise her ability and devotion to the law, a South African who had lived on the wrong side of it in a detention cell. But he doesn't say this. The appointment would be an advance in her career towards taking Silk. One day. He wants that for her; as her Baba had wanted her to be educated. —Of course, I'll still be able to do work at the Centre in my own time.— She's questioning herself?

Missed period for the second month. The doctor looks up from examination: pregnant. Stupid not to have gone to the doctor at once. It seemed so unlikely. Or some atavistic hangover. Baba's women running a gaze as wisdom over a flat stomach: husbands expect sons for their perpetuation. Her man is different. She doesn't have to tell him. Couldn't explain how this happened to them, her usual precautions, no impulsive take-a-chance lovemaking.

Do they want a third child? There are other kinds of fulfilment for us. For him, at this stage in the chancey development of the university; of course he's too optimistic about her taking Silk, it's a love wish . . . but there'll be much wider experience, the variety in common law cases as well as constitutional ones, so much to know, need to learn.

Another? Sindi blossoms every day, top of her class, at just the right kind of school to prepare for *now*. Gary Elias. Perhaps trouble to be expected in trying to understand him; anyway he seems to have been right in choosing a school for himself, he's far from withdrawn these days; if the closeness is more with the Mkizes than at home.

The doctor is a comrade, from the time they were in detention together, women's prison where the so-called matron accepted books from a prisoner's father because he was an Elder in a Methodist Church. In the brief chance to talk in the exercise yard this comrade had seen the future only as the passion to study medicine. Abortion is no longer illegal, a dangerous backyard matter, except for the Catholic Church and some other religious or tribal edicts. It is skilfully done by the comrade's freedom achieved as a gynaecologist.

If they can't make love that night, men don't keep count of the days between bleeding, why should they, he'll think she has her period, their desire will fade away in sleep. Although the refrigerator is making a weird clinking racket, it's coming from the kitchen . . . Wethu has complained, you must buy a new one, more big one, too much inside.

Simplify tasks that have to go along with the purposefulness of living—working for justice to be done in the courts, working for the right of knowledge to be given in the laboratories of the science faculty—by buying each Saturday enough food for the week.

A normal life. (At last?) What is that. In what time and place?

Doesn't matter. A life where the personal comes first.

But it—would be—is—clandestine, like the Glengrove Place one. Not 'the same'; 'like': which resembles in some way. (Glengrove isolation was by decree.) There's Outer Space on Earth between our people, and the others; what space-craft can be launched to make it humanly part of the country. While she offers her little bit of justice, he offers his scrap for education.

A resort from it all. In such time as they have to themselves he reads these days more than he ever has, and differently than she does, the law means so much delving into precedents for each type of case to learn why the tactics of a particular prosecution or defence have been decided on.

At his Reed family traditional school he was taught Latin, not Greek. But Sindi/Antigone's fair pick-up of the local demotic of the language, her growing interest in bringing home to meals the fascination of philosophy and politics which she knows as Greek myth, moves in him an impulse. To look to another age for some enlightenment—help—with a present one. Take from the university libraries the works he wasn't privileged to, in the privileges of his white school. And that urgent faith of his youth decreeing him in a factory mixing chemical elements for explosives instead of paint, kept him from. As with most of the supposedly well-educated of his white generation the names of ancient Greek sages were tags to describe characteristics, derived from those whose works and thought the users didn't know. Call so-and-so epicurean, doesn't have a capital initial, that's someone who indulges in fine wine, fine food. A luxury-loving fundi. As some ministers in the present government take to Cuban cigars, not a badge to show brotherhood with Castro but as a right to what the capitalists kept to themselves.

He brings home a translation and interpretation of Epicurus from the philosophy department for Sunday leisure reading after the newspapers. The cast of ministers, government officials, members of parliament in the arms sales corruption serial is relegated to the inner pages as old news, that week, this week back on the front page. She has no inside information to keep up with her intention of relating what justice was being done to deal with the hostel students in that other university, where black cleaners were gleefully abused; there was none. What happened seems to have been willed away, on hold. The hostel meanwhile simply closed.

Here it is. Epicurus believed in an uncreated universe unguided by a creator, his moral teachings affirm human freedom to pursue aspirations, live better, increase pleasure, a condition that can be created only by self-constraint in dealing with others, respecting the principles of justice which ensure that condition's very existence. The right to happiness. That's a normal life After the Struggle.

You're never alone in a room, always some other form of life is there with you. She moves to close the window against the rain in the air and she's signalled to by the slither of a silverfish moth out of one of the books in the shelves she is passing.

She tries to stamp on it with the bony edge of her thumb joint but of course its form is made for escape—gone. She clatters out books from the stack of four or five into which it's vanished and several more of the creatures fall from the pages. It's more difficult than swatting flies. If they live on paper it is easier to get at in the loose form than between the covers of books. There is an adjoining tier of shelves she and Steve bought from a made-to-measure carpentry store in a mall partly owned by an Indian comrade who has become a successful businessman—Steve's academic documents and papers are haphazardly piled there. What a feast. She begins to stir among them, taking out a bundle, and a few sheets, some newspaper cuttings, escape scattered on the floor. No silverfish to be seen; but the whole paper collection ought to be tidied up, she straightens at least the shelf she has disturbed, and gathers to replace what has fallen. The newspaper cuttings are flimsy and falter out again. They are in the familiar format of advertisements; all have in heavy black type their product: AUSTRALIA. The dates on which they appear, some almost a year back, some recent, are in his handwriting. AUSTRALIA CALLING AUSTRALIAN MIGRATION AUSTRALIA. Australia needs your skills today! SERIOUS ABOUT AUSTRALIA? She begins to pick up snatches from one to another—she must slow down, read the texts while her mind in another mode of attention, intrigued, tries to answer why he should cut and keep these. ARE YOU INTERESTED IN LIVING IN AUSTRALIA ON A TEMPORARY OR PERMANENT BASIS? LOOK NO FURTHER. Explore hidden opportunities. Trustworthy, spectacular success rate. For ONLINE ASSESSMENT AND INFO . . . IMMIGRATION AUSTRALIA. Consultancy will be holding a free seminar. The seminar will cover recent immigration announcements and what Australia has to offer. We are specially interested in those people with degrees. Immigration lawyer will be available for one-on-one consultations . . . cost applies . . . AUSTRALIA. Hosting a seminar. Space is limited so please call to reserve your seat. Available for appointments to inquire about our upcoming Australia migration event covering various migration pathways. Click on Immigration Seminars. Please join us for a free seminar on . . .

If he is thinking of writing something about the phenomenon, skilled people leaving the country (an issue for the university) how is it he hasn't mentioned this, said anything, as we do, to each other. I would be interested, he knows. Show me this stuff.

Hidden away as if they were love letters from some woman.

Because she would not allow herself the explanation that she couldn't believe, consider, she found herself at the door of the Andersons, as she might have dropped in from a walk. Unthinking, it was not likely anyone would be home at this time in the afternoon: at work and the boys still in school. She herself wouldn't have been back in the Suburb if the property dispute case she was engaged in as attorney to one of the advocates in the firm she had joined, hadn't been remanded and he'd postponed the discussion until the next day. But Jake opened the door, after a wait. He was rumpled, hair and clothes, must have been resting, back early, he often suffered headaches since the hijack attack. Barefoot, he led her in. —Isa's not home yet.— But if without realising it she had wanted anyone it was him, the comrade who was Steve's fellow male. The small talk. Asking Jake if he was all right, how was he feeling. He waved hands down himself in apology for dishevelment. She held out the cuttings. —Do you know these?— He moved them between thumb and first finger, as with cards in a game. —Of course, they're in the papers regularly. Why?—

—I found them today, fell out of some journals and things Steve keeps.—

He's scanning; while taking time to read what she's telling him. —So? I suppose he keeps lots of cuttings, many things happen to us, you find you've forgotten . . . get dates mixed up—then you need to—

—If he's writing something for the *Umkhonto* veterans (just come to her) he hasn't said anything about it to me.— As if it were a question. —Not to me. We haven't taken much notice of guys taking the plane for Perth, whoever they are.—

Why has Jabu presented these cuttings. What does she want him to say. Steve's pissed off. We're all pissed off with what's becoming of the country.

Jake lifts eyebrows in avoidance and rubs a hand across his face to rid himself—weariness or refusal. —How do I know.—

He knows. Puts the wad of cuttings—evidence she's seen—from one hand to another. And gives them back to her.

There's nothing more for them to say to each other.

His lawyer woman produced the evidence to him that night when Gary Elias had been persuaded to go to bed, Sindi was already in her room listening to Michael Jackson, and Wethu in her chicken coop cottage with the TV Steve had bought for her in compensation for loss of the company of collaterals in KwaZulu. The place, the room where the momentous is about to be raised, *to happen*, comes out of ignored familiarity, to a new focus that will be stored when paper cuttings have been eaten by silverfish moth and the change of existence they propose has either been effected—or never existed. The much-lived-in room of the house in the Suburb occupied since Glengrove Place, the chairs bought to provide missing comfort, the pictures painted by artists in the common kind of experience, one in Brazil, the others in Africa, shared with the house occupants, the school blazer left lying, face-down books, cracked tray with sunglasses among coffee cups and half-empty bottle of wine, a ballpoint pen with Mickey Mouse head: witness. She looked round in inventory as she took from somewhere in the cotton dashiki she liked to exchange for her court clothes, some of the cuttings AUSTRALIA.

—They fell out when I was cleaning up this afternoon. From your papers.—

—Yes.—

Now she is waiting for his recollection: commonplace curiosity, something for chatter round the Dolphin pool.

He had picked up the tray; he lifted from it Gary Elias's Mickey Mouse pen, balancing the burden with the other hand. He placed the pen on the table.

—I wasn't getting into your things.— Comrades respect privacy however intimate and long-tested a relationship. He stood with the tray; at once it had become her responsibility to speak, say whatever there was to say.

But—urgent between them this is not an argument. —You've never said, I mean, you were keeping this—about Australia. What for.—

Another silence. His eyes are on her, they see each other in a way they do, not in the familiarity dear to them, if sometimes taken for granted. —I was, I am going to talk to you.—

—Australia.— She is slowly working not just her shoulder

but her body. She doesn't want to go on. —Tell me, you're not really thinking Australia. Us.—

—I have been. For us, Sindi, Gary Elias. I know how you feel, it's how I feel too—felt.— He went away carried the tray to the kitchen she heard it meet the metal surface of the space beside the sink.

He brought the declaration back with him, standing it unfurled to them. —Was this what it was for, what we did— The Struggle. Comrades—reborn clones of apartheid bosses. Our 'renaissance'. Arms corruption, what's the nice procedure in your courts, the never-never—the Methodist dump just one of the black cesspots of people nobody wants, nobody knows what to do with—'Rights' too highfalutin' to apply to refugees—shacks where our own people supposed now to have walls and a roof, still living in shit, I could go on and on as we do, the comrades. I'm in the compound of transformation at a university, schools don't have qualified teachers—or toilets—children come to learn without food in their stomachs.—

At the Fifty-second Annual Conference of the African National Congress in Polokwane: Jacob Gedleyihlekisa Zuma, Praise name Msholozi, Chief of Intelligence in *Umkhonto we sizwe* who had been a prisoner on Robben Island for ten years, and operated in exile from Mozambique and Swaziland.

He was elected President of the ANC by a majority against a breakaway faction as well as supporters of the country's President Thabo Mbeki, who had dismissed him as Deputy President over the case, two years earlier, of corruption, President Mbeki making whatever the court verdict—the court decision was that the indictment was set aside—a moral judgement of involvement with a charge of this nature as disqualifying a man from the second highest position in the land.

There was tumultuous celebration, particularly by the

youth, who sang with Zuma his theme song '*Awuleth' umshini wami*', bring me my machine gun, an *Umkhonto we Sizwe* war cry which (if not to be used literally) was surely going to bring them jobs, houses, cars, feast of the good life when—again taken for granted—he would be next President of the country. He had testified in court he was aware the young woman with whom he had sexual intercourse in the rape charge was HIV-positive: in his victory speech at the Polokwane Conference he declared 'all structures of government should actively participate in the fight against HIV and AIDS in all facets of the national strategy—prevention, treatment, support for families affected, infected.'

Zuma President of the Party.

—Your father will be elated.—

If it was meant wryly to share her feelings, it was a mistake. She turned her head in her familiar gesture of finality. Stupid of him, he saw: how could she, as they both did, deplore the result and, as she would have to, accept in the privacy of her relationship with Baba, her father's satisfaction.

What he could do right: he enquired from a friend (if not a comrade) at the university who had often spoken of the joys of a cottage on the Cape Coast, whether it might by chance be for hire during the Christmas and New Year period. It belonged to the friend's father-in-law, and as the family was going to be overseas, this was arranged.

He took the liberty of making the announcement of distraction, Holiday At the Sea, to Jabu and the children as a treat offered rather than a decision to be made between him and her . . . Coming out of love and concern. She could hardly reject the proposal as irrelevant—in the face of the children's excitement, Gary Elias announcing at once he would go surfing, his friend had a board he'd borrow.

No Christmas visit to the KwaZulu home at present:

understood. —Gary'll have his time with the cousins in the Easter holidays.—

A New Year.

There was one of the many beaches, clean sand runways to the sea and the sky shown in tourist brochures for foreign visitors. The cottage only a walk away through the bushes. If it were not for newspapers and the radio—no TV in the father-in-law's retreat—Polokwane, Zuma and what the consequences might have been left behind the door in the Suburb. Australia.

When he came back to the right umbrella among many, with fruit juice and ice cream from the beach shop —And the papers?— He didn't have to return. Jabu ran loping off across the sand.

They both read with the compulsion that matches thirst with which Sindi and Gary downed juice and ice cream. Sea and sky blotted out in newsprint: the split in the Party confirmed at the Polokwane Conference, rivalry even over the name chosen by the breakaway faction for their new party, 'Congress of The People'—COPE—claiming both the masses and the ability to meet their needs. Congress of The People. —Well . . . how can you take the title of an actual, a specific event of ANC history, how many years ago?— That's what it was.

Flips up her sunglasses. —Why can't you? It's a statement, what it promises it's going to be. Anyway does the name matter. Just the Zuma crowd angry that anything claiming 'the people'—they're its property, his property, even the words.—

—It is a *threat*. Look what we've lost—Lekota to begin with.— Both have strong convictions of the political integrity, intelligence, honesty of Mosiuoa Lekota, Struggle man known as Terror Lekota until with peace-and-freedom that's too suggestive of terrorism although in fact it was a nickname celebrating his fame as a football player. —Terror gone—that's on ANC's cost of the bill for infighting, back-stabbing, who's taking bribes from whom, the whole Shaik mess smeared on the party . . . COPE. This name's not *nothing* it's the sign of take-over from our party's failure, failure of ideals. Promises?—

And that final word has a tone which questions what it means. The election of a new President, new government, new promises. Only a year away from this New Year which has arrived at the beach.

—Don't we have to have promises—

—Even if our leaders don't—can't—keep them.—

Sindi gets up to go and swim.

Sindi hitching at her bikini. Sindiswa's adolescence, summons of attention to another current of time running with change, she's walking now with the side-to-siding of buttocks Jabu had when he first saw her in Swaziland, the side-to-siding attractive to men black women have. His daughter in this kind of present.

Gary Elias is out of sight fishing with pals he'd immediately made on the beach. They are coloured, like himself, and various, some black as well as white, nothing remarkable about that, to them. But unthinkable remembered from another childhood: playing on the Whites Only beaches. And at last Sindi and the boy are getting a decent—a human education; but this is because the parents—we—can afford (we've ducked comrade principles enough) to send them to private schools. Open to any child of the people. Whose parents can pay.

They're alone under the umbrella. He takes a swill from a bottle of juice and holds it out for her.

As if she doesn't see.

—Has something happened at the university.—

The jostle of waves and the hush of their retreat. Doesn't

she understand. That's not it. You don't come suddenly to the stage of considering, at a certain point in the living of it, your life, the multiple living of Sindi, Gary Elias, Jabu and self. A shock at some academic decision taken by the Principal he trusts? No. An *un*covery—like the recent one the science faculty dealt with so well, that one of his own brightest students was peddling drugs on campus. The culprit's defence: to pay hostel fees. No. Or a bypass, when a colleague was given a promotion of responsibility above the Assistant Professor's own? No. That's not it. She always had ambitions for him he didn't covet, care about for himself.

Zuma is going to be President next year. The breakaway— hardly a party yet, COPE's unlikely in the months before election to gather enough votes to dent Zuma's support: and Zuma's the ANC's choice. How can party comrades through prison, bush and desert, not cast the vote *Umkhonto* fought for to the African National Congress.

—What's going to happen under Zuma, and after? Who is going to follow if he's overtaken after this first term, who among his performing worshippers singing for his machine gun will see it as power *right there* in his fist, want to grab it in their own. He's promising them everything, how much or little is he going to deliver. The ANCYL, Jabu it's not the youth group of Mandela Tambo and co. who transformed the Party to the need, then, of forming *Umkhonto* because that was the only way left to kill racist rule. '*Awuleth' Umshini Wami*', the youth singing for him now will be a different tune for Sindiswa and Gary Elias to dance to and God alone knows, if he exists doddering helplessly up there, whether the way Zuma's failed won't have led to a new Ubuntu—dictatorship—

She's waiting.

—Sindi, Gary, growing up; to that.—

She's still waiting for it: Australia.

—So must we, should we be here as you can see it coming. Are they growing up to another Struggle, this time Brother against Brother, it'll make Congo, Zimbabwe, look like pub brawls. At least . . . for them, something else. Something else. We can't force on them our AMANDLA! gut-strings to a country that's not the one we believe in.—

—But does that mean . . . comrades working together—at least a beginning—it's useless. You're in a university where have you forgotten?—Black medical students weren't allowed to dissect white corpses but white students could dissect black ones. No one could marry you to me. Sindi may soon have a white boyfriend, no one will look twice at them, they won't need to hide from the police, Gary maybe fall for a black girl, like me.—

—A new class? The class above, out of the race divide, race war, yes: elite, that's ours while the mass of the brothers and sisters, still the blacks left down behind. D'you really believe in the classless society we were making for. Our old freedom dream stuff? We've been woken up. Had to be. There'll always be a hierarchy of work, not so? The professions and the factory hand—set aside business tycoons all right, black as well as white, for a moment—the street cleaners, has to be someone to take away the dirt—one of those workers and the advocate, the assistant prof, the editor, the surgeon, they're not always going to be planets apart, *prestige* as well as money, economic class? It's political power now that's the Struggle and it's going to be between Brothers.— And the unsayable—colour.

When the looming of a threat has been made undeniable there's the instinct to confirm closeness by confession of mistake. —I don't know why . . . I just . . . I went over and showed Jake the cuttings. He was alone, wasn't feeling well.—

He does not ask what Jake said. Accepts apparently that

hers was an impulse: maybe he is to blame for feeling it was too soon for the purpose of the newspaper offering, recruitment for another country, to be brought out, to her.

Done now. Comrades have always been open with one another, it had been a condition of survival and it survives as one of the forms of honesty necessary to justify a 'normal life'. For some among the cadres that life was taking on the option—duty?—of the new political kingdom, ministries, responsibilities in parliament and governance. Give credit for that even if it's turning out to be an option for the rainbow nation few to survive in luxury.

J ump in the deep end. Steve himself brings up: Australia. Among the full complement of Suburb comrades back at the church pool on a Sunday, the company joined by his brother Alan. It's turned out that Alan knows the Dolphins through circles among gays.

Steve presumes it is to be taken for granted that Jake told Isa and Isa told the Mkizes and so along the trusted chain, of Jabu coming with a handful of newspaper cuttings to find Jake at home with one of his headaches. So far as honesty is concerned, apart from playwright Marc, the Dolphins are unlikely to have any particular interest in stigma of someone's leaving the country, just as anyone would move to another city within it to better opportunities or because of personal attachments.

There is frankness in a veteran's bonding. Jake asks what she has stopped herself from presenting further, with Steve. —Have you been to one of those, what's it seminars?— This doesn't have the tone of accusal.

—No . . . I didn't think there'd be much for me to hear about in business opportunities.— A brief laugh nobody joins. But no outright rejection, denial, of what's being contemplated. —There is one coming up next month I've registered for—

—You have to register, can't just walk in? So many people interested . . . ?— Jake's lips remain apart, taking breath on his own naivety.

—Exodus. The flight from Egypt.— Glib as a line from his advertising copy: Alan.

—This one's about the professions.—

—So the Aussies want our teachers, academics, as well as civil engineers, opticians, doctors, nurses, all down the line to our refrigeration mechanics, crane operators.— Jake's remembering randomly from the cuttings she brought for him to read.

—Well, there're plenty of mechanics, artisans unemployed, factories laying off, here, if they can be assured of jobs.— Is she just showing loyalty to her man, despite the shock with which she had found Australia calling him, or has Jabu come to taking the call herself. Although Jake saw no mention of lawyers in the listed opportunities.

She remarks at supper one evening while everyone is around the table helping themselves to spaghetti drooling from the bowl's serving spoon—she's going this weekend to KwaZulu, it's been some months since she's visited. Wethu enthuses—*Bheka Baba!* See Baba! His good girl that's right!—

Sindiswa goes along to KwaZulu only on occasion when it is understood that everyone goes. Gary Elias, Wethu's usual companion on visits, attacks—Ooww no, not this weekend, we've got some guys from Pretoria, our first team against them—I've got to be there, we must vuvuzela our guys. Who's going to take me to school sports, Saturday?—

—I am of course.— Steve will not be going to KwaZulu, not expected to share all daughterly duty.

After the meal the children and Wethu watch an episode of a television thriller they follow and she is in the kitchen with the two mugs of coffee she makes every night for the Suburb's patrol watch he has suspected of being personnel of *impimpi* veterans.

—Anything special happening at home this weekend?—

—Not that I know of.— She lifts the mugs in a gentle hint for him to open the kitchen door for her.

She's gone out to the front gate to hand out what has become the men's comfort.

Back in a few moments, and stood while he locked the door behind her. He turned and smiled: forgotten something? But she wasn't looking round the kitchen.

—I think I have to tell him about Australia.—

—But why. What for?—

He's saying what has it to do with your father.

—What he would think about leaving. Us leaving. Me leaving.—

—I can't see how that can have anything to do with us just looking at—What's got into you, we're not taking the plane tomorrow, are we, we've made a hell of a lot of decisions, we've always had to have all the circumstances clear, simply considering. Why does he have to know—right—it's 'common knowledge' gossip among comrades even, I've picked up although I don't know how it spread, by someone's Twitter Face Talk or whatnot, to the Faculty. But how would this have reached the village . . . the school, the church.— While he is speaking: her leaving. What business is it of anyone. What the Reed clan would think about him leaving; a son has opted for a superior degree that will qualify him for a post in another country while civil engineers are needed for the future of this one. 'Her leaving'—her Baba. Yes her Baba. What Baba thinks in every decision for every move she makes in her life, the life he propagated and that is deep in her being as Sindiswa and Gary Elias were embedded in her womb; it matters to Jabu. It's not a question of influence; between her and Baba, his comrade wife and her Baba there is an identity. Final one?

What is called the intake of shades-of-black students at the Faculty of Science has increased at least sufficiently to more than compensate for those who have failed their year or abandoned the idea of becoming an industrial chemist, engineer, and other scientific professionals, either because they've run out of scholarship support or the best intentions of band-aid classes have not proved able to subvent poor teaching of maths in schools from which they came. Research has become part of the curriculum, study of climate change, as well as alternatives to fossil fuels as producers of electric power. The university Business School has the largest number of new students, no longer seen as a dead end if you weren't white and had the footprints of a businessman father to lead you into company directorship, banking, commerce. There are black directors in mining cartels and shopping mall complexes, insurance companies. It's encouraging, while understood, certainly by an academic that attending lectures together, working in labs, libraries, side by side at computers and canteen takeouts is the simple side of transformation; so long as students live at home or in some pad in the city. Hostels bring together in the intimacy of shower stalls, adjoining beds, place for the need of differing personal possessions, the skin colours and habits of young people who have never lived together in the same closed space before. There've been some incidents of minor spats at the 'mixed' hostels—mixed only in the old jargon of race—these students play hard rock recordings when others are trying to study, this guy blocks the wash basin with combings from his hair; nothing serious as inference of racism.

A New Year.

The newspaper report of what happened last year at a university, in a part of the country that still has its old Boer Republic name—Free State—long preceding apartheid, dating from Boer defiance against the British (fellow) colonisers—it's hardly credible in the version now revealed by whoever the informant or informers were.

There are accounts pursued for months by journalists on the Internet from individuals anonymous, reluctant to be interviewed, and then—photographs. Somehow got hold of, clips of a video apparently made by some of the participants in whatever the event was supposed to be. White students at the traditionally Afrikaans university of The Free State held out the ultimate hand of non-racialism and no class prejudice by inviting the university cleaners of their hostel, black, to a party customarily marking the initiation of new students, usually a very private clandestine ritual. The mostly elderly four women and one man whose role in these students' higher education was to clean up after them, danced in drunken freedom, and then on their knees forced to help themselves generously from a pot of stew. One of the students had pissed into it.

What was the progenitor.

Yes. yes. Need to know. It goes that far back, initiation. Beyond ancient history, not of battles and kings, tyrants and slaves. Back beyond all that—into evolution. But not how apes stood upright and lost their tails. So very far: back to the intimate anatomy. If you're female, Jabu is a girl, you have a definitive initiation in your body. The day of that is when you bleed. (What it must be like to put your hand between your thighs and there it is.) You have become a woman. As a male, a boy, for us nothing so drastic as bloodletting. The rising of the worm you pee through, become a stiff upright, it happens apparently in the womb and you can make it happen through childhood by toying with it. Must have experienced when the attention of your hand became urgent and there was fluid spurting excitement, pleasure. So. Then you were not a boy: a man.

Rituals the body has.

Was there some sort of other, gleeful ceremonial in the dorms at the high school where Reeds have been educated over at least two generations. Don't remember so could not have been significant either as good or traumatic. Must anyway have felt by it totally recognised, safe and accepted, in that manly white enclave, sons of those who mattered.

University. Could you call it recruitment outside the curriculum. Nothing so authoritative. Initiation; beginning to understand a contradiction in the ways of living, let alone thinking—that's political initiation. Didn't really come out of the bibles of revolution read: rather the disappearances into Swaziland, putting into practice tentatives of what theory called liberation, contradictions resolved by action, you *can* choose sides, you don't have to *belong* in the one you were born to. Guts not obedience. The proof of it later at the paint factory, ingredient of concoction of explosives to blow up power substations and rupture the service of apartheid. Initiation: what you yourself did.

And *Umkhonto*. The comrades who went for the first time on raids, into battle across the desert and through the bush, to kill the apartheid army and be killed by them—what student hostel initiation, if it is to test endurance, did *they* need.

Religious initiation. But of course how could you remember that you must have yelled as you were snipped—when do Jews do it—before two weeks old?—at some atavistic whim of your mother married to a Gentile (if not observant Christian). Muslims do it at a stage in development, marriage, when at least it makes more sense to become a man by ordeal of some sort; we males don't go through childbirth. And the justification, for non-believers: it's not mutilation but a hygienic advantage. And there are differing opinions apparently, among women frank enough in gender freedom to come out with these: intercourse with a circumcised penis is more/less rousing than with an intact foreskin. What will she say. It'd imply a wider experience than with me. Before me? Since. You don't ask such opinions of your woman.

As with Jews and Muslims, initiation to manhood is tribal among Africans. AmaXhosa circumcise in adolescence or adulthood, in time to be considered a man ready for marriage, Zulus don't, any more. It's probably not in the traditions observed now by her Baba.

Not only is the coffee hot in the Faculty room. Westling from Psychology should have something enlightening to say on the Free State. He is professionally beyond disgust, judgement: —Suffering. Doesn't have to be surgical. It seems adult initiations all involve that other form: humiliation. You have to show you can take it, the jeering and taunting by your peers. And then you get drunk with them. That's exactly what it is, what it's supposed to signify you become one of them, behaviour of your own adult-kind, as in turn you will initiate the next student.—

—But it is exactly that what has happened at that university was not.—

Lesego is ready. —What do the people who scrub the floor flush the shit from the lavatory have to do with students becoming men? It wasn't, can't be *initiation*. Tell me, say it, into what? Those students accepting them as their own, same as themselves? Out of despising those men and women who clean their dirt they trick them into something you can't even think about. Was the come on in, the worst insult of all; invite these poor blacks to party with the students, get them drunk, make them dance for you—and then eat from a pot one of the same students has pissed in. It's all there, filmed on video.—

But the academic colleagues don't commit themselves to probing revulsion, disgust, and—understood but not breathed—something *like that*, unimaginable as it is, could happen *only* in that province, that university.

Disgust. Disgust can't be the end of it.

* * *

It's raining and instead of the church swimming pool the comrades are in Jake and Isa's house.

—Who're these superior louts receiving higher education—no, tertiary, eh in our new 'dispensation'—sounds less discriminatory between high and low opportunity? Who are these superiors themselves more degraded than any filthy degradation into which they initiate their 'inferiors'.— it's Jake.

Some things you can argue out only with yourself. He is hardly aware of his own voice —Were those young men so brutalised, don't let's call them beasts, beasts are innocent, hunt and attack only for survival—did their parents' torture of so many in ingenious crude daily apartheid routine—did this seep into their DNA—do what?—haunt them into some hideous farce of repetition.—

Jabu launches across the room at him; for everyone there. —So they can't help it?—

What had to be said—excuses? There cannot be any kind of haunting justification of present behaviour taken from that of grandfathers, uncles, fathers, who were the torturers in their Special Branch, their police, their army! Is there a skin-branding of shame which scars into defiance, indecency, the extortionate unbelievable?—So you don't have to take any blame for your kind that an old bloodied coat can't shrug off.

Only Pierre, the Afrikaner Dolphin can speak about the Free State, aloud: —Boere. Afrikaners.— Pierre's taken on the hardest kind of recognition, responsibility for what his people have done to themselves.

While they also produced a Dominee Beyers Naude who wouldn't preach in a segregated Gereformeerde Kerk.

In that only refuge from what's happening elsewhere, another university—in bed again away from all intrusions, there was tension to be felt in her. He stroked her hip where his hand lay. She drew away as if she were going to speak, say something that among crossing voices hadn't been heard.

How not to have understood! He and the others mindblown by what had been done in the name of the white-skinned; themselves. She is part of the old women cleaners, the men lured to drink with the sons of the past masters, fed in a stew all that they'd had thrust down their throats all their people's lives, the whites' rejection pissed out as blacks' share of life's abundance.

Make love to her, would be the tender healing, most respectful acceptance of what she couldn't release herself of without cursing him in the wordless sense of what his skin represents. But for once, first time ever, since the bold boy-girl desire met, ignoring the Reeds, ignoring Baba, in Swaziland, he could not expect to enter, taken in by her. How long will it be—it's the country in mind now, not the Free State, no-no it's too easy to say it's colour, race, Jabu has multiple identities in living: in her convictions, ethics, beliefs, along with the congenital. A love between them, her Baba and her, which that other love, woman and mate, has not supplanted. Her bond with her Baba survived the disillusion and pain of that other visit the day when she went back home to KwaZulu after sitting—witnessing—at the rape trial and found her father outraged by the trial and triumphant in the dismissal of the charge against Zuma.

Also easy to miss within her multiple identities something you would rather miss. The attachment tangle, strength beneath any acquisition to selfhood, of that history called 'tradition' (didn't colonials dub as a basket of customs anything other than their own ways dealing with the events of life and death). The attachment, not in sense of emotion but of a history alive in the present which he cannot claim to share with her and her Baba. Must face, like it or not—comrades and lovers as they are with their definitive shared history of the Struggle—leaving is different; for her, Jabu. Call it Australia. Whatever. He's not leaving what she's leaving.

What her father knows, she's leaving.

—What did he say.—

—Nothing. At first. I almost thought he hadn't heard me right. What I'd told.—

The father removed beyond belief. She read the conclusion taken, this one of the communication facilities of growing up together not as children but as adults. —No, his way of not being pushed, you know, taking his time . . . you see . . . for the meaning of what's been said. He just opened the door in his room and sent a boy to fetch tea and only when we started to drink—Are you and your children going too.— Like asking a man in the family who's off to a job he's found in the city. I said again, opportunities . . . you've heard about. —Australia, England, America, Ghana—he said it—'all the same'.—

Opportunities. Quoting from the cuttings—as a circumstance, reason Baba would perhaps respond to that she herself had not shown any recognition of to himself, Steve; but this was her Baba who had seen sending her away to education in Swaziland was his decision of opportunity for her.

—And then. He was angry. So then—

She pinches in her nostrils a moment, concentration to repeat her Baba faithfully, of course they would have been speaking in isiZulu. —He changed to English, 'There are many white people going there, I read they call it something, relocating, that must be the word they took when they put us, black people into Locations outside the towns.'—

—That's all? Didn't ask anything, more about you.—

What about her; first thing she knew was coming upon the cuttings wasn't it.

She smiled with closed lips and paused—before the evocation of Zuma's man, the father. —*Uzikhethele wena impilo yakho!* You made your life, I let you choose, you must live the way it is in this time.—

What is she saying, comrade Jabu, that whatever her betrayal of her Baba, his bitter sorrow, her rejection of him; her betrayal of herself, Ubuntu, her country: a woman, in the order of her Baba's community, she will live this time as ever on the decision of her man.

Australia, I am leaving with him, leaving our country, KwaZulu, leaving you. The woman goes where her man goes, that's the ancient order understood, but *he* knows, Baba knows, had his own kind of revolution in nurturing his female child to independent being. Wouldn't be deluded, would accept that she was emigrating—that reversal of what brought foreigners to take the continent, Africa which was not theirs—as a wife obedient to her husband. Baba will still force her to meet him on common if not equal ground—he is the father, ultimate authority after the Word of God—he had provided for her. She has to defend herself on the choice made for the children, hers and thereby Baba's lineage, children of Africa, of the Zulu nation.

Protect herself from knotted liens of nature her man must recognise, always should have recognised, liens he didn't have. Being born here is not enough. Even in the equality of the Struggle.

Sindiswa is about to be fourteen. When she's asked what she wants as her birthday present she says one of the new mobile phones where you can see movies and read books, the pages passing, you don't have to turn—her cell phone is old stuff.

—Oh please—must she be like all the kids (and his students) a clamp on her ear, apparently talking aloud to themselves.—

He keeps his 'old style' mobile in the car—for hijack emergencies . . . ? There are breaks in real communication in the faculty room just when someone is putting together an argument worth hearing and he/she is claimed by a singsong sounding somewhere under clothes like a digestive gurgle. When a student comes to him to discuss a formula not clearly grasped—that's what he's there for, a teacher always available—he has bossily made it a rule that the thing must be switched off. He's not cool, Prof Reed, although they say he was one of the whites in *Umkhonto*.

—Everybody has them. Gary's nagging too.—

—Exactly.—

Brenda has called—for Jonathan's sake, Steve is a brother after all, even if their ways were parted during the bad years—everyone agrees now they were that, although not personally involved except in being white. Brenda keeps tally of family anniversaries and birthdays as calendars mark Christmas and now Muslim, Hindu, Jewish and so on, holy days. She'll just pop round and drop a little something for Sindiswa, big girl, no more toys, what would she like?

—Your aunt—

Sindi comes from her room enquiringly —Baba's place?—

—Your aunt Brenda.— They chatter, Brenda has an assumed understanding of young people (it works) who are balancing on the edge of adulthood.

The outdated landline is handed back happily to Jabu. A natural connection has been made by her daughter and the wife of Steven's brother. —Won't you and Jonathan eat with us when you come to wish happy birthday, no party, I'm sorry, because she's taking her school friends to celebrate at McDonald's that evening, believe it or not.—

The receiver resounds Brenda's dismissal. —Of course I believe it!—

—Just lunch. On Sunday, then. How many of you?—

—Only Jonny and me. As you know, Ryan's overseas and the others all make weekend plans.—

—Should we have a *braai*.— Jabu's suggestion, for his approval. She's such a South African, this descendant of amaZulu warriors!

—Whatever's going to be easiest for you, m'love.—

She doesn't mind family occasions, even on his side (why does he make the distinction) although their kin, his-and-hers, are the comrades. That progeniture is the one they live, survivors, while Ruth was blown apart as she opened a parcel, the gift sent to her, Albie lost an arm and the light of one eye . . . who else? The great ones.

They're moving to eat on the terrace, the garden table upgraded with a cloth. Jonathan is volunteering to carve the leg of lamb that was decided on, although there's putu with beans as well as roast potatoes Reed style (or what Jabu knows as white style). Steve grants expertise to his brother. While Jonathan tests the knife for keenness he's telling of his son Ryan. —It seems he's been working hard, and the great standard of the courses—you know he got into the London University School of Engineering? He's still found time, ay, to fall seriously for a girl, sister of one of his top student friends. He's bringing her to show her, not us—Africa, sometime next year, the swimming pools and the lions.—

Brenda proudly amused. —Sindiswa, you better get ready to be a bridesmaid. A wedding in the family. We'd like him to graduate first, but it's not our *affaire* to decide!—

She has given Sindiswa a beribboned packet. Sindi is fitting something from it round the principal recognition of her birthday, the iPhone she has chosen. The gift is an elegant cover for the mobile. Sindi must have told Brenda in the kitchen, Steve didn't want her to be just 'talking to herself'. —But these things are educational as well as a good safeguard for us parents, your child can always reach you if she's in trouble in any way, this place, you never know . . . this dangerous city.—

The weekend papers he was out early to buy in addition to the two subscribed to. Scattered about, the image of Jacob Zuma is the front page.

When he has made coffee, his share of tasks of a meal, with some aside of excusing himself nobody hears under the table's rally of voices, Jonathan is teasing flattered Gary Elias about the sporting prowess he's sure of the boy, Brenda has another social gift, orchestrating subjects and gossips about celebrities which animates herself, Jabu and Sindi in femininity if not liberation, he goes to the living room and snaps on the screen, the roar—

Awuleth' Umshini Wami

Weeks go by, when they don't speak of whether he's still in contact with the possibility/opportunity, Australia. Normal life takes up attention and energy. The immediate on its track. There was a connection apart from what they customarily share when a winter school on the interface between law and social sciences was organised at his university and she, Jabu the freedom fighter-cum-lawyer was one of the invited participants, some from other countries in Africa, the USA, Brazil, India. He left the Science Faculty the day she was a panellist on the connection between law and public access to power and heard her speak, with interruptions of applause for the points she expounded. As part of an audience, to see, hear, one you know intimately, sexually, intellectually, in temperament, oddities, as nobody else does is to find that no one knows anyone utterly. He's sat in on a few court cases but there she was a modest member of a legal team, one of the attorneys assisting advocates, a combined presence. Here, up at a microphone with the attention of all around him on her become oddly, strangely one of them, sees the supple length of her brown neck above the small well between her collarbones as she raises her head to acknowledge the audience in her relation to them; the iconic image in the elaborately wound cloth giving height to the piled hair it holds, a few locks painted with coloured strands free from it, moving in emphasis while she speaks. She is in African dress not the businesslike garb for the courts. Which is hers: Jabu's? Why is she dressed in this one for an occasion whose subject is the law. You have to be in an audience to come upon, why; what you should know and don't.

*   *   *

In the July school holidays Gary Elias went as usual to spend part of the time with his grandfather and the boys of the KwaZulu collateral. It was for him a privilege above his sister, a girl of course, he wanted to offer his buddy Njabulo to share. They—the authority of his parents who were also always his friends, said there might be other plans made for Njabulo, and when Gary was sent by Steve and Jabu to ask Peter and Blessing if the boy could come along, this was so. That family was going to Blessing's sister whose husband had landed a job in the parliamentary complex—through knowing the right ANC person at the right time, Peter tells confidentially— wouldn't Gary like to join Njabulo there instead? Gary's unspoken denial in wide-opened eyes and straightened body brought from Blessing and Peter, oh after all wouldn't it be a better idea . . . opportunity for Njabulo to go with Gary to his grandfather's place? KwaZulu. The Mkize roots there had long ago been dug up and transplanted to more industrial-ised parts of the country. But Njabulo opted for the sea. And there's no question that Gary Elias would forego his prince-dom in Baba's kingdom.

She was putting together Gary Elias's clothes and necessities when he walked in to their boy's room. —D'you want me to come with you.—

She sends her free hand out behind her to feel for his, pressed a moment, then she needs two hands to fold a shirt. —It's all right.— Australia between them: he would bring it with him in his very presence before Baba. If she's alone that might give some sort of assurance, however false, it's not going to happen.

She left early drove without pause, the chatter of Gary Elias and Wethu the accompaniment—a present for her mother a warm shawl, a book for Baba, reprint of Dhlomo's *An African Tragedy* he might not have, and after eating with the family, the aunts celebrating as usual the visit from the city, left the same day with Wethu. Australia was not present; she was not led apart to the privacy of Baba's cubby-hole.

Steve and Sindiswa had prepared dinner or rather shopped together for takeaways at a supermarket owned by a Greek South African, maybe Sindi was a schoolmate of his children.

—You can see how happy Gary Elias is! Doesn't ever want to come to say goodbye to his Babamkhulu. Too busy-busy with the boys. *Hai!* I never see him here like with them, they are best friends to him—and they make a fuss for him, *eish!*— Wethu entertains in Zulu and in English, because Steve only half-understands the Zulu tongue. Wethu has by now made her transformation to the country the government tells the people is in the process of becoming. *Eish*—we are all South Africans. She comes back from the home village to her converted chicken run in the Suburb, at home in both.

MIGRANTS SOUGHT TO STIMULATE ECONOMY

He had attended—that's the inadequate word for action of a kind not relevant to his life—their life—a free seminar. Migrants sought to stimulate economy. The flattering inference, for those wanting to leave their country for another, that they would not be immigrants simply received charitably but would indeed be serving the needs of that grateful country. The Australian consultancy was particularly interested in—first of a list of desirables—people with degrees. He had in fact sat through the process as if secretly—clandestine form self-awareness: what are you doing here? There was among the attentive gathering in a conference room of one of the five-star chain hotels a single face recognised while looking to typify the attendants by class, the crude tape-measure, businessmen in suits and ties, others in informal outfits declaring their difference—someone from a faculty of the university. Unknown by name, but seen about, as he himself must have been recognised by the individual. Brothers under the academic gown invisible over their shoulders, no acknowledgement called for. One black man only. Difficult to read in classification because while wearing an elegant dashiki, not the cheap ones for sale in the passage at the Methodist Church, his crossed legs were in pinstripe trousers, his briefcase unscuffed fine leather. Why be so surprised? If there were some millions of black men invading South Africa out of poverty at home, why should there not be a bourgeois black man for his own reasons wanting to emigrate. Over there. Down Under. Some have already gone to the West, doctors opting for higher pay and better working conditions in hospitals.

One of the unimagined circumstances in the clandestine possibilities of what he had not abandoned was that you still had no one to talk to about it; an inhibition. Not even her.

The Australian representatives conducting proceedings were unpompous and friendly in their speech-making, even when warning the proviso 'conditions apply', and affable in exchange with those who asked complex questions, from educational policy to health insurance, income tax. Nobody asked about crime; whatever the safety situation might be, must be better than the one prospective emigrants would leave behind. Flee. Wasn't that a morally acceptable reason, against betrayal of patriotism.

An immigration lawyer, registration number supplied, would be available for any one-on-one consultation. 'Cost applies.'

Peter and Blessing play a tooted phrase twice in greeting whenever they drop Gary Elias after fetching him with their Njabulo from the chosen school. It was Wednesday, rugby training (that English game) after classes, so late afternoon.

—Comrade Steve home yet?— Peter calling from the car.

She was on the terrace helping Sindiswa with some research for homework—hoping to win the argument that the child should go to the encyclopaedia instead of, as second nature to her, Internet to save the trouble of turning all those pages.

Through the house to show herself at the front door. —He's not back. But come in.—

—No, won't disturb you, Jabu.—

—I'm pleased to be let off Sindi's homework—you're welcome, *nafika kahle!*—

A slamming of car doors, Njabulo and Gary Elias immediately disappear about their own affairs, the regular thump of the oval ball panting through the house. The three embrace cheek-about-cheek as comrades signal one another. Wave a hand—there's Sindi at the computer on Internet . . . Exchange parents' tussles with their children's ideas of education, laughing critically; Blessing's proud and jealous. —They can learn anything, we were stuck in our little books.—

The precious books decoded in detention. Without them how ever would Jabu have become a lawyer. There's a swerving crunch over gravel in the yard and he's arrived, Steve. It's often a reminder—how attractive, to her, he sometimes is, other times you don't really notice each other; today it's as if he's gone away and then come anew, there again, in everyday.

He carries radio batteries she asked him to remember, along with his university stuff, and an early edition of the evening paper under his arm although it's delivered every evening. It drops on the cane and glass table (survivor of Glengrove Place) beside Peter, as if for him. —News of what the principal's doing about it?— no need to identify as the head of that other university.

—They're going to 'deal' with it in the university before a disciplinary committee. How does that sound to you.—

—Oh it's just a student *prank*.— Peter's lips twist and work. He makes the word a foreign one.

—Oh sure, high spirits, a *jol* that went a bit over the top.— Across whatever Jabu is beginning to say. —They're not going to expel them?— Blessing's high voice cuts in —Not even the guy who— A gesture will do.

Steve reaches for the newspaper. It's one that just gives the facts. —The disciplinary committee will decide on 'appropriate action'.— With his files of student work brought home to mark he has another newspaper, less cautious in producing what's coming before the disciplinary committee, board, whatever. It's a press that is attacked as a rag by politicians who don't want to see in print some of the things they've said or done. Open it and here's again the picture taken from the video one of the students kept as a souvenir, trophy?—didn't have the sense to destroy. Gloating grinning faces applauding the stream of urine going into the *potjiekos* from one whose back's to camera. Legs sturdily planted apart.

—I don't want to see.— Blessing's hand up to her eyes.

Peter with a laugh bursting as a rude noise. —I don't know why you're all in such a state—man, isn't it what you'd expect? Having what's for them a good time.— But turning seriously on himself —So if the principal expels a couple of them, which ones? And divide the rest up, some of the guys sent to this hostel, some to that? Punish them by having to live with students who see them as rubbish? Must be some in that place who know what that is, even in the Free State *University*. But what'll they care, the rubbish. They should be kicked out. Not accepted at any university.—

So. Anger. Revulsion to be satisfied by in-house punishment rap-over-the-knuckles of the 'rubbish'. The law, justice as she learnt early on in an LLB correspondence course, is founded on the principle of perpetrator and victim. —None of us— not the newspapers he's brought—is talking about the cleaners, the lowest at the bottom of our pile. Who's thinking about the men and the women invited to the 'party'? Who's asking if the university Convocation, their academic justice is *justice* for these people? There's the law, redress under our Constitution. That's the only justice.— The comrades (surely he) ought to see that. She's donned authority like a black gown worn in court. —A university committee, senate, convocation— go as high as you like—they cannot send down a decision in terms of the Declaration of Human Rights. The students must come to account. A criminal indictment against them. Charged. Nothing else. Nothing less.—

The relation, lover and comrade, to each other, is contesting, come alive. He trusts her suddenly come out in this aspect of herself, from her withdrawal that first day. A lawyer is *for* the victims, not one of them, no matter other, personal identification.

—How does anyone go about it?— The others turn to her, on her. It is recognition, something comrades learnt, had to, demand of one another's qualities, chance of effectiveness, in the Struggle.

The eagerness to see action instead of settling for condemnation by disgust; she sees they have higher expectations of her familiarity with the process of justice than she can offer, straight off. Justice Centre elders will know how, by whom, what criminal charges should, can be made.

Jabu has long overcome what she had to admit, face that time when she went to her father after her day at the Zuma trial and found the poster image celebrating dismissal of the case at her Baba's place, her home. If you live with someone through successive phases of your life together, you don't, can't know how he or she has come to terms with them, the disillusion and the pain, can only sense this has come about. She's gone back on a visit to the village where the Elder of the Methodist Church, the school headmaster, decrees the way of an extended family's life, his synthesis of what are known as traditional values and his rightful claim of whatever gained at such a price of centuries' loss and indignity (you defy tradition and send your female child for education in the coloniser's culture). He certainly supported Zuma for triumphant election, president of the ANC at Polokwane, as preliminary to becoming president of the country, giving the weight of his voice to electioneering among collaterals and the village. But does not expect, it seems, obedience from her. There was the customary welcome for this daughter and the grandson who successfully belongs both to the colonial-style city school and the country cousins on their soccer field. Offered to teach them to pick up the ball and run with it rugby-style.

So she's tough, Jabu. Tougher than a Reed. Although together—they've grown through bush camps and detention as their initiation. No—not tough, this gentle woman of his, soft flesh on her hips and more on backside now, in confirmation of black women's femininity. No other ideal adopted; not conditioned like his mother, dieting to stay young beyond successive stages. No, not tough, strong in the way he never could be, of course. A matter of another conditioning, her people, her Baba, all the generations behind them have survived those centuries of everything determined to demean and destroy them. His drop of Jew's blood? If he'd been the survivor son of German Jews who were shoved into Nazi incinerators; if he were a Palestinian in Gaza, he would be tough in her way, maybe.

Now she has the resources she's earned, she's able after that initial retreat into victim as along with the cleaning women, to use all these advantages combined within her.

She keeps the two of them informed on the understanding that it will be a long process, there are many devices of the guilty for delaying the law: the Judicial Commission may have to be involved before there's public demand for justice to be seen to be done before the Constitutional Court. Maybe he could get going movement at his university beyond its certainty that such horror could never have happened there.

How certain. Change, change, the past had to be overturned but what crawls out of the rubble can surface in some form anywhere, even in institutions undergoing real transformation: there are more black-of-all-shades in the Faculty of Science this year than last. Remind himself; some reassurance against disgust.

*   *   *

There is between them the realisation that he had not discarded, ruled out consideration. Did this mean she is convinced it would not, could not come to pass, but she must grant him the freedom to research what he knows he is putting before her, and what he is putting before their daughter and son. He receives some further information he applied for by email from the immigration department of the government of Australia.

Yes yes conditions apply. A positive response, a sign. He takes it to his lawyer—wife, comrade, for interpretation beyond his: interpretation for them all, Steve, Jabu, Sindiswa, Gary Elias, applying to them all, if it comes to that; comes about.

S eptember, spring, season of burgeoning.

The African National Congress Youth League has a new spokesman, he says of the call to 'Kill for Zuma' the League won't use the word again but 'will stop at nothing to see Zuma elected as the country's next president'.

Peter Mkize is promoted general manager of a group of communication enterprises, mobiles, data modems.

Blessing has now her own catering firm in partnership with Gloria Mbanjwa who used to be a waitress at the coffee shop Isa frequents; a BEE opportunity.

Isa has opened a gallery selling indigenous art, with one of the artists himself.

Jake is in insurance, with good prospects, a company where one of the ministers of the present government (may not be around next year after the elections) sits on the board and has investment.

Jabu's place among comrade ex-combatants, in her career both prestigious, likely to become prosperous, while devoted to justice against the past and for justice in the present, has been the first to see something like the Black Economic Empowerment policy in evidence even if only within the class of the Suburb.

When the Suburb gets together each in this trusted company can unburden frustrations, unforeseen situations, unexpected successes of their piece of the jigsaw, argue where it will fit in to make the map of the new life. Not everyone sees the same cartography, anyway. These are the mountains to sweat your way up—no, these are the cesspits still to be drained of the shit of the past, no, they're the green fields in the dew.

—What d'you do with leftovers when you make all that fancy food for government people, what happens to it I wonder? Do your helpers eat what they like? Takeaways?— Isa tick-tocking a finger at Blessing.

—It goes to any orphanage or old age home, school—you know, that's near, we've got our fridge van.—

—Caviare for the kids.— Jake makes affectionate fun of Blessing.

Peter joins in. —You're not jealous she brings things home for me. I'll call you next time she has a bottle of wine under her apron.—

There's also development of another nature, would seem entirely personal if it were not that all their situations out of their pasts are personal to the ex-combatants' comradeship of the Suburb. Marc was now often not among the Dolphins when the Reeds brought their young over for a Sunday swim. He was missing in the lively adult playfulness around the church pool; assumed with his growing success that he was busy staging his new play in some festival, another part of the country. He walked in one night late when Steve and Jabu were about to go to bed and told them he had fallen in love with a woman. He was going to live with her: his first time, ever. He wanted to talk. Never been bisexual. This was a decisive discovery—they would understand. He who'd become their comrade was no longer a Dolphin.

Summer and he's in court again, Jacob Zuma: the charges of corruption against the President of the African National Congress are withdrawn in a High Court judgment. The statement later that this order was made while it was the judge's belief that there had existed political interference in the defendant's case was not the reason why he held that charges against Zuma were unlawful, his belief was merely a response to the State's desire to have the allegations struck off . . . it was 'an adjunct to issues of law': the national Department of Prosecution had not, he said, given Zuma a chance to make representations before deciding to charge him.

—This did not relate to Zuma's guilt or innocence in the criminal charges against him—what the hell does that mean?— Now it is Jake who turns up: at the Reed door. She's home, the lawyer comrade, and it's to her that a page torn from a newspaper is thrust.

Steve brings beers and a packet of chips to one of the Suburb's usual sites of discussion, the terrace.

—You're guilty or you're not guilty, isn't that what the court decides! What else does the whole rigmarole, evidence, counter-evidence—

—Oh hold on Bra, you're not a lawyer, neither am I, but there's the case of extenuating circumstances, I remember that time when what's-his-name, Fikile—

—*Extenuating* all right, the charges have been hanging on for a year now, no hearing.—

Under this, she has been rereading to herself the newspaper report she knows from a copy of the judgment at the Justice Centre—there were calls for a commission of inquiry. This means he says he was not in this specific corruption case handing down judgment on the arms deal—Zuma's involved there, too, through allegations of his money-making tenders conspiracy with Shaik and the French arms company. —Look, Zuma's had threats of prosecution over his head for years.—

—Commission of Inquiry. Not to worry, delay, delay, and it'll all j-u-s-t go away.— Jake's sweep of the arm to a future. It is set before them: this is what the years in prison, exile, deaths in the bush battles were for.

And Zuma himself was ten years on the Island.—

Wethu has seen Marc at the gate and brought him through the garden, the Reed and Anderson, Mkize boys come along from the street with their steeds, a rivalry of ikon-adorned bicycles.

—What's making your cabal so long-faced, losses on the stock exchange, you should be so lucky, afford the bull and the bear ring, ay? Don't you listen to the radio, this evening's Friday programme how to appreciate booze was on whisky, enjoy the single malt from the unpolluted streams of Bonny Scotland, not that beer you're swallowing brewed with urine from streams around squatter camps.— He's come to invite them to church, not the church pool but the Anglican one where he is going to be married, and to a party with the Dolphins after. —They're reconciled to my defection, not only same-sex marriages are respectable, kosher, now.—

The flash of laughter changes the aspect of everyone.

Isa swings round to reach him with a knowing embrace, they're laughing together as if in some secret shared. Yes, of course, he, the Dolphin was the one who came to take care of her and the children while Jake was in hospital after the hijack attack, when no comrade made her- or himself available. After the celebratory neighbours left with the future bridegroom the mood remained. Jabu who rarely makes any intrusive remarks about the Suburb's private lives, softly, barely mouthed, —D'you think she . . . did it that time when they . . .— He spluttered again into laughter, now at her, his turn an urge to embrace her as if in example. —Are you telling me our Isa initiated him!—

And then recovered, asking himself—why are we heteros so joyful, is he a trophy for us, do we still have a trace, throwback contempt for the third sex, righteous about any conversion to our kind, the only way to live; to be.

*   *   *

A week after Jacob Zuma had again walked free out of court not on a charge of rape but of corruption, the National Executive Council dismissed the President of the country, Thabo Mbeki, from the National Presidency. It's the landline that's summoning not the Michael Jackson signal on Sindiswa's mobile. Jake: —So the vacancy's there for Zuma!—

The Christmas season—not in climate sense, the southern hemisphere is summer holiday time. Instead of snow for the old man's sleigh, time of peace and goodwill brings also the time of summing up the academic year ended. Total enrolments, 97 per cent of the country's children are in schools, 40 per cent are now no-fee schools. Recent statistics show 67.4 per cent of schools have no computers, 79.3 per cent have no libraries. And 88.4 per cent no functional lavatories.

Under the 'Outcome Based' education system (what's happened to 'Results'?) due to the National Student Financial Aid Scheme black enrolments doubled this year: black students now may enter universities with a lower academic qualification than coloured, Indian or white students. —The freedom hierarchy.— No one catches Lesego's low bass, or if they do, takes him up on devaluing his own university. Between Faculty room farewell exchanges of who is going where, sea or mountains there is the rumour that our universities are going to lose accreditation in the world because here students are accepted without adequate qualification.

Over the seasonal get-together drinks at house or church pool in the Suburb it's not the comrades' academic who turns within the holiday mood to interrupt, it's Marc, there with his bride, who's brought up the subject —How do we know that the students are not granted degrees on the same principle, that's the *Outcome* of Outcome based education . . .—

—How are you going to open up higher education without making some concessions for blacks to get in—

—But that's still exactly where we were months, a year ago.— Since the injury to his spine Jake has a tic of gathering himself to pout his chest. —Can you tell me the 'advancement' in granting degrees to students who're going to enter professions unequipped to do the work they're supposed to do. What's the sense? So people are happy to say—see, dumb blacks! That's perpetuating the racist 'inferiority of blacks' brains', that's apartheid dolled up as Black Economic Empowerment.—

In the flying decibels of voices these are directed at Steve, the university professor. Although the comrades know about Australia: what has he to do with what happens, is going to come about in education, here.

So what right has he to be asked. To give any answer. Are they pretending *not* to know about Down Under, avoid, deny judgement of him, one of their own.

Presuming the comrade still has the decision for Australia in mind whether or not negotiating it; at the university Lesego in African Studies and one or two other academics sometimes speculate on who might have the chance to succeed him in the Faculty of Science; an opportunity, however come about. Everything in what's known as the country's new dispensation erupts, and then drags on, become somehow everyday life. The country is in its adolescence.

The Christmas season.

By chance brings return of one of those violent happenings whose consequences are resolved by Jake's other gesture, his sweep of the arm, delay, delay, delay, it'll just go away. The initiation of black cleaners by white students into the barbarity of white culture seemed to have done just that. There had been now and again a few inner-page references to what the university's intentions were to be 'dealing with the incident'. These apparently were whether the students should be allowed to continue with their studies; whether or not the university's concern included the consequences of the 'incident' for the cleaners wasn't mentioned. But while the year was running out the incident of the year before untimely surfaced; as black and white unemployed men took the Santa Claus job in supermarkets under the ritual beard, one of those students gave or sold a copy of the video and more photographs appeared in newspapers. Greeting of the guests, circus of prancing drunken display under the glee whip of encouragement, heads bent over the pot the guests were uproaringly forced to eat from; again the back of the student pissing in preparation of the *potjiekos*. It hasn't just gone away: a reminder. But maybe at the wrong time. Everyone preoccupied elsewhere.

For him the reminder was, could be taken as to himself. Although happenstance, he had received after an on-off of contacts with Australian consultancies, slow progression to the education authority, some finality to be approached: presentation to specific universities. Academic credentials, CV stuff; he could and did ask Professor Nduka to write a character and personality recommendation for him—Nduka the man who had left for his reasons his own Nigeria to take up a foreign appointment. Could not approach one of those in cabinet posts whose supporting testaments would really count, the Struggle comrades who had known him in that time and could vouch best for what were his qualities—this comrade leaving the country.

An *impimpi*. In the new life: caught a glimpse of himself in that shop window.

Applications for a post in the Faculty of Science are very encouragingly received by the three or four he approached. The consultancies supply glowing pamphlets describing the climate, flora and fauna, sports facilities, cultural activities, likely to be decisive for an intellectual of wide interests in the community where each university is situated. He tells—University of Adelaide, South Australia, Melbourne, Victoria State, James Cook University, Queensland. After a pause —Show me the map.— Sindi has an atlas handy among her school books she lends her mother without curiosity about the purpose, she is gasping, conspiratorial, into her mobile as called from her room she brings it. The children don't know about Australia, there has been care that they don't overhear—too soon.

Only Sydney and the Great Barrier Reef mean anything conjured up visually, it's consideringly admitted. But not that there are actual institutions, universities named and placed in the unknown; simply possibility confirmed as existing. Nothing has been spoken of opportunities in the practice of law. The acceptance of his opportunities as if understood, of course also hers, in common.

He had seen in those first advertisements of welcome to Australia, civil engineers, opticians, nurses, refrigeration mechanics, armature winders, crane operators, no lawyers on the list of desirables. They had not talked in the private hours where they might have, of what would be open to her—there. Not as someone's wife brought along in his baggage. Whether her LLB degree was a recognised one in that country's judicial system. Whether Australia has enough lawyers, thank you. Whether her present experience as an attorney in a Justice Centre is a plus in the capacity of an appointment to commercial legal practice or a social service created to provide defence lawyers for people who can't afford to hire them.

—You could ask about that.— Ceding to him the possibilities for her.

So they have been living on Baba's customary law that a woman will as ever live on the decisions of her man.

—Look, you ask, you're the one who knows the ins and outs of law. There's a seminar next week, some hotel.—

—What day. I've got to be in court Tuesday—no, Wednesday.— Her casually practical response was the answer: she is independently with him in the decision of the possibility—Australia.

Unaware of its significance between these two at the consultancy seminar on Thursday, a hotel one of whose five stars was a Thai sauna and karma massage centre neither had ever heard of. The conference room was not full of chancers, but men and women mainly in early middle age, from the look of them, and confidently prepared questions by them; young men and girls both with gold loops in their earlobes, Australia's apparently known as not fuddy-duddy square, if you have the skills they need, and there was what must be somebody's son whom BEE might have discriminated against because of his lack of pigment, who has with him an old woman, face defiantly made up. Jabu the only black. She was dressed in her African complexity, the high cloth around the pile of her hair more sober in colour than usual, and no locks escaped. People in the room noticed her covertly; few individuals want it witnessed that they too are giving up birthright. Defeated? Defecting; it's known as taking the plane for Perth.

Jabu surprises anyway (now they turn to look) by the precision of general questions she asks that they themselves are here to pursue, as if she's doing it on their behalf, and better, in presentation of matters they don't have the knowledge of jurisprudence to follow. The law is present, somehow, in their favour. It turns out she is a lawyer married to the white man beside her. He's a university professor who's in correspondence with some universities already interested in him; his questions don't concern that advance alone, however, but whether appointments in any capacity of employment are restricted in terms of a valid period or are permanent immigration granted. And what is the position in regard to membership of professional associations, may immigrant workers in industry join trade unions? Not employed on the cheap—no benefits?

Isn't he putting his foot in it for everyone by dragging up politics! Is it because he's got himself a genuine black wife (look at the Black-is-Beautiful power outfit) he's unlikely to be discriminated against in jobs for professors here at home—so what's the reason for the pair going to emigrate?

But this conference room isn't the place for exchanges across the floor among would-be immigrants, it's not good form to address one another. He gets his information, she gets hers, and is told there is further available in the brochures.

There has been the mutual experience, to break tacit non-communication, so now it's all right to speak. Going down in one of the elevators the man with the old woman engages him. —You've already had some responses from over there? You're lucky. 'Explore hidden opportunities', 'all visa-types', 'in-depth accurate, honest assessment', 'spectacular success', blah-blah. 'Welcome' they advertise, and the guys at these consultancies are gung-ho encouraging, but I've had no response to my applications, firms they've put me in touch with. I'm beginning to think about New Zealand, what's your take on the country? Of course you're a university man, I see, I suppose you have a better chance than I do with all the 'conditions apply'—the small print. Every time I come to these meetings the consultant gives me a different story, whether they're actually from Down Under or some hired local lawyer . . .—

The old woman has the lowered blue-painted eyelids and tucked lip corners of one who has heard all this before, dinned many times over. To everyone pressed together in the confinement carrying them, she speaks. —I'm taking the final emigration.—

It's all too solemn; someone titters patronisingly kindly,
—You're doing the tourist trip to the moon?—At your age?—
—No. Cremation. You go up in infinitesimal particles to
infinity.—

They are in Steve's car bundled with presents and contributions of Christmas food, for once the complete family, Gary Elias off to his second home, Sindiswa acceptant after having exacted the assurance they'll be back in her home by New Year's Eve when she's invited to a party with her Aristotle schoolfriends, Wethu humming some hymn she knows she'll soon be singing in the Elder's Methodist Church.

Baba himself called to invite them all; when Jabu told this was uncertain—unlikely that there would be some obligation to the Reeds, but the comrades, the Suburb, the Dolphins and a new body round the pool, Marc's defection, had some party plans. Yet it seemed to take for granted, between them, that if her Baba summoned, they would come to her home-place. The rape case was behind; and the corruption case set aside although appeal against that judgment being proceeded; Jacob Zuma remains, he is, the African National Congress's nomination for the presidential election in the new year.

There's an ox slaughtered in the village, the meat butchered from it isn't in plastic packets from the supermarket, it comes straight to the great iron vessels straddling the women's cooking fires. For Sindiswa, who doesn't often visit in KwaZulu this is not exotic; at the birthday party of a Greek schoolfriend there was a sheep on a spit he and his pals, directed by his father, were turning.

Steve's drawn into the football game with Gary Elias, the boy cousins, along with other fathers in Baba's collateral clan. Many of the men who live away in the industrial towns, miners, construction workers, are Home-Boys back for

Christmas. They form their own enclave drinking the supply of canned beer they've contributed as well as *imbamba* that has been generously brewed. They are amiably drunk and then there's a discrete breakaway by a few who protectively surround a woman bowed and weeping among the laughter and chatter of a good time; her son has died in some city where he found work. Jabu goes with her mother and other women to console, when she finds herself nearby.

He's given himself half-time from the football match.

—It was AIDS.— —Who?— —The one who didn't come.— Her tilt of eyes to the city workers. He and she followed the toll of AIDS, she could quote straight off the latest infection count published but so far no one either knows has died. At the Justice Centre she meets men and some women—out of fear of disgrace they are even more cautious about letting it be known—who are HIV-positive, on antiretrovirals, and even some who have AIDS. They are people dismissed from their employment because they are infected with the virus: she's involved in court actions against employers illegally ignoring workers' Constitutional rights.

Who knows which among his students is positive, aware or not; a lecturer in another faculty has made what's called his 'status' public and addressed the students in every faculty, urging them boldly, like himself, to take the test, and if it is positive start treatment immediately; if it is negative, wake up, be sure in your love-making you take every means of protecting yourself and your partner of whatever sex from infection.

There are two comrades—not of the Suburb but theirs from the wider association of the shared past—who are out of the closet and on treatment that will keep them alive maybe without developing AIDS. The Dolphins? Don't fall into the wishful belief that it's a homosexual curse passed on to heteros.

Still flushed by a football game taken unseriously by everyone, fun—like the absurd contests there used to be sometimes
in camp lulls between action, he goes to join the workers in
their loss. But they come from dispersion in whatever jobs
they've found all over the industrialised country, most will not
have known the man as grown men, and if there were a few of
the man's comrades—fellow workers, they will have mourned
him, away at the graveside; it's the mother's sorrow revived by
the son this year missing among the Home-Boys returned for
Christmas. These welcome the white man the church Elder's,
headmaster's daughter married, exchanging happily, interrupting each other's anecdotes that come from the kind of
life the towns and cities offer them, hostels where you must
survive violence, the cost of backyard rooms if you manage to
find them—there's the thigh-slapping story graphic in their
mix of isiZulu and English, of one who's got himself a share of
a room on the skyscraper roof of what used to be rich whites'
apartments. Up there, the servants lived, now the new tenant
class don't have live-in servants, and the building's owner
rents sky rooms to anyone—there's a shebeen run by some
women at weekends, there are kids up there, men and their
girls, *Izifebe Onondindwa*.

Sindi is speaking isiZulu she learnt from her mother since
the first words heard as a baby in Glengrove Place to a cluster
of girls who find they have the same jokes and complaints
about boyfriends although her freedom at her kind of school
is something unimaginable to them at the girls' equivalent of
Headmaster Elias Siphiwe Gumede's school for boys.

Instead of going home for Christmas, the Zimbabweans
fleeing from home in tens of thousands, finding a way to that
other Methodist Church, the beds of city pavements, the
empty suburban lots. New Year a week ahead bringing the
elections, another post-apartheid government; the hiving-off

of ANC heroes to start a rival party—no one's talking of this, these are the KwaZulu Home-Boys, back drinking home brew. It's going down plentifully to the great promise—the promises of the idol, Zuma. Jacob Zuma will change all that hasn't been changed to make better the better life for all. Msholozi, his praise-name: one of them, the workers; Zuma, their own.

Her Baba has given her husband his share of the presence and attention he distributes among everyone in traditional hospitality both of the Christian in this holy season and amaZulu feasts of celebration. He has the easy male subject to introduce—having to buy a new car. —The garage man tells me my old model isn't worth repairing any more, and the tyres—our roads you know—a new set would be a lot of money thrown out . . . they say you must buy a new car every six years.—

—In that case, mine should be in the scrapyard! Nearly three years out of date.—

—And you got here with Jabu all right? . . . of course . . . of course if I do have to replace, I must have my wheels, there's a Japanese model or maybe I should stay with Ford.—

Their expressions show each has other things occupying their minds, but this is friendly talk on safe ground in respect of whose this is beneath where they sit. No venture to mention a corruption trial lingering above the certain election of Jacob Gedleyihlekisa Zuma, as if allusion first would be an offence to the host, and second could be tactless in consideration of the politics whatever they might be, of the daughter's husband. Her reactions when she paid that visit after Msholozi was found innocent in the rape trial: she will have influenced her man. Or his could have been the influence on her attitude. A daughter of mine.

They passed a night in comfortable spirits at her parents' house, sleep understandably delayed by the singing and rising scales of ululating joy, background static of the radio commentary until some uncounted hour. The children were distributed where they elected to be among collaterals their own age who were delighted to make place for them, Gary Elias of course sharing a bed he occupies on his regular visits.

She didn't have to ask if he would come with family led by the Elder to church for the service on Christmas Day.

—Am I all right?— He wore a jacket despite the heat, and the tie he'd thrown into his duffle bag, remembering decencies observed in the Anglican church attended with his father.

He would pass; she had brought her formal Pan-African outfit and although this elaborately distinguished her from the simple traditional dress of the other up-to-date women and the tight tailored skirts, flowered hats hung over from the colonial period of decorum worn by a few old women, her beauty as a tribute to worship of the Christ Child, coming from their continent of Africa, was admiringly received. Their headmaster. Their Elder, in the line of his family's distinguished leadership in this, their church, had educated his daughter for the world but she had not forgotten to come back, bring something, symbol of her achievements, to them.

Enjoyed himself. Really. He felt—at home. In her home. In place. Is it because the personal life can become, is—central over the faith—political faith? (That's heresy . . .)

He's *got over* (unthinkingly there) his rejection of, no wasn't that—his detachment from the Reeds, Jonathan. A reconciliation brought about by Jabu, by life with her? Yes, a comrade; but she has never given allegiance to their faith—Struggle— as a religion, substitute for religious faith. She's free? What an easy way out. But she doesn't take easy ways.

It's killingly difficult to accept a priority between choice of existences in the meanly allotted human span. Oh, stuff the philosophy. There is her heritage KwaZulu Africa as exemplified in her father with whom she is bonded although parted from by the poster she came upon on the fence.

Tonight he sees her reading and making notes on the information supplied by the Australian consultancy on the jurisprudence and legal system Over There. He's addressing her to himself by her full name: has Jabulile Gumede accepted, decided for Australia. They discuss the move practically, they've talked about schools, about whether it would be more to a lifestyle perhaps envisaged, to be in a city rather than well, some suburban outback, a suburb, not the Suburb?

That's not a decision, an acceptance within the self, herself.

It is expected that some time after the return to the Suburb, as promised, in Sindi's concern to be back for her schoolfriends' New Year's Eve party, there'll be an afternoon or evening with his mother—perhaps the last before she moves to Cape Town—and whoever among the Reeds may be around her.

Jabu has made the arrangement, it's an evening. Jonathan and Brenda are there, the Jonathan-Brenda daughter Chantal who with her mother's ebullience hugs cousin Sindiswa whom she has seen only a few times in the childhood almost outgrown. And Ryan the son who is studying engineering in England for a degree which will favour him to take up a post there or anywhere. He hasn't waited to graduate, he's married, his Welsh-English wife Fiona is with him, Sindi won't be a bridesmaid after all. Ryan's speaking confidently of life in London, acclimatised in every way—even his South African English has somehow naturally lost its old inflections which come from the way the language is used by the Babel of citizens, isiZulu, Setswana, Sepedi, isiXhosa, Afrikaans—all notes sounding up and down the linguistic tune.

His wife works in an art gallery in Cork Street and her brother is first violinist in a chamber orchestra that performs all over the world. —Not just the stress and strain of engineering structures I'm wise to, we never miss an exhibition of developments in art, trends, the different conceptions, what art *is*, I mean, taking in new technology as means the way paint brushes used to be and then of course the music— Fiona's brother the open door to concerts, everything new that's happening in music, fantastic, post-Stockhausen to post-Jackson.— As if suddenly remembering the concerns of Steve and the beautiful—yes, she is—black wife. —And we don't have to feel why am I having all this while people here are living in shacks still kicked around— Wrinkles his nose, and then tosses the situation, as it should be for the evening, away with jerk of his head.

—What about the Muslims in England?— Jabu's gentle witness-interrogation voice.

—Well there are, there've been nasty incidents, of course you'll always get thugs who'll take out their own frustrations on people who don't look like themselves.— He arches his eyebrows to make known he's not among them.

Australia wiped out its aboriginals. Almost. So you don't have to feel guilty of privileges, there. The few who're left, the descendants, are mostly specimens, they have no real part in national life?

He isn't hearing the exchange continuing between Ryan and Jabu.

Neither is Jonathan, who's telling him, —I'm looking for the way to finance buying a house for the young couple in London or wherever he gets a post, most likely one of the big construction companies—maybe even a municipality or what do you call them, county. My lawyer's busy with control hassles, how to get permission to send the money from here, there's the provision you can own one property abroad, you know . . . oh, conditions apply. Officials go nosing into every nook and cranny of your finances. However. I've got some friends who know their way around.—

So the son's not coming back. Home.

As was clear when Jonathan came to ask for advice about the best university faculty of engineering for his son. Home is transferable. It always has been. Long before tribes coming down from the equatorial North, the Dutch following the reconnaissance of the Dutch East India Company, the French and their viniculture, the English colonial governors, the indentured Indians for the whites' sugar plantations, the Scottish mining engineers, the Jews from Czarist Russian racism and later Nazi Germany's persecution, the Italians who took a liking to the country during their spell as prisoners of war here, the Greeks whose odyssey launched by poverty brought them—all these and others of distant origins made home, this South Africa. It hasn't managed to wipe out completely the San and Khoi Africans whose homeland of origin was taken from them.

You can make of somebody else's your home anywhere. It's human history. But it's less complex if the indigenous population has been more or less disposed of.

Has Jonathan heard of connections with the Australian consultancy maybe through a friend who has noted who else was there at a seminar; or has Jonathan beside him read his mind. —Ever think of England? You have such good connections haven't you, that conference you went to? You could surely get a pretty good appointment in a university. But I suppose you have your ties here . . . no reason to . . . Brenda and I— the awful violence growing—we talk about it don't we all, but when you come down to nitty-gritty I say . . . *everywhere*. God knows what country's safe, and I just have the idea that once the world recession's over, investment, business is going to boom here; well, stick it out. The metal industry, we're not doing too badly even now, my outfit, we've managed to redeploy—not so many worker lay-offs in our show. But that doesn't solve the question of getting money out for Ryan's house.—

They laugh together, Jonathan aware that in this matter his brother Steve is not the man to ask for useful advice.

England. Other consultancies. Yes. Why never think of England if you have such great thoughts at all and are pursuing them. Connections. The influential academics at the conference where all arrangements were efficiently managed by the official with a man's name in its female version. 'Home' to England where father Reed's line came from. Life in England: a few days in an old mill converted to a private place.

The old year is seen off at the Jake/Isa venue, but all were joint hosts, Blessing and Peter Mkize, Jabu and Steve, the Dolphins, including renegade Marc and his wife. The comrades in the sense way back in the Struggle and now in the Suburb commune, ignite one another in enjoyment just as they are ready at hand when anyone among them is in trouble.

Dancing, she and he are the clandestine lovers in Swaziland where Baba sent her to be educated and the university student was evading the Special Branch. They circled Marc dancing, nuzzling his wife as in parties round the church pool he used to one of the Dolphins—his lover?

Jabu whispering after an unaccustomed extra drink or two.

—What d'you think there was about her . . .—

She means in particular that attracted Marc; what—in the one who's not a male . . . ?

Yes? Not easy for himself a man who's attracted only to women, to place himself in Marc's—what—body sense and aesthetic sense.

Into the small ear close to him. Wine speaking. —She has a beautiful long waist.—

Connections. (Jonathan had brought them up.) England.

The one with the feminine version of a man's name, she has a waist that your hand goes smoothly down from the intimate armpit to the hollow at the hip.

Time hasn't materiality, the New Year's arrival is aural, cheers jetting with fireworks from the Suburb and the city all around, the stamp of drums and farting blare of vuvuzelas, supermarket clone of the oxhorn that used to be blown to honour tribal dignitaries, not in its plastic evolution deafening crowds when a goal is scored on the football field. From whatever was their partying in the yard the sons have appeared among the adult embraces landing where they will, the hugging, shoulder-thumping half-triumphant to have made it through an old year, half-expectant of the new one—and the seeking out, alone among all the press of others, a special meeting, embrace between those who live each-to-each. They are clasped as one body, but they kiss for the first time—never before in the time that is now, this year, he sees tears magnifying her eyes in celebration. She laughs and they're kissing again.

This is the last. To be the last change of time in the Suburb, with its normal life claimed.

Subject Ozl: OUR PEOPLE

It's the heading of information pages come online to his room in the faculty. Australia the world's smallest continent and sixth largest country etc. (all that's in the cuttings read before). Indigenous people lived on that continent up to 60,000 years ago; their lives were changed irrevocably after the British claimed Australia in 1788. British colonisation began as a penal colony with convicts shipped from Britain. Free settlers from there were joined by people from other parts of Europe, and Malays, Japanese . . . they started the pearling industries. By the 1930s the indigenous population was reduced to 20 per cent of its original size. Today a little more than 2 per cent of Australians are identified as Indigenous (seems 'aboriginal' has become a no-no, like 'Kaffir'). Large-scale immigration began after the Second World War . . . and after the abolition of the 'White Australia' policy, migrants came from many parts of Asia. Recent patterns show more coming from Africa.

In the years that followed European settlement the indigenous population declined significantly as a result of increased mortality. In 1967 the Australian Constitution was changed to recognise the indigenous for inclusion in the national census. (So earlier figures must be guess estimates?)

RECONCILIATION. Six years into the twenty-first century that population had increased by 11 per cent to 45,000 out of the country's total 21 million. In 1992 in the High Court of Australia, Eddie Mabo was the first Indigenous person to have native title rights to land recognised on behalf of Indigenous people. The Mabo decision led to the establishment of the Native Title Act 1993 which recognises native land ownership throughout Australia. In 2008 the Australian Prime Minister apologised to the Indigenous people for the 'Stolen Generation': the Indigenous children who between 1910 and 1970 were forcibly removed from their families, inflicting profound suffering and loss in Indigenous Australians. Education, health, housing. Fewer Indigenous students attend and finish school than non-Indigenous Australians . . . overcrowding is associated with poor health outcomes, 2004–5 health survey found 27 per cent of Indigenous were living in overcrowded conditions.

White South Africans didn't apologise to black South Africans for the abuse suffered by blacks from whites, seventeenth century to apartheid's final perfection of the means. Didn't apologise for anything—didn't have to, *they* were dealt with in the retribution that counts most—their last regime finished off by the Struggle.

Humans lived in Australia 60,000 years ago.

The San, humans living in what is now South Africa 200,000 years ago, joined by the Khoi Iron Age people from the north of the African continent; these also have managed to survive under whites that saw them as hardly human— some must have done so by clandestine breeding with other blacks, the whites' Malay slaves—and even the whites? They got the vote along with everyone else in 1994. They now have radio stations broadcasting in what has survived of their own languages. They live wretchedly degraded in poverty, the freedom transformation of the country to which they belong more than any others in the population.

So it's not emigration. What's left behind? It's not another country, if you're an aborigine, over there.

At home in their living room, he has the information at hand to show her. She's worked late at the Centre, it has taken on a case against mining companies which have for years dismissed with token or no compensation workers who contract asbestos poisoning and develop TB due to conditions breathed in underground.

She gives it back in the gesture for later.

—Not going well?— The case, he's aware, has been lost in two lower courts, now it is for the Constitution height.

Doesn't seem to have accepted the question. She's telling him something, nothing to do with the day's work. —I stopped by the supermarket for grapes Sindi wants and one of the men who hawk brooms in the street came up to me, now, as I was leaving. I gave the usual sorry, don't need, and he said Headmaster Gumede's daughter, I know you—recognised me from home, even my name. He's one of Baba's schoolboys but he hasn't found a job since he finished school two years ago. Come out of Baba's school really literate, numerate . . . all he can do to feed himself is try to sell straw brooms he says Zimbabwe refugee women make.—

She has an aspect of being unreachable. How say to her, give her the other handout, the man's one of thousands. But this is one of Baba's charges, educated by Baba for the new opportunities. She's describing exactly how the man approached, the mask of the beggar's confronting face that comes with the calling as that of the preacher or the judge comes with theirs. What he is seeing is that what she, Jabu, is experiencing is guilt. Why? She's guilty of belonging to the new black class that is not out on the streets. Not a cadre along with a Home-Boy whom Baba hasn't been able to give freedom as he gave it to her to pursue. Guilty of false pretences.

That's what this country is doing to its people. Guilt for the better life for all not being delivered by themselves. If you stay put long enough perhaps that will just go away, away, a court case not heard. Only Jabu giving judgement on herself.

So long as she lives here.

He's taking cuttings from newspapers and printouts from Internet not only on Australia; about here and now. She doesn't ask for explanation of this, she has it in herself—surely he's also realised it has no purpose. He is in negotiations with universities Over There.

Unless—will we still follow. What happens, is going to happen not just to our own we've left, Baba KwaZulu; and even his Reed family he isn't close to. The transformation; it is going to come now. The date of the national election this year is soon to be announced, already there are the promises from those hoping to stand for parliament. Shifting alliances of politicians' bargaining, power patterns; the new kind of Struggle. What changes are coming, inevitable. At the Justice Centre, it's the judiciary in debate.

—Too many white backsides seated on the Bench and too few blacks, that's the first contention—

—Judgments affecting government ministers and high-rank public servants influenced in their favour by government—

—Hold on—perceived to be, ay—

—And if there is—must be—democratic balance in proper proportion to the black majority—that's going to change pardons for pals—

—Conclusion. Don't clean up connivances, call corruption what it is.— One of the advocates from whom she has learned so much has the right to reproach her.

—What's the future of the Judicial Commission? Who'll survive. Will the Commission continue to be the independent body to appoint judges, with the president-whoever-he-is—

The colleague is interrupted —What d'you mean, whoever—
(someone barks a laugh, they all know it will be Zuma.)—
The President putting up his chosen four along with rubber-
stamping the Commission's choices—won't he simply dis-
band the J.C., make all appointees to the Branch himself.—

—Himself! Zuma he's been on the wrong side of the law.
So that's his qualification for knowledge of who is and who's
not fit to be a judge.— At once names of some come up who'll
understand the obligation to keep the President's men out of
jail. She brings this insider disquiet back to the Suburb, the
bedroom night talks, and to exchanges with the comrades
whose concerns these are going to be. He has for her a cutting
from the night's newspaper in his hand, not yet added to the
storage box he's keeping on the shelf the Australian immigration ones fell from. Nine million illiterates out of a population
of 48 million. That's a figure to sleep on before you begin to
think about her KwaZulu Home-Boy wandering the street
with straw brooms hitched against his shoulders.

Neither is surprised, but although he's Assistant Professor
at a university, the lawyer is even less surprised than he.
—That was one of my first functions when I was a junior. I
sat for hours with witnesses reading aloud to them, explain-
ing the meaning of the terms, words. Many couldn't read for
themselves. They were able to write their own name painfully.
I used to think the pen was like a handle they couldn't get a
hold on—it was awful, so embarrassing for them and for me,
black like them— Paused and drew first finger and thumb
down either corner from her fine full lips to her chin. —If
I'd been white it'd have been natural I know everything they
didn't.— Another moment. —Wonder how it would be for
Sindi and Gary Elias, they're *both*, on the look of them.—

At least, there are apparently other Africans, blacks
emigrated, accepted for migration. It's an aspect that hasn't

surfaced, is Australia what she's applying this thought to, rather than concentrating on witnesses in the defence of Constitutional rights in court. Australia's become an element of the normal life. How they, Down Under, see beings who are both black-and-white, though not white-and-aboriginal, of course. And—of course—there's Obama, since last year, how he's to be seen, that may help identity in the world.

At the Vice Chancellor's meeting when the university opened for the first term of the New Year, comrade Lesego from African Studies was a commanding speaker. The matriculation results: only 62 per cent of 'learners' had passes. No improvement. But his voice rose with his hands as he reminded that 69 per cent of students enrolled at the university during the past year were black and over half were women. There was the stir of applause his volume and gesture expected.

Another hand flagged rather than held up—academics are not 'learners' seeking attention to speak in school. Here it is again. —Those among the sixty-two per cent making application to the university this year—it's on entry standards differentiated between higher school results required for whites and Indians than lower qualifications for blacks. Look at the consequences for those of us who're going to teach them at undergraduate level.—

But it was not the time or occasion for Lesego to take up, disinter the situation. The term must begin positively. When he with Steve and a few other colleagues went to their pub for a beer, he used his same decisive rousing as he lifted his glass. —*Eish*, here's to more and longer bridging hours! Bigger intake this year!— Foam slopped over the lip of the glass and made the prospect of heavy responsibility, flippant.

Would he be there to do whatever could be, had to be, done?

* * *

Looked as if it would be Melbourne not Adelaide. The 'remuneration'—compound term—offered a good level of academic status as well as excellent salary and housing allowance, settling-in benefits. Enquiries about the legal profession were misunderstood: Jabu wasn't an academic, it was not an expectation of some lectureship for her, in the deal. He had made some enquiries, nevertheless, not mentioning this to her, for the law department here among his colleagues to give information on the legal profession in that far, other country.

Sometimes had the sense that Australia . . . it was the return, a recurrence of the time of the conference in England: something existing, in him, not revealed, beneath the practicalities exchanges discussions with her—Jabu, there beside him within touch, as the woman with a version of a man's name was at the mill. A subconscious deception of his own woman. Subliminal, not memory; some sort of constant in the flaws of being.

Promises. Promises.

No election date yet. But election manifestos budding: or shedding leaves already. Newspaper cuttings. The thirteenth day of the year's first month report the African National Congress promises to rescue South Africa from global recession. Cut unemployment to less than 15 per cent by 2014.

Over with Jake at the Mkizes' watching a cabinet minister on TV. 'Change and continuity' (contradiction?) to reassure investors fearing shift to the left—but faster change (at the same time) assuring the poorest 50 per cent of the population that mantra 'service delivery', water, electricity, refuse removal, will be accelerated. Almost half the country's 'learners' dropped out of school last year. The number of university students who failed to graduate was high. A major renewal of the education system, 15,000 'trainers' (not teachers?) to strengthen performance of schools on maths, science, technology and language development (literacy?). Ensure teachers are in class on time.

Jake waggles one leg across the other. —No slipping off to the shebeen to get *babelas*.—

Denials. Denials.

Shed by a split in the Party, one of its most popular Struggle leaders, Mosiuoa Terror Lekota is lost defected from the ANC to lead a new party, Congress of the People, with its smart double-meaning acronym COPE. COPE calls for scrapping of the policy of Affirmative Action by which blacks must be employed when black and white are applicants for the same post, the criterion uncertain whether their qualifications are equal.

Gone dark.

Peter snaps off the voice and the wide-mouthed image. —Affirmative Action, it's simply more jobs for cousins, in-laws to join the black elite—our Brothers—that's joined the white elite.—

A columnist writes as if speaking for the one who is snipping the cutting. 'The National Prosecuting Authority, government and leadership of the ANC, should take notice—the endless power games the different parties are playing: prosecute or not Zuma.'

She doesn't need to read it. —It's time for him to defend himself in court, he's forgotten he said that's what he wanted—he should stop his legal stalling tactics. Corruption, racketeering, tax evasions should be put to Zuma in the High Court on a date to be set for *next week*. Look, if the opposing parties aren't ready for a trial now, never will be. Zuma probably will want the Supreme Court judgment against him tested in the Constitutional Court.

Let that arbiter of human rights decide once and for all whether there's any reason to believe the conspiracy theory that the Zuma camp says charges are purely the vendetta against him, rivalry in the ANC itself to keep him out of becoming President.—

Next week? But there's the real alternative . . . delay, delay. Once he's President, cannot be charged. It'll all go away.

Gary Elias and Sindiswa see many kinds of mass celebration that exists for them only on the screen; but it's even bigger than the international football one with Maradona playing. The footage of who knows how many cameras can't encompass the size, the whole.

A commentator has made himself heard.

—Eighty thousand people, that must be a guess not an estimate.— But to their children the sight and sound of such is familiar; while to the parents it's some sort of consequence—of a different kind, of the protest crowds defying apartheid laws, police guns and arrest. It is Jacob Zuma's launch of the ANC's election manifesto. The date of the election still not given but in the air; and the triumphal joyousness as if the result has already been won. 'Awuleth' mashini wami' Zuma sings, the chorus that soars with him is exaltation both of himself and the people themselves.

The cohesion, mass transformation of what are individuals can be uplifting or an assault. The effect of whether you are down there at one with the mass in their purpose, or reject it. Gary begins to dance along Zuma-style, back-jacking from the knee, enjoying himself. Sindiswa with some schoolbook in her lap looks distracted and goes off to the family computer.

Comrades are not accustomed to being onlookers. He gestures—enough!—the control in hand. She frowns no, stoical. If they're not there, they're part of the Party constituency, share responsibility for it as they did in action. There are going to be plenty of other gatherings of the Party in its election campaign, and not all a pop praise song.

She assumes the Mkizes, Jake and Isa, will be coming with Steve and her to the one in the city. Jake's low voice—is it poor reception on a cell phone. —I don't want to hear him sing, I want to hear him in court.— Isa is laughing in the background and her message passed on, of course they'll be there . . .

It's what was a depot for tramcars way back when the city had tramways—for Whites Only. Must have been long before this distinction was named apartheid, that term that's even used—comrade Jake, not a Jew, often insists, to characterise mistakenly the situation between Israelis and Palestinians. Nothing to do with the justice of returning the West Bank and East Jerusalem to Palestine. Both peoples with ancient claims of origin to the same territory, whereas we whites in South Africa have no such claim, no common origin with local aborigines—unless you accept the palaeoanthropologist discovery of the origin of all hominids in The Cradle of Man, the site in this African country.

A huge skeleton shed is crowded to standing crush at the entrance. Way is made for the mixed group, either in amused recognition of the novelty among them or as a small sign of reconciliation that's supposed to exist. A woman buffeted, answers Isa's apology. —Welcome, my sister— this electioneering event is in one of the 'safe' areas of the country, confident of Party votes. 'Kill for Zuma!'—some youths have declared— Isa looks about, quoting in mumble. Jake prods her along by the elbow: —Well, suppose Zuma's 'Bring Me My Machine Gun' is heard as permission.—

—See any AKs.— Peter is gazing around from where the comrades from the Suburb have found a bench and people in possession have shifted to make cramped space. There's nothing to signify in appearances, anyone who isn't too fat is like the Suburbans, in jeans; there are the usual hair constructions, more spiky than Jabu's, some Afro-bushes dyed redhead, noserings and shackling ear-baubles. Isa's appreciative of political participation. —That's how we are . . . you can't tell which is pop group and which is Youth League showing signals of having outgrown wisdom from Party leaders—

—Heritage isn't a grand old pile out of which nothing new must come.—

—Stevie— Blessing, head on side. —Shame, they mustn't rubbish it.—

—Mandela and Tambo, the young ones, changed Luthuli's ANC, the great man for the reality of *his* time—for what they'd say, 'knocking on the back door'—youth came up, eh, and brought the Party to *Umkhonto*.—

—That's it! That's it! We need a youth group, wild to keep us awake, know it's *now*—*a luta continua*—but it's a new one at home and globalised, Internet, blog.— Peter repeats in a mix of isiZulu and isiXhosa, for the benefit of the sharers on the bench he hears speaking in their tongues.

—So we've got to take up the AK to fight a free and fair election?— He hasn't waited for Peter to finish the translation amid the delighted attention of the beneficiaries.

His own vehemence registered by Isa; he's aware of the questioning blankness turned on him: her usually expressive face.

Zuma has not come to address this gathering. Kgalema Motlanthe, interim President of the country since Thabo Mbeki was dismissed, is up there. Jabu, just loud enough to be heard —He was under pressure to appoint an inquiry into the arms deals.—

Motlanthe repeats Party promises, he doesn't charm, sing or dance. Speeches have had their place, electioneering is taken over by the crowd. A man has heaved to the vacated stage a bulbous street-shiny successor to the cowhide drum and stretches a crane of arm to haul beside him a small boy clutched round an example of the old kind. The man performs, with all fury of a star preacher, angry hysteria of victory to bring about an event to come, and turns a gasp for breath into command for the boy to lift his child's head too big for the body, and flail tiny hands expertly over his drum. Out of the battle-song chorus of the crowd all the women have risen and are wending widely round and round, up and down, they are the breasts and belly foremost of an anti-privatisation move- ment's expectation, government takeover of the mines, gold, platinum, uranium, coal. The stark echo of the tram shelter becomes itself their voice.

Jabu beside him sings with her sisters, from where she sits; one of the men sharing the bench legs up over it to cheer AMANDLA!, brotherhood granted he leans to put an arm either side on Peter Mkize and the academic who has the promise of professorship in Australia. AMANDLA! It comes out of this one along with the Brother, Jake, Peter and Isa. But not Jabu; as if now she hasn't the right? Although she cannot help singing. AWETHU! the others respond with the call from the crowd, power to the people.

Was Isa bewildered, after all, by his presence; was that what had come to him from her moment of blankness, earlier. What do hopes in this election have to do with Steve and Jabu, now.

Life goes on. Whether or not there is a future in common. It's a life of contentions when national elections announced for 22 April may bring personal as well as social change some will receive as justice and progress, others as defeat and danger to these.

The trade unions in ANC's Congress Alliance produce a booklet attack on COPE. There's accusation of Struggle Heroes, COPE President Mosiuoa (Terror) Lekota and his Deputy President Mbhazima Shilowa having deserted the African National Congress to 'pursue an agenda of the capitalist class'.

And there's some sort of division already in the breakaway party itself: a pastor nobody but his congregation seems to have heard of, a Reverend Dandala—his face is the one that's appearing instead of Lekota's on COPE election posters. So is this the leader of the party now?

—How can Terror be ditched, what for! It's mad.—

He has the answer for her, she ought to have known. —To capture from Zuma a big haul—rural Christians who'll follow a man of the Church, God's will, *ei-heh*.—

Election time. The ANC in the Free State finds it a time to decide the other kind of initiative, the students' 'initiation' in that province hasn't quite gone away: it's time for a black principal to 'undo the damage' at the university. Political pressure is now on to find one. The racist nightmare of last year will shudder back—no excuses. Principal Fourie, white, must be replaced; but the ANC complains there's not much effort by the university to attract a 'progressive' candidate. The four students about whom headlines of the urination into a pot of stew for blacks went around the world will go on trial—later—in August this year, charged with *crimen injuria*.

August. The same month. Jacob Zuma's lawyers have formally proposed the date 12 August for his application for his corruption prosecution to be permanently quashed. He has promised his application will detail a political conspiracy behind the corruption, racketeering, money laundering and fraud charges against him.

The precedent in other countries is that the President cannot be charged with alleged offences committed before his election to Presidency. The election of the new government and a new President will be on 22 April.

August: four more months later. This charge really will go *away*.

Additions to the store of newspaper cuttings are continuing. In particular concerning education. At a university of technology students reported to be horrified at rubber bullets fired on the university's workers who had rejected a wage increase. The university says 'Trying to match wages with other human resources—the challenges are still primary'. Women living in a hostel where 800 people share four toilets in one of Johannesburg's old 'locations' are demanding decent housing the way industrial workers use the streets for protest but in the higher register of women's voices and the different spectacle of female bodies. Some group on a high have announced the launch of the Dagga Party to join the electioneering roster. Shabir Shaik, Zuma's friend and financial adviser in the arms corruption case is released from prison on medical parole grounds of a state of approaching death and is seen driving his car around his city. At a university other than that of the initiation *potjie-kos* the principal has aligned himself with COPE, making an impassioned speech of support at a COPE convention; as a result the Congress of South African Trade Unions, part of the

ANC alliance, says it will campaign until the principal steps down from office. Study for Democracy at yet another university declares that the principals must be non-partisan; the Chair of a Parliamentary Education portfolio committee says there is no law against voicing one's political affiliation.

Fallen leaves, paper sweepings on the shelf. Among hard news, the writer quotes from an open letter to Nelson Mandela by a poet long away in emigration, an Afrikaner freedom militant jailed for years during the apartheid regime. Breyten Breytenbach to Mandela. 'I must tell you this terrible thing . . . if a young South African were to ask me whether he or she should stay or leave my bitter advice would be to go. For the seeable future now, if you want to live your life to the full with some satisfaction and usefulness, and if you can stand the loss, if you can amputate yourself, then go.' A fellow Afrikaner Max du Preez answers in his newspaper column 'It is not only possible to live a full and useful life in South Africa of today. It is indeed easier to do it here than in, say France or the US . . . or Australia, Canada or the United Kingdom, other favourites among white South Africans.' And there are the last lines in the ragged cutting 'Don't allow bad politics to drive you out of the country of your heart.'

Election time. Among Suburb comrades there's not much exchange of the usual parents' talk about their children, except in the projection of what form of political perspective—no longer rising sun post-apartheid but the present freedom's storms—will mean for the generation. Whether this child is showing aptitude for maths, that one is sulky, this is ignored, aside, when the determinants of coexistence are all-demanding.

But the private school for boys Gary Elias chose to be with his pal Njabulo Mkize has its news headline somewhere down among the heavy-type of the municipal workers' strike leaving the streets turned slum with trash, the transport workers' strikes leaving commuters stranded; darkness, lights out when power fails. (And it's not due to *Umkhonto* homemade explosives placed in substations, now.) A group of seniors living in the youth hostel lined boys up against a wall for an initiation. They beat them with golf clubs and cricket bats until their buttocks bled; a mother has laid charges of assault against the school; her son was forced to rub a powerful substance, 'Deep Heat', used for the relief of muscle pain, on his genitals.

Njabulo and Gary Elias are not boarders in the school hostel. Of course they are back home safely in the Suburb with Blessing and Peter, Jabu and Steve, every night.

What kind of assurance is that.

Jake's house is the tribunal for whatever affects the comrades, although the Anderson boys don't attend the Mkize and Reed boys' school. But as the calm survivor of peacetime violence, robbed of his car and dumped unconscious in a vacant lot, succoured by homeless people dossed down there for the night, Jake is the one who can be counted on to see situations objectively; what he has been able to come to in himself he can arrive at for others.

It's Peter Mkize who has been to the school, walked in on the headmaster; been assured a teacher in charge of the hostel has been 'suspended', the head boy at the hostel has been 'removed'.

—Where?— Jabu would have pursued: and does. —There's only one hostel.—

—Is that enough. Everything's OK. *Finish and klaar.*—
It's Marc who has no children. Marc and Claire (the shift to think 'Marc and his wife') have dropped in by chance after Jake called the Mkizes and the Reeds to come round without explanation needed.

The boys whose future is in question are out taking part in a cycling marathon the school arranged to raise money for the fund it has created to donate sports equipment to rural and shack settlement schools who can't afford golf clubs and cricket bats.

—How come our hostel boys have *golf clubs*—we didn't know private schools provide coaching for the future chairmen of boards—

—But Jabu, don't forget comrade Thabo Mbeki, when he was president, he revolutionised the status of blacks on the golf course from caddy to player, taking up golf, low handicap he had, himself.— Jake gets his laugh.

—D'you think the leader should be expelled?— Isa seems unaccustomedly embarrassed by the Mkizes and the Reeds with whom until now so much has been shared. Anderson boys are not at that school, don't risk being initiated or initiating others—so far as the Andersons are aware.

—What'd you do if it'd been your boy— The playwright, dramatic. —I mean how'd it feel for anyone to know your own kid had somehow become so brutal, where did it *come from* in his life, the decency he must get from you—you'd know, wouldn't you—he wasn't a kid you'd let torture a kitten.—

—It's not just the one they've 'removed', there was a gang, can a school expel a group maybe most of them in that hostel have been through the ordeal, proud of it, expect others to be tested the way they were—one of these manhood rituals *eih*, isn't what's really behind it is that a male must be made killer enough to be conscripted to kill in some war your country decides on. Peter—blacks, you have your initiation, circumcision school whatever you call them, in the bush, and look at the cases when the job is botched, the victim suffers horribly to 'become' a man.—

—We Zulus don't circumcise, Steve, don't you know that—
Reproach: white ignorance.

A Christian father, yet ritually, as a baby, made a man, the Jewish way, was that *really* what my mother couldn't have known: preparation for the Struggle . . . and finally a man for the contradictions of a decision.

—Violence is—cool—even if the hero wins in the end it's also by violence—all this comes to our children on TV. We allow them to see hours of it— Peter's head is jerking, his eyes squeezed, then wide. —What happened last year not in a school—a university? Right, not on TV, but d'you think those boys haven't followed that shit, what's to be done with the big brothers at schools whose filthy kind of initiation has been got away with—that's manpower all right? They followed . . .—

—Subconsciously.— Marc supplies for Peter.

—*Eish*, I wouldn't know how to explain it, perhaps someone else . . . ? Something in the . . . what we breathe—

It's Blessing, who listens more than she speaks. —We haven't asked our boys. What they want us to do about—school. How they feel.—

It is not easy to find the right time, the place in a day to bring the subject up with Gary Elias. His subject. She's threading new laces in one of his football boots while he is threading the other, and naturally, without a choice, she finds herself asking —What's it like at school now. Have the teachers changed, are they more strict with everyone . . . did you know, I mean . . . any of those boys.—

—Oh they're matric, not in class with Njabulo and me, but Raymond, he's one of them, he's our top goalie, first team.—

—Were you very surprised he'd do—things like that. Does it make you . . . Njabulo and your other friends unhappy. In school. So awful such a thing happened.—

—Headmaster had us in the big hall—you know, I told you and Dad that day. There was Father Connolly from the Catholic's church and Reverend Nkomo our school pastor, they were praying and now every morning at prayers those boys are there, we look at them— He breathes slowly on his hands deftly looping long laces.

Quickly lifts his head. He's smiling directly at his mother to comfort her. —They're mad.— Vociferous scornful dismissal.

It must be said although she has the confident answer already. —Gary, you don't think, you wouldn't rather be at another school.— If nothing else (he's dealt with shock, disgust by declaring the perpetrators freaks) is he not afraid that as he advances to become a senior, the age at which such 'madness' takes place, he could be a victim.

Or—how could she ever have thought—a ritualised 'man' subjecting others to torture.

The freedom comrades fought for.

—Our boy is strong.— She's telling how the necessary moment came about, of itself. —He's not afraid. And not to worry. He'll never become a bully. He won't take on that 'madness' and he doesn't want to run away to another school, I could see he already knows what happened is something, the sort of thing that is going to come up anywhere. As you grow, make your life.—

Even in Australia. He does not feel bypassed as a father; she has opened the way for him. —It wouldn't come up at Aristotle. Ask Sindi; she'd freak out, as she'd say, even at the idea.—

It lies between them where their bodies and shoulders touch in bed at night, their hands encounter, settling for sleep. A conformation brought from clandestinity of Glengrove to that of the Suburb and wherever they may go. —Suppose it doesn't make sense anyway—move school when there's only the rest of this year here.—

He's the one who took the initiative, if the process has been, is being followed by them together. —I just wish I could have taken up a post now. Bad luck it was too late for this year's academic entry, all that paperwork, emails dragged on so long.—

—We're stupid to think of it, crazy.—

Take him out of one school? Put him somewhere else? New surroundings, new teachers, new kids—and he and Sindi are going to have to deal with all that, new country, people don't even speak—no, what is it, yes, don't pronounce English like we do— And she breaks into a little snort invading the clandestinity of the darkness.

W e're going to hear Terror.— One leg then the other, shaking off the shine of drops as she gets out of the bath. It's a statement.

He's shaving. —Yes.—

And it is not a simple agreement, it's a consent. She will not question, for either, the right to be at gatherings at which declarations will be made for the present and future of the country. The question which Isa's moment of blank regard had realised in him at the ANC meeting.

Neither the Andersons nor the Mkizes would be asked if they would be coming to hear the Congress of The People gathering.

There are some comrade faces they know in the crowd neither as tight-packed nor palpably at one with each other as at the ANC parent-party electioneering. In the courage to break with the political fortress of the shared Struggle, defiantly exuberant voices exchanged, there is the unaccustomed shrill timbre of defection, inevitable in human self-consciousness no matter how convinced of the political validity brought about by the parent Party's own betrayals of its battle-avowed politics. There are whites present; a few prominent ones, also defected from other parties? Prospective or already COPE committed? And maybe relics who regard themselves as not before having found a political home which might be their own: roughly awakened to the push and shove of the country's situation, a never-before. Perhaps you can't now be apolitical, that old solar topee of colonialism?

Lekota spoke with the individualities of his personality— the Terror of the football field—and the standard raised fist of rhetoric dedicated to victory, but smiling intelligence rather than berating, and he neither danced, pranced nor produced an armed theme song, while leading the cry and response that belongs to all who defied apartheid, his AMANDLA! bringing AWETHU from a following avowing themselves to him. The Reverend whoever-he-is, standing by; he has his turn invoking Christian values in COPE under the restlessness of the gathering's preoccupation with Lekota.

Sling-shot questions from the people around him and her, praise and disagreement dart to the platform, some verbal litter without hitting target, a few respectfully join the Reverend's invocation of God as a member of the new party; the pertinent ones find Lekota ready for them.

—It's true COPE says blacks shouldn't get the jobs instead of whites?— The man is referring to the party statement that race as the determinant in the policy of Black Economic Empowerment would produce only a small black elite.

Lekota rallied to the opportunity. —I called for Affirmative Action to be scrapped because it doesn't provide the real answer for us, our own people. The big one. Giving a man or woman the post because their hands are black like mine doesn't make our economy equal and opened to all, if that man or woman has been historically deprived of acquiring the skills you need to do the job, to fill the post with the special knowledge it demands, and the young are still not getting these skills and knowledge to take up what is theirs . . . You won't improve the living standard of the workers and the poor until equality in our education standards inevitably makes Affirmative Action out of date, into the waste-paper bag, simply by the number of qualified blacks who'll be able to fill the senior positions. Our country needs everyone, never mind the skin. That's the issue. That's justice.—

Through the ears the mind takes immediately some statements more tellingly than others. With the closing

AMANDLA! rising from the crowd to the platform the leaders' chorus response AWETHU, Lekota came down and mingled, arms about people he knew and greetings to their presence for others made brothers and sisters by hearing him in his new political identity. On the way out through groups, ignoring, in their eagerness to be heard, the obligation to clear the exit, he may or may not have recognised Jabu—she had once been in the background of a legal team he was consulting. Anyway, he turned a moment, to ensure he had seen her, remembered (perhaps he too has Madiba's faculty of face-recall among crowds, over years).

She took up her part in the moment. —When I was a young girl that book you wrote in prison . . . *Letters To My Daughter*, it had so much in it for me—what made me.— Of course (it is in his eyes) this is a recognition beyond that of the identity of himself he had just been creating up on the platform—but his arm was tugged by a handsome youth with black spaghetti dreadlocks. —Why dinnen you say wha' about Zuma's corruption?— And before he could respond (to the eagerness of those who'd heard the challenge) he was pulled the other way by somebody else.

There's something of a moral assertion, responsibility, that the decision to leave the country doesn't mean you don't go to hear what the contesting parties' hypotheses are if they succeed in coming to power; or in holding onto it. It's not become an abstraction. What you hear, there, confirms—or contests, within that decision. Without changing it. Perhaps it will be contested within, for ever, without denying its validity. That's the reality in all decisions. No reason to make a subterfuge out of going to hear Zuma or Terror.

—Jabu and I've been to the COPE election meeting. Last week. You weren't curious? Seems the—other—parties won't even have the chance to get hands on power unless they make alliances which contradict their individual aims, Where-They-Come-From; the ANC's the only one with a sofa-size throne more or less able to contain nationalism, communism, traditional leadership—so far.—

He knows Lesego will be with the ANC, split or not.

He and Lesego are having their usual Friday lunch together in what used to be known as Chinatown (the Chinese, who had been segregated, but closer to whites on the colour scale, have moved upmarket in freedom) although now it is a street of Indian traders whose shops are closed and takeaway curry and Bunny Chow stalls left unattended during noon prayers at a nearby mosque. There's one Chinese restaurant left. Lesego speaks of Lekota as of one dead—well, 'passed on', the euphemism generally used is perhaps apposite in the different, political sense, for Lekota. —What'd Terror have to say for himself. I just supposed I'd read it all . . . Lots of people turn up?—

—Full. But of course he's not the one-man-band of Zuma.— Spring rolls arrived and mouths were occupied.

—Were there any of ours there, heckling from the youth group?—

An appreciative swallow of the bite dipped in sweet sauce. —Not that we saw. Someone did ask the big question and Terror answered well, or rather turned round on itself to his own advantage.—

—Oh he's cool. That he is.—

Lesego started his won ton soup, tasting a spoonful, pausing to add drips of soya sauce, applying himself again, while he heard the account of Lekota's response to the haltingly posed question about the call to abandon Affirmative Action. Between spoonfuls, he once waved the spoon licked clean, go on go on. —So you and Jabu were there. Heard it from him.— And as the colleague who had reported, turned to his soup,

Lesego above his emptied bowl was beginning gestures not concluded . . . opening lifted hands, fingers running a scale, drawing a long breath through a scenting nose.

He was silent, as if he were the one now occupied with the soup. When he saw the last mouthful captured and he was sure of attention, he leant a little across the table and then drew back. —That'll be one of the nails in the coffin. You'll see. He's attacked head-on by Cosatu. The new baby'll be buried before it gets to squawk in parliament. I've got hold of that booklet the unions've put out, they're saying COPE could cause great damage to the workers if it came in to power. It'd roll back the gains the unions and the poor have made since '94, even if it drums up a small number of votes, gets a few seats in parliament. It would put brakes on policies to create jobs, cut poverty, accuses Lekota and his deputy Shilowa—big businessman, they're cosying up—they've left the ruling party 'to pursue an agenda of the capitalist class, international capital and its local allies'! The booklet's to set the record straight, my man, so voters won't be cheated by COPE. Lekota's handing on a plate ammunition against himself, scrapping our genuine African herb medicine, Affirmative Action, that national *muti*. Man, it's heresy to list our open sores for which it's no use.—

There on the floor. Lesego must have slid the booklet under the door of his room while he went to the laboratory for a class after their lunch. Was it a sign, some sort of hesitant encouragement taken from the fact that Steve and Jabu went to hear the election speeches of the Party, congenital for them in the Struggle whatever's become of it now, and then followed the electioneering of its break-away—this seen to mean the comrades were not going; anywhere. Except where the country was going in this election. Otherwise what was the point of sitting among people whose lives were being ordained.

Her legal qualifications are insufficient for Australia: part of the information going back and forth on many aspects, requirements for visa application—permanent visa, working visa, probably if you just want to go and visit the Opera House with its wing like a bird (picture in all brochures) ready to take off over Sydney harbour, attend the Adelaide Festival, fish on the Barrier Reef, you can get the tourist one without more collateral than ID, proof of funds, and medical certificate you don't carry any communicable disease, what's it now—swine flu? Of course the Australians are justified (the professional qualifications), no one wants shysters practising law who aren't conversant with and observant of the legal system of the country. And she's informed also that this may differ in some aspects from province to province. It looks as if it's going to be Melbourne, but that is not settled. *Migrate@2OZ.co.za* had informed her she would have to complete additional legal subjects by correspondence from Australia through application to an 'Additions' Board. This study material is coming efficiently through email to the Suburb but she takes a batch from time to time to the Legal Agency's library to make clear to herself the precise difference between clauses in the South African Constitution under which she is living and their counterparts—in that other country.

His academic qualifications: if the post is confirmed, he will qualify for a permanent residential visa and she and the children would emigrate with him. She could take the new subjects while already resident as his appendage.

They were told the immigration process takes about a year. Which fits in with the academic year, in Australia, just as in his university in South Africa, opening in January and running through November. Too late, for comments as he's had to accept, for this; election year. There's no haste.

She takes the material and her notes onto the terrace table at weekends and applies herself to what has no application to the life around her that catches her attention every now and then—Sindiswa taking the fashion and events pages from her father as reading weekend newspapers he discards these: the teeth-bared acolytes in the company of someone who must be famous. Gary Elias squatting on the grass with a bottle of Coke, swallows turn-about with a new friend, son of a KwaZulu countryman Wethu had found, attendant at the local fuel station.

He felt a touch ill at ease that she his lawyer would have to go back to school, while his qualifications as an industrial chemist and academic were approved. But looking at her on the terrace he would see that her application was absorbed concentration; Baba had given her a love of learning for its own sake, even if for an object like that of her present, as people who exercise regularly do so out of instinct of their bodies even if not committed at that time to some sports contest. She makes synthesis of the concept of law deriving from colonisation, and traditional authority—the cultural image of that crown of hair majestically mounted, thread-woven locks falling to her shoulders, like some ancestral memory. Come back, Africa.

The documents are loose on the passenger seat so driving home she can glance at marked clauses while held at traffic lights.

At the next she's at the back of a pile-up of vehicles having to wait edged close as each change to green allows only a portion to proceed—there's a strike today, this time municipal workers, and their procession has left hazards of rubbish spewed from their trucks blocking the parallel street. Nothing to be done, but for once *something*—impatience is occupied, she can take hands off the wheel and turn the pages of her study material to verify margin notes made when finding comparisons she sought in tomes at the Centre's library. A touch control sends her windows down for the breeze sluggish with bad breath of exhaust fumes, it brings cool, anyway—but something else, laboured breathing and—a sight, summons:

The open mouth.

The gaping down which the first finger of a hand is pointing to the wall of the throat that's where food is taken in. On the city streets there are often waylayers rubbing circles at their stomachs to indicate hunger, some it's obvious have found drink at least. This, this, is a bony articulated forefinger repeatedly stabbing through the empty mouth to the empty passageway. The owner is nothing behind jaws that have distorted all features; no face. This giving-of-the-finger comes to her as the final version of the insult of that gesture used, in the air, to end quarrels. She groans at the uselessness of the response: pulling her bag from under the emigration study papers and fumbling at the zip for the pouch of coins—and at once there are blaring horns, aggressive, cars ahead are moving, the return of the green light is at last for them, the bus behind her has the driver throwing up his elbows, the spaceman helmet of a motorcyclist is cursing her to fucking move, move—her foot falls on the accelerator, the mouth falls away from the window, somehow that shadow relic of what they in their vehicles all are, one flesh, must be slipping away between them, their onrush. If he's been hit everyone would stall again. Dead is one thing, barely alive, that's another. What could she have offered if the small change pouch had opened in time. The finger black, like hers. As she drives home to what is her own solution brought

about by Baba getting her a white education, her marrying into Them—she finds herself expressing within what
she hasn't, even in detention cell: hatred of whites. Election
posters on street lamp poles passing. Terror, Dandala, Zuma
Zuma Zuma. What will they do to wipe out, *make good* is
the term, what whites did and blacks must change, pointed
down the open mouth.

A private incident lost in the statistics. At the church pool
on Sunday where life goes on, talk of the power blackouts the
past week, the hell someone's having at the dentist's, Marc's
news of his new play may be going into production with a cast
from the rural villages, amazing talent, why do those ignorant
Yankee directors bring black Americans to play Africans in
their films. Peter asking in trust of comrades' shared experience
—Forty thousand jobs going to be lost. Is that *all* my brothers? Oh shame. That's nothing. Fourteen thousand more on
the line, in the mines, 'it's the global downturn in demand for
minerals'. Minerals are what we've got.—

—So the government says unemployment's down shade less
than twenty-two per cent—but more than thirteen million
are out of work—

—Never mind, you know this new idea of whether or not
you're employed? Anyone who hasn't found a job in four
weeks, you're officially unemployed. There you are, too broke
to take a bus to look for work any more, you sit selling a
couple of cigarettes outside the supermarket. Man! *Eish!*—

Everyone has their own focus in the profusion of what's being
uncovered beneath daily life—that thin layer—by coming
elections of those who'll take power to rule over that life.

—What's happening in the Alliance?— The lawyer has the
calm to raise.

—Cosatu going to force the ANC into a policy pact, no
more cosy mating, mixed economy—

—What else can they go for? They know there wouldn't be any chance in a breakaway—not à la COPE, but a big one—standing as a worker party for election maybe joined by little brother, the communists. They're counting on Zuma, man of the people to steer left for what the Alliance hasn't delivered so far.—

Jake concludes for others what they've left out. His laugh-bark. —The man of the people who's been sitting with frightened big industry and business telling them there'll be no policy changes? That means it's on hold: state ownership of their mines. If they know what's good for them, they'll go along with The People and vote ANC, that's *him*.—

—But what can The People think—whose side is their Zuma on, colonialist-capitalist or worker— He hears himself. Perhaps both; that may come out when/if the arms deal corruption trial ever does.

Read about it in Melbourne.

Isa presses her hands together between jean-covered knees. —Look, he can't shut that mouth, Zuma needs the support of the youth group, they might easily turn to Cosatu, why not? What are their prospects, why not just more marches with strikers, they're enough to choose from, burning tyres on the road, yelling for municipal-speak 'service delivery' for shit buckets to be emptied water taps to run.—

She doesn't happen to be the comrade to remark on it —There was one this week, right in town, I don't know what union made the chaos there.—

—*I'll kill for Zuma*, the ANC should outlaw Malema—call him Baby Face but he's no innocent.— Like the cry of a passing bird over the pool a voice from one of the Dolphins as he takes a dive; the Sunday morning swimming party has fallen away, as attendance at the Gereformeerde service did with the transformation of the church into a commune free of cages, political and gender, the Suburb drifts round there for discussion, not the pool. This young man defies the necessity: plunges enjoyment.

Jake is senior not alone in age but analysis, he's telling —Yes, we need the youth, even the brat—if Mandela and Sisulu hadn't come along and broken with Luthuli's knocking on the back door, we wouldn't have had *Umkhonto*, yes? But that youth group didn't waste energy bad-mouthing, ridiculing opponents, the tactics of Julius Malema. If they felt anti-white, and Gareth's right, why shouldn't any black after the Boers the British and all the other rag-tag-and-bobtail from across the sea—I'm myself descended from them, ay— stole the country. The Fifties young got down to the business of *taking back*—taking power.—

A lawyer's a professional listener; she comes with what perhaps has not been caught by others in flash back and forth. —Zuma's glad to have someone ready to kill for him to be President. He'd better look out for Julius Malema planning to take over from him, not too far off, one of these days.—

Blessing is offering some small flag—seems out of character. —When he's President, I mean—Zuma won't be fighting to get up there, any more. Zuma may be good for us.— What is she saying: everyone condemning bad-mouthing is also bad-mouthing, in advance, the Brother who is going to be only the third Freedom President? Impulse or fairness? More likely she has a Baba, distant authority; troubling to discard.

They are reading aloud to one another from a batch of
school prospectuses which have come with a friendly
letter for parental concern from a civic educational organisation he found a way to contact. Over There. He rests the
affirmative length of a hand on spread pages. —This's the one
for him.—

—For her.—It's co-educational.—

—Yes yes—but for *him* now's the time—that's the chance
going to a new country, everything will be different. When
you're that age you're adaptable— (She'd forgotten she'd been
sent off alone to Swaziland) —we'll all be together.—

—He doesn't like being at school with girls.—

Remember Aristotle. Another place another time. —Give
him a year, a year older and he'll be chasing curves.— They're
laughing. —That's the advantage he doesn't know about
yet.—

Shouldn't he be called from the garden and fruit-box wicket,
he and Njabulo are teaching Wethu's protégé to play cricket,
the game popular at their school where bats are also weapons
for another kind of initiation, shouldn't their boy have a say.
These are parents who respect children's rights, don't they, not
only at the protection level of the Constitution familiar to her
as ABC. —What does he think . . . considering—

The new life to be served upon him and his sister.

His mother—Jabu pronounces authority —We decide.
We'll apply for him at that co-educational. Him and Sindi.—
The tone final, not in manner of judgment handed down in
court; something parentally fundamental making itself heard
to her.

—We'll think about it some more—over this weekend.—
It's Easter interregnum anyway, when Gary is expected to be
brought for the holiday weekend with Baba in KwaZulu.

Yet then—she's gathered the prospectuses now, cover on
cover of impressive school buildings laid out in gardens, the
kangaroo emblem as the lion is in Africa; she looks up not at
him; no. —I don't want to go.— As if speaking to herself.
—Will you go. Mama told me on the phone yesterday, there's
going to be a huge gathering—election—he's organised, he'll
introduce the speakers, his choir from the church, freedom
songs she says, if Msholozi doesn't come himself it'll be one of
his closest. Can you take Gary.—

The moment outside the Glengrove Place door. But no threshold to carry the bride over. She asks him, alone to take the boy to
spend the usual promised weekend there, her home KwaZulu.

I don't want to go.

Her Baba. The consequence: meaning this—it can't be
questioned, dissuaded—what an intrusion he feels that would
be of the commitment of love, the confidences kept, you for
me, I for you, in areas I don't, others don't, have access to. The
mystery of sexual intimacy, that's called upon, unknown.

All he could ask in response to their need, the specific need
of Jabu in her torn bonds with her father was take to her what
practical reason could be the lie he must produce. But he has
it: she is involved in a difficult case, cannot miss the sessions
of preparation required of her by her senior advocates—what
else, the Elder of the church, headmaster of the boys' school is
one who strictly observes the pre-eminence of duty.

Sindi of course had other plans anyway. Wethu has also cried
off. She has become so popular in the women's league of the
city church she chose that they insist they need her with them
for the rising from the dead of their saviour.

There's the poster he was told by Jabu she saw after she attended the rape trial. It was honouring the not guilty judgment in celebration then, still does; many more posters are tacked up now, including an example of one of Msholozi's marriages, picturing him and whatever wife in full guise of flesh and leopard skin.

Even without the daughter of the village who had given legitimacy to the presence of the white man in the extended family by marrying him, he was familiarly welcomed with accompanying grandson of their churchman, schoolmaster. Elias Siphiwe Gumede observed male protocol, greeting him before allowing the interrogation of questioning eyes: was his daughter back gathering something from the car, women always at that sort of arrival fuss—and here is the boy, tall enough, this holiday come home, to put his arms round his Babamkhulu in joyous cityman style, why not, that the other grandsons around would not dare. The high greetings were in their language; standing smiling by, he caught the assurances not questions coming from the grandfather that the boy was happy, happy to be back, heh, and the boy's gush of names, how's Sibiso, is Xamana here? —Where is your mother, already with the women?—

His Zulu could pick that up. And he began in isiZulu but had to resort to English. —Babawami, Jabulile sends a special message to you (quiet a moment, Gary!) she asks me to tell you, explain for her, she couldn't come home for Easter although she very much wants to be here with you and Mama—there's a terribly important case coming on and she has to be with the advocates the whole weekend, meetings preparing for it, no way out of this, she instructed me—she apologises, she said, but Baba he'll understand.—

Not home for Easter, sorry sorry (she would have used that bowed-head jingle before him as a little girl); these are the inspiration come to him in a lie.

—What trial is this? Did you bring papers?—

No lie stands; it has to lead to others. But necessity makes this glib. —Too bad, it hasn't come to court yet so there's nothing in the papers, she would have given me these for you . . . there wasn't any document she could, unfortunate . . . she says—

And the next lie, to offset any mood, absence darkening over the occasion. —At least I've brought Gary Elias for you, that's what she absolutely insisted, and you know what Jabu is when she wants you to do something!—

—You are always welcome here.— Out of a phrase book. As if granted, between Jabulile's two men, that without her he doesn't count.

Elias Siphiwe Gumede is already disciplined to the pre-eminence of what this weekend is: not the Easter devotional celebration of Jesus rising from the grave to which each year the daughter was respectful for her father's sake even if for her the rising was that of the Struggle from the grave of apartheid; this is the Easter when her father will be the man who has brought home more than an election meeting: a gathering for the congregation of Jacob Gedleyihlekisa Zuma.

There is no soccer game for Gary Elias and team of extended family boys. The open land that was the field is an amphitheatre of planks being totteringly tiered by the usual home-boys back from the coal mine and the cities' factories (it's still the Whites and Indians who own them) along with old men back in their birthplace to die, and the schoolboys for whom this is another game. —It's all us guys!— Gary Elias is off to join them; the dignitary whose namesake he is gives the stern flourish of a permissive order —*Hamba ushone.*—

Good Friday is not one on which the usual weekend drinking in city bars, shebeens happens; here the Elder might come out of his house and wither with authority of disapproval any groups of men squatting round liquor which the daughter's man joins whenever she brings him to her home. But one of the group that always welcomes him hears he's arrived and sends a child to beckon—there's a private Friday, just displaced to someone's mud-insulated house that's more or less out of sight of Baba's range.

Msholozi, in what would have been the persona of his clan name, did not come, either, to honour Elias Siphiwe Gumede, his influential campaign organiser in the village and surrounding communities, including shack dwellers from around the coal mine. The substitute wore no leopard skin (perhaps he was not at that level of traditional authority) but was dressed in the well-tailored dark suit, tie and fashionable pointed-toe shoes as if already a cabinet minister, anticipating Zuma's government. He spoke with impressive cadence bringing out all the beauty of Jabu's mother tongue, that she sometimes said was becoming lost in the adoption of it to pop slang, *tsotsi* talk, American and international substitutions for isiZulu's own forms of expression—she caught herself out in the practice she accused.

This isiZulu ringing over the football field-cum-stadium with pauses as if to take breath, but actually skilfully handing over to calls, chanting, cheers, was clear enough to get the gist with his limited grasp of the language his son had turned to so effortlessly the moment he stepped onto his mother's home place. What was caught in the full spate of words was the same litany of Zuma's speeches, as expected; who would presume, in the entourage of the man to deviate from what was so successful even without the rousing of dance and battle song 'Awuleth' umshini wami'. The home brew downed in secrecy with the home-boys perhaps released a facility to understand some of this; perhaps to feel not rejected; a response—what would Jabu think of that!

Gary Elias as usual had to be called, sought out again and again when it was the day and time to leave this home for the other. He has over visits gathered to himself a rather special place among the boys, they clung and pushed about him, playful punches and trippings-up as he finally appeared at the car, and an always unfinished teasing exchange continued through the window as he was driven away. A flushed face twitching animation, joyful sweaty presence beside the father. His last yell, —*Ngiyokubona ngontulikazi—Nagokhisimazi! Khisimazi! Shu!* See you in July! . . . And Christmas, Christmas! *EISH!*—

In July; yes. But Christmas. If the Melbourne post was confirmed, just a few minor details still, but the certainty is there, the departure would be latest November—it was expected at the other end that the immigrant family would come with the provision of weeks to get accustomed to the way of life, settle in, before the university and whatever schools the children were entering began the year in January. A New Year.

While the formal preparations are being followed in accordance with a process by the parents, in the jostling public presence of election time in a free country, normal life goes on for children; suppose to Gary Elias and even Sindi . . . Australia is an abstract (as 'when you grow up') with no effect on the day-to-day of school and weekend pleasures. They haven't known loss. It'd be difficult for them to feel, while the parting is so protracted, what it will be to leave behind bosom friends and buddies.

What about the house. Jake, who found it for them, has asked, as if it were a detail forgotten in the total decision made, with all its implications comrades cannot intrude upon.

—Yes. Of course sell it—for occupation at the end of this year. But don't agents always want immediate sales?—

—Or let it. For then.— Jake has the alternative. Does he refuse to believe the departure is lifetime, no return. Or has he a friend ready in mind, wanting to rent. Bringing up the subject, is it a sign of end of sensitivity in a friendship, Jake is not affected by the departure; or is it an indirect reproach. Australia.

When he speaks of Jake's suggestion to Jabu it becomes referent to something else; the home of their daughter and son—for themselves Glengrove Place was home, the first, the original possible for them. They ought to consider the meaning for Sindi and Gary of this one; ready them more considerably for change, not explicitly, something looming, but as preparation making Australia part of life in the present.

Again the matter of the right time—not to make it heavy. Favourite food is always the adults' resort to counting on a good mood shared, it maybe comes from that between the woman and the infant when it is sucking at her breast. He and Gary Elias went to a takeaway to bring pizzas, each for everyone's individual taste, including one to put aside for Wethu who was out with her church women somewhere.

The mother has her courtroom confidence. —We've found what we think is the school for you, I'll show you the photographs, curriculum and so on, subjects extramural—to choose along with the usual—drama, music, there's even a special communications high-tech group in the science department, space exploration, it's called astrophysics, stars and planets, and of course all sports, there's a fine gym near the swimming pool.—

But no. Gary Elias is quick. —A school for me?—

The father's turn. —For both. You and Sindi.—

He can't believe it. —A boys' school for me.—

Sindi's private smile of approval to her mother, for the moment they look alike although Sindi is not as beautiful, only a man (himself) would recognise that the DNA mixture hasn't worked so well aesthetically, this time, although it so often does. The boy is the beauty.

—A co-ed, like Aristotle.— Her mother and father know she won't agree to be separated by gender, that's old stuff in education, her father doesn't teach in a single-sex university.

There has to be male response to a male. —I have to enter you for next year—now. But when we are there, November most probably, we'll go to the school. And you'll see for yourself. I've had the best reports about it from someone who'll be my colleague at the university, he's got two sons at the school—and he has no daughter, so—

He'll have to talk to the boy alone, just the two of them over the coming months; he's the educationist yes but Jabu is the one who affirms their comrade-and-lover conviction that there's an end to all nature of segregation. Under whatever rubric. Apartheid. It's over.

—And you, Sindi—

—My friends think I'm so lucky, have the chance. Travel to new places . . . I mean you know— Spoken as might a woman complimented on her enviable shapeliness.

What he was really searching is how she accepts in the other emotional life-upheaval of adolescence, itself departure from the familiarities of childhood—Australia. They have given her books, she's been a reader since she learned to recognise words at the age of six, journals of the glories of the country supplied by seminar organisers.

What is the process of acceptance. The 'envious' remark of Sindi's schoolfriends was really of the excitement of holidays; not deportation. Gary calling from the car in KwaZulu, Christmas, Christmas—the summer holiday he'd be back.

*　　*　　*

The concept of belonging is a pile-up junction of private footpaths and public freeways in a month before there's going to be an election and the country (can you honestly call yourselves a nation only fifteen years after you've been centuries divided by cleaver, black and white) will get new governing parentage. Jacob Zuma, electioneering, says the ANC is a 'child of the church'. The support of Christian leadership is in line with the commitment made when the Party was formed: three founding presidents were priests. Two thousand churchgoers pray hand in hand with him.

The church leaders have said they will encourage their members to ensure an ANC victory at the polls, and also undertake to fight against moral decay. On the same page of the newspaper she has taken up—not in the mood to force themselves to turn over the rejection by the boy—there is the report that the National Prosecuting Authority is still considering whether or not to drop sixteen graft, fraud and racketeering charges against Jacob Zuma.

—I can't make sense, who's in opposition to whom, if the NPA is really after Zuma, or putting on a front for justice. Keep refusing to say whether they'll ever explain the hold-up of the trial.—

His private lawyer has her knowing head before him. —A few days ago a brother of Shabir Shaik told university students about the possible scrapping of Zuma's charges. That's the kind of inside information the Shaik family would have. What happens to Zuma also happens to Shaik, he's on 'terminal illness' parole from serving his fifteen-year sentence for corruption and fraud but if Zuma comes to trial Zuma's financial adviser will be arraigned somewhere along.—

She has ready every legal convolution in the continuing saga, Australians are lucky acquiring this astute mind from South Africa. Another byway, criss-crossing: there has been given a bit of press space even while electioneering commands the pages—an announcement. Australia slashes immigration to protect its workforce. No more foreign bricklayers, plumbers, carpenters, hairdressers and cooks will be accepted. Academics in science and their partners in the legal profession who meet the local qualifications are not on the list disfavoured due to world recession. He has made certain anyway that he and his family—every requirement in place, only the specific date of arrival to be settled—are not affected.

Except by the presence of rising unemployment around the enclave of a university and whatever residential suburb are part of what's to be left behind. The finger pointed down the empty gullet, surely she won't have that, pointing at her over there.

The bishop from the Methodist Church has applied for defence against a group of shopkeepers taking the church and city to court in demand of enforcement of by-laws, the removal of toilets set up along the street. The church is inundated with something like four thousand more refugee arrivals in the city since a refugee camp just this side of the Zimbabwe border has been closed. When this was being discussed, who from the Justice Centre should go to the street and church for first-hand evidence of the situation —I know it. I've been there, months ago.—

Since, it has become normal life of the city while the political parties make speeches and the Suburb argues about the hidden agendas for power and the rifts between party leadership. She'd sat with Steve and the Mkizes, Andersons, attending round TV a COPE rally where Terror Lekota and the good Reverend Dandala again appeared electioneering together. This time footage showing each had prepared separately with a walk-about among the people and prayer at different churches.

Jake. —God puts his money on nobody.—

The Terror he and she were familiar with was saying
—Reverend Dandala and I are on the same track.— People
like Dandala in the South African Council of Churches cared
for his family when he was imprisoned on Robben Island. He
vociferously denies the public appearance with the Reverend
alongside has anything to do with—(camera on crowd in
cock-crow debating among themselves).

—What was that, didn't get it— Isa's appeal.

Steve and Peter crossed-voicing: —Mbeki, Mbeki, Dandala
supposed to be linked with our ex-President— —Mbeki's
maybe muscling into COPE against Zuma—

The track returned to, Terror and Dandala embrace. Holding
hands, they dance together, now Zuma's not the only one to do
the traditional African high-kick for the voters' pleasure and
reassurance: one of them.

There's a pair of wide pyjama pants hung over the branch of one of the shrubs that once were planted to dignify the street outside the magistrates' court. The pants shelter from the sun a child asleep. She can't see a face, it will be one of the faces of those playing in the gutters or hanging from a woman's hand; the soles of the feet at drawn-up legs are not black but worn grey with the friction of paving and roads. All is just as it was, only twice as much so. A continuity which overturns what this word generally means, the ultimate of disconnection: chaos. There's no longer space for the ingenious normalcy of an old man rolling cigarettes out of bits of newspaper round tobacco scavenged from cigarette butts, the woman dividing railway lines through hair, attaching false locks on heads. The defiant culture of poverty. Culture's the term she's come to use, like everyone else, for an activity that's seen as an ethnic response—the politicians dancing—and it is missing around her walkabout, this time. These people— brothers and sisters—now too destitute even to make a culture out of nothing; or they're others come, haven't been in this situation, at this destination of the Methodist Church long enough yet to do more than overrun the 'culture' established there to the disgust of the city. Well what do I know. I'm not a refugee 'problem' in somebody else's country. I'm here a lawyer following an advocate's instruction to investigate a case—scene of crime, Jake said when she told the comrades that was what she was going to be doing. Jake always ready with a wry take. You can count on him.

One of the Suburb comrades who's member of the Communist Party—not much volume of electioneering from their small ranks but at least a few of them in government, veterans of the Struggle and likely to be in a continuing government alliance—the comrade's theme is that race, pigment, are going to be replaced post-Struggle by class struggle evidencing itself already with the new rich, the blacks, including, don't ignore, the youth leader Malema in designer outfits, never mind the shares it's said he has in some big engineering industry.

A member of the class of the legal profession in her home country; not like those Brothers and Sisters whose close bodies her own is gently pushing past through the church doors. Not now. The present. But the present doesn't last—have tenure, the legal vocabulary comes to her although Baba, before, made sure she would have a constantly expanding contemporary one for her future—even books in detention. Some of these placeless people blacks like herself are educated, with professional skills; on the wrong side of the political palaces. Baba's Zuma, what would follow Zuma's time, tenure, would the Youth ready to kill for him now, is it not on the condition he shall make way for them—euphemism for overthrow, discard him and take the country for themselves. Suburb soapbox talk: —Luthuli had to make way for the young, didn't he? Mandela, Tambo, Sisulu breaking down the doors the old man was knocking at.—

—They weren't Julius Malema ready to kill in time of freedom.—

Refugee Brothers and Sisters lying on the wrong side of political palace walls of Idi Amin, Mugabe, Malema. Sindiswa and Gary Elias on some Methodist Church pavement. But no neighbouring country available as refuge, refugees from those themselves seeking a pavement to sleep on.

Australia.

She is not the eagerly confiding, open young one, his girl in the Swaziland discovery of sexuality as a natural part of political discovery: you were not white, she black in the risk of prison, torture threat to both on your short-lived existence that was set fighting to end existing categories of power, custom, what-have-you and create in their country a human one out of all the divisions bedevilling the hideous past. Working with law, its sane obstinacy defending justice within the new varieties of injustice, she has come to act as determinedly.

Ah . . . *I don't want to go*—no echo there also in the decision of their future? They don't need even to suppress the subject, there's no distance between them: she's there for him, for departure; the leaving. They're in it together. In their bathroom, taken off the bubble of her shower cap, with the other hand she's lifted the stiff tumbled locks released, they are dancing wildly pointing the hair about her head. —Medea!— He's amused. But the reference is unlikely to have visual meaning for Jabu, just as in Zulu image or metaphor often her reference has no meaning—match—for him. In Australia at least however they'll both not have references to the local foreign images, metaphors. That in common.

But if references not known between them at home are sign of the intimately irreconcilable, coming from their different 'cultures', aren't they, haven't they been from the beginning the fascination of what's called the Other!

The aspects of the election are divergent for the different concerns of groups each in its familiar enclosure: coffee-room focus is that in its last weeks before dissolution of parliament the government has made a farewell announcement. The Ministry of Education is to be split into two departments: 'Primary', for schools, and for universities and technical institutions, 'Tertiary'—avoiding the old-style category 'Higher Education' with its suggestion of class distinction. Probably not coincidental that in this last month before the Day of the Vote the Education Minister visited the university to inspect improvements in progress. A bank has funded a building which will provide new lecture halls, a student centre and tutorial rooms. —He doesn't know how the guys and the gals are going to miss the necessity to squeeze up close.— It's old Professor Miller from Maths who enjoys showing he's cool. A new appointee in the History department, Hafferjee, a thin gold earring winking in approval. —More Internet connections for students—

—Facebook, Twitter—enough enough!—what they need is somewhere to live, what about shortage of beds and bathrooms.— Lesego in Nelson Mandela dashiki turns to Professor Neilson in his form of academic dress, impeccable suit-and-tie, everyone has a constitutional right to traditional attire, with official uncertainty about veiled Muslim girls in school. —Three-ninety-nine million the university's asked for from 'Tertiary'. The man won't be in his ministry after April twenty-two, he won't be there to see we do get it.—

Overture to that day of election is deafening against everything else even if he reminds himself he will not meet what comes after. The Secretary General of the Party—His and Jabu's, the Mkizes'—says of the brain drain, professionals follow opportunities as a result of the country being part of the integrated global economy.

Nothing to do with the prospect that the new President at the crest of fervour for the man of the people, will be a President with seventy-two charges of fraud and corruption against him?

She's uncovered that 20 per cent of the people living in the Methodist Church and the pavement dormitory are not refugees from Zimbabwe or any other country but are destitute South Africans, thrust finger down the open mouth.

Hasn't Zuma's corruption case caught the delay wind.

—There have been calls for a review of the Constitutional Court decisions.— Lifting not his machine-gun song but the weapon of Christian values he accuses the judges of 'behaving as if they were almost close to God'. And in the same cycle of this country the National Union of Metal Workers is calling for the nationalisation of a mining company owned by Struggle veteran Tokyo Sexwale and Patrick Patrice Motsepe; black, two of the wealthiest men in the country. Brothers betraying the egalitarian ideals of the ANC? South Africa—mixed economy—is still largely a capitalist society—if only one in which laws preventing the emergence of a black entrepreneurial class have been abolished.

A voice from under the bonnet. —You can't attack white fat cats without pointing at black as well. Double standard.— The friend of Peter Mkize joining the Suburb comrades to give advice about the faults of acceleration in Blessing's car, is one of those who are members both of the ANC and the SACP. —We won't exempt class betrayal by brothers profiting on capitalist enterprise.—

Peter can place him. No offence possible between them, no contradiction in the policy of the ANC alliance. —Who's arguing about that, we're equal now whether exploiting or exploited, isn't it, *aih*, sinning or sinned against, all got the vote. The workers have the same boss if he's black like us or white like Stevie.—

—Ja, we've heard it all—(whether he means: even down in the engine's belly)—*Eish* man, we know, tarara black capitalists generate new wealth the white capitalists tell us, how's it go, they make job opportunities, they have to pay taxes that increase money for social grants poor women get something to feed their kids—

Isa and Jabu coming out with coffee and a tray of mugs; Jabu is there with the figures. —Inequality, it's increased more than fourteen per cent, that's since two years after the first all-race election (as if prompted the horn blurts from inside the car's engine where Peter's friend must have touched a wrong part)—alarm bells, you see it in the service delivery protests. At the Justice Centre we have reports, political connections work in favour of prominent ANC members winning contracts for upgrading township water supply, electricity, over tenders of firms lower priced, better qualified. We've seen houses where the roof's blown off in the first storm after tenants moved in. People rewarded with tenders are making millions. There's the risk, street protests will lead to black class conflict, Zuma's going to have his hands full. You can forget about xenophobia.—

Always he finds himself curiously in the same relation to her as are other people while she is speaking from a professional perspective. Instead of that indefinable identity called wife. Other women are desirable, that's the basis of man-woman, but there's no woman other than she who could have been, could be the identity of all he has found in her. He's in recognition.

Jake —That's why the big man has to make sure the hands of support are well greased!—

Is it a jolt back to personal reality or a diversion . . . Gary Elias's school. Another 'incident'. One of the matric class who was involved in the initiation affair apparently not directly enough to be named then, has lined up senior boys on a grandstand for what he called 'haircut inspection'. He swore at a boy about his unacceptable haircut, kicked him in the chest, thrust fallen to the ground.

When he comes home from an after-hours meeting at the university she is with Gary Elias sitting close, on the terrace. Wethu is there; she groans a soft accompaniment while mother and son tell what happened.

—Must have been yesterday, we only knew today, the headmaster didn't call us to the hall he came to our class, every class, first we didn't have a clue what it was about.—

So their boy didn't see.

She explains —The football team had been taken to play in a match at another school.— Gary Elias has been spared violence, even the corrupting spectacle of it, not on TV.

—We won, six-three, easy.—

—Blessing called while she was driving the boys home from school today, the line kept breaking . . . I'd left the Centre, was here at the time she dropped Gary.—

They shared relief each can confirm unspoken, Gary is not frightened; in fact shows again sense of importance of one who is connected with the sensational at second-hand: he could have been in the school when it happened, it might have been experienced not only as he is conscious of being present at the battles of space monsters on television.

Julius Malema in the news channel switched on out of habit tonight. A clip from the twenty-ninth birthday party of the

ANC youth leader, who has said the youth are ready to take up arms and kill for Zuma, is with one of the successful businessmen and the premier of the province where the birthday boy was born.

Nice shot of political connection between rebellious youth and new capitalist. But doesn't say this to her, doesn't belong in their present moment.

He and Peter Mkize go together to the headmaster of the school next morning. Not along with the usual transport to school shared by Mkizes and Reeds; they agree it's better not to add to the impact on their boys by showing how disruptive the 'incident' is of reassuring routine. They'll go later without the sons knowing. He's called the faculty to arrange for someone to take his class in the laboratory, Peter waves away any need to explain late arrival at his firm.

The headmaster can't refuse to see parents but the secretary asks, do they have an appointment.

If the man is unable to be prepared for dangerous bullying in his school he hardly qualifies for the formalities. The fathers will sit it out until the headmaster returns to his office from whatever he is about. There is a whispered consultation behind computers and a young woman is sent, evidently to summon him. Her ankle twists on a stalk-heel shoe and is embarrassedly righted, as she passes. The office staff must have been told to say the headmaster is unavailable. —Doesn't want the press to get hold of this.— Peter is accustomed to waiting, it's the timetable of the blacks' apartheid past, when he was a youngster.

But Mr Meyer-Wells (good mixture of origins in that name) arrives in full stride. Smiles as if they are people he's called upon. He's recognised: two father-friends from one of those new suburbs where black and white live as neighbours. —The son of Mr Mkize, good to see you. (One of the few black lads,

the school should be able to attract more.) Professor Reed—
it's been too long! Gary Elias is doing well, and going to be
one of our sports stars— (A coloured, actually the school has
more of those, along with the Indian intake.)

In the principal's office the young woman who went to
summon him brings tea. There's determination to make this
a friendly occasion of a request to see the master of the school,
not a confrontation by parents, one a university professor, who've come in academic and business hours to speak
to him. Yes, it happened. The problem is—how to predict
these unfortunate things. And the learner (nomenclature in
accord with a progressive private school) this boy is not a
boarder, we cannot know what influences he might encounter that his parents aren't aware of. —Of course they are very
disturbed. He's apparently a friend of one of the matriculants
although he's in a class below. He may of course—think of
the behaviour a couple of months ago as assertion . . . You'll
know from experience with your own offspring, childhood's become very short these days, I've no experience in
this regard with adolescent girls, but in twenty-six years'
teaching the male young I think I can claim knowledge of
change—adolescent boys now take charge of themselves
before they have the moral judgement to succeed, if you
follow me, they experiment with mores and morals—behaviour—to reject the intermediate stage of life they feel we
impose on them *in preparation*. For the world they're going to
live in; and with modern technology they're so much more
exposed to the kind of world it is than other generations I've
taught. It's a world of *display* isn't it—you must show who
you are, and the way to hand is take power loud and abusive
over your peers.—

A fluent analysis—but if his experiences can't see the signs,
can't predict. —Have you thought of some combined group

of teachers and boys—the boarders and day boys, like ours—to talk together, why they think—see—these things happen among them. It won't be easy, they may be quick to button up in suspicion of being recruited to spy. Tell-tale. But you can deal with that; if your staff's open, make clear this is absolutely not a disciplinary tribunal. It's their school.—

The principal feels obliged to listen attentively to the academic; he teaches, too, and the campuses have their troubles—and then some! He rests chin on fist. —Perhaps you—one of your colleagues, a young lecturer himself not so long out of school, mh?, he could come along and meet our boys, talk to them as the young men they're going to be.—

It's not a bad idea but what is the headmaster himself going to do about the peer group that follows its own code of discipline in the school, probably they've never heard, been taught about fascism but the fact is they're young fascists in the making, Mussolini-style, Nazi-style, Apartheid-style. History's always ready to make a comeback. The man can't regard what's happening as a mishap in his school's production of a free-thinking generation in a free country.

Each must go his own way, to the city, the university, now's not the time to talk about what they, parents, have to do . . . There's only the shared frustration—what use was the confrontation. Alone in the car, addressing himself. Poor devil's having to deal with developments coming to him from outside the school walls. Julius Malema's harnessed himself bucking high to the election campaign, pulling the great eager mass of black youth (brothers of Njabulo and Gary Elias although without the privilege of private school) behind Zuma. For the time being not singing his adapted hate song, the generic 'Kill The Boer' which in Struggle days meant not the Afrikaner farmer but the white army of apartheid. On the subject of discipline—Malema's still successfully ignoring any edict against hate speech, with gibes, insults, racist and sexist, at opposition leaders. If not a hero, he's created a climate which sweats rebellion.

Peter draws up alongside the open car window as both are driving off. He's in some agreement with himself —Not much sense, *aih*, taking the boy out in the middle of the year, I think let him finish it and then start somewhere else, new school, next year.—

—Peter's going to leave Njabulo to complete the year.—

She prompts with questions the account of the principal's response to Mkize and him.

—And then?—

He's aware what both are thinking.

It's end of summer but still warm enough for them to exchange the day on the terrace where the Dolphin's welcoming gift of the hibiscus plant is blooming man-tall. —Njabulo'll be in another school next year; that's it.—

And doesn't make sense for Gary Elias to leave the school, now. Next year. He won't be here, in the Suburb.

Whatever she said then was drowned by a plane trampling the sky, grumbling away.

Australia.

The public relations department of the university—where every detail of his post has been confirmed—has considerately sent a photograph and description of the residence assigned to him and his family. It is larger by several rooms than their Suburb house where they're handing round the photograph and obviously has no history of the kind this house has, taken over from the community of the Gereformeerde Kerk transformed into a Dolphin pool; it is the colonial version of open-plan Californian, attractive, which suits sunny countries like South Africa and Australia. There happened to be a racing bicycle against the façade wall when the picture was taken. —Is that my bike— Gary in joking anticipation.

—Is there a pool?— Sindiswa speculated. Some of her boy- and girlfriends at the school she will be leaving have swimming pools at home taken for granted; she has been the exception.

There are conditions her father could not meet in the adventure, another country, which her friends see privileging her. —I shouldn't think so—but there's an Olympic-size one along with a gym, apparently the team swimmers compete nationally.— Quote from a brochure. Sindi takes the photograph of the house. —I'll borrow it to show Aretha.— A friend whose family have a house on a Greek island.

Gary flips it from her. —Give here, I'm going to let the Mkizes see.— But on the way he changes direction and goes to the Dolphins. The pool is a watercolour painted by the setting sun. The men are in the house, with Marc and Claire, he remains part of the Dolphin family although she is, in a sense, a foreigner, they are drinking wine and watching election meetings, exclaiming over speeches on TV as Gary would heckle at a televised football match. —This's the house my father's got for us, over there (he's picked up the geographical colloquialism) isn't it fantastic. I'm not taking my old bike. I'll be getting a new racer, like this. Cool.— The notion momentarily dismissed the co-education school about which he never speaks. But the Dolphins and the woman pass the photograph between them with abstracted glance taken from the screen or hand it on without notice. Marc gives him a welcoming punch on the shoulder while his attention stays with that of the passionate crowd hailing a bear-hug of Msholozi Zuma and his pop-star acolyte Malema, who, going beyond confidence of his own presidency, he predicts as a future candidate some day. —Where're the folks— Gary Elias is just a sprig of the Reed entourage. —At home? Be a good guy and call them to come over.— The boy draws past his buttock the mobile in his pocket—although he hasn't yet been granted one of his own, has filched his sister's. There's some sort of questioning from the other end—what're you doing at the *pool*, you said you were going to the Mkizes'—but in a short while Steve and Jabu arrive amid welcoming laughter at the invitation coming from their son. Who then leaves to proceed to where he was supposed to be, the Mkizes'; in the interim he, too, has been watching the crowd out of habit as at any spectacle on TV, without taking in the exhortation of the speeches, he's too young to be recruited as a Malema disciple—or just not black enough, only half-half and middle-class nourished, Julius Malema at the age of nine was a poor black child demonstrating protest against apartheid and rejoicing Mandela's release from prison.

The Dolphins and comrades continue to follow the electioneering but their counter-crossfire to the blast prevails at the touch of a remote control that drops the politicians into night.

Wherever Suburb comrades and comrades of the Struggle are together there is now an underlying strain felt almost in the juxtaposition of the familiar bodies, the known characteristics of crossed legs, cracking of knuckles—they may have become strangers. Since the split, breakaway in the party, each unbelievably—unacceptably—does not know how the other right there at the Dolphin pool, in the Mkizes' house, on the Reed terrace, under the Jake and Isa garden umbrellas—is going to vote. It has become a fact of life in common, better left unsaid. Unasked.

This can't mean there is no exchange of impressions, arguments over the tendencies, Left, Right, uneasy Centre—politics no longer simply white against black.

Peter Mkize, *Umkhonto* cadre, is a scornful descendant of tribal society, the—nevertheless legitimate?—base of the black Traditionalist party. —Are they Left, Right, Centre? What? If you sit yourself in a European model parliament, that's what we've taken over from the colonialists, that's what we've got, my Bras—you have to position yourself—see what I mean—in the way that House knows politics, like the way followers of the church see Catholic, Methodist, Seventh Day Adventist, so on, everybody knows the different kinds of Christians all expecting to be saved.—

—Sharp sharp! But no no no.— Lesego, all colloquial in defiance of being an academic, has come to the Mkize house with Steve, this time. —There's nationalism, the African nation, wasn't that how it was, early days of the ANC, Mandela, until the SACP brought the light of the Left, scared some people it might be kind of Outside: colonial. There's nationalism in power in many countries on our continent, maybe under a different fancy African name. For them . . . The rest of the world can go to hell, not Brothers in the Underdog we still share.—

Jake looks to Steve for his concurrence. —We're as a *nation* committed to switching away from the old North–South, South–North axis, yes we're getting good trade and other connections, India, Brazil—

—China.— It's Mkize again. —I'll bet everyone here's wearing jeans made in China. Including me. Our textile people can't compete with the cheap price of slave-labour stuff. Has Zuma or Lekota said anything, what they will do about that. China coming. Already own twenty per cent in our biggest bank.—

At election time you question the intentions of those whose political eloquence is hooked for your vote. He can't ask—but what if the Party whose human aims you share, even risked lives for, is snarling against itself, now in what is only the third election in freedom—which side, now, in the break has what you and she believe in?

Where you 'belonged'.

Other political parties are of no account to members of the African National Congress although they're disgusted—embarrassed?—by the behaviour of their own Youth League's crude insults to a white woman, leader of a liberal party generally regarded as white with a growing tint from voters in its territorial majority of descendants of the indigenous San and Khoi aborigines, mixed with blacks and colonialist variety, the real people native to South Africa. Babyface Malema said the politician was a white whore who selected only white males for her provincial cabinet because she sleeps with them all. A political wily caper: at the same time he also claims respect for women's rights. Anything goes in platform audacity.

The two halves of what was the unity of the comrades' Party.

Zuma—of course—its Presidential candidate—his sacredly danced promises of integrity to the Party's great vision, the mantra 'Better Life For All', is obsessively seen and heard.

Mosiuoa Terror Lekota shares his COPE platform with that Reverend Dandala who turns out to talk some sober sense on what could be done for the better life but hasn't the flair of Terror to suggest COPE could achieve it. Terror has been joined by another deserter of the Party, Tokyo Sexwale, a stronger ally than the Reverend. But maybe a risk as a rival to head COPE?

Insecurity added to the great breach between Terror and Zuma, broken apart in this other Struggle—it's Jake who's said it, and repeats —Who could ever have thought. We'd come to this.—

What are we, Steven and Jabulile doing here, giving opinions like our comrades, about what the politicians actually are dealing with both when they declare their policies of government are those the people need and want, and when they attack (not with Malema's obscenities but just within the limits of free speech) the hopelessness of other parties to meet these.

Comrades; about to vote. Each sees in the familiar aspect of the other—is it to be loyalty to the Party, Mandela's, that brought freedom. That means: Zuma. For the purpose of power to the Party.

—Tales of corruption among his peers are being unearthed, tattered and dirty; who revealed state security information in exchange for how much.—

Zuma is the Party now. If its self-severed half is the alternative—and for the comrades there's no third—has Terror Lekota taken the ethos of the Party in his pocket, rescued it. To keep it alive: a shift of the loyal vote. That means: Lekota.

The decision the comrades are having to make exists as a state somehow in common rather than as it is, irrelevant to the two among them who have taken the option of leaving behind the obligation—no, giving up the birthright, to vote for what kind of leaders, what government commitment to justice there'll be in the fairy-tale slogan.

Jake can't keep his mouth shut even to spare himself. —Who're you going to vote for?—

Some sighs to reject the intrusion, others laugh at exposures that could threaten comradeship, and no one remarks that he and she laugh with them.

The bookshop and university library have few books by Australian writers compared with, say, literature of India, contemporaries from Satyajit Ray to Salman Rushdie, novels, poetry, within that country and its relation to the world. But the presence of India is historical. The population's share of South Africans of Indian origin: indentured labourers in the nineteenth century, through the years of Gandhi's presence and influence on the early liberation movement; the enterprise of a shopkeeper class despite segregation: the emergence of South African Indians beside Mandela in the Struggle and continuing prominently in freedom politics. Australia; that country to which people emigrate doesn't have a pervading presence among local images. Online he can order Patrick White (whose early books he'd read long before there was any idea he'd ever live in the country they invoked), David Malouf, Peter Carey, Thomas Keneally. Jake says he'd better not read Germaine Greer, and he's therefore ordered a work with a kick in the butt title *Whitefella Jump Up* and the subtitle claim, 'The Shortest Way to Nationhood'. It turns out to be a skilled tirade with some home truths about the attitudes of white Australians to the remnant of Australian aboriginal people. He comes to a page where she says 'it was only when I was half a world away that I could suddenly see that what was operating in Australia was apartheid, the separation and alienation South Africa tried desperately and savagely to impose on their black majority . . . I want to see an end to the problemisation of aborigines. Blackfellas are not and never were a problem. They were the solution if only whitefellas had been able to see it.'

She once owned a rainforest property in Australia and for a time divided her life between professorship at a university in England and her home forest.

The half-and-half cop-out.

They've never talked about it, but there's no question there'll be a change of communication. Nothing foreign as there so often is in a decision such as theirs. English. Their language, except for her for whom it was once a second language, and there's family usage of what was her first, passed on as some sort of accomplishment inheritance to Sindiswa and Gary Elias. There is indirect allusion, for him, when the talk around the coffee machine is of frustration of teaching in English while the student's home language is one of the African nine. —I find I'm resorting to pidgin concocted by putting together with a first-year student a common concept, just differently expressed, he may have in his own tongue.—

The Leftist refusing to face facts. —Couldn't just be the student's lack of intelligence you're finding.—

—That's not what Steve's saying, it's the chaotic failure of the schools—

—The 'learner' has been 'learned' way below the level of literacy where scientific terms and processes have to be acquired as part of whatever world language is to be used—

—Because you have to have one—

—Is English as our entry to the world a survival of colonialism? Many of us blacks see it like that—

—And French, Portuguese the same, the old masters—

—Should a country that's got rid of them demand world entry for an indigenous language—let *them* understand *us*.—

—So which among the nine that were here before the Europeans came—

Christina van Niekerk is such a quiet woman, usually it's not noticed if she's there (why isn't she in an Afrikaans

university)—stands sounding her Afrikaans rounded vowels.
—Some among those whites evolved a language that mixed
something of their Dutch with the words of Malay slaves they
brought from countries they'd invaded in Malaysia, but without inclusion of languages of the indigenous San and Khoi,
except for words that describe what the Dutch didn't know,
animals, customs, landscape of the natives. So we claim the
taal, Afrikaans is an African not a European language.—

—And our English? Such a *taal* of cockney, Oxbridge posh,
tribal Scots, Liverpudlian, mispronounced names of Huguenot
origin, turns of phrase 'you should be so lucky'—translated
from Yiddish of grandfather immigrant Jews—we can't claim
it to be an African language? Just a relic of colonisation?—

Hominids have lived in South Africa for nearly two million
years. Australia inhabited less than 60,000 years ago. He's
been reading that like the San and the Khoi, the indigenous
Down Under had languages of communication between themselves and the reality of their environment before the English
came to colonise, first with convicts exported. But there's no
question—Australians recognise as *their* language and lingua
franca, English. Their created *taal* is known as Kriol: it's not
a mix of settlers' tongues from Europe, but the indigenous
people's language with some English, the need to make themselves understood, by the masters.

—Whites don't speak indigenous languages, even Kriol.—
Professor Rouse invited to the coffee room from Linguistic
Studies (Lesego trawls people from various faculties in
eagerness to bring exchange between what he calls another
apartheid). —Maybe not in Australia, but come on, you can't
say that of us—many whites, particularly males brought up
on farms, they played with the farm workers' boys, they've
grown up isiZulu or isiXhosa or Sepedi speaking along with
their parental English or Afrikaans.—

There's another way to have your English language boy speaking an African language; this time a mother tongue since the boy's mother is Baba's daughter. But it isn't appropriate to bring that up—Lesego and others who know this is their colleague's last year among them—would be thinking, much use isiZulu will be to the boy where there are no Zulus.

She's the one to bring up what they have taken for granted. The co-educational school they've decided on for Sindi (of course) and Gary Elias, his strong reservations dealt with by the promise he will be taken to look it over while in November there's still time to make a change.

—Is the school for anyone, we've never asked, really. The black children.—

His reading doesn't give an answer to a question no need of asking. The emigration people haven't for one moment in all the to-and-fro of acceptance as desirable citizens shown any reservations (For Christ's sake! As father Reed would say of the preposterous presented) about a black wife, she's been there before them, the lawyer but in all her assertion of formal African dress, regal adorned head, from that first day at the seminar—what could the children be but black and white, an identity, not a 'mixture'.

He'll ask, although there cannot be any question on what Jabu really is raising, which is about those Australians known just as indigenes rather than black in any degree or variation. The young woman at the emigration agency is a South African employee who makes an assumption on necessity to reassure a white, like herself —Schools are open to all races, of course . . . it'll depend where the schools are, if it's not a school near where most blacks live, there'll probably be only a few . . . you know, the ones whose parents . . . you know, can afford private schools—

He relates this to her like a feeble racist joke.

Julius Malema is in a bid to be taken seriously these last weeks before the election, his child prodigy leadership of the Youth celebrating Zuma in triumph they'll be voting to bring about for him. Malema's reinventing himself again, new avatar as peace envoy. He's getting a good press now (although it was the bad capitalist–colonialist press that ridiculed, demonised—and thereby first, *made* him) since he's gagged his cry 'We'll kill for Zuma'. His arrogation of leaders' right to make promises there'll be a new, *functional* country run by an ANC united (forget COPE): the Party has the Youth vigorously empowered with testosterone, along-side or ahead of it. A count of potency to match Zuma's own, sexual and political.

You have to be young to ignore or be unaware of what that future may look like. A schoolfriend of Sindiswa has asked, —You'll be coming back?— Sindi answers in a variation of emigrants' assumption of reassurance. —Oh in the holidays— not this Christmas we'll only just have moved there—but next year, oh sure, maybe—they have the same winter and summer as here, I think the same school holidays.—

She hasn't told Gary of this question. But as the family eats Sunday evening takeaways he asks —Are we going back home, I mean, to see everyone, sometimes.— His father gives a gentle lesson in realities children must be trusted to under-stand —It's very expensive, the flight for all of us— —You can send me. I can stay with BabaMkhulu.—

—Are elections the same everywhere, other countries?— For Peter Mkize the choice of a government is a right he, Jabu, and everyone else tanned with a black DNA have experienced only twice before. The first, the euphoric freedom one, Mandela from Robben Island, prisoner to President. The second his successor Thabo Mbeki also a Struggle man despite being an intellectual who forgot that a man of the people doesn't quote Yeats to comrade voters who are half-literate, have had poor schooling even in their own languages—and then he's President betrayed by his brain in refusing scientific evidence that AIDS is a disease caused by a virus.

—Comrade—elections are about rivalry. For power. That's all.—

Marc takes on Jake. —How can you be so cynical. Where'd that get us. This party has its policy, that one has another, we choose between how we think our country should be run, develop.—

—Democracy's only about power? Well, democratic Zimbabwe's one that proves it.— She speaks and Peter's reminded —Jabu, what's happening—the refugees—we're all so busy with this election—they'll still be pouring in when that's all over. Or if the new government gets the door shut at the borders we'll still have how many thousand already—how long now. The church guy, is he still running that shelter or has the city council got onto him again.—

—They're there, on the pavement and the street, he still has his church full. And soon it'll be winter. There was a move to take them to some abandoned building but they came back to where they get food, and some sort of pickings from street trading. And it seems the camp at the main border point people enter, Messina, it has been closed, it was supposed to prevent the drift to the cities. We're acting for the church, our Centre lawyers. But I'll take you down to see—right beside the Magistrates' Courts the city's had to put up portable toilets, the kind at sports events. And now the local shopkeepers have gone to court against this.—

—Choice. Did you see? One of the columnists has guts to write: we've the choice of a balance of thieves to vote for—

Isa claps her palm a moment over her lips as if this is what she's really doing over Jake's. —Why's my man such a bad-mouth, he'll be first in the queue to make his cross—

—Because . . . *my love*, ay—you have to face the facts.—

—At least you don't say 'the truth'.—

—Let me finish? The journalist says there are some good ones thrown in, sharp, sharp, *aih* Peter. Our ANC has luxury German cars as canvassing fleet, where we're getting our funding—shhhh—no one knows he says, how many millions from the dictators of Libya and Equatorial Guinea. Can't call these bribes can we, no, just sweeteners to be sure our foreign policies will support the sugar daddy donors to our democracy when their totalitarian states get hauled over the coals by International Human Rights. The opposition? The Independent Democrats have a murderer on their list, the Zulus' IFP has a convicted fraudster, another has a churchman—not Dandala!—convicted and then pardoned. Well, can't complain things are dull. The Trade Union S.G. tells workers Malema may become the next Mandela. Malema's now called Helen Zille a colonialist, that's much worse than when he called her a whore. She comes back at him—do I pronounce it right—*inkwenkwe*, whatever that insult is.—

Blessing blurts cheeringly —Stevie, it's my language, isiXhosa, 'uncircumcised boy'.— Her man Peter to the comrades —You don't know our insults, that's about the worst thing you can call a black man.—

Malema's repartee allows election-mode freedom of speech become general. —The shit hits the fan— And Isa leads the laughter, as Steve ejects the words.

She has insider reflections to bring back from the company she keeps at the Centre. The advocates in their exchanges pronounce, the Zuma corruption indictment hasn't safely blown away. And what she confides isn't legal gossip, that's not her responsible nature. However the provisions of Constitutional law brought this about, right to appeal is upheld, and the withdrawal of the charge is judged as invalid—overturned. For complex procedural defections you need a lawyer in-house, to follow.

Jacob Zuma goes to the polls with charges reinstated against him, to be heard again after 22 April.

—When he'll be President.—

He says it for her and for him, as if already an event in their past.

22 April.

She often is kept late at chambers when a client has to consult after hours and she must be there with the advocate leading the case. Wethu has microwaved the lamb stew taken out of the freezer, so he and the children with Wethu are at the table when she comes in tossing her briefcase to a chair and running a hand along her tailed locks.

—There was such a crowd queued up.—

That is how she is telling.

His eyes hold hers, question—and answer: she—Jabu—has come from a polling station. She kisses each child and him, flutter of a passing moth come in to the light as if her apology for being late, before serving herself and sitting down to eat with them. Gary Elias mocking his mother's own admonition—You didn't wash your hands—while holding out his plate for a second helping.

The bedroom—that non-conformist confessional. So she cast a vote, well that's her right, it was withheld over so many generations from her people she's entitled to use it for them, even on her way out.

She has another choice to admit. —I voted COPE.—

There are too many confusions to be questioned between them in the process of packing oneself up, each must trust the other. The accord in the Struggle—that was another time.

Baba taught her to have her conviction, duty (among many others to be observed and of which, turning away from the poster on the fence, she is in default in respect of her father). To face for herself what others expect of her. But she has no obligation to tell the gathering of Suburb comrades Isa has insisted must receive together at the Anderson house twenty-four hours later the final results of the day, 22 April. The mood—rueful, it's Zuma—congratulatory, the Party has anyway defeated the lucky dip of rivals; of course whatever their doubts the comrades of the Suburb have all voted for the Party. It's as if in the emotion of the day the coming final defection of two among them is forgotten. It is—understood?—Steve and Jabu did not vote.

There is no surprise in the televised announcement above blare of crowd, ululating women, farting vuvuzelas—a sound majority.

—The scary shift to the Left that might have put some crosses in the wrong place—

—*Who* would have?—

—The whites who're afraid of Zuma, the rival blacks, House of Traditional leaders—

—Didn't happen.— —Oh it probably did, but Zuma had Malema herding the Youth!—

Then amazement. Final analysis: COPE gets 8 per cent of the

vote—they've been in existence how long, three months?—
—*Two* months, for God's sake!—Terror must be dancing as
well as our Zuma.—

Her vote in the count, that is as clandestine love once had
to be.

The doubts the comrades had about Zuma as their
Party's choice—there were preferred names of those not
potentially damaging to the country, less compromised by
corruption and sexual shenanigans, although no one knows
what the power virus may manifest against the antibodies
of trust—are overcome by evidence that the Party of liberation, Mandela's, Tambo's, Sisulu's—it's still in charge! The
loyalty of intelligent people, some battle-scarred, isn't the
uncritical slogan fealty. All the better for that. Viva ANC
if not Viva Zuma! There is zest in the fact of victory, third
time, over sham elections of the past, whites only, same
as the signs on the public lavatories. Jake and Isa brought
out wine, beer, and the whisky bottle for those who had
advanced to it in the present. The children—except for
attentive Sindi who played Antigone in her school's curriculum which naturally includes politics as an element of
everyday history from ancient times—had only gusted in
and out, irritatedly gestured away by Jake during the result
announcements that will affect their lives if not determine
them. They burst back along with Blessing's contributed
snacks. Jake and Isa's Nick slid a CD to play what his parent
liked from the unimaginable distance when they were
young, a Miriam Makeba, and the folks, he knew, wouldn't
resist it. While the boys finished Blessing's curried chicken
wings Peter took Sindiswa by the elbow, up to dance. Marc,
swinging sexy gyrations round his serious choice of a new
gender partner, wife Claire; Jake and Blessing circling Isa's
hip-shrugging solo.

They see Sindi their schoolgirl; dancing as a grown woman does with a man.

Sindiswa in Glengrove Place, proof of clandestine revealed: forbidden intimacy. Growing up in a second freedom, in another country, from burden of the past.

They dance wildly as they had in their beginnings in the Struggle, Swaziland, Baba's girl and her white boyfriend.

A week or two later President Zuma's multi-million celebration is a bash, the press didn't hesitate to remind, on taxpayers' money. Wethu had gone home to vote where she was registered, KwaZulu. She came back—Happy Happy! Her refrain as she unloaded the gifts of emerald swatches of spinach you don't see frozen in supermarket packs, woven shoulder bags, straw and reed origin of the plastic version city women wear, and for Gary Elias a little clay figure of a boy clutching a calabash as a football, modelled by one of his holiday pals. He laughed with pleasure and scorn at the arms without hands; his father challenged, —You couldn't make anything like this out of mud, could you?—

Wethu brought greetings and what must be a message rehearsed with school principal Elias Siphiwe Gumede. She paused between chatter about and for nobody in particular to recall to his daughter faithfully —Baba says we must thank God the country he said it's in good hands—how was it—oh for us, our country. And we—we can be—proud amaZulu.— This was a translation, polite in a house where English was familiarly spoken. She gave the message again in its original isiZulu with the gravity in which Jabu's Baba had spoken it.

The Justice Centre is preoccupied with the immediate. Situations in which its lawyers are likely to have to take on defence for individuals singled out by the police among mass protesters from 'informal settlements' outside this town or that where there's rioting over that colloquialism for bucket toilets, water supply, electricity . . . 'service delivery'.

—A car burnt, shops stoned, the clinic set alight, a local government official seriously injured. The Minister of Cooperative Government and Traditional Affairs who's been making speeches condemning violence was supposed to go to the settlement to calm people, hasn't come. Instead he's threatened to crack down on what he says are instigators and perpetrators. Three arrested, who knows whether they shouted louder than others or actually got there first in the attack on the official. We're going to apply for bail on Monday.—

He turns to her perspective they're living with just as before the election victory euphoria. (Morning after: still *babelas* from the first in 1994.) —But let's give your Zulu countryman a chance, he hasn't even had a month, never mind the American President's hundred days.—

She looks at him, half-smile down the corner of her mouth. So fair-minded he ought to be a judge. There's irony that didn't exist in the clarity of cadres, you were for or against, simply a matter of life or death, apartheid the death-in-life.

For him the immediate that was preoccupying the university was happening not in this university but can't be ruled out as not to happen. The university at which it was, is where students in the Young Communist League threaten to make the university ungovernable by mass action until the principal agrees to step down. —So it's not Black Empowerment issue, that vice chancellor principal's as black as ours.— Lesego has come to the Science Faculty to talk.

—Not much in that—well, shows we've moved on. It doesn't matter whether the man's black or white he's responsible for what's wrong at his university even if he says it's due to government underfunding.—

—What can the university do to stop the Young Communists from disrupting mid-term exams. Mass action, bring in the National Students Congress, that'll mean some of ours joining. *Eish!* You know what they say, 'We usually sing loud as possible to ensure our demands are heard'. Call in the police to beat them up?—

At home Sindi asks —What are the guys protesting about, what do they want?—

—Twenty thousand have been refused permission to write exams because they couldn't pay their tuition fees this year— her mother explains.

Sindi's clamped teeth and tightened shoulder blades. —When I'm at university, I've paid fees, I don't want people stopping me from writing exams. I don't want to be in it.— She has the—privilege?—they've paid for it, for her: the principle of Socratic argument not violence, for everybody.

They don't either of them remind. You will not be here.

P resident Zuma has declared the African National Congress will rule until the Second Coming.

Along the streets there are men and women thumbs-up for lifts, the bus drivers have been on strike for almost four weeks. Blacks in their locked cars don't stop to pick up stranded workers any more than whites do; he's a white among them. Class makes unity in consciousness of hijack danger. She does take on the signals, from men as well as women, swerving to the kerb. She hasn't told him she picks up commuters along her way. He warned her against this, it's risky, but there is no man other than Baba who has been able to tell her what not to do.

City parks gardeners and cleaners, administrative staff in the municipalities, social workers, prison warders are ready to strike if pay packages agreed upon two years ago are not distributed within a week. 'If it comes to the push we will bring the country to a standstill, we have no option.'

While they are handing the Sunday papers between them she folds a double page down the middle and slides it over the one he's reading—there's a picture spread of black and white doctors picketing outside the hospital named to honour a white woman who spent years in prison in the Struggle, Helen Joseph. WE'RE LIFE SAVERS NOT SLAVES MY PLUMBER EARNS MORE THAN I DO.

Round the first fire of the coming winter, at Jake and Isa's, Peter Mkize repeats precisely the President's assurances as if testing the vowel sounds for genuineness. —Corruption and nepotism will be fought under his administration.—

Jake grants —You have to have the nerve with which the man *doesn't* begin on himself. Anyway, there's a new code of accountability to us, the nation. The Minister of Transport gets a million-rand present from transport contractors and dutifully asks the President if he should give it back.—Peter's glass staggering its contents—Our President's advice, no, man—keep the present after you declare according to whoever's in charge of—who's it—the government's code of executive ethics.—

Isa flips into the fire a skeleton twig claw from the bunch of dried grapes on her vine the birds have missed. —Box of wine, Gucci outfit—

Jabu's asking—Remember?—Zuma's promise to stay in touch with the voters, people's president. Someone from the Centre was at the Maponya shopping mall in Soweto last weekend when Zuma came from a church where he'd been to thank the congregation for praying for the ANC victory in the election that would make him President. Zuma Zuma people yelling ran to keep up with the electric golf cart he sat on going through the mall, the movies and fast food sections, kids went wild, and outside—a crowd waiting for him. He said he was there to thank them for voting for him, when we were campaigning we told you, we were coming to you not just for votes. Today's the start of staying in touch . . . first stop Soweto because this is the place that symbolised the struggle of the people, I came here because this place tells a new story, here you can walk into world-class shops and buy what you want, you don't have to go to town, this is a story of our freedom.—

—To spend, spend, if you're not unemployed— Jake hails with arms in the air.

It's as if she feels she must be the one to acknowledge between them, if he wants to spare her what might appear as reproach: it turns out the party she voted for, COPE has its own share of corruption. A huge parastatal fuel and other energy sources company (she reads to him from a document) has COPE strongly represented on the board. Bonuses of 1.8 million and 3.5 million rands have been awarded to top executives of the company. Lifestyle. Everyone has corporate membership of a golf estate which costs a princely initial fee and there are yearly fees on the matching scale. The company's spokesperson says expansion plans require its executives to engage in networking initiatives with current and potential business partners, customers, investors.

At the eighteenth hole. Whatever he may have felt about her defection (said nothing of this at the time) both share a general outcome.

President Zuma again declares the ANC will rule until the Second Coming. The Council of Churches has objected to his statement as sacrilege. (Jake evokes —Shades of the Mohammad cartoon in Denmark? Don't demean our gods.—) In the confusion of public tightrope acts, while students riot because they can't afford university registration fees, 'Financial Exclusion from Education' is the subject on the tacked-up posters' call to a mass meeting at the university and among the discussants, student union leaders, heads of departments, known 'activists' Lesego and himself, are three-piece-suit Professor Neilson and his one or two other colleagues from various faculties who usually absolve themselves, now, from public protest. A Brother (or is it a Sister) university last year saw a 154 per cent increase in student enrolment. First-year maths students sit on the floor, have to share desks. Other 'tertiary' institutions: one failed in the last financial year to spend 142 million made available by the government for bursaries. What's happened to the money? Nationally, mid-year marks of engineering students in a developing country short of engineers dropped to 35 per cent passes. Like the voice of authority unexpected from an opened tomb, it's Professor Neilson speaking. —There is everywhere, among all of us, enormous—a staggering strain on teaching staff, on our possibility of educating, our dedication to disseminating knowledge on required levels for this country.—

The Old Boy product of exclusive educated class, clubman, has never before been applauded at present gatherings.

There's an Australian exclamation picked up from the books in the process of being read: Good on him!

What is the difference between not doing anything, and having arrived, while desperately opposing yourself, at recognition that what had been believed, fought for hasn't begun to be followed—granted, couldn't be realised—in fifteen years—and right now, every day degenerates. Oh that fucking litany, Better Life, how often to face the dead with it, the comrades who died for the latest executive model Mercedes, the mansions for winter or summer residence, the millionaire kickbacks from arms deals and tenders for housing whose brand-new walls crack like an old face. Who would have had a prescient nightmare of ending up sickened, unmanned of anything there is for you to take on, *a luta continua*.

She has been 'lent' to a firm of lawyers in a case of rape. Although any violation of the human body would seem under rights in the Constitution a case for defence by the Justice Centre it would first have to be heard in a civil court before, lost or dismissed, going on appeal to the Constitutional Court. She's been chosen because it's remembered she has done so much in her early time as a recruit to the Centre preparing disorientated people to bear witness; her natural empathy would be an advantage in a case of this nature. And someone may have noticed her presence in the crowd at the President's rape trial.

—Have you ever known a woman who'd been raped?— Surely no one among the women they knew, but the country is said to have one of if not the highest incidence in the world. Maybe if it had happened, a woman wouldn't want to talk about it. Not even an Isa, much.

—How would we know. Among the girls at the university. Did we know that one in four men in the country is willing to admit committing a rape? Statistic: I'm so amazed, can't believe . . . you . . . can you believe it.— She is asking him not as her husband but as a male, whether this is an instinct all males share but all don't follow. Calling her up not as a lawyer but his lover is his certainty that the instinct or whatever else it may be has nothing to do with his making love to her impulsively perhaps demandingly sometimes not in their marriage bed but as they had to on the run against the law. Might as well have asked if he could understand murdering someone, yes? What is turned up under these stones. If you kill in a revolution for freedom that's not murder. Too late to question.

—Senior Counsel says these one-in-four men, they're boasting . . . to him that's perhaps the ugliest manifestation of the—she pauses for precision—the 'commingling in South Africa of culture of impunity with one of masculine sexual entitlement'. That's how it's put. Conviction rate of those men who do go to trial is only around seven per cent.—

—What are the police doing about this masculine entitlement.—

—Police don't have any real ability to prevent rape, do they—not the way they can catch thieves escaping with cash. Unless they come across *flagrante delicto* in cars, bushes . . . most rapes take place in private places. Homes: the men are friends of members of the family.—

—State of the nation.— His voice is as if speaking to someone else. —State of the nation address after he became President, Jacob Zuma, himself accused of rape, saying the most serious attention would now be given to crimes against women and children.—

She is the one, not he, who faces the victim in whose defence she is present at Chambers of the firm to which she is on loan. The victim isn't a woman but half-woman-half-child. Fifteen years old. There has to be unlimited patience to draw her to tell. To be called upon at all is like being brought to the headmistress's room and you wouldn't be there if you hadn't done something wrong.

It's not drawing blood from a stone, it's looking at the blood and semen that ran down the thighs; there is the medical report from the doctor on night duty at the hospital where a taxi driver, evidently the lover of one of the women in the house, took the girl 'because the auntie (there was no mother) didn't know what to do with her'.

The looks and manners of the lawyer woman who was asking the girl to speak about It—nothing like a headmistress, this beautiful lady out of TV, what an African woman's supposed to look like, wearing the cloth wound high round the head and the smart jacket-and-pants suit you see in shop windows, white women wear. She's what you would like to be; and she must have been a black kid, too, some time.

Yes I know the man, he comes to the house and brings things, a bottle for auntie, she likes brandy, and takeaway, chicken and stuff. That Friday the others were out, even the little brother her sister's kid, she washed her school shirt for Monday and the man came up behind when she was ironing it, he said shame, they's left you all alone, shame, I just laughed, and then he said come talk to me a little while I take you to get us curry rolls from the Indian's then he took the iron away, his hands were big, he turned me around and he was . . . kissing, I began to hit him, kick, and then he pulled up my dashiki I had on for the weekend how can I say—I screamed but he didn't care he knew there was nobody in the house lots of noise in our street—He got the zip and opened my jeans, I fought I tried to bite, he pushed me on the floor there's a rubber mat there by the sink and then with the other hand he was doing something at his clothes—

Of course she began to weep a jumble of words and snot.

So she must have been intact—what's known, with biblical reference, as a virgin. Or maybe did have a boyfriend who entered her secretly as it was long ago in Swaziland. But it was the brutality of this man that brought her blood and his semen running out of her.

To go to her, take her in your arms within a bonding of the common language—the girl is Ndebele but the language is through old tribal conquest close to isiZulu—that's not in lawyer's protocol of objectivity essential for extracting truth from clients' emotions, but she takes the girl's wet hands firmly in her own. Although the girl comes from what's emerged as

354

a background of poverty, a household of women managing an existence—where have the men disappeared to after insemination?—she's not a bedraggled frail slum child. Something in the highways and byways of African DNA, a strain of strength and grace has sustained her. She doesn't go to school in a dirty shirt on Monday. She is tall, for fifteen, with good long legs from what can be seen of the calves below the rolled-up jeans, a narrow waist above our jutting buttocks, and our African lips. Her story, evidence. She didn't thank the unexpected kind of questioner but the dazed relief in her glance was an expression of this.

Fifteen.

She could be Sindiswa. Shades of brown deepening where the light catches the flesh. As Sindi would be. If Sindi had more share of me than share of her father.

Professional detachment by which you live now as you could not in the Struggle—misplaced as if it's a document put down somewhere, can't be found.

This is Sindi with the one man in four in our country.

The advocate on the same case met them cheerfully at reception and forbore to murmur aside to his attorney and expect an answer, how did it go. She left him with her tidy pad of notes. Many thanks, I'll call you at the Centre, he patted the notes as he spoke, an assurance between the code of colleagues that he was confident in her special qualification for this case. These are worthy, not reprehensible situations when race does count.

She's fifteen.

—The girl is fifteen years old. Same age as Sindiswa.—

He turns his head swiftly away and back again; does she have to be reminded this is not one of her cases to be told about with Sindiswa in the room, lately interested in her mother's, a lawyer's work; she and her schoolmates are being engaged seriously, at that school where there is a curriculum assumed responsibility with what pupils are going to do in life, for others, within the career they choose for themselves. What you going to be, as the schoolmates put it. Butcher-baker-candlestick-maker, oh no no no it's nothing like the old jingle—television film-maker, advertising copywriter, sports coach, actress, five-star hotelier—teacher, doctor, lawyer, architect, engineer—these last are what the school hopefully advises while not encroaching on individual freedom of ambition.

He and she never had had the idea that you don't bring your work preoccupation home with you, enough is enough as the phrase goes, one of those that have come into the country's English from the colloquial of a long-mixed population, pre-colonial indigenous and immigrant usage. The university is about to send students and academics—himself—out on the winter vacation, with the poor mid-year exam results, solidarity with protest against inadequate bursaries, poor living conditions at hostels—the endemic of tertiary education—until these reassemble for the new term.

The month is ending with doctors again on strike. In a province that has the name Mpumalanga, 'Rising Sun', a town which still bears the name of a Boer War leader against the British, Piet Retief, two are killed as a mob round pyres of burning tyres, brandishing 'traditional weapons' clubs and pangas not out of date, protest against what's dubbed 'service delivery', a non-existence for them, their needs, water, electricity, refuse removal ignored with promises for fifteen years. In frustration they rage indiscriminately destroying what they do have, what's passed for a clinic, a library.

She speaks about the rape once more.

Gary Elias was at the Mkizes where Njabulo is allowed to

call up Facebook on his father's new computer and they enter themselves to be received by others they're unlikely ever to meet within touch. Sindi has Mandoza playing so batteringly that the walls of her den and the walls of the living room seem to act as drums resounding. He got up and made to go to her. —Don't—no, leave her.—

It was imperative; he smiled, the objection in court; but his legal representative counts on the volume to ensure privacy, the daughter won't overhear. —She could be Sindi. Could have been her, I had to stop thinking.—

He must concentrate on what he can't know, what it was like drawing a woman—a girl, to tell what rape is while it is happening; to have the body, the opening that can't resist forced entry down passage to female being. —She's not Sindi, I mean it's not what we'd want to admit, but look, that one comes from the shacks, there for any man to grab—that's the fact.—

—She'd remind you of Sindiswa.—

She is black. Living as the fag-end of racism. Can't say it. She's not the product of a Baba who sent his daughter away to Swaziland for the evolution of education, and of the white Reed breed whose offspring evolved into a revolutionary comrade, she isn't the product of an Aristotle school where the origins of democracy are taught relevant to Here and Now. Can't say this.

But they are too long through many circumstances for her not to follow. —Girls are forced into cars when they're taking a walk to a shopping mall in their suburb, a gang gets over the security fence and breaks into a house, one rapes the woman while the others collect the TV and computer. You've read about it. An eight-month-old baby was raped, at the Centre we're looking into a commission of psychiatrists to explain this.—

—Male entitlement.— He supplies.

357

She doesn't bring home the rape case again until the week when she's going back to her work at the Centre, the rapist has been found guilty and sentenced, his lawyer is applying for an appeal, but her bit-part is over.

—Nothing to be done?—

Her voice closes a file. —Nothing.—

Apparently she is not seeing the girl; probably handed to the care of one of the organisations for abused women which Blessing Mkize is supporting with leftover food from the weddings and corporate dinners, as she does for old-age homes.

It's noticeable—the interest of his documentation on Australia; lately come, as if only now she sees on the calendar that November is four months near. It's not on the practical settlement arrangements, the school decided for Sindi and Gary Elias, that she is turning pages. It's the legal profession in a country which is not a republic under a president but still some residue of a British Empire, in the Commonwealth, a federation where the Queen is the highest authority as represented by a governor-general. What conditions are going to be the immigrants' in relation to the statistics of crime, the nature of crimes. She has struck up quite a lively Internet exchange with a group of women lawyers Over There. Of course—not strange—logical if we look at the map, that what Australians call their dialogue partner is South-East Asia, those nations, people nearest to them. They signed a 'Comprehensive Partnership' (she's reading it out) two years ago, political, economic, socio-cultural and on security, transnational issues including terrorism.

He and she each walking over in projection their own future field. Sometimes afford the other a glance there, afterthought. —There are women on the judges' bench . . . city hold-ups in certain quarters . . . low incidence of rape.—

He had had his self-accusing doubts, was he forcing her

to leave because they belong together as proven in every circumstance and solution. Now she has made her decision for Australia, down under in herself, to pry into it would be to admit some macho misuse of intimate freedom.

South Africa inhabited by humans for almost two million years.

Australia inhabited by humans for less than sixty thousand years.

He's called up online. 'Australia at the time of European settlement in the seventeenth century the Indigenous population with its highly developed traditions reflected in a deep connection with the land was estimated at least 315,000. The Indigenous population declined significantly as a result of increased mortality and by 1930 was only 20 per cent of its original size.'

Colonisers solved any future problem of liberation movement by killing off the natives, one way or another.

'There was no population referendum until 1967, after 250 years of colonisation. The Australian constitution was then altered to allow Commonwealth Parliament to make laws to include aborigines in the national census.'

Before that they didn't exist.

'The 2006 census. The Indigenous percentage of the total Australian population 23 per cent. But with an average annual growth of 2 per cent compared with 1.18 per cent for the total population.'

Poor always breed like flies.

'Just over half Australia's Indigenous population live in or close to major cities but as a proportion of the total population Indigenous people are far more likely than non-Indigenous people to live in remote areas. Nationally, Indigenous people make up 24 per cent of Australians living in remote or very remote areas and just 1 per cent of those living in major cities. The expression "native title" is used in Australian law to describe communal, group or individual rights of aboriginals. In a decision of the High Court of Australia in 1992, Eddie Mabo was the first Indigenous person to have native title rights recognised on behalf of Indigenous people. The court rejected the idea that Australia had been *terra nullius*— land belonging to no one—at the time of British settlement. The Mabo decision led to the establishment of the Native Title Act which recognises and protects native title throughout Australia.'

End of Outback Bantustans.

'The Australian government is committed to the process of reconciliation between Indigenous and Non-Indigenous Australians. Reconciliation involves symbolic recognition of the honoured place of the first Australians and the implementation of practical and effective measures to address the legacy of profound economic and social disadvantage experienced by many Indigenous Australians, particularly in health, education, employment and housing. Fewer Indigenous students attend and finish school than Non-Indigenous students. Today Australia has a population of 21 million. More than 43 per cent were either born overseas themselves or have one parent who was born overseas. The Indigenous population is 23 per cent of the total.'

In South Africa everything in reverse. Whites 12 per cent of the 49 million population, still dominate the economy, the black majority which overcame also produces those who join the white class and take freedom as the advance to corruption and distancing from the majority living jobless between shacks and toilet buckets.

Take the Down Under information to her; familiarising herself with law over there, unlikely she's not aware . . .

The fact that she's never brought it, to us.

We've paid our Struggle dues: and the result? What our son and daughter must grow up to be here, at home, by birth and genes, responsible to a Zuma, a Malema.

Gary Elias is practising on his newly acquired guitar and Sindi, Jabu and Wethu are watching the news on TV, Wethu doesn't want to see again alone in her cottage the excreta of city's life where she found herself that afternoon, the rotting food nesting flies, the shore of dirty paper, broken bottles, torn T-shirts cast by municipal workers on strike again, when she was there to buy some special headache *muti* demanded by a sister back home in KwaZulu.

Education:—no, mustn't allow himself to be distracted by sections on agriculture, bird life, entertainment, Internet cafés. Education: over the past decade the Australian government has committed to halving the gap in literacy and numeracy between Indigenous and Non-Indigenous Australians (that's a humbling admission in identity, imaging South African whites agreeing to call themselves Non-Africans!) . . . Although it's admitted there's still a long way to go to increase the educational levels of the Indigenous, the progress is encouraging. Out of the country's total population the number of Indigenous children attending school has increased to 4.2 per cent . . . universities: the proportion of Indigenes attaining Bachelor or higher degrees, 5 per cent of the national intake—

And at that moment, darkness—Oh fuck! from Sindiswa, a wild thrum from Gary Elias—electricity blackout.

He and Jabu share the moment. Just some piece of the vast equipment that misfunctioned. Probably failure to be routinely checked. Or, other times, the explanation, cables stolen. Evidently you can get good money for them from metal dealers, one of the ingenuities of having no job, the culture of unemployment, as a professor coined it at a social science seminar last week.

Dark is not—like a sudden flare of light, a disruption. The fumble around for candles, the bed the place of darkness as another kind of reflection: back at the results published end of term on the boards, 23 per cent dropouts missing. Earnest dutiful bridging classes a finger stuck in the hole of the flood wall against the failure of schools to provide 'learners' with education. The indigenes of this African population.

Some of the indigenous homeborn, homeskin, emigrated from poverty to the status of money and political power, the indigenous mass left behind, below, to do the work of fouling the streets in desperation for pay to survive on. *A luta continua*. Where's the cosmic gap least, if never closed, in continuation of freedom's revolution? Sweden, Denmark, Iceland? Too far. Too cold.

What to do with the house; the Dolphins don't want it to go to strangers who won't fit in with the Suburb, near-neighbours to themselves. They have found two men who have always fancied the possibility of extending the Suburb's character by moving in, so to speak. The Suburb has been and will continue to be, if the Dolphins, Isa and Jake, Blessing and Peter have anything to do with it, a place, a home where colour, sexual partnership, have nothing to do with the qualities of living in freedom. —Even as an enclave in the tsunami— Dolphin Eric says —of revenge for the hideous old years, *gimme my tender to build a World Cup Stadium, I'll stash up millions in your ministerial pocket*, you're all welcome to keep afloat in our Gereformeerde Kerk pool.— (It would be a good line in one of Marc's plays, neh.) The care the Suburb comrades have for one another has meant that although the playwright doesn't live there any more he has made a deal whereby the prospective buyers rent the house to the former owners until these—depart. The new owners will take possession on 1 December; but the price of the sale—the playwright is shrewdly wise on the comrades' behalf, is to be paid in advance; now. Unusual. But Foreign Exchange regulations on the flight of capital mean we may not be allowed to take it all to Australia. —You better go wild and kit yourselves out. You Can't Take It With You.—

Gary Elias wants to know —When'm I going to BabaMkhulu's for the holidays?— Two weeks of July have already gone by. Maybe when you are too young, and one of the protected, to have experienced ruptures in your way of life (they've even avoided this against their own better judgement by following the Mkizes' decision that the boys stay on at that school after the initiation exposure) you have no precedent to bring sense to parting and loss.

Jabu has given the boy a date: next Saturday.

—I don't think you have to come.—

Not have to come, does she mean this time? Or any time before the daughter's husband finally has to make his fare-wells; face her father with his own male responsibility. Nearer the time she said. Compassionately, why burden her Baba with appalled attempts to assert authority to prevent the rejection of home, country. Place.

The poster of Jacob Zuma when the rape trial—went away.

Is *she* going to say goodbye? Now. Goodbye with Sindiswa, Gary Elias: her children who are also the headmaster's, the Church Elder's, the grandmother's, the aunts', by lineage and blood children of KwaZulu.

The question of his, the Reed family, no likelihood they would have any reaction of personal or clan abandonment, there is their pride in Jonathan's qualifying as an engineer at an English university prestigious enough for him to find a good position anywhere in the world. His mother: she has surround of sons, daughter and grandchildren to accept his absence as she and his father had to when he disappeared in that fight against apartheid. She will certainly come to visit in the other country for some reason chosen rather than Britain; many people are relocating.

It wasn't a good time for Jabu to have to accede to Gary's rightful demand, although it made sense in another way; it decided when the actual date of departure would be—how to say it—put before Baba. The present coincided with a time when the Centre was concentrated on the development of the highest seat of justice in the country, the Constitutional Court about to appoint new judges to replace retirement of the four originally appointed by Nelson Mandela himself.

Someone has tacked a piece of plastic over the Zuma poster ragged but still there.

The boys are on the lookout for Gary Elias and colliding with each other run to meet the car, Wethu and Gary Elias announce arrival, and the boys yell back throwing the football up to the volume of their voices. The women have heard, led by her mother come clustering. Wethu has her bundles of fulfilled requests for city products to hand over to a clamour of joy, Sindiswa is embraced by the girls, the little ones clinging round her legs, the young her own age admiring her knee-high jeans, touching a forefinger to her double earrings, one hoop above the other in each twice-pierced lobe. Someone calls out in proud recognition the name of the TV star whose style this is.

Her father awaits his daughter in welcome; Baba, on the veranda of the house which is the place of the church Elder and headmaster of the boys' school with a standard of education exceptional in rural areas. The house not like any other in the village.

The homecoming visit the same as it always is—was—Gary Elias coming to spend school holidays or an extended family gathering at Christmas, these years—although the Struggle that had taken her away has ended, she and the white man she had chosen within it meant another life for her—she had never come home.

Her mother has confidences to pass on in the kitchen when she joins her to help with the skills learnt as a female child obliged to have tasks there since she was lifted from her mother's back and set down to shell peas, happily eating many on the way to the bowl. Hear about Eliza Gwala. She and her husband took in Es'kia Zondo when his wife died shame she was only forty-something, he had nobody to keep him to his diet he's diabetic since a long time, and next thing he's getting into bed with Eliza when Gwala on night shift you remember he's at the coal mine? We all know but we never said . . . Now she want to marry Es'kia, she tell me she's going to town to see about a divorce—but you know, it's your kind of work, a lawyer, costs a lot. And Sophie passed on after you were here last time, she was my best friend, Baba never liked her but he arranged the funeral and everything the son nobody knows where to find him, he was supposed to have a job some Indian's factory in Durban, they say he left to work at the docks—I must say Baba tried *everything*—disappeared, it's easy in Durban so many people there from all over—they say you can hear every language, not isiZulu. Everything changed . . .

As wife and daughter come out to the table, laid on the colonial veranda, with the women bearing pots and dishes it's as if from familiarity with the mother's preoccupations Baba takes up where the conclusion he didn't hear, left off. —Murumayara now has as hard a time as Mandela had—in a different way, and Mbeki didn't take it on, he failed, so it has all come up for Murumayara Zuma to deal with. But he's strong. Ready. With God's will. And ours.— The injunction about will, in the language that is theirs, all of them gathered without him (her man).

A better life for all. She doesn't say, what's become of it— that wry observation among comrades.

What is Baba's demand to everyone at his table, she receives as directed to her. From his mind, that time she came from Zuma's trial for rape. Reproaching—no, tutoring her—which while she rejects she has the confusion of feeling part of— close with, not *to* him—an identification that is called love. In the Suburb there is the intense exchange over shared food and drink, perceptions of what's happening around and to them, their conception of the country now, as much a sustenance necessity as what they're reaching out forks for, swallowing. Here at home there is no such compulsion to the reality that contains them all, KwaZulu and the Suburb, the commuters stoning the trains that leave them stranded, the doctors on strike in hospitals so ill-equipped in one month a hundred babies have died, while although the money from sons out of work in the city isn't coming any more, here the hens are laying and there was a fair crop of mealies for the winter, the matric passes at the boys' school were the highest in the province last year and the headmaster has every intention (the will) to bring the mark still higher this year. It is only in the late afternoon when he comes back from a church meeting that Baba and daughter can find themselves alone. The women are about women's business, you hear now and then the anecdotal exclamations, a drift of song. Distant thump of the ball on hardened winter earth, the boys on the football field, Sindiswa with one of the girls who is making herself a dress, showing intrigued Sindi how to use a sewing machine powered by foot on a treadle.

—So COPE is in trouble. What a mistake Mosiuoa Lekota made ever to think he would get away with it—but maybe Zuma is better off without him.—

They are at home; in its own language.

He knows her so well, from her promising childhood, better than the sons of which more could have been expected (he's never disguised his disappointment in her brothers' lack of attainment, no lawyer, doctor or politician among them). Perhaps she voted COPE. He will not have, he never will forget her reaction to the trial that was a ploy to disgrace the future president.

—Baba, we need an opposition. Not those little old clubs of whites, or new black ones.— She in turn knows he wouldn't betray Jacob Gedleyihlekisa Zuma even for the kingdom's traditional one, the Inkatha Freedom Party. —You know history better than I do, you've been teaching all your life. Without real opposition you get dictators down the line. Idi Amin, Mugabe. No democracy without opposition.—

—Zuma is the guarantee of democracy as our President. He was a poor boy growing up in the worst time, he knows what it means to be hungry without rights, he was a freedom fighter for what?—to make sure our people will never again be ruled by any power from outside, we'd have a government where we all have the same rights—isn't that what you mean when you say democracy? And in that government—if there are men who want power against it, quarrel with their own brothers, like Lekota, turn against the man the people want, Zuma their man no doubt about that, if those men work in government against him, is that democratic?— In English now, its colonial origin better suited to betrayal. —So they try their little opposition party game, what can they offer our people that the ANC doesn't? Nothing. You'll see, some will come crying to be taken back by Zuma into the Party. He is the man to make our African democracy.—

English best for this. —Everyone's talking about millions being spent on making a palace out of the President's state residence—what a time to spend a fortune on one of his houses where he'll spend only a few days a year and the housing target promised for our people living in shacks doesn't show any sign of being met. Well the President's big spending started right off, the seventy-five millions his election party cost.—

Doesn't answer, contest. Maybe Baba was invited to some such occasion held by the traditional leaders of the AmaZulu in celebration of one of their own as President.

What's left, at last, to say between them.

—The mess in the streets where you are? I don't like to think of you and the children—

—Not where we live. The central business parts . . . and on the marches to the big employers' headquarters, transport authorities—bus and train drivers' strikes, the municipal workers—

—Someone is putting them up to it, for sure . . . it's all part of plotting against Msholozi. What is it like for you, going around the city.—

—They don't need inciting, Baba, they're miserably paid, they're poor even if they still have jobs, not yet laid off.—

—Of course Zuma couldn't have taken on our country at a worse time, the recession hitting us from the world.—

That's his explanation.

—But Baba, trashing the streets is all that's left to get something done for them. Negotiations drag on, the workers demand fifteen per cent they're offered five per cent they come down to eleven, they're offered eight . . . on and on. The worst time. I see every day in the city people with nowhere to live and when Steve and I drive past at night, they are there, they're sleeping on the pavements in the cold, it's a bad winter this year.—

He must have the last word with her on Zuma; his advice, her father's. —Our President has only had a few months. How can he be made responsible. *Singa mubeka kanjani icala na?*—

There is no subject, Australia.

Baba has accepted (as he did, although that was a matter of his decision for her, a bright female soul should not be disadvantaged educationally, enlightenedly, by being female) that whatever he thinks of the desertion, the betrayal of heritage of Africa, it is her own made by right (fault?) of his ambitious evolution of her from the status of the sex that stays behind in every sense while the brothers go to school. He believes, she sees, it's out of his hands; in God's hands.

And this shows he's gone further than ever in his trust of her? Terrible must be for him to hold this while she disrespects, rejects the future of the country to be achieved led in the person of a son of the Zulu nation.

Sindiswa has always been uninterested in, resistant to KwaZulu visits, finding reasons for staying behind in the Suburb; at this stage of adolescence in the time to be calculated before the adventure of Australia her school friend envies she is getting on intimately (blood will tell?) with her cousin contemporaries. It's television that has brought them together—not blood will tell—they all envision life, sex, love, ambition, popular aims, gains of success, fear failure, from the same sitcoms and soap operas. Almost every mud-plastered house has the altar of the box, now. Baba himself has the same wide screen in his house as installed in his school, both to provide the informational and educational material available; the programmes on culture and politics in the world brought by the image without the opportunity or need to desert. No one and nothing whatever is permitted to distract him from the sight and sound of every public appearance, even on state visits to other presidents in distant places where President Jacob Zuma is received by the President of France, President Brother Obama, or the Queen of England. The hour of each newscast is a knell that silences all interruptions in Baba's house. She sits with him now in the old instinctive ordinance to his interests, the privileges she had as his favourite child. Six o'clock and there is Zuma eloquent as he concludes a dramatic appearance he has made in a KwaZulu district where a rival party has the majority in provincial elections but nevertheless is confronted with a community burning tyres, attacking the mayor over failure of water to run from the taps, lack of medical supplies in a clinic where the women give birth.

Msholozi has the infallible instinct to take in his upraised fist the failure of the rival party to meet the demands of its followers and vow his government will not tolerate the deprivation of the people of their rights anywhere in the country, he's in process of nationwide inquiry, those responsible must answer for their neglect and lack of action. As if the water has begun to flow into the taps with his words the angry disarray of the crowd has become a song and dance of celebration for the presence among them: ZUMA ZUMA ZUMA. He is them they are him, their suffering, the man of the people, is his.

A flick of the control in the father's hand dismisses whatever might follow, on- or off-screen.

Baba leads her out to the veranda where Sindiswa and the girls are drinking Coke, the boys lobbing their football into the midst, demanding a share, the sight of Baba and the appearance of aunts with the mother quietens the scene without lowering the pleasure. Some of the Elder's fellow members of the church governing committee arrive with homebrew and the women mock protest, two of them striding their bulk zigzag to bring out as well the hospitality of the house. One of the men has been to see the site for a stadium to be built for the World Cup event that has been won, against all other world contenders, for South Africa next year. KwaZulu is to have the honour of one of the stadia which will hold fans coming from all over the world to see international countries compete. The boys are all gabbled questions. What's it look like, how big, bigger than—but the man can't find any comparison grand enough. Gary Elias from the city is fully informed, these country people haven't a clue. —The Orlando one's m-u-c-h bigger. But they're all e-normous.— One of the boys insists —So what's it look like?— The man who's been there is grinning, lifting his chin to the scale of magnificence planned. But Gary Elias has the answer before him. —It's not up yet!—

—Yes, they're only clearing the ground, sixty-one thousand three hundred and twelve square metres they told me—

—Wow!—

—D'you hear—

—So how big would that look?—

—*Mfana awazifundi izibalo zakho na?* Don't you learn your maths, *umfaan*—

The boys tease excitedly, punching each other. Gary Elias triumphs, he's been with the Mkizes to see the vast changes already in progress at the stadium in Orlando. —That's where the action's gonna be.—

—And we'll have our stadium in KwaZulu, d'you hear—

—And we'll be there, we'll all be there!— Chorus, the boys are linked, Gary Elias in the middle.

The headmaster reminds. —That depends whether you've passed your exams you must all be going up to grade nine or ten—

—Except Thuli—

—Yes well he is a year younger so he'll have to be up to grade eight, he'll be the exception if he's worked hard this year.—

—Baba's getting tickets for everyone in the team—you'll come.— Vusi with assurance to Gary Elias as one of them.

Baba never needs to acknowledge boasts on his behalf, it is understood he has influence on this occasion as in many others that concern the community of the family. —We must not count the chickens before they are hatched. *Ungabali amatshwele engaka chamuselwa*, the tickets will only begin to be available perhaps early next year, it's going to be a process, a great many, whole lot reserved for the people overseas, all the other countries with teams taking part, America, England, France,

Brazil— At the pronouncement of that South American country a cry goes up even though you don't interrupt Baba; after
the home team Bafana Bafana the Brazilians are the favourites.

He allows the enthusiasm. —I have arrangements, soon as
tickets will be available for us in our own country.—

The women laugh and slap open palms of one another.

Baba and her alone together, he had not for a moment taken
attention from her in a hold that penetrated, appropriated
from the statement of her pauses anything being withheld
in what she was saying to him, for him. Here among the
company where they belonged, his wife, her mother, the boys
and the girls half-grown women among the family women, he
did not pass a word or glance to her, it was as if she had taken
her leave of him, already in her car, gone. Later there were the
customary farewells, turnabout, as there had been the gifts of
arrival, new-laid eggs from the ranging hens, mealies from the
winter's store, all in baskets where purpose and beauty met in
the first art form she had, unconsciously, known, that of the
extended family women who gathered the reeds and stripped
sheaths of cobs to weave strength, each in a personal pattern
through the agility of fingers. For some reason—parents never
seem to think it necessary to give this honestly—this visit
was to be shorter than usual. Gary Elias had been brought
late in the second half of the school holidays, and this time his
mother would come back to fetch him after a stay of only a few
days. He happened to hear from one of the uncles who would
be making the trip to Egoli where a son, once an outstand-
ingly clever pupil nurtured in the headmaster's school, had
just been made a director in a food-chain enterprise—the
uncle would be happy to have the chatter of the boy to accompany him. The proposed date coincided with the end of the
school holidays. Gary Elias was eager to accept. If he took the

lift with the uncle he'd gain four more days with the team. Wethu would stay on, too, and take the same ride with the man who was known to her by some generic in the complex of family relations.

Baba has come to the car with the women, as is not his custom, although he keeps his space from them, he's there. She and Sindiswa open the doors, linger, get in, lower the windows so they are still in contact.

The football team has run up in claimed possession of Gary Elias. Which one calls out, not needing to name Jabu —You gonna bring him for the World Cup?—

No matter from where.

As she turns the ignition key it comes. The realisation that Baba's ignoring her among the goodbye talk of others is his acceptance that if this is not the last time, before she is gone farther and further than any other time life has taken her; it may be.

Australia. Leaving like the men, the sons who for generations have left to work down in the gold mines, and now are gone Home-Boys, she'll be coming back maybe as they do for a funeral. The long flight for the World Cup; the boy Gary Elias to witness it with his team.

Withdrawal now while they were among others is her Baba's final permission for the future she and her chosen man have made without her father. It is Baba's unspoken blessing on Down Under. Another journey. Beyond any he could or had ever planned for her, an unspeakable kind of freedom he couldn't foresee.

It's not something to tell.

Sindiswa is gossiping with her father about Gary Elias's clever snatch at the chance to stay on with his football mates and get a lift later with some man who's coming to the city.

—So you don't have to go.— He's guiltily relieved she won't have to fetch Gary Elias, a trip he ought to have offered to make if there hadn't been a solution.

—I won't go back.—

When they are alone, she says it again —I won't go back.—

So she has said something other, told something different from casual understanding of an alternative arrangement.

—Wha'd'you mean . . . ?—

—It's only a few months to November.—

He's waiting.

—We don't have to say . . .— She cups a hand on his arm, a little pressure on the biceps. —Goodbyes would be so disturbing for them *eih*, and Baba doesn't like emotional things. I always had to make the partings with mama, and then he'd put me on the bus or train whatever with that sort of salute he has—you know.—

Yes, he sees it; commending the daughter to God, her father has this authority conferred by belief—she's wrong, there, it's surely the highest emotion there is, something genuine about it even while you don't believe in its reality.

—Baba's got the privilege to buy advance tickets for the World Cup match that will open the stadium that's going up, great coup for KwaZulu—tickets for the boys' football team and it's somehow understood we'll be there with Gary Elias, make a visit next year.—

He's drawn a slow breath of time for comprehension.

—I don't think I have to go back. Before we leave.— She is smiling almost with anticipation that seems to have come, as a gift to her, from her father.

Arm around his neck bending his head to her, breasts nudging, mouth on his. Embracing Australia with him. He knows as the kind of total sense of being which is happiness, that what he has not been quite sure of: he has not forced her against some instinct in her, she is an African as he after all can never be, to become an immigrant in someone else's country.

The municipal cleaners' strike had lasted so long the rat guerrillas who exist holed up in every city had multiplied on the abundance, resource of rotting trash in the streets and when the strike ended and the feast was cleared away they began to appear scavenging in the suburbs. In the Suburb. Blessing screamed high and shrill at confrontation with one in her kitchen, Peter thought she was being attacked by a thief who'd somehow breached the electrified security system and he grabbed the Peace handgun as he would his AK-47 back in the Struggle.

On the first day of August telecommunications workers began a strike of 40,000 union members. The workers at the zoo in the capital city Pretoria were on strike; local animal lovers called upon themselves to help feed the animals and clean cages. A metropolitan railway strike continues. The union says the offer they've rejected would have resulted in members losing pay because overtime would be cut. In some provinces no trains to get other workers to their work; where there are a few manned by scabs a commuter has died and four were injured, falling in the crush from packed trains.

As if turning momentarily in the subconscious away from all this—the Suburb's place in citizenship responsibility, comradely identification with workers existing on no-work-no-pay; and unexpected new middle-class frustration felt at disruption of telecommunications—Marc suddenly tells what's come up. The sale of the house arrangement. He's speaking as if from a lost note scribbled during an unwelcome interruption. —The guy's chickened out. Our deal's off, I'm sure he's lying about a change in his life, the partner, some hint—he's pissed off and he's going to forget the idea of a move to the Suburb.—

What can he say—giving her the news, such as it is in comparison with the news within which, still here, they are living. A house to vacate. Sell. The shacks of how many homeless thousands: no market value upfront. You don't have to say it—her brisk silence, getting up, jutting the chair from her, the pause with which she stays herself as she strides to the door, turns to him with a lift of shoulders, is admission and defiance for them both. The TV screen is filled with footage that could have been that night's or last night's reportage, same thing, heaving arms thrust as weapons of bone and flesh against batons and guns.

Later she is her pragmatic self: the house must go public, handled by an estate agent for possession after they are in Australia. No rent-paying clauses. There will be a board outside, now, For Sale. She's right. Departure. It can't be a Suburb comrades matter.

While he shaves and she's in the bath next morning he, also, is practical. —What about the money. You know we can't transfer the lot.—

She bloats a sponge with suds and draws it the length of her lovely thigh, bends the knee up out of the water and carries the gesture down the muscle of her calf. —The Centre could administer it with my father. I think they'd do that, for me . . . One of my comrades. For use when Gary Elias comes. When there's a visit . . . any of us.—

Zuma on the poster.

KwaZulu. The man standing apart, at the entrance to the house unlike any in the community of the Elder of the church where the Gumede clan have served and been honoured for generations, the headmaster whose faith in education, achieved under strict discipline the best results in the province against a national record of dropouts and failures. —He'd be willing?— —He'll take it on.— Although he hasn't been asked: she is the daughter.

She is right, her Baba doesn't oppose, no matter how much he must be in pain against it within the fundament of his being, his identity, ancestral and present—that she is through her identity with her generation's experience of Struggle, and her educational opportunities bringing understanding of the existence of Struggle throughout the world—a free citizen of the world. She fought for liberation of her people. It must be granted as earned that she does not have to take on the present Struggle, in place of promises, promises, the better life for all.

Experience in the world outside may make her think differently. White kept choice to itself, Black has choice now.

They don't make love much these days—or rather nights, too many things to complete, do. It's not premature, what they decide must be taken has to be set aside in the mind, from what is left behind. The bulk of their lives, what they decide must be taken will have to go by sea and that means well in advance, the road transport to port in Durban, the ship in a time warp of one of Captain Cook's voyages, crossing the Indian Ocean. What each of the four—Jabu, Steve, Sindi, Gary Elias—find can't be left behind is an insight to what they don't know about each other. Gary Elias doesn't want to take his racing bicycle, pride of his last birthday, where somehow has he got the idea that there'll be a better model waiting Over There? Sindiswa insists that the version of the ancient Greek statue of Antigone, high and heavy, carved by the art students at Aristotle and presented to her in honour of the performance, must be cargo, and Jabu for some reason that doesn't match her lack of attachments to objects so easy to transport, such as elegant KwaZulu baskets, includes a hairdryer—must be a special type? He and she go through the shelves of their books (there's the shelf where she came upon his cuttings, Australia) setting aside the essential while dumping others to be given to the university libraries. There was the sacrifice of some law volumes, famous so-and-so against such-and-such, but unlikely to be of interest anywhere else, and education reports in the same category. Before throwing away: a last look at reports of a university where white students pissed in a stew and forced four black women and a black man, cleaners at the student hostel, to eat it. They've apologised since. What's left behind is that no one so far has brought to the courts the case of the cleaners to receive justice as victims.

There was nothing, nothing he wanted that it is possible to transport.

'Our members are determined as hell. End apartheid wage gap, black workers are still earning lowest pay.' Now the post offices stay-away, that euphemism for strike.

Who cares, everybody has email, SMS, Facebook, who needs some face behind the post-office counter. Metro rail not running, clinics closed, patients not receiving their HIV and AIDS antiretrovirals, threat of darkness as the National Treasury refuses to give money to meet claims of electricity workers: people live with all that. The newspaper falls and slides rustling under the bed.

They have not kissed goodnight. Inert beside him, dozing, there's barely awareness of her there—out of nowhere the hand—her hand on his penis. The pyjama pants cover is a token, he's there. She's found him.

She's there amidst everything else that surrounds them. He does not wait in the erotic response but turns to her along with the other, to all that is desolately happening in that better life for all. He's able to confirm in their embrace: confirmation we're leaving, casting behind all we 'cadre veterans' are useless to change, street dirt only the shit symbol of it.

Or there's just the confirmation of persistence of desire. That equality in rich and poor; even in this country, which he's just read is the most economically unequal in the world.

Can't live the cheat, travesty. What use an assistant professor and a lawyer where education is the sum of schools producing pupils to be accepted as university students without the level of comprehension for their course; the law dodges corruption charges of guilty comrades high in government. It's a worn holier-than-thou to cite your children when you make decisions. But Sindiswa and Gary Elias growing up to *all that all this*. Children in whose very conception there was faith in a present that hasn't come. No sign of the equality of their black-white fusion in the country, born of Struggle, which is the most unequal in the world.

It's been taken without mention that Wethu will simply go back home to KwaZulu. What sort of goodbye gift would she like, when the time comes; but shouldn't the time be now, when all the other sorting out of what departs from what remains is being done. There's also the circumstance that what's been applied to Baba, the emotional one applies here: avoidance of a vision of Wethu insisting on being at the airport farewell. Sindi is particularly attached to her, she's been a kind of extension of schoolgirl friendships, probably confided in with secrets as mother Jabu is not. Wethu will go back these few months earlier in a sense as one of her usual visits; only this time it will be homecoming.

—Perhaps we shouldn't be putting it—telling it quite like . . . I mean . . .— Baba's daughter and a human rights lawyer is sensitive to what might seem to be dismissal.

—D'you think she would've spent the rest of her life here if it hadn't been—

The expressive face goes through considering changes. Of course Wethu's not a servant; family, in a way. An accessory life: is that a Better Life. What is said is different. —In the things she sees in the streets, the abandoned old buildings that some of the friends she's picked up—through the garage men—they live in, the way she's become streetwise, they've taught her don't go into this park, keep away from the traders at that taxi station, don't go out of the Suburb when you hear there's a crowd of strikers on the freeway, shots can fly wild and hit you while you're watching—how can she want to live here.—

—She's been, well, it looks as if she has.— The chicken coop cottage he built for her: her independence. Away from the collateral family under the jurisdiction of Baba. —Her emigration.—

They give a shrug-smile at the category, he goes on —Who knows how this applies to other people.—

There's still so much to conclude. Professional colleagues, comrades, are moved to mark them with recognition of their work, their loyalty, their different modes of friendship, understanding, support—despite Down Under. The cop-out.

They are even involved in obligations to the appointments of their successors in the niches they've functioned from. Steve at the university, his activism beyond teaching, to transform the institution in its needs. Jabu, her commitment to justice as legal defence for the country's people too poor to pay for it; above any ambition to become a better life phenomenon, a highly paid black advocate (maybe on the bench some day?). He is taken in by the dean of the Science Faculty and called privately for his opinion on the successors considered for his place in the laboratories, lecture halls (the coffee room never mentioned although, for him, it was from there he achieved anything—which was doubtful—that had been argued for and conceived). At the Centre she was asked to add her informal talks to interviews with applicants as essential advice in the Centre's choice for her replacement. Rather the way as a novice in law, she had been assigned the task of preparing in the languages she shared with them, nervous black witnesses for answers to be given under cross-examination. The way she had made herself useful in the case of the young girl, not Zuma's victim, raped.

It seems there are more occasions to be together, get together than usual. Lesego's brother is down from Uganda where he's in some international conflict-resolving position, the brothers in general are spread all over, now, in various opportunities. There's a big bash on Saturday, it's a family reunion but you and Jabu must come along, open house and go on most of the night into Sunday, a getaway from the troubles in Uganda and ours, here. Marc comes back from rehearsals in Cape Town of the play he's at last found—may have found—financial backing, only here for three days, up to the eyes in hassles with the money bags, but will Jabu and Steve, must see them . . . Peter and Blessing have a calendar when they come over. —There's the long weekend, ay? Njabulo said something the other day, all the boys at school talk about the parks they've been to, elephants round the camp at night, lions eating a kudu, I don't know what else—but we've never taken our kids. And you? Your Sindi and Gary Elias ever seen their Africa. They all know it on TV like the English and the Yankees, right?—

He and Steve take, grinning privately: 'our Africa' shared in *Umkhonto* bush camps—but this, something other, their children ought to have now outside the animal prison of a zoo: a sense of the birthplace they share with animals. Used to be a luxury only white children had, the Kruger Park; while blacks were barred entry, except for warders and camp servants. Peter made the booking and Blessing would provide the food from her catering business. —What are we going to bring, my man?— —The booze of course. Steve, you load up the beer, Coke for the kids.— They occupied thatched rondavels with bathroom blocks and took their place in bush and riverbed, shared the vast enclosure of freedom with animals as the ancestors must have shared the whole of Africa—Sindi contributing unexpectedly what she had learned at her enlightened school. Africa is the origin of all *humans* in the world—despite that the Suburb comrades were moving in warders' vehicles not on foot among the three-toed elephants, the hooves and claws of buck, leopard and lion. Time out. Nothing to do with either present or departure.

While they were away Wethu continued her comfortable habits as if they were there, church on Sunday, settled that evening to the house TV with its wide screen in contrast to her small set, all there was space for in her cottage. The volume high for her to follow while she was heating *inkomo* stew to accompany ground corn *isitambu*, but she heard a repeated call from what must be the back gate, imploring again and again. She remembered to switch off the gas flame beneath the pot, picked up the gate key and went out into the twilight yard: must be one of her friends calling to the cottage. She pushed up her glasses, they were only for TV, she was farsighted but in this half-light couldn't recognise either of the figures at the gate, just hands stretching through the bars as she appeared —Ousie, mama, please some water! Please please, just some water, water, we been running far, please.— In English like hers, whoever they are, expecting a white person to come from the house.

Poor boys—she signalled a hand and went back into the kitchen; didn't want strangers drinking out of one of Jabu's good glasses, filled a plastic mug and hurried, slopping water a little, to the gate. As she handed the mug between bars it was dashed from her hand, the key chain dragged from her wrist tearing the skin over knuckles and twisting fingers. Panic knows no pace. At once, the two men were in the yard, she screamed and a fist was half in her mouth, she gagged and was thrust arms pinned behind her back, to the kitchen door, thrown into the house. —Where they keep the money, the guns— One was pushing her into the passage, a smooth strong young arm tight round her neck against the chin, the other man legs wide prancing backward —*Checha wena!*

You know! Money and guns!— She struggled her head free, gasping a shout —Don't know! How can I see they put . . .— There was a hefty canvas boot tramping on her belly, she was screaming and suddenly saw the youth's face as it came up in the moment before he hit her —I can be your grandmother!—

As it was still too cold for the pool to keep him on form one of the Dolphins working out on his bicycle and making for home in half-dark after completing four kilometres he'd set himself, heard screams coming from the direction of Steve's house. The Suburb's not a squatter settlement or sleazy Hillbrow where domestic quarrels and gang rivalries mean this is normal; but sometimes the children of these straight comrades play games that raise alarms. Once home, he thought he better call the Steve and Jabu house anyway, to see if all was well. When the phone rang and rang, not picked up, he hitched the mountain bike out of its stand again, thought he'd go round. No one came when he shouted at the front gate against the screams and gabble for help coming from the house, the back gate was open and light was a path from the open kitchen door. Kitchen empty. In what must be Steve and Jabu's bedroom the woman who's some sort of relative of Jabu lay sobbing and calling, tied up, in the midst of wardrobe doors gaping, desk drawers spilled to the floor, a dressing table with mirrors pushed wildly away, reflecting make-up, purses, a rifling search, bedside tables overturned— that's where there'd be a gun . . .

The Dolphins were wonderfully efficient; more than could be expected even of comrade neighbours. They summoned police and watchfully accompanied them in the search of the house—these days some of them might be light-fingered— helped hysterical Wethu with her statement, made coherent her familiarity with what she could tell had been taken, the widescreen she had been enjoying, the machines—didn't know what a word-processor, fax, photocopier, were called—all was gone along with clothes, DVD player. Cut loose of her bonds she went frantically from room to room taking stock—even Sindi's TV shame, shame, they should be ashamed of themselves— She had Steve or was it Jabu's cell number but for some reason it made no connection, Wethu knew they'd gone to look at animals but didn't remember the name of the place. The comrades from the Gereformeerde Kerk transformed in the time of the country's freedom and their genders also, took Wethu home with them for the night, calmed and cared for her. As if she had been their grandmother.

Steve, Jabu, Sindiswa and Gary Elias arrived back in the Suburb on Monday afternoon of the weekend apart.

That was what was happening while we were reconciling with Africa in the bush. He doesn't say it. As if it could be heard as some contribution to justification for the approach of November.

The house: it was not there. He was seeing it, deserted, displaced. She is with Sindi and Gary Elias at the Dolphins' being cared for in shock along with Wethu.

The house.

Things were gone—material *things*, don't matter: order is gone. In advance. What's been taken? Perhaps that's relief, fewer things, less stuff to be packed up with what's stacked already.

Jabu took Wethu for an extensive examination at the family doctor. She was badly bruised, trampled purplish the brown pigment of her flesh, fortunately no ribs cracked or vertebrae damaged. While describing over and over under the doctor's attention to her body, what the attackers had done to her she included or perhaps his hands released recollection—one of the men was someone among the out-of-work she'd seen often hanging about the garage where she'd come to know a petrol-pump attendant, he gave them odd jobs in return for some bread or a couple of cigarettes.

This alerted Jabu professionally, away from the guilt she was struggling with, in herself acknowledging to Baba that she had left helpless Wethu alone in the city climate of savage lawlessness in which—yes, there's no racism, Wethu's black as you are while you kick and hit her.

Jabu stops Wethu's monologue. —You are sure. You'd recognise him? We'll go to that garage and you'll point him out. Show me. If you are sure, quite sure.— There'll be a warrant for his arrest. Grounds for bodily harm as well as housebreaking, robbery. —To the doctor, fellow professional —I need a detailed report on her condition as result of the attack on a woman her age, physical and psychological.—

—Yes, blood pressure's high, that could be stress. I suppose you don't know what her level was, before—at her age . . . blood pressure problems quite common.—

Wethu is weaving her head as if being accused of the crime of age. And Jabu as if deftly discarding a piece of evidence likely to be negative. —I don't think back home she will have had blood pressure check-ups . . .—

Several visits to the petrol station with Wethu bring no possibility of arrest, of finding the attacker among the people-within-the-people, potential burglars and hijackers, street muggers. The young man whose face was recognised as he hit her was not to be seen. *Eish*, she was sure, Wethu was sure. She talked with her petrol attendant friend, they exchanged description of eyes, dreadlocks, scars, nose and ears; the man was no longer among the layabouts at the filling station. Did he, streetwise, know she might remember him? And the other attendants didn't want to be connected with any trouble, have the police questioning them, a presence alarming to clients— where the police are there's suspicion that crime is a risk to

your person and your car—better drive on and fill up somewhere else.

Sindiswa has moved Wethu into the house: her room. Sindi
did not ask permission. With Gary Elias's help simply carried
Wethu's bed from the outhouse cottage while Steve and Jabu
were at the Dolphins' in one of their many needs to thank
them for what there were no adequate thanks. The move was
discovered only when already accomplished.

The daughter gave the order.

—She can't live there alone in the yard any more.— Sindi
has a dependency of attachment to the member of Baba's
extended family she doesn't have to—whom? Her mother, her
father? She is a member of the extended KwaZulu family now.

It's something unexpected; to be understood. Sindiswa's in
a way more affected than Wethu herself. Whenever they can
be alone, away from the laboratory, the Centre, Gary Elias—
Wethu—Sindi—they must try to reason about this. Sindiswa's
disturbed by everything that's happening—it's not only the
awful travesty of Wethu, the Wethu she loves—at that school
(it's what we wanted for her) the seniors are made aware, they're
kept informed, there's no privileged shelter from facts that
there are schools without electric light or desks, no libraries
or laboratories, the kids live in cardboard and tin shacks, this
winter a candle or paraffin lamp fell and children were burned,
died . . . And what about us? We adults, we're always talking
strikes, the rights of workers—some of the kids on scholarships at her school come from slum townships, the father isn't
paid enough to provide decent food, back in their homes.

So what Jabu is saying: even children cannot be innocent.

She has her precision. —Not guilty of the exploitation but
not innocent of knowing about it . . . it's all too confusing. For
a child who isn't really a child any more—not here. She told
Wethu and me—one of the girls saw how the man who has a

township store near where her family lives was beaten and the store set on fire, the girl's proud of this, says he was cheating people, charges high prices for bread and baby food and fire-wood. Was he a man everyone knew, one of themselves? From the description given by the girl, and passed on by Sindi, seems to have been a Somali.—

Xenophobia is being discussed while senior lecturer from department of psychology and adjunct professor of sociology are drawing coffee. Steve remarks aside to Lesego how what is externalised as xenophobia has wormed itself into a schoolgirl, classmate of his daughter, against the high human principles taught at that school.

The man was a foreigner? But if he'd been a local who was overcharging? You don't believe he'd be attacked, you don't see that a capitalist (oh, a *capitalist* now, even a spaza shop-man's screwing the poor is a class issue, my Bra, economic). You think he'd've been allowed to exploit them if he'd been one of their own?—

—Long as he was home black—

They can have a down-mouth laugh, just between them at Steve's, the white man comrade's subconscious fear of racism in reverse—a local strain of xenophobia? That's economic, too, isn't it.

Wethu lives with Sindi in the house yet still holds court during the day in her cottage with city friends, women from her church and the petrol attendant from the filling station, his seems more than the empathy from the church women; a kind of responsibility expressed for what her association with him brought upon her, the disrespect of vicious blows from a man who could have been her grandson.

The right thing to do is send her, take Wethu home to KwaZulu. Baba. She would have had to be returned in good time before November anyway, that had been decided upon for unwanted emotional farewells, now more certain than ever. Wethu must feel threatened; horror proven to her there is no shelter, in the Suburb from the city that Baba's daughter and her husband could provide, good people, family, though they were.

Nothing is what's expected: the old woman appeared not to hear when she was told she's going home, even when Jabu went to her in the privacy of Sindiswa's room, that temple of female adolescence, and gently explained in isiZulu, with all the traditional reverence between young and aged, that she would have been parting from this extended family soon; she knows they are going to another country.

Sindiswa had walked in and listened.

She followed her mother out, and to the living room, where her brother and father were about to play chess. Gary Elias set up the board and men while Steve watched at the flimsy distance of a television screen municipal strikers threatening weapons—sticks, clubs, anything they could pick up—against nurses, before angry, terrified patients in a hospital, a plaster-encased arm flung back and forth jerking across the camera's vision.

Sindiswa's voice reduced everything else to mere noise. —Wethu's coming to Australia.—

Jabu's eyes sharply silenced, stopped him, her knee rocked the chess table shivering the men as she cut off the other reality, of the city in whose midst they were. —I hope you haven't given her that idea, Sindi.—

The child (could you be a child while grown-ups made violence around you, entered this house of theirs and tied down trampled on the body) wasn't to be deflected. Not only could Wethu not be returned to the chicken coop he had converted into a cottage, she could not be left behind where there is no respect for one of the grandmothers who could be attacked and beaten in exchange for a television set.

—Wethu will go home, to Baba, she'll be able to forget what happened here.—

Sindiswa was scraping her foot up and down the floor in hard-won patience. —She won't. She came here, she wants—she'll go with us when we go.—

Now he speaks to forestall Jabu. —Sindi. She'd be lost. Absolutely. In Australia. There's no one there for her, lonely, lonely.—

—She'll find friends.— Sindiswa turns to challenge their discrimination. —If we are going to, why shouldn't she.—

—She speaks hardly any English . . . It's entirely different, we have the same language, we've led the same kind of life—

Does he, how can he explain to this exception, this child of—'intimate integration', love unknown to racism: the facts of life in this society aren't the story of the bees and the birds . . .

Fact is. The Suburb is the bourgeoisie of the comrades. We're not, even in our mix, like the old-style whites, but we're not living the life of the people though some of us are black—the Mkizes and Jabu, our syntheses Sindiswa and Gary Elias. Out of the mouths not of babes and sucklings but adolescents from the privilege of progressive schools your own pretensions are brought to you.

—She's got spirit, all right!— Jabu grants, Jabu exclaims.

—But our Antigone standing for the wrong cause, your Centre wouldn't brief her.—

—Oh I think we would, not in this case, but for some other . . .—

Bed is their tribunal, so little privacy when handing over, packing up not only the furnishings at what is resolving as a stage of life (as he had to carry her from the clandestine hideout over a threshold to the first house) but the certainty—the Absolute of the Struggle, left behind along with a present: a liberation, in a form that could never have been believed could come about. Happen. Well. A signal of the new generation always comes to take over. Mandela and Tambo from Luthuli, and on and on, the next and the next, an insolent Antigone . . . The freedom-born generation and how they'll deal with the travesty that's being made of freedom. 'A better life' lyric of a pop song outdated, into the trash emptied on the street by workers paid a wage the price of a cabinet minister's cigars. How to get to sleep. Only animals can sleep at will. But it's possible to do so on authority of at least one conviction.

If the present could never have been foreseen you don't therefore have the right to condemn Sindiswa and Gary Elias to grow up in it.

The groups of the Left—communists, Trotskyites, probably no old Stalinist survivors—'are hardly more than a curiosity' (triumphal sneer wheezed by Professor Craig-Taylor in the coffee shelter) *a luta continua* having been taken over as a black national rhetoric by an innocent-faced young man with a resuscitated Munich Beer Hall delivery, Julius Malema—he may be the Antigone in the era of sex change (that's Marc's quip as one of the Dolphins who's got himself married, to a woman).

There is a force which does not belong to the colonialist past that has asserted its rights in the African millennium: a political party. Traditional leaders in parliament, whether or not they are representative of all tribal origins with all nine languages, they support the customary rights of each. The amaZulu don't circumcise, the AmaXhosa do. And this rite of entry to manhood has become money-making. —Like everything else.— Peter Mkize at a meeting in the city called under some acronym of human rights on the report that in the winter season of circumcision twenty boys are dead. —Why doesn't our Minister of Health prosecute the crooks who butcher our young on the cheap, cut-price offered to parents who don't want to pay the cost of the traditional practitioners in circumcision 'schools'?—

As a Zulu comrade Peter better be careful about sticking his neck out like this on the subject of manhood rites . . . The amaZulu rite decrees that their young males kill a bull with their bare hands—including prodding out its eyes, slow torture of the huge animal. An animal isn't human, of course, but there has been an outcry by animal rights groups since this year's performance of the ritual, made public when cameras reproduced the agony of the death. Zuma himself must have taken part in the ritual long ago, and you don't go around questioning the humanity, morality of how the President attained his proven manhood with many wives and other women. Although she is the one who wanted them to accompany Peter to the meeting—Baba, did her father fulfil the rite, too . . . before, along with the rites of the church? It's not a thought to repeat to her.

In the coffee bar they turn to afterwards, restless with their reactions, a young man attached himself, confronting Peter where they sat along the counter. —Man, you one of those educated who want us to stay for ever doing what whites do, all the white shit, let men marry men that's better custom not circumcision to make men, your brain from the old colonial time, it's not Africa, for us, now.—

—My brother, that's not what I said. We keep our ideas, what's called customs. But we must also keep them *right*, way they were before, you know what that means, they weren't a way of making money—you hear what I'm saying? Circumcision, always done by our special men—experts, you understand? They knew how to do it and nobody died, no boy had what he was going to be as a man's body messed up for him? Now anybody with a kitchen knife tries to do it, it's cheap, you don't pay much and you're *finished*, for life.— Peter made a slashing gesture between spread thighs.

—The AmaXhosa do it. If it's done properly by people who know how, maybe it's a good custom, helps against HIV and AIDS infection, never mind if or not it makes a man. But our amaZulu killing the bull with your bare hands, such pain, so cruel. Not because you're hungry. To show you're strong. And as you really grow up to be a man you're going to find you have to show other ways to be strong for the trials that come.— The young man didn't expect to hear from a woman, what do they have to do with male rituals.

Jabu had swung round her stool to recognise a *mfowethu* by his features or his home mannerisms of the language they share. So she takes the challenge rebelliously, personally. Would her Baba believe it had come to this: her sense of a right of leaving all this behind. What has *all this* to do with Baba—but everything was always to do with him—otherwise I wouldn't be who I am; where I am. Where I'm going. To be.

He, the descendant of colonisation, wouldn't be here beside her wouldn't be taking her, no, going with her of her own volition to another country, as if he really understands the brutality. People need symbols.

Yes—oh yes, of their power over nature is it? Over other people or to please the gods? Yes. But they've changed since those times haven't they, the Mexicans don't sacrifice their people to the gods any more. The bull hasn't done anything wrong. It hasn't angered any gods, it's only an animal. You'd think by now it'd be enough—as a symbol—at least slaughter the bull, eat it, not torture it to death.

Slaughter humanely. To be confronted by her with the obvious—they eat meat, he and she, and there are so many unspeakable happenings skin-to-skin close, human to human, real, not symbolic, around them.

The converted chicken-house isn't empty.

Lesego is representative of the university's African Studies in a national association exclusively of black South Africans which attempts no more successfully than Left, Christian or human rights organisations to condemn and halt violence against immigrants in recognition of African brothers. Lesego himself doesn't accept that the African continent is extended family, for whom space everywhere in the continent must be made as the reason why they should not be rejected. Being Lesego, he goes to meetings of the association as his own-appointed representative of the living conditions of South African black communities so deprived, degraded that their last ragged hold on existence is broken by the invaders.

—That's why our South Africans turn violent.— Lesego's angry saliva shines at the corners of his lips as he has the figures coming. —Twenty-three per cent national unemployment, and this when guys whose employment is to wave you into parking space aren't counted, up to half the children in shacks don't go to school, parents can't pay, provide more than a plate of pap a day—it's poverty, the cause of this violence.—

—What're any of us, veterans of the Struggle, eh, going to do about it? Zuma was our Head of Intelligence—the *President*, what's he doing about it. Why don't you come with me, see 'on the ground' one of the settlements where people were beaten up, kicked out—two killed—last week.—

—Jabu and I've seen, months ago, the people who had to get out of Alexandra, they've made some kind of slum camp for themselves on open ground just across the street from houses of the old and new rich in a security-tight suburb—great indignation from the residents black and white.—

—And what was done about it.—

—I suppose the residents got them cleared out. A threat to safety, the value of property reduced by what was on their doorstep.—

—So Steve we're sitting around talking ... *shocked* ... *Eish!*— Lesego dismisses, he's forgotten for the moment, that Australia is the response for not going to do anything about it.

—'Xenophobia', a future no one in the bush the desert thought of.—

—Just a minute, hold, my brother—how could we know then our countries round us would turn their liberation into dirty power struggles with their own people, the Amins the Mobutos and now Mugabe, so their refugees would flood in on us.—

Seen it all before.

In Lesego's car, it occurs. —Isn't *umlungu* going to be unwelcome whitey. I don't want to make them suspicious of you.—

Lesego doesn't so much as consider this. —They know me, their non-racial frontman. At least I'm a black prof of African Studies at a university where white profs used to study us. They'll think you're a journalist I've brought to write about what happened to them back home. Not to worry.—

Wasn't worried about the possibility of being abused, harsh words, anger that might spill over an emigrant from his local white world no, but that people could be offended at being a spectacle for him.

Once Lesego left the highway there was a jumble of burned tyres on a road to be manoeuvred through. It seems from newspaper pictures and TV coverage there's an endless source of these, they are the flags, the logos of protest. Lesego, as if remarking on a passing foreign landscape —Must have been cleared from where they barricaded the highway.— The road was a ploughed track of swerving levels, boulders washed up exposed from past rainy seasons, holes to be avoided or if too deep and wide, bumped through in low gear. Taxi buses taking their right of first way somehow missed hitting the car as they aimed for it: Lesego's experienced with these conditions. There were the remains of vehicle skeletons. A couple of stick-limbed and a lumbering fat boy yelled from the game they were busy with in one of them. (Can paediatricians explain why undernourished children can be either painfully thin or somehow blown up like empty bags.) Now there was the beginning rather than entrance to the place. Men stood about talking each other down and an old woman sat on a packing case before what might have been a house was someone's life exposed, three walls of the same kind of cardboard she was seated on, one buckled sheet left of a tin roof, the fourth wall missing or never existent, a neatly made bed there with a bright floral cover, shoes, pots, some shirts hanging on a wire, a tin bath, a poster of a football star.

Some man who recognised Lesego gathered him among men telepathic awareness brought from behind what was left of shacks and houses. Nothing appeared intact, not as if explosives had fallen indiscriminately but wrecked by individual intention. This place, invaders have simply moved in on local people living there perhaps years and somehow become settled enough to acquire possessions. Probably gleaned stuff dumped by white suburbans who have too much clutter, or stolen by the jobless turned housebreakers—no refugee could have brought with him the old upright piano lying among its torn-out white keys, a creature that has lost its teeth. A spaza shop which had the enterprise of displaying special offers with grinning client posters as in the supermarkets gaped on empty shelves and the spilling of loot, trampled, apparently not worth taking. Someone was picking over the remains of a TV—no electricity here, but television can be run on a car battery—the few cars were not more damaged than they normally would have been—windscreens one-eyed with patches, autograph dents from daily encounters on that single road; the owners must have driven them off to a safer place when violence began brewing potently.

The Zimbabweans didn't flee, this time, this place, they resisted the violence of rejection with violence. The men about Lesego indeed must think he's brought someone who'll make the world hear their story of invasion, so it has to be told in a language the white man with him will understand; what's vehement must be sent out in English. The voice fired from the coming and going babble of the group. —Who is give them pangas and guns, where they do get, who give them knives from butcher shop, who paying those people come to kill us, they want this our place.— A woman lifted a wail that drew theirs from under the black shawls of her old women companions. And suddenly a note with the cadence of Afrosoul soared somewhere on the low horizons of destruction. Whose voice. She's just one of those who're growing up in this place; an inspiration not interruption —Where're our jobs they take. There's jobs at the paint factory, the building going on over there-there Jeppe Street, the cleaners for the hotel—those people they take our jobs, they take any small pay, the bosses don't want our wages they must pay us the union says—

Lesego breaks away with one of the men and signals. —He asks us to go with him.— The shrug for the man's privacy. He questions him under his breath.

Too difficult to follow the gist of the isiZulu that follows; so without being able to make out the purpose, just be an appendage of Lesego. Seeing more 'on the ground'. Women have three-legged pots standing in fires, children are bowling, quarrelling over turns with the wheels of a bicycle corpse. Another woman, backside assertive, is stirring cement rather than food alongside a man patching bricks to close gaps broken in a house that had a luxury of a wall instead of corrugated tin and cardboard. There's an instinct in human settlement to be aligned as if you were in streets but some shacks are faced away, at the choice of the individual, from what is the rough conformation of a line of occupation; that's the freedom of destitution. Lesego calls his greeting to men swinging rhythmical hammer blows on what's left of a scrap-metal roof and they call back cheerful with the acknowledgement. There are everywhere underfoot—kick aside to get along—the twisted plastic containers of whatever, cigarette stubs, crumpled publicity handouts, beer cans—only in greater accumulation than what is shed to the gutters of formal living in the city.

Here at the shacks there's no municipal service to pick it up. Why should the parents of kids teach them not to throw away trash when their home is made of trash. —So they're not to be allowed to learn self-respect?— Not even that. She's not there with him but often when he's with others it's as if she's presenting him with unexpected aspects of himself. And sometimes he's giving her some of herself she's not aware of.

A shebeen coterie although they're in what are obviously rescued chairs from somewhere, each different with a lopsided leg or a seat replaced by double cardboard, drink beers from the bottle, maybe this battered shed is or was a shebeen, it's withdrawn, can't say protected from whatever's happened to it, by a tarpaulin as a devout Muslim woman hides behind a veil the compensatory visions for the ugliness of life. Children rat-scatter; and there are a few hens, not much shattered glass you'd expect of violence, because shacks generally don't have windows but there are shard reflections from smashed mirrors, whatever else people can't have, it's clear from mirrors seen still to survive in wrecked shelters, hung up somehow, men and women must have their image, to shave and (young Afrosoul voice) make up; have sight of themselves not just as others choose to see them.

The man stops evidently come to what he's making for. It's a shack like any other but iron railing, the kind of screen put up to protect a store front in a risky street stands propped over what would be the entrance, and some piece of broken furniture hung with a cloth image of the President in leopard-skin regalia blinds anyone from being able to see inside. A woman with the facial bone structure recording she was once beautiful (as Jabu the lawyer is beautiful) interferes with Lesego's man shaking the bars for attention. —They say there's somebody very sick, that's why you mustn't worry the people— The man jerks a shoulder to back her off in reproaches. A voice comes from in there, questions, and gets an answer in their shared language that satisfies identity. A man pregnant with a belly that means his belt only just holds up his pants below it at the crotch appears round the side of the curtain. He signs to approach and heaves the iron screen sideways, it's not flab, that belly, at an angle for the arrivals to push in.

There's a double bed with nobody lying in it. A young woman tending a baby among jars, mugs and a head of cabbage on the table. Confusion. A shack is a dwelling-place all purpose in one, a motorbike, piled clothing, mobile phone, stroller strung with limp toys, a car seat has two neat white pillows on it, must double as a bed.

Lesego was introduced to the man who bore his belly so confidently, names, elaborate greeting exchanged. And Lesego presents: —Steve, my good friend.— The man might or might not have been reassured by what came from a white, the traditional handshake—forearm grasp. The young woman with the baby on her hip drew up: and as if now remembered —My daughter.— Lesego asked the name as he greeted her and touched the baby in salute. —This's Steve. We teach at the university together.—

—Oh great, that's nice.—

What to say. —Are you all right? It must have been terrible for you.—

—They were trying to get in but that iron—they tried and tried and there was such fighting in the street they got mixed up in it and went to another place, a woman we know just near us, she was killed.—

Her father is impatient with the platitudes of circumstance. He swings the belly to a stained blanket hanging from where the tin sheet of wall meets the tin roof and lifts it enough for the three men to see—a gap there; it's open on a lean-to shed made of whatever, propped to the battered relic of a truck door. There's a man standing. Looking straight at them, where he would have been thrust before they were let in past the storefront guard.

He's a young man and he's wearing one of those bold bright-patterned topknot balaclavas women sell among sweets and single cigarettes on city pavements this year. It crowns and covers—his identity?—over the ears and down to join under the jawbone.

There is close and intermittently argumentative exchange between Lesego, the master of the shack and the man who led to this confrontation with what has become circumstance rather than a crisis. It's the dialogue all over the country.

What purpose in being here with them. What are any of us veterans of the Struggle doing about it. (Sitting around . . . *shocked . . . Eish.*)

The exchange has ended in abrupt conclusive silence. Lesego turns from it. —We have to get him out of here.—

The company stoops back under the cloth of the shed, hidden man follows. The girl looks about with random instinctive foresight, taking up this and that, the foresight of what can't be done without anywhere, piece of soap, razor, into a plastic bag, underpants and small towel, chemist-labelled pill bottle along with a leather lumber jacket folded into a carryall she empties of baby clothes.

He doesn't take off the elaborate headgear that surely will draw attention; he'll be exposed a moment when he comes out from behind the storefront guard to Lesego's car. But no— of course the thing is what every young black is buying this winter for warmth—shows you're cool, man.

The young man is talkative in the back of the car beside the one who led the way to the hideout. In the rear-view mirror see the topknot bobbing with nervous loquacity. He speaks English with more confidence than many South African brothers although obviously he isn't one of the class of some immigrant Zimbabweans, teachers and doctors—reminder that Mugabe started off well, reforming and advancing education out of its colonial limits. —I can't follow what's got into them, the people around Josiah's place, we were good mates, we worked in the same kinds of jobs we could get, Nomsa and I, we all partied together I was best man at the wedding of one of her friends—that I have to be afraid when I'm living with her . . . Some of the others, Somalis with their shops, they think a lot of themselves, annoy people, but most of us in those shacks, we give each other a hand. I couldn't believe Joseph first when he told—I mean even the people next door, round about, we drink and dance together between our shacks, we did, this Christmas even—now they're after *me*! All of us! Out! Out! They think if we're thrown out, they kill us, they'll be rich in our jobs can you believe it, the pay we get? They'll stay poor like we are—

But where will Lesego take him; Lesego must be thinking in the silence between our seats. The shacks are left behind, no one stones us from the trap of the dirt road to be travelled to the highway, no one's recognised an enemy from Zim known to them and tried to drag him from the car where a white man was one of his protectors.

The silence, against the man's monologue as Lesego drove, held, with the response of occasional throat-clearing sounds, syllables to show the victim he was being listened to.

—Where to take him. Who will.— Lesego in low bass just for that shared silence.

You can't ask the young man if he knows anyone, anywhere. So there's no answer, and that confirms they must keep thinking: where. The Methodist Church asylum the last place, now, must be overflowing the usual overflow—unless it's been raided for its Zims.

Lesego seemed vaguely to be following the way to the Suburb, maybe considering somewhere else: or first to drop off the comrade seated beside him without hope that either will have a solution to offer.

As if come to a realisation he began again in the same confidential bass. —Jabu's whatever-she-is, she doesn't live in the outhouse now?—

—She moved in with Sindi—after what happened.—

Lesego doesn't take his gaze from the road to accompany what he's saying. —He could be there, couldn't he— An observation. As if in anticipation of an obstacle in mind —Jabu might not like the idea . . .— A moment has to be left for response. But in the delay —I can't take him to our place, the parents are with us these days, there isn't even a bed—Jabu—oh maybe Jabu can fix something so at least he can become a legal immigrant.—

—Forget it. The Centre acts for people who're being denied their Constitutional rights as South Africans. Anyway since when does 'xenophobic' ask whether or not you've been let in legally?—

What the purpose is in being there, in a passenger's seat, in having been there in the shelter of shacks and the bashed relic of a truck door. What any of us is doing. Brought down the crowned centuries of colonialism, smashed apartheid. If our people could do that? Isn't it possible, real, that the same will must be found, is here—somewhere—to take up and get on with the job, freedom. Some must have the—crazy—faith to Struggle on. Past the Gereformeerde Kerk pool choppy with winter wind to the house that will be occupied only until November; the outhouse is already empty. The passenger door opens just as Lesego switches off the ignition. —I want to go in and tell Jabu we've brought someone. Who . . . again?— There was a name, mumbled by the authority of the belly. Lesego thinks, Albert-somebody.

Saturday afternoon, Gary Elias and Njabulo in their football shorts and pullovers after the game, sprawled at ease while another sports match on television is vociferous blast. Concentrated by it they don't hear Gary's father come into the house. This generation inured to disturbance, muzak the atmosphere, commentary the broadcast chatter in public places, registering only the one side of cell-phone intimacies and banalities. Their aural senses are going to be worn ragged before beards begin to sprout. (Yes. But didn't you have the Beatles going strong while you studied.) Sindi's not there—where would she be but absent with her friends on a Saturday. Jabu's taking notes from tomes dealt out around her—brought home some research from the Centre, concentration stops her ears against noise. She jumps up in welcome and dread. —Was it awful . . . why isn't Lesego coming in.—

She gets the signal. Not that the boys would overhear. In the passage he makes for the kitchen but she takes his elbow, there's the rhythm of chopping something, Wethu must be busy in there. —A man's in the car—he was hidden by the family he's been living with in the shacks. He wasn't among all the other Zims attacked last week but people know where he is and they're after him, now.—

She's waiting.

—Lesego doesn't know right away where to put him.—

Is some suggestion, solution expected from her.

—Lesego's place isn't possible, full house, the parents are there. We'll have to take him.—

Her head is still lifted questioning; but not the unexpected.

—Lesego remembered Wethu's place. I didn't want just to walk in on you without a word.—

She turns without one, instead her lips, a quick kiss, not explained.

Lesego and the man came in and were welcome. —Would you like some tea. Or a drink, maybe that's better. I'm Jabu Reed—our son Gary and his pal.— She's silenced the sports match.

The stranger now takes off the headgear as the boys titter appreciatively, this is a sharp guy. He sets down the carryall; in this house.

It's a claim recognised by Jabu. —I'm not going to ask what happened to you, it's all been—we see it. On TV . . . the papers, hear the radio . . . — But the man: become by Lesego, *their* Zimbabwean. —It's terrible—our people, whatever our people here feel—

He has a beer and again tells his history, the packer at a wholesale electrical appliance firm, truck driver, fast-food waiter. A dossier, three years of acceptance.

When Lesego swallows the last of his beer—he wasn't offered

his usual red wine, it's not a usual gathering—and gets up to leave the other does not attempt to follow; it's understood. But to be sure. —You say I can stay here . . . Meantime.— He thanks Lesego under Lesego's dismissing protest.

Jabu appeared with bedding under her arm. —Steve'll show where you'll sleep, it's not part of the house but there's a bathroom and so on. If you need anything . . . Supper'll be late we don't hurry when there's no school next day.—

In the brief argot of domestic intimacy —That camp bed, when we went with the Dolphins to the Drakensberg—oh Gary Elias knows where you put it, Gary?—.

And then as he leads the stranger out to Wethu's chickenhouse cottage. —Shouldn't you slip him some clothes, your jeans'll be best, he's smaller than you but you wear them tight they won't be much too big . . . that shopping bag all he has with him.—

Gary Elias and Njabulo are rounded up by her to find the dismantled camp bed, release its bandy wooden legs in flourishing style and stretch the canvas its length. Gary Elias is roused to a grievance —When can we go camping again, we never go any more.— Any more. Not the distracted moment for a father to remind him what he's been told, there's another wilderness of bush Over There; just as the bush that has been his adventure holiday place here is not the Angolan desert, bush, where his mother and father were in the Struggle. So what. That the boy, their boy, my boy, knows the bush as happy adventure, that's a small gain—in the better life that hasn't reached people in the shacks, so that they need to defend with fire and panga possession of the scraps of the survival they can't share.

Over supper for which Wethu had been chopping carrots and celery for the salad everyone listened to stories, accounts of

Zimbabwe. When you are twice displaced—first the long rough trial of escape from conflict and hunger bringing your country to ruin, then rejection in a brother country—perhaps it's a need of unconscious return to sanity symbolic of what was at home—before. What doesn't exist. Any more. There was the dragged-on palaver over independence and then the fighting years, the battle of the Smith imperialists (that's the label for them freedom fighters learned) against the African people. But always there was the village with the Christian Brothers school, good teachers, there was the river where the uncles and grandfathers taught you to fish, there was the stick-fighting contest to make men of you, there were the drinking parties and the very old men who told of fighting lions way back. Before, before. There's the motorbike bought from the white farmer with cash saved, two years' work on the cattle farm—that's another skill along with the variety of employments; he's expert at culling. And he's explicit, for Gary Elias, on what this means. Wethu ignored him, the Suburb is a place where many friends from the working lives of Baba's educated daughter, a lawyer, and Steve, a teacher at a university, are brought to this house from time to time. Sindi was spending the night with a schoolfriend, she'd be given the news of the arrival if Wethu could get in first, Sunday morning on return from early church service. Jabu: responsive to the man as if taking part in village occasions he described; and when he spoke of Mugabe, asking pointed questions he evaded. Her lawyerly habit of going into areas of witness confusion between—fear? Residual loyalty in the victim to the power that had turned against its own constituency flesh? She is matter-of-fact. As the meal ended she asked whether the guest wanted to call anyone, perhaps a cell phone was missing in the essentials of the shopping bag and—as her man would be expected to assure—was the geyser in Wethu's place functioning, hot water for the bath.

There was a cheerful goodnight exchange, now in isiZulu, she chanced apparently rightly that in three years the man would have picked up enough of that most widely spoken of many languages in his workplace.

He glances about and picks up the headgear, puts it on his head.

In that place of discarding the happenings of a day along with jeans and underwear. —He said nothing to you about what he left behind in the shack.—

—What d'you mean.—

—There's a girl with a baby, she suddenly found a photograph pushed it at him for the bag, in tears.—

—Her father'll take care of them. Her, the baby.— She knows that. He knows that. It's the circumstances of generations in KwaZulu, Baba's village and thousands of villages, the eternity of colonialism, doesn't matter whose, the recency of its apartheid evolution, Bantustans, and its circumstance now in freedom. You have to eat. The men go off to the industries, the factory farms of chickens, wine, and Baba and *magogo* are left with care of the wives and children conceived when the men come home on leave, with money. It's their emigration. She's known it; this form, all through her childhood, her companions grew up in the absence of fathers. Even though she was by chance the exception, her father: the headmaster, in place.

The present is a consequence of the past.

Including the newspaper cuttings she found.

She and he have the same intense conception of horror at the degradation to violence people have descended against Zimbabweans. She, he—poverty is what it's about, again and again, reality that's avoided under the useful 'xenophobia'. If they didn't share this as they do within them their lives in the Struggle, their ultimate relation in love with one another wouldn't remain intact.

He sees now with this disaster come indoors to them right in the Suburb, enclave of human variety where at last race, colour, gender are simply communal, that she has an ancestral surety he hasn't, never will. They—*hers*—have known and know how to survive what his antecedents never experienced.

The end product of colonial masters in Africa even if he's redeemed himself in *Umkhonto*.

If he'd been born a generation earlier and in Europe, that capillary thread of Jewish blood from—a maternal grand-mother was it—could have resulted for him in that other kind of ancestral surety, known and knowing how to survive escape extinction, Holocaust.

All this crowds, remote, out of mind, what is going to happen is happening in the present to everyone everywhere, the whole planet. Nature's holocaust coming with the effects of pollution. And the result of this human self-destruction, or—some scientists/philosophers say, a recurring phenom-enon over the existence of planet Earth—climate change to destroy the resources of life.

The man in Wethu's chicken-coop cottage is also of course a ward of Suburb comrades—some answer against the inevitable shame and revulsion the impact of 'xenophobia' his situation brings among them. At least the humiliation of charity can be relieved while he is there—the idea Blessing might give him some sort of job in her catering venture, which is doing rather well, was offered—and then realised by everyone as unsafe for him, among her staff there could be resentment at a Zimbabwean being employed when they had brothers and sisters out of work. The Dolphins while assuring him he'd be welcome to swim but brrr water was still too early spring cold, asked if he would be willing to help with the clean-out of the pool they did at this time of year, and he was enabled to earn something from joining this task with them. Isa had put off the need to have two shabby rooms painted and here was the opportunity of employing someone to do it. No one wanted shelter to be a handout; though when Jabu passed Albert a clip of banknotes in concern of needs of the baby whose photograph he had among his few essentials, he took the money with a curt thank you of something owed. Wethu did not object to his occupying, for the time being, her cottage, while keeping him aware that this was by *her* permission; although—*that* night—she hadn't been asked by Jabu. She took for granted he'd take his evening meal with him from the kitchen to his borrowed quarters although he had his mealie-meal, bread and tea with her in that kitchen when the family had gone to work and school; but Jabu made the statement of laying a sixth place at table while she and Wethu prepared dinner.

How long would he, could he stay.

November.

The man had some unexplained inner assurance—couldn't be questioned about? Things would settle down in the shacks, he who had been living there with the people, three years, a South African woman and a child his compact with a life just as theirs (he determinedly would nod in agreement with whatever his own assurance was) he would go back. Soon. It will be all right. Soon.

Every week there's another collection of shacks crowding to be a settlement, identified popularly if on no map, by the name of a Struggle hero and taking up another kind of struggle against people from over frontiers. In some areas the problem was solved by Better Life development as an industrial zone or country club, then it's everyone out.

Soon. November. There'll be no Wethu cottage. The new owners will move in. —They didn't buy a Zimbabwean *bonsella* with the price.—

Confronting Jabu and himself. This kind of farewell.

The Mkizes, no. Jake and Isa . . . take him in; take him on?

She's looking at discovery: —The Dolphins.— The words don't have a questioning lilt.

But how does she *know* these things; he has nothing less demanding to offer—for the meantime, which is any time between when the man thinks he can go back to his wife and child in the shack, and when there'll be a Zimbabwe fit to return to.

Only Dolphins Donnie and Brian are at home, indoors with the newspapers and their glasses of good Cape Pinotage before a pinecone fire for the beauty of it, winter's nearly over. Brian is a telecommunications expert who often has feasted them his other expertise, his jambalaya since they moved in to their welcome in the Suburb.

—No problem! There's only junk we should throw out anyway since Marc's got himself a wifey, it used to be his studio, he called it, but you know he's never painted, no Picasso or Sekoto, always wrote plays there, he's said he'd come to work back there in peace—whatever that tells the tale about life with Claire—we'll just need a bed, if you have a spare—

They will have everything to spare of beds, tables, cupboards, chairs, freezer, TV—no, the new living-room widescreen will go along with furniture Wethu should have, perhaps Baba might like to give away the desks, keep his daughter's, for himself—when transport is arranged, time come for her to go to KwaZulu. Soon.

When that time comes, if 'meantime' still needs it, the Dolphins will shelter the man with the topknot crown of city pavements. Imagine the ghosts/ghouls of the old Gereformeerde congregation: the sinful *moffies* in God's house—now they even have a black man to bugger. Who's thinking this, himself or others when Steve tells them the Zimbabwean will not be cast to the streets . . .

Autumn of parties, in summer. An ending.

The children are possessed by TV-Land, somewhere. He and she are on the stoep, that's what the terrace was called when the house was built in the forties, as the Dolphins' poolhouse was the Gereformeerde Kerk before there came about a comrade takeover. Eyelids of light open upon the Suburb from houses on another hill, the conversation is that of cicadas rubbing legs together. But watchface glanced at in half-dark— they're expected for another of the unacknowledged farewells. At Jake's now.

They're tardy. The comrades, Blessing and Peter, the Dolphins with their sexual renegade Marc and his honorary Dolphin woman—the comrades have been drinking before the arrival. Jake's trying out one of the new vintages from an old well-known vineyard taken over by German (or are they Chinese) entrepreneurs with the precaution of one of the new black capitalists drawn in as a partner. —Why should whites own the wine resources as they do the mines—and there're high voices in the ANC Youth none of the prosperous white oldsters are hearing yet—toyi-toying, calling for gold, diamonds, platinum industry to be nationalised.— Jake is even more loquacious than usual rather than drunk on this experimental Pinotage, unstoppable, uninterruptable (if there isn't such a word there ought to be).

He and she—they sit on an unsteady swing couch. Hand within hand while these are not touching, not held.

—ANC'll have to dig the wax out of ears before the elections come in 2014, that squalling prodigy Malema rallied his generation Brothers to vote first time Zuma Zuma Zuma,

Zuma'd better start worrying whether they'll dance with him all the way knee-high next time. Isn't Malema lifting his to lead the dance himself? If not this time . . . after. One day. Soon. The five hundred thousand jobs Zuma promised as President? So where are they? The multi-million election victory celebration. The four hundred thousand he spent on a birthday bash for his daughter, and what about his nineteen or so other offspring and by-blows, will they all have birthday bashes at our tax expense? How many houses could have been built for three-generation families slumming in those abandoned downtown buildings, how many roofs could go up from the bill for French champagne gone down and pissed out by government ministers—

—There've been about two million houses. *Eish*. That's nothing . . .— Peter is talking over Jake not defiantly but dismissively as if compensating for some congenital circumstance Jake himself—comrade—cannot be aware. —I'm the lucky one I have a house (spread hand waves to encompass the Suburb) I've got not just a job—it's what we call a position, my wife has a business of her own, yes. But I—black, all of us, the beggar and big boss—I can walk where I like, move about my country, live in any place, city, get on any bus come in any door, send my kids to any school. That's not nothing.—

Jake accepts—flinging right arm to catch his left below the shoulder—what a white cannot experience. But there's no stalling him. —Strikes, they're the employer these months, telecommunications, transport, electricity, every public servant from dustmen up, they're taking over the country with blackouts and no-go streets they're the worker-boss as full-time marcher to the headquarters of this commission and that. And NOW—the army, *army*—who can blame them, the ones it's counted upon to do the head-bashing on workers if it comes to that. The army. Yesterday didn't you see, the South

African National Defence Force, three thousand rampaging under their banner at the Union Buildings, that's boss government itself. Those supposed to protect us are the lowest paid government employees—

Blessing laughs out —So that's the place to go! When there's a strike I'm without my two cooks, although they share our profits, they want to show solidarity with other workers, their husbands from the municipality, one son with a bus company . . .—

—Since when do they have a union?— Eric of the Dolphin pool was in the apartheid army, remembers what doesn't change with any regime. —Soldiers never have the right to strike. Jesus! Haven't you heard call-in programmes, people saying the guys should be thrown out of the army in disgrace. Who cares if our 'military force' earns peanuts while we can send them off to earn us kudos, Congo and anywhere UN organisations are trying to prop up peace against oppressors—who those are and aren't—

—Who's for peace—

—Who's doing the oppressing—

—ESCOM's strike's suspended anyway, going to be 'allowed negotiations' of the sticky issue, housing allowance—so we don't risk rolling blackouts—for the time being, maybe.—

—What we ought to be worrying about is the mines, my man, platinum, the output's about three thousand ounces a day, that's worth fifty-eight million to the economy . . .—

—Wage settlement agreed today, strike continues tomorrow, tomorrow, all the tomorrows . . .—

—Tomorrow, tomorrow, Zuma's connection with the arms deal's gone away, e-eh—never brought to his day in court.—

—Three thousand ounces . . . The mining industry's going to cut production, labour, avoid paying nearly fifty times more to its compensation fund for miners who've contracted silicosis

TB over years. Some of them never saw a cent: went home to die. The owners got away with slow murder during apartheid. And after. Now, it's part of our transformation: owners expect some compensation could close their record on exploitation if they paid up. Even if you can't give men their lungs back.—

Jake's drumming fingers are against the chest of all —ARMS. Hear me! Our free country at peace, we sell arms to countries with human rights records like Libya, Iran, Zimbabwe. Deals 'allegedly' approved by our National Arms Control. Right, Jabu? You've got it all in the Centre's files for sure.—

(Cuttings come upon, dusting.) —The global village is too involved in arms trafficking to make laws against it.— Probably no one hears Jabu; Jake is the voice from the mountain, he's thrusting a new bottle of wine round at each glass, potion all must imbibe from him in unspoken farewell toast: Australia. —Where are we. For once when he's not in a tantrum Malema blames the old race of government ministers: whites. An accusation. But it's a race whose characteristics have been adopted smartly by apt blacks in their ministry seats.—

—At least women're recognised even though they're white—Gill Marcus Reserve Bank Governor, Barbara Hogan Public Enterprises—and she's a Struggle veteran.—

—Are these powers given to display the regime's above revenge, in reverse for traditional white condescension that African—black—wasn't capable of directing such portfolios? Or is it to woo the white voter for next time, 2014?—

—Marc, no prizes—but who is it who defends the 'minority appointees' white, Indian, too-pale-to-be-black? The SACP Communists say while they're opposed to ugly 'chauvinistic' attitudes which persist in some places, a country's narrow African chauvinism simply reproduces what does he call it, its counterpart.— Jake is lifting this phenomenon with his wine glass. —But our Zuma he opposes Lindiswe Sisulu, head of our ANC's Social Transformation Unit, over her proposal to debate this kind of—symbol is it?—of race transformation. We pride ourselves on being a multiracial organisation, she says, and Zuma comes with 'the debate will take the country backwards'.—

Ragged chorus —Don't let's talk about race— —It'll go away— Isa fondly removes from Jabu the burden of the glass of wine she's not drinking.

Jabu and Steve are an example of those for whom it has all gone away. Away.

—Where's Albert?— Dolphin Eric notices—no, Albert isn't here, these days he's present at any gatherings on the Reed family terrace but perhaps he knows he'd still be a stranger on the terraces of others although soon to be part of the Dolphin household; how he'll fit in with a way of life not only his refugee status but a gender one he's going to find unfamiliar . . . cleaning a pool was sharing a job not the intimacies of everyday.

—His wife was to come and be with him today.— Jabu's locks shaking from the pinnacle of her fine head. —There's no response from the cell phone, he doesn't know what's happening with this new violence. Trouble. As far as Steve and I can find out, it's not in that place yet. But we had to stop him from going back there to see—if he hasn't gone away after we left—

—Who knows how many Zims are in South Africa. Three million the government said—three years ago? What's that new count, the other day?— Peter expects Jabu to be the most accurate with the figure.

Her way of running finger and thumb down an earlobe to the earring. —Nine-point-eight-four million. Twenty per cent of our population. Unlikely? Other officials' and business organisations' count is meant to be reassuringly lower.—

—You know what one sane man among us says and nobody wants to listen.— Jake is standing as if before not just the Suburb: the city, the country. —'It's time to accept that migrants have been the lifeblood of this city since it was founded'. That's the black mayor of Johannesburg.— Lifeblood of the country. The tribes who came down from the north of Africa to conquer the San and the Khoi Khoi, the Dutch and the English, Scots Irish landing from ships.— He's propounding. Will he get to the Jews who came from Latvian *shtetl*, made African, *eish*, at last, a descendant of the colonialist Christian father and the Jewish great-grandmother while another descendant brother, Jonathan, turns from the man on the cross back to the scroll in the synagogue.

Blessing as one who provides, no matter what, the comfort of good cooking has her confident interruption of Jake —We've got the World Cup next year, already such a thrill . . . the stadiums going up, people—

—Buying the logo T-shirts made by slave labour in China, dirt cheap compared with those made by our garment workers who're underpaid—on strike . . . People need bread and circuses, this binge is the big circus that's going to take bread off the mind of our population that's supposed to exist on two dollars a day—why anyway does the world use that currency as the standard for survival everywhere. *Tell* me? And for how many millions that's not pay it's handout to the unemployed, the destitute, and here's where what's surely the lowest form of our shit-art of corruption—it's not only the fat cats finagling the profits of tenders, it's the small fry who pay our old-age pensions, grants to feed children—they have their level, faking grants for themselves, Social Security just closes one eye . . . *Do you hear me?* Their loot from the poor has been more than a hundred million between last year and just *so far* this one!— Stricture in Jake's face. Fury. —UBUNTU. One of the African words everyone, all of us, any colour, we know—we know it means something like we are all each other— shouting —Say it! Say it! Say it for what it is. Turned out to be! What we've produced! What we're producing! Corruption's our culture. The Spirit of The Nation. U BU U N TU UBUNTU U U

They sit alone together, in this company of comrades.
  —UBUNTU UBUN-TU UBUNTU-U U U—
  Suddenly—facing this comrade Steve:
  Jake's gut, stomach, lungs, sucked back to the spine under his Mandela shirt, spews, —You lucky bastard—*you're out of it*—

The moment holding a life.
  —I'm not going.—